The Scorched–Wood People

*A*nd who has made this song?
Who else but good Pierre Falcon.
He made the song, and it was sung
To mark the victory we had won;
He made this song that very day,
So sing the glory of the Bois-brûlés.

Books by Rudy Wiebe

Fiction:
Peace Shall Destroy Many (1962)
First and Vital Candle (1966)
The Blue Mountains of China (1970)
The Temptations of Big Bear (1973)
Where is the Voice Coming From? (1974)
The Scorched-Wood People (1977)
Alberta/ A Celebration (1979)
The Mad Trapper (1980)
The Angel of the Tar Sands (1982)
My Lovely Enemy (1983)
Chinook Christmas (with David More) (1992)
A Discovery of Strangers (1994)
River of Stone: Fictions and Memories (1995)
Sweeter Than All the World (2001)
Hidden Buffalo (with Michael Lonechild) (2003)

Non Fiction:
A Voice in the Land (ed. by W.J. Keith) (1981)
War in the West: Voices of the 1885 Rebellion
    (with Bob Beal) (1985)
Playing Dead: A Contemplation Concerning
    the Arctic (1929)
Stolen Life: The Journey of a Cree Woman
    (with Yvonne Johnson) (1998)

The
Scorched–Wood
People

a novel

Rudy Wiebe

Fitzhenry & Whiteside

First published by Fitzhenry & Whiteside in 2005.

Published in Canada by Fitzhenry & Whiteside, 195 Allstate Parkway, Markham, Ontario L3R 4T8

Published in the United States by Fitzhenry & Whiteside, 121 Harvard Avenue, Suite 2, Allston, Massachusetts 02134

www.fitzhenry.ca   godwit@fitzhenry.ca

10 9 8 7 6 5 4 3 2 1

Library and Archives Canada Cataloguing in Publication

Wiebe, Rudy, 1934–
    The scorched wood people / Rudy Wiebe.

ISBN 1-55041-323-6

    1. Riel, Louis, 1844-1885—Fiction.   2. Dumont, Gabriel, 1837-1906—
Fiction.   I. Title.

PS8545.I38S3 2005   C813'.6   C2004-904061-8

U.S. Publisher Cataloging-in-Publication Data
(Library of Congress Standards)
Wiebe, Rudy Henry, 1934–
    The scorched-wood people / Rudy Wiebe.
[320] p. : ill. ; cm.
Originally published: Toronto : McClelland and Stewart, 1977.
Summary: An authentic portrait of Louis Riel and his commander-and-chief Gabriel Dumont, portraying an agonizing chapter in Canadian history.
ISBN 1-55041-323-6 (pbk.)
1. Riel, Louis, 1844–1885 — Fiction.   2. Dumont, Gabriel, 1838–1906 —
Fiction.   3. Indians of North America — Fiction.   4. Riel Rebellion, 1885 —
Fiction.   5. Northwest, Canadian — Fiction.   6. Revolutionaries — Fiction.
7. Politicians — Fiction.   8. Métis — Fiction.   I. Title.
813/.5/4 dc22   PZ4.W643Sc 2005

Fitzhenry & Whiteside acknowledges with thanks the Canada Council for the Arts, the Government of Canada through the Book Publishing Industry Development Program (BPIDP), and the Ontario Arts Council for their support of our publishing program.

Printed in Canada
Cover design by Karen Petherick.
Front cover illustration and type by Paul Morin.
Interior design and typesetting by Daniel Crack, Kinetics Design.

*This book is for
Eric, Doris, Aritha and Tom,
who got me started and
sometimes even helped*

Contents

1

Riel's Province

"If, by trying to say that the Manitoba Treaty was of the delegates of the North-West, the Canadian Government wanted to avoid the fact that I was a being at all, the whole world knows that it is not so; they cannot avoid me."

— Louis Riel, 1885

_1_

SIXTEEN years later Louis Riel would be dressing himself again, just as carefully. And he would remember then this dressing in Fort Garry, remember the exact ruffles on this shirt and this frock-coat black against the log wall, his face so stone white it betrayed nothing of his ancestry shifting on the stained silver of the Hudson's Bay Company mirror as though it were whorled, brown water. Time then within twenty-one days of four perfectly completed fours of years. He wouldn't have a mirror then of course, nor need one for the grey prison coveralls they would give him to wear out into that morning brilliant with hoarfrost; and certainly not hear Gabriel's voice boom in the next room, men laughing with his gigantic laughter. I know he will hear only his own feet slur a steady prayer down the corridor, moving him to the wood he has heard them hammering together on the prairie outside his window, to steps he will obediently mount while a bulging sun burns the hoarfrost into sheet gold; there to be hanged by his neck until he is at last, perfectly, dead. O my God have mercy.

Laughter again covered Gabriel's huge voice in the Company

mess. The chair he sat in groaned, and the laughter roared even louder. Riel smiled, but at the water beading his own face: washed and in such clothes at least he might have been presentable to Prime Minister Sir John A. Macdonald, or President Ulysses S. Grant, perhaps to fat Victoria herself, tiara and all. If he were ever presentable. If they could stand unnoticed with him in this tiny room off the officers' mess like three–add Lord Carnarvon of the Hudson's Bay Company since all four thought they held divine prerogative to Red River–like four ordinary human beings hearing Gabriel tell of the McDougall hunt, of that violent surround bursting up black out of the burning snow–the laughter would be too strong for them, the faces, the leather lived and sweated in. Were they actually people, those great–names, nothing but names–did they ever look in a stained mirror at the pore and follicle pattern far too familiar on their faces, feel triumph teetering like fear in their stomach at a nailed door that suddenly lurched open, that had to be walked through? Ever think about what they looked like to the breathing people who stared at them, the millions they inevitably ruled?

From beyond our untouchable divide of wilderness and blood I often, like Riel, considered the existence of lords and rulers; once I even discussed with him how it was possible there should be such; but certainly Gabriel Dumont in his buffalo-calf shirt tanned by damp poplar smoke in some Saskatchewan ravine never thought about them. At least not yet in November, 1869. He never thought of how he looked either, never saw his own face like a cliff undercut by a prairie river from one year to the next; he and his brothers and their people were their own lords, their only rulers the sky and the long land and slow muddy loops of prairie rivers, and the buffalo, their true king and ruler who gave them everything for life and happiness. The day before they met Ambroise Lépine and his eleven men riding from Fort Garry for the border, Gabriel and his three men had found a few buffalo between the north ridges of the Pembina Mountains. The beasts were down in the snow, fat, digging for grass, and Michel Dumas thought a cow would be best but Gabriel agreed with Isidore, why drag it if you don't have to, and he dropped a young bull near spruce ready for their fire. That was their first fresh-meat camp since they had heard of action at Red River and left their families and the other hunters on the Saskatchewan to ride four hundred miles just to see, maybe it was something interesting. But they had met no people at all, and for a week Michel had been moaning, "We're so far south already, why don't we just ride to St. Joe for a drink?" And Gabriel always laughing at him, "There's a lot more friendly girls at Red River." But now they all rode south together, and Lépine said,

"I don't think we'll get to St. Joe."

"Okay with me," Gabriel said as Michel grimaced. "I'd rather get warm fighting anyway."

The snow had come early that year, and the low sun had glazed it to a crust now covered by fresher snow. That's hard on a horse's legs, so Gabriel let the others break trail for a while. Louis Schmidt was riding back there too, and he nudged his horse over.

"What'd you hear about Red River out there?" he asked.

Gabriel hadn't been inside a building in seven months and to him Schmidt looked strange, dressed in cloth like a Company big shot, though they never rode anywhere and would probably have split if they tried to straddle a horse; his face so washed under his clean cap he must really be freezing. The only one without a rifle, at least.

"Uhh..." and this was not time to talk, early morning, men and horses moving. "All kinds of–pushy Canadians–surveyors...."

But even a few words and Schmidt was in business; cold didn't bother him. "If they'd told us what they were doing, told us anything, but these Canadians all titles and mighty come stomp over our land and the colonels or what are supposed to be in charge can't do anything with–the officer on the road crew just about got kicked into the river by his men and they had court about it, and the surveyors pushing people around, cutting their survey lines right across farmyards, not one of them could say more than 'non!' in French—"

"Through yards, where the people live?"

"Sure! They've got this square-mile system from the States and it always stays square, even if a farm cuts across three loops of the river it doesn't mat—"

"Bull! My father'd never let any big-ass cut a fence across his yard!"

Schmidt laughed, breathing white clouds. "I know–but the Canadians never got to his place. Louis Riel stopped them in St. Vital, André Nault's hayfield."

"That was one thing," Gabriel said. "We never heard anything about this young Riel on the Saskatchewan before."

"He's the oldest son of Louis Riel, St. Vital—"

"Yeah yeah, the famous 'Miller of the Seine' who never milled nothing, yeah, but his son–where's he been all the time?"

"He's never been on the buffalo hunts." Schmidt's voice had such a clear edge to it, Gabriel had to look at him again. He could ride all right, the washed fancy bastard. "Bishop Taché sent him to Montreal when he was thirteen, to school, and he worked there, and in the States. He reads a lot, writes..."

"And sits around, dreaming?"

There was only the creak of riders, the horses feet crushing ice into snow; Schmidt leaned across in his tight coat, his voice a delicate hiss,

"He thinks. He thinks."

Gabriel was too much a gambler to change his expression. "Yeah," he said, "we need thinkers, yeah, we've got enough doers already and if those whites want to shove us aro—"

But Schmidt was hot. "Riel's a doer too, a real one because he knows Canada and law and he's thought things through, long ago. We talked about this all last winter for hours, every night, instead of drinking and gamb—" Schmidt's eye suddenly glinted up, apprehension there, and Gabriel had to laugh, huge dirty head thrown back in the sunlight. "...Riel knew exactly what to say to freeze those surveyors in their tracks and—"

"And he's no savage, he talks English." That was Lépine's growl, his horse's rump abruptly in front of them. Schmidt looked up, startled, then noticed the men were spread out, riding abreast in a single curved line.

"Isn't this just about the border?"

"Just about," was all Lépine said.

"We can't cross it," Schmidt said. "We have to be careful, that would be an act of aggression." The steady jog of the riders, the silence.... Schmidt had to continue, abruptly, "What if McDougall has lots of men, what...?"

Lépine glanced at Gabriel, said nothing. Lépine is very big and has a general's looks and good voice but when Riel chose him I told him Lépine had no words. I told him Cuthbert Grant, not a day older than I was in 1816, already had the words that could persuade us of anything, that made us feel we could gallop over the world before we rode out to face Semple at Seven Oaks, and Riel just smiled at me, his face so young and already so aged. "I'll give them the words," he said. But he answered nothing when I asked, "And when you're not there?" Maybe Schmidt had heard us talk. On the frozen prairie it was so obvious to Gabriel that Schmidt needed words he almost laughed out loud; thinking, if this Riel sends these two on a tricky job, what kind of a leader is he? Schmidt's face seemed one blotch of frost-bite and Gabriel grinned at him.

"Then we surround all of them," pointing to the riders moving steadily outward at the wings, "and run them like buffalo."

The near men laughed but Lépine didn't. That's what I told Riel too: Lépine never laughs either. But now he was looking to the far right: Isidore Dumont there had pulled up on a small rise, and signalled. Lépine and Schmidt and Gabriel rode over.

If you can find a gopher mound–and that's not too hard–to mount on Red River prairie, on a clear day you can see for fifty miles. Straight ahead two, maybe two-and-a-half miles south, people were coming: it looked like four riders and one, no, two sleighs–but the sun's glare in the dusting snow was so fierce it was impossible to tell exactly. Lépine swung his arm to the riders and the line started forward at a trot.

"You think it's them?" Schmidt asked.

"If it isn't, it won't matter," Gabriel told him, and nudged his horse. Soon they were at a canter, then a gathering gallop, and it almost did feel to Gabriel like a winter run, the hunters stretched in a tight line and the beasts dead ahead not yet catching their smell, but Lépine was captain here and the black cluster on the snow did not bristle horns suddenly, did not wheel and spread like birds flying. The hunters looked at each other, their horses at a flat gallop now and they could hardly believe it.

The two sleighs were galloping towards them! One directly behind the other and the four riders–there were only four–pulled in tight against them: all together like that they actually tried to drive right through our Métis boys. It was so stupid the hunters were laughing aloud. Lépine and Gabriel, in the centre of the line, pulled up a little, four wingmen swung around ahead and each took out his rider, and Gabriel hardly had to lean over to drag the lead team around by their bridles in one gigantic spray of snow. The second sleigh just piled up against the first, and our two wingmen had to pull the team down or they'd have run all over whoever was still sitting in the lead sleigh and still so piled over with robes and blankets they hadn't gotten their heads out into the cold yet to know what was happening. The lead driver was screaming through the noise in English–no Métis would have tried to drive like that

"What the hell you bastards trying–this is a public trail—"

"Shut your mouth," Lépine said and cocked his rifle as he swung it up. Even that stupid American understood him.

Michel Dumas and Elzéar Goulet had hauled the second rearing team back on their haunches, off Gabriel's sleigh where two fur mounds were breaking open, two very white gentlemen popping into a cold world. One wore an English officer's beaver cap, the other a moustache like two long brushes hanging down past the corners of his mouth, all white though no frost could have touched it under all that fur.

"What–what is the meaning of this outrage!" says White Brush, but the officer, obviously a bit swifter, shook him by the arm, gesturing at all the rifles. The driver was leaning down, scrabbling at his feet for something, and Gabriel nudged his horse a step closer. He didn't touch his rifle, just leaned across the butt: the driver was certainly big enough.

"Want to try something really brave?" Gabriel asked gently, and the driver's green eyes flicked up, sharp an instant, and then glazed over milky like they do when a man's heart suddenly jolts him with a complete, bottomless terror. Gabriel had seen that often enough, it didn't look as if he'd really get warm there.

Louis Schmidt was talking; he was sitting up straight on his horse well behind the action and with paper in his hand he looked happier than he had all day.

"Are you William McDougall?"

A man with a paper White Brush could handle; he was standing among the crumpled robes, moustaches quivering:

"I'll have you all in jail for this, every one of you–bandits! I am the appointed Governor of the North-West and this is my appointed Chief of Police, Colonel Dennis, and in that sleigh—"

But Lépine was on the other side of his sleigh. "Shut your mouth," he said, and his rifle was so close even that McDougall understood what he meant. "Read it," Lépine said to Schmidt behind him.

In a flat sleigh like they had there was only one place they could hide anything, so Gabriel swung down and started throwing robes off their seats into the snow. There seemed to be a long box, a chair under the thick soft wool, buffalo hides–an armchair on a prairie sleigh!

"My man," Colonel Dennis leaned down, very confidential and unruffled English, "you make a grave error. We are fully authorized by the Canadian Government to—"

Gabriel's hand grabbed the corner of the robe he was standing on–there were nice hot stones beneath to keep their tootsies warm–and jerked. If Dennis hadn't jumped, fast, he'd have landed on his fine beaver cap; as it was, he landed on his ass, McDougall's chair–it was really a chair all wrapped in sheepskin–crashing down beside him.

Big Elzéar was laughing so hard the team he held almost shook him loose.

"Get out," Gabriel said to McDougall, who had with great intensity found some paper and was searching his furs for more as if he had the six-day fleas. Dear God, that was our everlasting Métis laugh, McDougall scratching himself and finding at last what he was looking for and hopping obediently, clutching that paper which would prove everything and Schmidt, not seeing him, of course, clutching his paper and already reading into the wind the words he had carried seventy winter miles from Fort Garry:

> For Mr. McDougall: the National Committee of the Métis of Red River orders Mr. McDougall not to enter the Territory of the North-West without the special permission of this Committee. By order of the President, Louis Riel.
> — Louis Schmidt, Secretary of the Committee.

But McDougall, like any paper man, hadn't heard a word; he was too busy thinking about his own words pondered so long, written so carefully; he was plowing through the snow to throw the weight of his paper into the case and thereby prove once and for all everything that had to be proved. Gabriel was down to the wooden box on which Dennis had been sitting and it was exactly the length he'd expected, though a little bigger around, and finding that he'd forgotten the driver until suddenly in the corner of his eye there was movement and he turned, fast: the driver straightened up with the rifle he'd been going after before. Gabriel had to grin at him. That was very good, to get over a first terror and then this with a dozen rifles around–well–it was really laughable because he had come up at the wrong end! He was clutching the barrel, and from his horse Lépine said, very sharp,

"Don't turn it around," and the driver glanced quick at Lépine sitting with an almost lop-sided grin on his face, not lifting his rifle from across his saddle, and Gabriel knew Lépine would let the driver come for him if he wanted to. The driver was really tempted; he was big enough, they were on that narrow sleigh together, and he had the long rifle for club or spear and Gabriel had his bare hands. He knew Gabriel had seen him afraid, but he couldn't know why Lépine was letting him try this if he wanted to or where it would get him if he did crack open that huge shaggy head grinning at him. So Gabriel helped; he moved quick, right, and the driver raised the rifle like a club and Gabriel dived in tight as it swung down, faster than he would have thought possible, and it caught his shoulder and if he hadn't been twisting aside as he went in he wouldn't have used that arm for a few weeks. As it was it hurt so much he bellered like a wounded buffalo when he clapped his arms around the driver's middle, but that one jolt numbed it and he grabbed his dead left wrist with his right hand and hauled in: the driver had a gut like an iron kettle but he'd stupidly let all his air go in that big swing and Gabriel got enough into that one pull to straighten him up, rigid. If he'd so much as twitched, Gabriel would have broken his back. The rifle slid down, thudded, and Gabriel threw him on his ass into the snow.

Lépine slid off his horse and came to see the box. "You warm yet?" He ripped the boards up without dropping his mitts. A neatly oiled nest of new Enfields, about forty of them. Their long barrels blue and beautiful.

McDougall was busy shifting papers and Schmidt was bending down, looking at all those famous signatures the Canadians had been yammering at us for months,

"...and you see here, authorised by Sir John A. Macdonald, right there, my commission as Governor, and here is Sir John Young's..."

There was nothing broken in Gabriel's left arm, he could feel that; he could *feel* so much of it he felt like smashing–something, anything smashable, and those rifles would have done just fine, but Lépine blocked him like a boulder and Gabriel couldn't open his mouth, or move, because then Lépine would certainly know how his arm felt. At that moment Michel, God be praised, ran up with a box hoisted over his head.

"Gabriel! Gabriel! Look, in their sleigh, look!"

Twelve big bottles of Scotch whisky, shining like jewels.

Lépine suddenly wheeled, was actually grinning as he reached across Gabriel and took that box from the startled Michel as easily as he would a handshake.

"Only the Company brings that into the North-West. You know."

Michel's mouth fell open; he couldn't believe what he heard. But McDougall, faster here than with rifles, was already plowing back, yelling,

"That is my personal–personal–medicine and if you–you touch it I'll..."

Lépine swung his arm to the men, and they whirled the horses and sleighs around in the snow, furs flying; the driver and Dennis scrambled to leap on as the horses, whacked, went plunging back the way they had come. McDougall stood there, still yelling clouds into the frozen air,

"...on the authority of the Governor General Sir John—" when he finally saw the littered trail and his teams a white dust retreating south. His face burst so red behind his white bristles it seemed possible he would explode.

"I'll have you all shot for this! Shot!"

He glared about, at them all so sun-black on their horses in an open circle, motionlessly watching him. As if they understood nothing, wordless brutes in greasy leather, what had he been sent–he turned, stumbled after his teams, the sudden prairie stretching before him empty as endless steel.

The drivers wouldn't be able to turn those teams for two miles. Gabriel looked up at Isidore and his hard face split in a grin.

"How about you and Michel give him a lift."

Michel forgot the whisky Lépine cradled in his big arm. He was astride his horse and they were dusting down on McDougall's flappy coat tottering towards the States over the torn snow. They were on him, tight on either side before he knew they were after him, and scooped him up under his arms, up, and off between them at a gallop, his legs still churning in the air, fur hat flying in a spray of snow. Thinly across the prairie came his scream,

"Put me down! Put me down you savages! you sons of...!" till they caught up with the sleigh and tumbled him in, Dennis grabbing him so he wouldn't bounce out again.

Our boys were all laughing; Gabriel had to hold his gut with his good arm. But Lépine hadn't yet cracked a smile. Schmidt sobered a little, and said,

"Riel said you shouldn't be rough with him."

But Lépine never moved. He was watching the distant sleighs, the two riders wheel, slapping themselves in laughter; he glanced at Gabriel, and knew suddenly that ultimate humiliation of McDougall had been too far beyond himself even to imagine. Gabriel Dumont. Schmidt grunted,

"And you should have taken the rifles."

Abruptly Lépine jerked a bottle out of the case and squinted through it at the sun. There was a terrific quiet, then one by one saddles creaked like long, careful sighs.

"We got enough," Lépine said. He was still studying the whisky."We got these four savages from Saskatchewan."

Lépine tossed Gabriel the bottle, and he caught it in his right hand, halloed to Isidore and Michel, waving it. The riders yodelled, jumped their horses into gallop; Gabriel snapped the bottle neck off clean on his rifle butt and god above forever he was drinking cool, sweet fire. Everybody was around Lépine, laughing, and Schmidt didn't have a word to say. All he had was a hand reaching, a mouth open like an empty cave.

"And that's *all* we got," Gabriel roared in the mess hall, "for stopping those buggers running over Lépine–a slug of whisky and an insult! Huh!"

"How about your chair?" someone laughed.

"This chair? I'll tell you, my snickering friend," Gabriel would be leaning forward, pulling their heads in tight about him, "this magnificent chair will be the most famous seat in the North-West. I'm gonna set it on two long poles and train the best buffalo runners in–shut up, I've got them already! –and they'll carry it between them like a bee-utiful bird's nest, swaying so gently, and I'll train two midgets like you, Snicker, to ride them horses, and we'll run buffalo on the wide prairie, me leaning back like a prince floating in his goose feathers and rising up to fire...."

The mirror wavered, became...the young moustached face in it moved, shimmered as if rippled through the violent hooting laughter from the neighbouring room and then, before he could really see the surface that a moment before had seemed to be there, it had passed through him into something else, the sound and sight weaving through each other as if they were blended into water. The summer he had left Red River for Montreal, when he was thirteen and praying almost consciously moment by moment O God use my life for your glory, give me the vision of your divine call, the face of his sister suddenly grew in the mirror as he leaned forward, washing apparently, and her mouth opened, said at his ear, "What did you see?" Sara ten, and always like that, watching him intensely, knowing when he wasn't really in the room though his body moved as if it were, but that was the first time she spoke directly. And perhaps it had been his going away so long that he could answer her. That he could tell her he had seen nothing of his school boy's face, plumply innocent and all dark eyes sober as a priest, rather tree roots curling downward below water as if they were shaping a heart–sacred?–between them in the grey sand, the single grains shifting deeper and deeper into clusters as if moulding themselves into a new world under the subterranean breath of God.

"But that isn't wat—" she began, but stopped, for a mirror was new to her also and the knowledge of looking into water, once learned, cannot be removed by silvered glass. It is like the knowledge of looking behind your own eyelids, at the aura which flames at the surface of your own perfect purple sun. If you have one.

"...end up like Ireland, everything we have and ever will have shovelled over into fat English banks by fat English lords who...."

But now nothing alive moved beyond the surface, nothing shimmered in colour. There was only white and black, coagulating, like Collège de Montréal basins where there were no mirrors either and the cold water broke into grey soap curds gouging eyes, a rusted file drawn through the eye dearest God, he tore himself back, warm water in his hands cupping his face warm, warm.

"...Macdonald Orangemen shovelling it outa here into banks in Toronto, Ottawa–Louis, will you for once listen! John A. won't take this–I'm talking to you! Will you?"

Will O'Donoghue stood in the doorway, his voice tilted forward on his gaunt body like a peering eagle. How long had he been there with his Irish-rebellion talk? Riel shook the water from his hands, groping for the towel.

"On the pillow," O'Donoghue said, not moving. "I saw my people by the hundreds lying dead on the roads of Sligo before I was ten, starved to death in green Ireland because those English bastards took everything till there was nothing when the drought came. You think I want to teach arithmetic to children with bellies hanging out, eyes shrunk into—"

"Washington is no different from London. Or Ottawa."

"It *has* to be!" O'Donoghue exploded, his arms leaping up so close to Riel's head emerging from the folds of the towel that the men in the next room quietened abruptly. "It's our one political chance, the only one we'll *ever have* to make our own deal with somebody else, not a goddam snotty English lord or Canada bigot Protestant!"

Riel picked up the ruffled shirt; I never met another man who could flay you so neatly, gently if he wished, with one phrase. "They don't," he said, "elect a new queen every four years."

"Victoria's just a old bi—" but O'Donoghue caught himself at Riel's swift stare, hesitated, and wheeled. Lépine was standing at his shoulder in the doorway, as tall as he and about three times as broad."Well she has that whole litter of kids, hell, she robs enough countries to afford them."

"You know the rule about cursing," Lépine said.

"Of course," O'Donoghue strode back to the small table he shared with Louis Schmidt. "The Hudson's Bay Company last year makes a profit of 36.8% on Fort Garry but you do not curse, oh no, I do not curse."

"I guess here's the profit," Louis Schmidt grinned; money was piled there, bags of it almost hiding their papers.

"One little bit, and we'll all pay interest on it too, one kind or another. Out of our skins."

"Should we pay every soldier in full?" Lépine asked. He filled the doorway, watching Riel fit the cuffs at his wrist.

"How many have signed up now?"

"Six hundred and thirteen, but over a hundred are less than a week."

Riel glanced from the linked buttons at his wrist to the moustached face floating between black flowing hair and white ruffles, eyebrows sprayed black; it seemed a thing he had never seen before. The eyes drew him forward; he might have been falling into them and imperceptibly the face paled, stretched between the luxuriant hair and the starched terrifying whiteness of shirt, the eyes sank, deeper, the tight skin sallow, straining taut and for an instant he saw the death's head he would not see sixteen years later, a skull with eyes still fixed, set out of a collar at its own peculiar, dreadful angle. "O my Lord, Mover of all, when will be the day of your fierce anger, when the earth will melt like wax before your wrath and the mountains cringe before..." but he shook his head. Violently, snapping the image, the sweet temptation singing in his head. He groped, discovered the black tie.

"What did you say, Ambroise?"

I know Lépine never saw about our people what Riel had already seen before Bishop Taché sent him away to school; Lépine simply believed, as enough Métis did not, that Riel could hold the North-West for us. But he saw, and worried, when Riel left his body like that.

"Eleven companies," Lépine said again, "haven't served quite a week yet."

"Everyone gets paid whatever time they have. Paid right after the ceremony."

"Rum too?"

"Is it necessary?"

Lépine shrugged. "They want to celebrate. Really."

"All right, one glass each and none for guards, until they're relieved. We can't give them any excuse to accuse us of anything, you hear? Anything."

"Yes sir," Lépine turned, walked past O'Donoghue who glanced up sardonically from his accountant columns, and Schmidt making sure once more of his words on certain paper. A

score of our men, the soldiers around the fireplace at the farther
end of the mess hall were watching Lépine come; Gabriel had
gone, leaving the tooled, golden leather chair gleaming momentarily empty in the firelight, and around Lépine's footsteps there
was silence, only the fire snap and crack and the distant snowy
crunch of people gathering. But then from the small rooms
where the prisoners were locked, rooms which like Riel's bedroom simply opened off the main hall where the men lived and
slept when they could, a voice began to sing, thin, mockingly
English:

> *The Coyote French will celebrate, celebrate, celebrate,*
> *The Coyote French will—*

Lépine had swung his arm up, and the guard slammed his
rifle butt on the door. Lépine spoke English against it,

"Dr. Schultz, we had an agreement. He does not sing,
nothing. You understand?"

Even the Métis who understood no English listened. After a
moment there came through the door, "We understand, yes,"
brittle, as if barely controlled.

At the farther end of the long room O'Donoghue had clamped
both hands to the desk to keep from exploding. "What a god
damn situation," he hissed to Schmidt. "We control the country
and Fort Garry and we have to sit here, smelly guards, and listen
to that Orange Canadian shit sing, one little desk between us; sit
here, so-called Secretary and Treasurer, and we control the
country! What the hell are we..."

"Give him time," Schmidt said. "You think he likes—"

"And Mactavish lies in his Hudson's Bay palace, eight rooms
for one randy old bugger dying!"

The door scraped open over a sill of snow: Father Ritchot
crunched in, hugely bundled against the cold; Schmidt scrab-
bled among his papers in relief.

"Oh Father, we were waiting..." he lifted the order of ceremony he had been worrying. Ritchot glanced over it, his shovel beard rigid with ice.

"There are a thousand people...what will you do with the flag?"

Riel stood in the bedroom door pulling on the frock-coat, his face bright with happiness. I can tell you Bishop Taché was never Riel's mentor, not after he returned from Montreal and Chicago and St. Paul grown and cassockless; as Louis Schmidt was Riel's disciple so this dour French-Canadian priest, with a peasant face above his black beard like the back end of one of the pigs he let run around the parish yard behind the St. Norbert church, was Riel's confidant and guide.

"Isn't the order right?" Riel asked him.

"Yes, but the Hudson's Bay flag, it..."

"It's coming down, just before our new flag goes up."

"That will provoke some of those people," Ritchot said. "Unnecessarily, I think. If you took it down now, before the ceremony..."

"Oh...no flag on the pole when we go out..." Riel turned abruptly to Schmidt, "Is Elzéar the captain on duty?"

In a movement Schmidt was at the door, calling, and Elzéar Goulet appeared. He was as tall as Lépine, but he had laughter the Adjutant-General never would have and he stood blocking the sun's glare off the snow, his broad face stretched in grinning anticipation; that would not have changed had he known the vicious way his life would end soon, all too soon.

"Take down that flag, before we come out," Riel said. "Without calling attention to it."

"How about we fire a cannon? They'd all look that way." Riel smiled. "That's for later."

"Yeah," Elzéar laughed, then bent, peered at him closely. "Your coat's real nice, but you need a mackinaw. It's seventeen below out here."

Riel laughed aloud. "Not the mackinaw," he said, "the capote. This is the day of the Métis!"

"Hurrah for the Bois-brûlés!" Elzéar roared our old, first name, turned and vanished in the sun, the men's answering shout following him. Riel was surrounded by their dark, heavy laughter, his face a thin gleam of happiness.

"Would you pray for us now, Father?"

"It is time, yes."

The men knelt as Ritchot raised his arms wide over them, with Riel kneeling as it seemed at their centre.

"Wanderers ready to perish were our fathers, and our mothers dwellers in darkness, but the Lord heard our cries; he gave us food in the wilderness and with his mighty arm destroyed our enemies. O Lord, who hast given us our land, and us to become a new nation, look upon us from heaven thy dwelling place. Bless us thy people, and bless the land which thou hast given us, which we have held from our enemies with the power of thy arm. O Lord our God, bless us today according to thy great mercy. Glory be to thee O Lord, forever and ever. Amen."

That was Noël Ritchot's great strength as a priest, and he learned it during the years he was with us on the plains for our summer hunt and knew the violent sun, the thirst and dust, the pain of searching and searching for buffalo while children cried in hunger and our scouts watched Sioux warriors on the distant ridges watching us; it was a strength Alexandre Taché, though he loved us, was our great teacher and finally Archbishop, never learned: prayer in a language we could all understand but still kept in that path of holiness it is proper to walk when approaching God. In that Ritchot, never anything but a parish priest, prayed like every good Indian; and that's even stranger since he was unmixed French-Canadian. Well, maybe that isn't so far from Indian anyway, like my father always said fondling us, so brown in his lap, for as Ritchot prayed over the mutter of people gathering outside in Fort Garry square, his face gradually pulled together in agony as if he already saw ahead through four Indian fours of years to this very December day in St. Boniface Cathedral when he would be praying again surrounded by several thousand kneeling inside and out among the snowy stones of the cemetery; a coffin nailed shut within a ring of these very men. But now while he prayed a small sound grew in the far corner of the hall where the prisoners were locked; inserted itself thin as scissor points between the kneeling men, snipping them out each into their separate hates, and O'Donoghue opened his eyes as if tugged by some stench; but Lépine on one knee lifted his head through Ritchot's gloria,

...the Coyote French will celebrate
Till wee-wee time in the mor-ning.

and in an instant had crossed himself and was at the prisoners' locked door. His fist hammered louder than any rifle butt, though he did not so much as raise his voice.

"Schultz. He sings once more and we whip every one of you. You hear."

Riel had noticed none of that; his thoughts were beyond Orange insult as Schmidt clasped the capote around his shoulders, the door opening brilliant sunlight before him. Outside we people of Red River were waiting for him, and he led his small party swiftly between the ranks of the Métis soldiers, their guns shouldered and their blue sashes more or less trimly tied, to the platform at the foot of the flagstaff standing bare now in the Fort Garry square.

We the people of Red River: we were a very mixed lot on December 8, 1869, but at least we French Métis–Bois-brûlés, my song name for us, now not much used; it seemed some no longer liked the implication of campfire, or colour–we were still the largest of the four groups. We still supplied most of the food, whether by our summer buffalo hunt or by going south for the flour in winter, and we had the only possible military organization at Red River in our buffalo hunters; they had now turned soldier under Ambroise Lépine, as we had once turned soldier under Cuthbert Grant when our dream of ourselves as The New Nation was born. The Scottish settlers we had fought in 1816 were now our neighbours and friends, as were the English half-breeds who lived as one with the Scots since their fathers were the Scottish servants of the fur companies who, when they returned to the British Isles with the fortunes they had taken out of us, invariably left their half-Indian children behind. But since 1849, when we French broke the Hudson's Bay Company monopoly in trade on Red River, more and more of the Company men remained with us when they resigned from service; after all, many of them loved their Indian or Métis wives as truly as any husband could and once a livelihood was possible on the plains after you had given your youngest energy to the implacable Company, why, many loved the plains as we did. The third group, the Americans, were mostly businessmen. Though their saloons along both sides of Winnipeg's main street created a stench that reached to heaven (I thanked God that we lived forty miles away at White Horse Plains, not across the river in St. Boniface and St. Vital), fortunately they were too few to have much effect politically. It was the fourth group, the Canadians, who almost destroyed us all. With confederation of the Canadas in 1867, the Upper Canadians–they were so *upper*–somewhere got the notion that Red River must be their proper colony. Of course there might be the odd furry Scot out there (that three generations of farmers had lived and died at Red River was beyond their comprehension), but mostly there were just Indians and "raw pemmican eaters," as Sir John A. put it–us–who obviously needed all-knowing Protestant Ontario to develop us to our fullest potential. Develop our potential! I burst into laughter in the middle of the blessed Mass at that thought but Canadians came, by the hundreds. People like the speculator Dr. John C. Schultz, whose wife, when our Governor Mactavish jailed him for refusing to pay a debt, led fifteen friends to the prison at one o'clock in the morning, overpowered the guard, and carried the handsome young doctor home in triumphant drunkenness; or the so-called poet Charles Mairanyone who tried to sing his verses while riding a horse would fall off in broken rhythm—who weekly sent long letters about how easy it was to make a fortune off the poor dunces in Red River to his Ontario brothers, who as regularly published them in the Toronto *Globe*. Contrary to general Ontario belief, there were persons at Red River who subscribed to newspapers; some could even read. And when Mair stated in one letter that "many wealthy people are married to half-breed women, who, having no coat of arms but a 'totem' to look back to, make up for the deficiency by biting at the backs of their 'white' sisters," the next afternoon when he arrived at the post office Mrs. Andrew Bannatyne (no totem she) not only lengthened his affected Byronic nose but counted his ribs with a heavy horse whip she had brought along for that very purpose.

A thousand of us, including our delegation from White Horse Plains, stood in the snow and watched young Louis Riel and his party stride through the ranks of our Métis soldiers. Father Dugas signalled frantically to his St. Boniface College Boys Band and presently they produced a squawky fanfare. The valves of one trumpet, however, were frozen shut and though the trumpeter battered it against his knee, the historic moment had passed him; he never played a note after he left school, but until the day he died sixty-seven years later he was known as Spittles O'Haligan.

"Our Mr. Riel has shown remarkable restraint," said James Ross, looking up the bare flagpole, "waiting so long to strike the Company colours when his savages have already occupied the fort for a month."

Andrew Bannatyne was watching Riel mount the platform. "When I see men stand guard saying their rosaries," he said, "I get no sense of savagery."

"Oh of course they're always praying," said Ross. "When they're not drinking."

Bannatyne sniffed in his direction and raised one hoary eyebrow; Ross laughed.

"Riel drinks nothing," said Charles Nolin beside them. To the day he died he was a Métis like that: if he could find a spot, he stood with the English.

"But what can I do," Ross shrugged eloquently, "my education wasn't the Sulpician College of Montreal, that sense of duty, the piety...."

"I'm sure Osgoode Hall," said Bannatyne dryly, "never taught anyone to pray."

"Only *in extremis*, before exams," Ross was reaching inside his coat. "Even for us half-breed natives, this country is so confounded cold, eh Mr. Nolin?"

"Enough people seem to want it," said our Charles.

"My friends, brothers, and sisters..." Riel stood above us, but so little elevated we could see only his head above the crowd. With him were Schmidt, Ritchot, O'Donoghue, and Lépine towering over them all. Elzéar Goulet, below them with the new flag folded over his arm, was so tall I could see half his grin above the clustered heads.

"When the day is cold," Riel said, his high voice clear and strong in the flashing sun, "it is good to see many warm faces. Especially from Winnipeg, and the far English parishes, Headingly, and Kildonan, and St. Andrews, and the French from St. Norbert, and White Horse Plains."

No one, not even the clever priests of Montreal could have taught Riel to speak as he did; certainly I never heard his father hold a crowd's attention with his first word. Perhaps his was the voice of some Cree orator generations past, perhaps it was the

Lagimodière blood: his mother stood with us, the pride of her family and her son stamped like granite on her delicate face. But Sara Riel stood there also, her Grey Sisters coif crossing her slender, beautiful face with a deep shadow.

"A few things must be said before we make our proclamation," Riel continued. "The people living along the Red and Assiniboine rivers, Indian and English and French, have always considered themselves a free people. We have hunted, farmed, freighted, traded as we wished; and we have been so free because for fifty years the Bois-brûlés have been wardens of the plains and their guns have repelled all those who approached our colonies with evil intent. And as the guns of our hunters have repelled Sioux war parties, so they have repelled Mr. McDougall. He was coming here with a sheet of paper and two boxes of guns to make himself our master. Then, repelled, from behind the protection of the border he tried with his illegal proclamations to incite us to civil war. The clear action of a fool! That we would kill each other for the benefit of Ontario! We have taken over this fort to protect the Company's property and to protect our rights as free and loyal subjects of Her Majesty Queen Victoria, whom God preserve long..."

The prisoners in the guardroom heard our cheers, and Thomas Scott best of all. He was not singing now; he had his stockinged feet on Jack Henderson's and William Farmer's shoulders, his head forward in the narrow window that opened into the cold, craning to see. The two below him staggered, and he had to grab for the icy bars.

"Jesus, can't you stand steady!"

"You try this!" Henderson muttered. "What's the bastard saying?"

"You don't have to bust your backs to know that," John Schultz said. He was sitting on the one bed and soundlessly, with all the delicacy of the surgeon, honing a long knife on his belt. "He's piling shit on the Company and on Ontario and on

Protestants." A key clattered against the lock and the knife vanished. "Inspection, get down!"

The two dumped Scott, cursing, to the floor as the door jerked open. Head guard Joseph Delorme glared at them from the open doorway; Riel's voice rang indistinguishably from the courtyard and, though we were cold out there, stamping our feet in snow, it was so rare to hear a strong French voice telling everyone at Red River, repeating a few sentences in English but telling the Company and the whole world in French what was going to happen, so rare we might have been hypnotised by a magician.

"...and Governor Mactavish, besides being gravely ill, has been as helpless as any of us. The Directors of his own Company that has governed us from London never asked his advice, never told him anything. They simply found it convenient to sell us. Like cattle! And the Government of Canada was more than willing to buy us. One and a half million dollars. We are people! The North-West is our mother. Here we were born, here our ancestors are buried, and here we will die. We will never be sold!"

Well, we cheered then! And not just us old people who had once lived and sung the glory of The New Nation and seen that vision slowly crumple under monopolies and laziness and more and more settlers and leaderlessness and buffalo fading west so our summer hunts from Red River became impossible and our people moved to Moose Mountain and Qu'Appelle, even the Cypress Hills, or like the Dumont brothers built cabins a month's ride away on the Saskatchewan while their father, too old to ride to the hunt, lived in St. Boniface: no, it was everyone cheering. What human being likes to hear he has been sold by someone he will never see, so he can never kick him where it will do the longest good? May God help us. Charles Nolin was yelling French among all the English, and Bannatyne clapping as much as his Presbyterian blood would allow; and James Ross too–Lord knows he was as much Cree as I, and that's twice as much as Riel–though he was shaking his head, whether in disagreement or in appreciation of a superb political speech it would have been hard to say.

"For two weeks," Riel went on, "we–all of us, English and French–have debated here in Fort Garry. We have not been able to agree on everything, but neither have Mr. McDougall's actions destroyed our brotherhood. For on this we stand together: Canada will listen to us! Sir John A. Macdonald wants the North-West because our vast country is the keystone of Confederation. Without us Canada is nothing but a puny Atlantic state. Some–not all, and we know those who have not–some Canadians among us have tried to bully us into hasty decisions and so our Métis hunters, under Adjutant-General Lépine, have had to imprison some who would have shot us, if they could, for speaking for our rights. The Métis guns have kept law and order, and I pledge to you they will keep it. We will not be rushed. We demand our rights as loyal British citizens, we will negotiate our allegiance to whatever country we wish as a free people. Therefore, I ask Mr. Schmidt to now read our formal Public Declaration."

Louis Schmidt had stiffened his backbone with more than a nip, that was plain, but it was a great moment for him. He had been sent to Montreal with Riel but returned home after three years, educated just enough to be useless in either the French or English world at Red River. For years he did almost nothing; when Riel returned in 1868 he was going south to Minnesota for the flour like any illiterate Métis, but he was so poor that when Riel invited him to live with him in his mother's house, he gladly accepted. And now he stepped forward, paper in hand, his glance flicking over us and snagging a moment on the Governor's Residence. At a window there William Mactavish, who had ruled Red River for five years at the pleasure of those lords in London, was watching Louis Schmidt and doubtless remembering that just a day ago he had had to turn over the key of the Hudson's Bay vaults to this formerly penniless half-caste, as the Company mostly named us in its correspondence.

No wonder Schmidt's voice shook a little:

Hear this Declaration:
Whereas it is admitted by all men that, when there is no
government, the people have the fundamental human right
to organize themselves for the maintenance of law, and their
own protection, and, whereas we the people of the North-
West have been abandoned by that government to which we
always gave faithful allegiance, therefore in the name of the
people of the North-West we declare that:

1. *We refuse to recognize the authority by which*
   Canada pretends to have a right to coerce us who
   have ever been free British subjects;

2. *We call elections to be held in every parish, and each*
   parish to send two representatives, freely elected, to
   form a council which will consider the present polit-
   ical state of this country and adopt such measures
   as may be deemed best for the future welfare of the
   same;

3. *Until such time as that Council is elected and has*
   reached decisions, we declare the Métis National
   Committee to be the Provisional Government of the
   North-West for the maintenance of law and order
   and the protection of its people.

   Relying on the protection of the God of nations,
   we pledge our lives and sacred honour to support
   this declaration.

GIVEN AT FORT GARRY THIS 8TH DAY OF DECEMBER, 1869.
Signed: Louis Riel, President
Louis Schmidt, Secretary.

Schmidt stopped, and for a moment Riel stood on the little platform, waiting. But there was not a sound; as if the crowd under

the long Hudson's Bay walls of Red River stone, the pointed bastions where the cannon sat, had finally understood what an ominous sound was here being made: we were all, suddenly, speaking for ourselves, and we would at last be held responsible for every sound we made. Let me tell you, it was enough to strike me dumb. Through the crowd suddenly I noticed a young Tourond–Patrice, I think, he was less than ten–but he was frozen as if on tiptoe, stretching his neck to see the men on the platform who had spoken such awesome words into the air, and like all of us he seemed not even to breathe.

"Raise the flag," Riel said quietly.

Elzéar moved, the ropes clanged in the cold, and then the flag rose out of the shoulders of the people. Not the old blue Bois-brûlés flag of chains linked for unity under which we rode down the Assiniboine with Cuthbert Grant fifty-three years before and swept through every Hudson's Bay fort on our way to Seven Oaks and which ever since had led us out on the plains, defying Sioux and Cheyenne and the dust and wind itself. This new flag had nothing of that North-West subservience; white, it slid limply higher into the motionless cold with the brown of a buffalo breaking a fold, a huge fleur-de-lis, and then, in a vagrant twitch, we saw a green shamrock straightening, almost exposed, folding again. It rang against the top, hung limply unseeable and all the people silent. I thought, by my sainted father this declaration is stillborn, Louis Riel rigid above us, praying for a breath from God to spread that flag and give life to his vision, praying–it was too cold, it would take a miracle–an Irish voice behind me bellowed,

"Vive le North-West, vive le North-West libre!"
and the rifles of two companies jerked up, exploded fire and smoke.

Everything exploded. The people were screaming, jumping, whether for fright or happiness it was hard to tell at first; but when the cannon in the river bastion boomed over our heads we knew why we were yelling. The Governor's Cannon! Rifles vol-leying smoke into the cold could not be heard above us, roaring for happiness.

Not everyone, of course. Among the large, dignified gen-tlemen there was clapping perhaps, but no cheering. Standing between James Ross and Judge Black, the Empire Britisher whose only reaction to the entire afternoon had been to jerk at the first volley but whose face had remained as stony as it always had been permanently frozen on the bench, Andrew Bannatyne said, clapping steadily, "This might not have been necessary, had Mactavish been well."

"After those surveyors in summer," Nolin stuck his head between them, "it was necessary, it *was*."

And in the prison Thomas Scott paced in fury, his curses a low, livid stream.

"If they hadn't caught your wife," Henderson muttered to Schultz still honing his knife, "with all them guns, they'd never have nailed us.

"We were sitting ducks, Jack, all that powder..." Schultz rubbed intently under cover of his jacket. "When they lined up the two cannon, no chance."

"Okay, the powder, but it was using your wife made them really mad."

"Riel's got them so jumpy about women, it was chance. And she got this knife past them, eh?"

"One knife," said Henderson bitterly, "all them hair-triggered pigs. We might as well sign his paper or we'll rot here."

The fourth cannon boomed outside over the shouts of the people. Scott wheeled, seized Henderson, almost screaming, "I won't perjure myself to no sonofabitching tincan Napol—!"

"Tommy!" Henderson pushed him off. "Tommy for god's sake, keep it down!"

"Yeah," grunted William Farmer; at White Horse Plains we knew him as The Great Stoneass because of his face and how he sat his horse when he rode through from Portage to Fort Garry. "Shut your mouth, or they'll split us up. They've let some others go."

Schultz had his arm around Scott's shoulders, paced him the four-step round of the cell. Both so tall their heads almost scraped the ceiling: impressive men until they opened their mouths. "Just wait, my friends," Schultz murmured, "just wait. They're nothing but little kids, they'll have to celebrate, just wait."

Father Dugas and his St. Boniface Boys Band were blaring a march he had composed for the occasion when the final volleys of the Métis soldiers lined behind Riel, who was smiling now but still at attention on the platform, suddenly echoed with shots from behind us, outside the walls. Everyone craned; the band lost their notes in their throats—perhaps McDougall, Dennis, those violent Canadians at Stone Fort or Portage—but the unthinking trumpeters, deaf from their own snorting, blasted the music on and a roar of laughter caught us all when through the river gate galloped wild Gabriel Dumont and his "savages," as we already laughingly called them. A whole company now, not just the original four who helped Lépine rout those prigs at the border, and behind them out of the whirl of dancing horses and rifles squawked Red River carts piled high with brush. They were spilling into the square among us, and Gabriel galloped one swirl through them to haul his horse back on its haunches below the flagpole, his shaggy horse and his worn leather quivering suddenly still as if hacked out of one gigantic rock. The last trumpets staggered out then as Gabriel swung his rifle up high in one fist and roared to Riel:

"The wintering Métis of the Saskatchewan salute the Provisional Government of Red River!"

The band blared to our cheers.

"We salute," Gabriel's gigantic voice bounced from the stone walls, "our chief, Louis Riel!"

I could not have cheered louder, but I did.

"And..." Gabriel's arm whirled his horse up so tightly the

animal spiralled, danced on its hind legs as if hung, "we have wood for fire; we'll celebrate like we know how!"

That was what built our unity in 1869: the planning and ceremony of Riel, the emotion of Gabriel. For twenty years after the breaking of the Company trade monopoly we people did not talk politics: we forgot what the word was and it seemed we did not need to know it; but by 1868 the only buffalo left were beyond the Missouri and the Saskatchewan, and grasshoppers had destroyed our crops. In February, 1869 there was so little food in Red River that for the first time in my memory–I was born in 1793!–we had to fish through river ice from White Horse Plains to St. Peters. Then in October of that year the Canadians, without a word of warning and without any rights whatever–Canada had no more right to us than did China–came surveying across our river-lot hay lands. Luckily they began with André Nault at St. Vital, and not at White Horse Plains; we Grants and Brelands and Falcons and Gariepys had no such educated cousin as Louis Riel to talk careful English with them–it was Riel and Lépine who rode into Fort Garry at the head of the two hundred hunters and told Company Mactavish they had come to protect him: not a shot fired and they controlled the heart of Red River.

Gabriel's fire ripped the quick December darkness into red and yellow tatters, the fiddles sent the night flying into the overcast with our flying feet. Riel had lifted his strict prohibition by granting each soldier one cup of rum, courtesy of the Hudson's Bay stores; and those off duty, their pockets full of pay, courtesy of the Hudson's Bay vaults and all carefully recorded, kept the snow between Winnipeg and Fort Garry singing. Dutch George Emmerling had a boy beating an up-side-down kettle outside his saloon, which probably meant his swill was worse than usual though no one thought of quality that night except perhaps the dancers feeling buffalo hides under their feet again. But for the Fort walls over us, it could have been a winter hunt dance on the prairie; a clean joy and the blessing of God to see people dancing on hides once more, their white and brownish and red scarred and deformed and silken young faces glistening with happiness, their voices calling to each other in Cree or Sioux or French or Saulteux or Swampy Cree or Gaelic or English in every accent that knows those tongues.

"I want to thank you especially," said Riel to the Grey Sisters standing at the farthest edge of firelight, "for sewing the flag. It is so beautiful, and you stayed up all night..."

There were four with Sara, the first of our people to be a nun as Riel was to have been the first priest, and they half-hid their young faces, smiling at this sudden incredible man so close to one of them.

"Oh, it was really Sara, all night...that fleur-de-lis!"

Riel's hand rose, he could not stop himself, and he brushed his sister's cheek before he forced it down, away from her beautiful face, down to the impersonal grey shoulder.

"It's just so plain," Sara said softly, her voice low as he would never forget it. "We couldn't do the elaborate Bourbon one."

Riel looked away, at our people dancing. "For us," he said "plain is really much better."

"...our two cannon balls crossing each other through Schultz's house," Elzéar was declaiming between dance and fire, "packed like it was with powder woulda blown every house in Winnipeg so high—"

"God save us, not Dutch George's!" someone yelled, and the gathered men roared.

"Just what I told Lépine," Elzéar hoisted a bottle momentarily, "but they all come out like sheep–swearing sheep, but anyways–and we moved in, that house where none of us ever got invited, goddam no, and there was young Mrs. Dr. Schultz lying all spread out in the big soft bed in a special room just for sleeping like—"

"Lépine never let you walk in *there* alone, eh?"

"No!" Elzéar bellowed above the laughter. "He went in first,

and the four of us, we had to hold hands so we wouldn't touch..."
Elzéar could time his audience beautifully, "nothing! Anyways,
she looks funny, bulging, like she's gonna birth a small buffalo
in that big bed and Lépine he stares, and we stare, we can't
believe our eyes, who hasn't watched her flying slim like one
little sparrow down King Street, but now she's so pale and looks
up at him with those bee-utiful Irish eyes and says, 'O General
Lépine, I am so ill!' and she looks it all right, and Lépine he hesitates. 'Please?' she says, and her eyelids flutter. And that's her
mistake, because like a flash Lépine's big fist's got that robe–
jerks–ha! you know what we see?"

They were all nailed tight into their expectations; even
Young Bertie of Lachine whose mind never got past childhood,
may God protect him, forgot the bottles he had been trying to
stare out of the men's hands into his own.

A squeak: "The whitest legs here to Ontario."

"No! Two cases of bullets and thirty-six Enfield rifles!"
Through laughter the big captain abruptly reached over, plucked
a bottle from an unresisting hand and thrust it at Young Bertie.
"Here...have a slug."

"You shouldn't really do that, to him," said an uneasy voice.
Elzéar watched the natural swallow, almost choke, then swallow
again.

"Ah the poor bugger," he said. "Easy, just slow and it goes
easy."

The fiddlers had drawn in more than just Métis now: everyone
was taking their turn on the hides before the fire, spinning our
dance. Blond Hugh Sutherland whirled with our black-haired
young people, and he beckoned to his mother clapping her
hands to the beat at the edge of the hides. A Métis girl, still
dancing, reached out to Mrs. Sutherland, drew her among the
dancers. We cheered as the tall Scots woman began to move her
legs, hips, her fine breasts, laughing in tiny bursts, self-conscious
but determined to move in her joy with her son, the dancing girl.

"Grandfather Falcon," Riel said beside me. "I am so happy you are here."

I was sitting near the fire with my thoughts, half roasted and half frozen in the way of an old man by an open fire, but I was too happy after such a day to notice. He hunkered down beside me and I looked at him as the people danced, shouted. I too once went to school in Montreal, long ago, and I saw all the great men there and read what Macdonald said, and Cartier, and the Americans Lincoln and Grant; I saw the great men who came to Red River–Selkirk, Robertson, Simpson, Howe, Taché, Tupper, Smith, Wolseley, Archibald–and not even Donald Smith knew I existed so they never protected themselves from my thoughts; every day I went through dust or snow to pray before the altar of St. Francis Xavier, and I have seen the size of men when they are called before the law, before sworn witnesses. Let me tell you immediately, Louis Riel was a giant. If God had willed it, he could have ruled the world.

No, no, hear me out, and you will believe it too.

"You were saying good words," I said to him then beside that fire in the quick darkness, December 8, 1869, his glistening curly hair bent close to me. "Strong words, and I remembered your father twenty years ago, when Guillaume Sayer was on trial: your father testified against the Company, and together they broke the monopoly. If...your father might have started what you are...per-haps not. He never prayed very much. Do you pray enough?"

Riel's black eyes stared into the crashing flames. After a time he said again, still motionless,

"Grandfather, how long must one live before he can speak for the dead?"

"I am nearly old enough to sing for them," I said, and his glance leaped to mine.

"You have made a new song for us."

And I laughed aloud. To be known again, our Métis glory! All of a day's driving from White Horse Plains, and my head bulging once more with words and music and rhythm, I chuckled and laughed until they all thought I was at last truly crazy, feeling again after years all those wild sounds of frogs plains and words clashing and liberators and lords drinking their death in enormous halls that had spun in my head for half a century.

"Yes, yes. You Métis boys have given me another song. About King Muck-Dougall."

Mrs. Sutherland had laughed herself out of the dance, but Hugh and the lovely girl–she might have been Riel's cousin, Lagimodières were everywhere and they lived forever–were now dancing very close. Not touching of course, which is impossible in our dances, but close enough to be locked together effortlessly far beyond the simple power of touch.

At the opposite edge of the firelight, away from the dance, Gabriel hunched over the buffalo bones; the circles of men around him deepened as the mounds of Hudson's Bay coin grew on the hide at his knees. Calixte Tourond now squatted facing him, watching his hands fly under the gambling leather, trying to concentrate that one bone into its place. Gabriel's hand stopped and Tourond's gnarled hand began to move, hesitated. The lightness of the last coin in his hand had caught him, and with that doubt he knew he was destroyed. He looked up. Riel stood behind him, eyes intent on the leather.

"Which one, Mr. Riel?"

"Left." Riel pointed without a second's hesitation.

But Young Bertie was behind him abruptly, making sounds in his throat, shaking Riel's shoulder violently, pointing right, moaning. The men stared, respectful before the President but held in the strange awe of a natural. No one plays lightly with the Lord's chosen, and for a moment the firelight even shaded them alike, their height, their intensity, their clustered hair...with a jerk, Tourond pointed left.

Impassive, Gabriel lifted the leather. The bone lay on the right. Everyone looked at Bertie, silent; then Riel laughed, clapped him on the shoulder and tossed a coin at Tourond's feet. But Young Bertie had already lost interest; the gamblers shifted aside from his furtive, slipping motion and Riel watched him go, the halo of his call circling him like snow, watched him walk between firelight and darkness under the stone walls beyond the fiddles still shrilling at the tireless people.

In the officer's mess, the guards had begun their mistake with Dr. Schultz and friends. Delorme had brought in tea mugs for the prisoners while two guards leaned against the door with rifles, bottles obvious in their coat pockets. Schultz half lay on the bed, and Delorme had so little experience being a guard he neither watched him closely nor the others near the window; after all, about a thousand people were cavorting outside.

"You celebrate," said Schultz, warm and friendly, "and we get tea. How about sharing a bottle with us, eh?"

Our people have problems: Delorme couldn't look a big white like Schultz in the eye. He knocked crumbs off the table with the edge of his hands, set out the four mugs.

"We can pay," said Schultz.

"Sure," said Scott at the window. "Get us a drink and I'll even tell you a funny story about—"

"Tom," Schultz said tightly, but Scott went on, tone nasty now, "...about down by the river where I slide Louis' pretty cousin around on my pole and her yelping like one happy little doggie to—"

Delorme understood enough English; he had wheeled on Scott, face black, but Henderson rammed Scott's shoulder with his fist and Schultz was talking very loud,

"Shut up, Tom! Don't listen to him, he's just crazy, that's all he does...just talks. Listen," Schultz said, standing now as Delorme turned to go, "if you get us a bottle or two—what will it harm, make us feel a bit better—I'll make it worth your while, you could get some extra for yourself. Eh? Two?"

And Delorme looked at him then, glance slipping aside to

the floor; when he should have been seeing Farmer, behind Scott and Henderson, gesture at the window.

The overcast night sky sat over us like a roof; Riel had looked into the fire for some time, and then he was gone. The fiddlers were tiring, so I settled my skull cap more exactly on my head and picked up my guitar. I walked around the fire, the rhythm already moving in me, and I knew this one was good enough, also, to be sung to the paddle stroke on the Assiniboine or the Saskatchewan or the Athabaska or all the way down the Mackenzie to the Frozen Sea itself. I hit one loud chord, the fiddlers stopped, and the dancers turned. I said nothing then, looking around at my happy people; just letting them know I was still showman enough to make them wait, a little. Cuthbert Grant would have been laughing aloud at me, "Pierre, you little chip of scorched wood, they'll sing your songs long after we're finished by the worms." May God rest his soul, his brave soul.

Thinking of that, so abruptly, I almost mistimed myself. But fire warmed me behind, and all about me the breath of our people rose from them like white prayer in the dark.

"My children, this is a day to be remembered when your hairs are as white as mine, and there is a song we might sing, to help you remember. As we were driving here from White Horse Plains, and my son-in-law is such a good driver, as you know, this song came into my head. From where it came..."

I shrugged, and they laughed.

"It is a song called 'The Sad Ballad of King Muck'...Muck-Dougall, that is."

Even Father Ritchot's solid face broke into a smile at that. He should smile: the songs of the priests—there were bits of my songs they didn't like, but they wanted the people to sing—helped us travel many a dusty, cart-squeaking mile when the terror of the Sioux was stronger than any blessing of buffalo. So I locked at him when I struck the first chords into the uproarious laughter: I had to keep him smiling. With my tune, at least.

Now where, the whole world over,
Could e'er be found again
A tale as sad as this one,
Of Muck-Dougall and his men?
　　But listen to me well
　　And the tale to you I'll tell.

Opposite me on the hides Gabriel roared the refrain as the people repeated it after me, leading them all as much by his swinging arms and his leaping body as by his bellowing, almost tuneless voice. Each refrain would go better than the last, I knew.

Muck-Dougall viewed our prairies;
He thought them his estate.
An Orangeman there could govern
Like an Eastern Potentate.
　　What's more, he actually was sent
　　By Macdonald and his government.
From Canada he started,
His chest swollen with pride.
He told his wife, when they parted,
"At last, I will provide!
　　With joy and rapture sing,
　　Bow down, I am a king!"
Muck's greed told him at Red River
A fortune he would amass;
And so he brought out nothing
But a throne fit for his—

This song should not give you the wrong impression of me. I am a pious man, I love to contemplate the divine mystery of the mass which I attend every day, but you should believe me that not even 'General' Dickson–crazy as only the bluest Englishmen can truly be, who called himself Montezuma II and wanted to hire, without a penny or credit, the Métis soldiers to help him liberate the "Indian Nations of Mexico"–not even Dickson whose unblooded regimental sword hangs on my kitchen wall gave me so much for a people's song. Now they could barely sing even the two line refrain, and Ritchot himself could not hide his laughter behind his hand.

There was no laughter in Governor Mactavish's luxurious bedroom. The sick old man lay high under the canopy of his bed, face like a death's head. His brother-in-law, Andrew Bannatyne, sat with him; and his Indian woman, even more beautiful than they usually had to be to serve Company officers, had just placed a chair for Riel. There was a silent moment, all of them hearing our roaring in Fort Garry square.

Bannatyne said, "Pierre Falcon really has them singing. Sounds a bit like his 'New Nation' song."

Mactavish's glance shifted from Riel. "You mean, the Seven Oaks one?"

"Not so new," Riel said curtly. "Fifty-three years ago."

Mactavish moved uncomfortably on his pillow, and the woman leaned to place a fresh cloth on his forehead.

"Somewhat before all our time," Mactavish said. "And no Company people have been killed, this time."

"This time," Riel said watching the beautiful woman wring a white cloth into the blue porcelain basin–the braided gold tassels of the canopy and the carved oak posts framed her across the bed–"they have been much more sensible, and cooperative."

Both Mactavish and Bannatyne laughed slightly, no more than befit the cooperation expected by seven hundred rifles.

"I understand you took," Mactavish's mouth reached for air, "...the keys and opened, the Company vaults, this afternoon."

"Yes. The men had to be paid. They have stood guard and ridden patrol on their own food for over a month."

"First our Fort, then our money, then...."

"You'll be compensated; O'Donoghue is keeping exact accounts."

"That man..." Bannatyne shook his head.

"...is the best bookkeeper in Red River," Riel said blandly.

"Yes! But a Fenian, a pro-American—"

"He is an excellent bookkeeper. The Company," Riel said to Mactavish, "always gets it back twice over–the men are spending it in your store right now."

Mactavish tried to laugh, his chest rattling. "Forty per cent perhaps," he said, "sixty for the, American saloons...."

We were singing the song the second time, everyone on the entire verse as I lined it out for them. The fiddlers were playing along, line for line, though they could hardly be heard as we came to the second last verse where the crowd, knowing what was coming, bellowed louder and louder,

Just as King Muck set foot
Upon his realm's fair soil,
Some men rode up and put
A stop to his progress royal...

I bowed my grey hairs to Lépine and Schmidt, leaning against each other, roaring up into darkness. I was turning to do the same to Gabriel, still centre, still leading, when Elzéar Goulet burst through the ringed people holding McDougall's chair high above his head. For an instant he seemed something devilish, the huge man with the enormous chair so marvelously carved and embroidered in leather they said there was nothing like it anywhere even in Canada, holding it high like a grotesque crown he was about to place on his own head, or perhaps Gabriel's, as he strode to the centre; but he lowered it gently to the buffalo hides.

"Sing Grandfather," Elzéar roared. "Sing!" And I sang the refrain, everyone's eyes on that unbelievably beautiful chair, already anticipating the outburst of the final verse.

They said, "That's far enough, my friend.
Right where you stand is journey's end."
But in dreams his crown he wears,
King Muck knows no defeat,
Though the throne on which he sits
Has a hole fit for his seat!

Such hoots, screaming—the refrain was impossible. I had no breath anyway. But not so Gabriel. Suddenly he had seized the huge chair and hoisted it high above his streaming black hair. He was spinning on the hides, his feet a blur, screaming the refrain I had no idea how he remembered,

Today that's all he owns,
King Muck needs no other thrones!

And with one surge of his immense body he hurled the chair high above the fire. Down it crashed, sparks spraying to the stars, down into the flames, and the sound torn from all of us then was the joyous scream of a woman, rapture and agony, delivered at last. That priceless chair blazed fire like grease.

Riel did not hear that celebration. He had just told Mactavish the Provisional Government would have to move into the Governor's quarters; the two Scots were looking at him in a rigid silence that our roars in the Fort square did not joggle.

Mactavish said, exhausted, "I trust I will, be left, my bed."

"Your bed, your dining-room table, your—" Riel burst out slashing his arm up and his furious eyes snagged on the Indian woman there, looking at him without expression, and he broke off as swiftly as he had begun. "Look. Your children are mixed bloods too—their, our ancestors lived here, we must stand together, we have called elections and we need this building for working room. We must all stand together."

"You know it's not, the Red River, people..." Mactavish could not continue.

"It's the Canadians causing trouble, you know that," finished Bannatyne.

"You know all about them, yes?" Riel said coldly.

"I trade with all who trade honestly with me," said Bannatyne. "How 'honest' do they have to be to trade...from that big powder magazine in your store?"

Bannatyne stared at him a moment. "Red River is my home too," he said quietly.

"So you sell no more than small shot to hunters," Riel said. "I know that. Good." His voice quickened. "We all know there is violence building, and we all know Ontario. Go to the guardroom and talk to Doctor Schultz, to Thomas Scott! I'll be hanged before I hand this country over to Upper Canada!"

Gabriel was dancing. On the hides, all alone, the fiddlers playing the power he churned in all of us, a magnificent male dance that frothed with Métis fighting spirit, wild and living and shaped in our people our strong horses and the wide, wide earth we rode. Clapping hands, chanting, the thud of moccasins on hide. I had seen no Métis dance like that since we defeated the Sioux in 1852 on the Missouri Couteau. Gabriel, short, ugly, strong as a buffalo bull, was the prince of us that night, stirring our blood like the memories of glory and power. Elzéar watched him clapping, his face pulled wide in awe.

But unfortunately the guards were also dancing; Delorme still held his rifle roughly steady but several others were dancing with Henderson in the mess hall, outdancing him easily even in their drunkenness, and laughing foolishly until Henderson looked at Schultz leaning in the open cell doorway, stopped suddenly, and staggered against the table.

"Okay, boys," he said, "you're better than me, okay. But how about Tommy–listen, there's the pipes starting–when the pipes play we *all* dance."

Farmer stumped past Schultz, face like a haggis, and the guards froze in stupored amazement as he began to shuffle;

obviously, he thought he was dancing! Then Scott's long shape was in the mess hall whirling patterns like cobwebs out of the firelight onto the wall. Two more guards had to move; they stepped, back and forth, cradling their rifles in their arms almost as they would women. Henderson and Schultz looked at each other; Delorme sat drinking, his rifle laid across the table before him. Schultz shrugged, caught a steady rhythm with his clap; and Henderson immediately joggled his feet into it again. Dancing towards Scott who, in his silent, controlled fury was inching around the table and into the dim reaches of firelight near the door. Schultz shifted his feet imperceptibly, clapping, clapping.

The pipes and the Scottish reels swirled everyone onto the hides before the fire. Sara and the Grey Sisters had gone to night prayers–and perhaps penance–but otherwise there seemed more people than ever in the square. Elzéar and the soldiers were now whirling reels with their women. Young Bertie's face blinked here and there between flying bodies, his intense unwinking concentration. I said to Gabriel, squatting back to the fire with me, his chest still heaving,

"We all know you already as the son of The Stander."

Gabriel's laugh showed his worn teeth, watching young Sutherland in the crowd try to persuade the lovely Métis girl of something that probably had nothing to do with dance.

"Reels," said Gabriel, "are a lot like standing off the Sioux, you need more leg than head."

"There are many stories about you Dumonts."

A woman with a gleaming face brought him roast meat on a stick. Young Bertie stood staring as Gabriel smacked the woman's lips as if he would drink them, then that blank face was gone in the spinning crowd.

"Maybe we can," Gabriel said to me through torn meat, "maybe make a few more. For you to sing, Grandfather, under our flag, eh?"

Our buffalo flag was stirring; a night wind must have been moving above the Fort walls though it seemed calm below. The good pictures on it opened, folded away again, sewn so beautifully by the Grey Sisters, and it would never be remembered exactly because that was the only one ever made. Sutherland and the girl were gone, like Bertie, and now I could not recognize anyone in the dancing crowd where a moment before every face was so familiar. The sky was black, icy with stars and that good flag opening but the people might have been Canadians celebrating: despite any yelling Métis the arch of white Confederation is already complete, burn the flag and nail down a railroad, cinch the North-West tight against Ontario and Quebec, forever. What piddling difference does it make, Ontario or Quebec–strangers all, laughing and fixed upon our potential. While we dance. I can see it, see it all.

Hughie Sutherland and the girl had followed Young Bertie though they were unaware of that. The natural moved in the shadow of the wall beside the River Gate. A Métis stood guard there of course, but at the moment he was draining a bottle with tremendous determination, his long rifle set carefully against the wall beside him. Young Bertie peered: the steady throb of the throat, the intense concentration; and slowly his hand crept forward, closed over the rifle, lifted it gently as paper from the stone. The guard groped for his beads, drank, head back and eyes closed in, perhaps, worship. He was still holding the two anchors of his life when, a moment later, young Sutherland and the girl also slipped past him through the gate.

In the officers' mess the guards still cradled their rifles in their arms, dancing to the pipes sounding more clearly than ever through the door now open to the celebrating people. The four Canadians had rhythmed, smiled their way past the crowd in the square, picking up a coat here, a scarf or a capote there thrown aside in the heat of dancing. Delorme snored, his face wrenched sideways on the black, worn table.

"Wait." Schultz gestured the others around the corner shadows of the fur shed; "There's a guard at the River Gate."

Scott did not stop. "I'll take him out."

"No! Jack, you–here, take this." Schultz handed the knife to Henderson; "But just enough so we get past, understand?"

"Yeah!" Henderson vanished while Scott jerked, almost beserk with impatience, in Farmer's bearish arms.

"Tommy listen," Schultz talked low, fast, "will you listen now! We should get across the border to McDougall, then go for Ontario, get them hot and raise men—"

"McDougall's a scared shit," Scott hissed, "and maybe you are too. Boulton's in Portage—"

"Aye," Farmer muttered, "we're Portage men, we'll fight."

"We'll get this cocksucker by the balls, he'll—"

"Will you fools listen! Portage! Fifty, sixty men? McDougall was stupid to tell Boulton to muster men, assault, break into any fort...Riel has all the cannon and seven hundred hunters!"

"Run to your Canada First *talkers*." Scott was so enraged he slammed his head against the log wall. "I'm gonna slice some throats. And if you're a man you'll head north to Stone Fort, get the Scots and Indians together—"

"Didn't you *see* what that Dumont rode in with?"

"No fucking half-breed scares Tom Scott, if you—"

"Dr. Schultz!" Henderson was at the corner of the building; he gave the knife back. "Let's go–I didn't need it."

"Where's the gun?" Scott asked.

"I dunno," Henderson was puzzled. "He didn't have one."

"What!" Scott stared from Henderson to Schultz, sensing a conspiracy, but Schultz said, as amazed.

"He didn't have one?" Henderson shook his head. "Shut up Tommy, we all needed that gun. C'mon, we have to get to Anne with the horses."

Riel had returned to the fire again, close to where I was warming my backside, but he said nothing. The dancing, the gambling, the laughter of our people which was sinking beyond celebration now into carousing, did not exist for him. He sat on his heels staring steadily and without expression into the fire, seeing perhaps the red and golden patterns of the flames, perhaps the crossed braces of McDougall's chair already burned into unrecognizability.

Young Bertie had crunched down the bank of the Assiniboine River until the Fort lay a long blackness behind him, firelight shooting gold above it at the flag and the starry night. He paused near river bushes, the forbidden weight of a gun finally in his hands, and he lifted it to his face, moaning for happiness: suddenly shadows moved! Someone stood there, horses stirred, a slim shape black in moonlight against snow. And then a low gasp: a woman's voice,

"Oh...Young Bertie, you–and you have a gun? A–a new one?"

The natural shuffled backwards; he could not see the face that was coming closer, but a woman's laughter, so soft...women were always dangerous.

"Will you show me your new gun, that must be a very nice one..."

Young Bertie hesitated. Near a soft woman was always a man, usually angry. This one's hand extended; the smiling, dangerous face advanced from the saddled horses clinking by the bushes; suddenly his legs hurled him backwards, were running him in complete terror back up the bank. Cursing under her breath, Anne Schultz ran after him; he must not reach the Fort!

But there were figures running, men, from the River Gate, and Young Bertie wheeled down toward the river bank again. Down among black bushes he dove down, thrusting the forbidden rifle out of sight into the snow, mumbling softly, desperately, if it was buried and not there he would be safe; if he buried himself like the rifle, the woman would not have seen him and he would be safe. He burrowed down, terrified, but then through the distant sounds near the Fort he heard–his heart leaped–footsteps beside him–a shadow–he jerked up the buried rifle, swung it around toward the gigantic shadow looming over him, fired. The shadow broke into two pieces, a man's groan, a woman's scream.

"Anne!" Schultz shouted, hurling himself through the snow. "Anne!"

There were running footsteps, somewhere, but she stood black against the bushes. "Here, John! Over here."

He was beside her, clutching her. "That wasn't me," she said, almost calmly, "it was someone, in there."

"You didn't scream?"

"A girl–she's running..."

Both Henderson and Scott had crashed by into the bush. Henderson's gasp, "My god, Hughie Sutherland!" spun them around.

"Hughie?" Schultz blundered ahead, "What in hell's going..." but Scott suddenly roared,

"And the idiot! With a gun!"

Young Bertie had not moved, his eyeballs blankly depthless in his gaunt face; the terrible rifle and the woman, it was too much. He was nailed rigid with terror against the scrub oak. Scott lunged for the rifle and they were down, rolling in the snow, Henderson too, and Farmer.

"Hughie, what in the name of..." Schultz tried to kneel down, to find something for his hand to feel in the slick, slippery shape on the snow, but Scott tore the rifle from Bertie's hands, was trying to beat the natural's head with the barrel and the rolling tangle of bodies blundered against Schultz, driving him almost prone over the, he realized it, already stiffening youth.

"Stop it, stop!" Schultz was tearing the men apart. "Listen!"

There was a swirl of men and lights up the bank at the River Gate. Gasping they listened, footsteps, running as they came. Young Bertie moved, groaning, trying to get to his knees and

Scott suddenly smashed the barrel down into his face. The crack snapped back from across the frozen river.

"Stop it—it's the town idiot, you crazy—"

Henderson and Farmer grabbed Scott as Schultz bent to Young Bertie. Anne Schultz was babbling suddenly, staring at the motionless body.

"He must have come here with a girl, that girl, and I scared... just with a gir—" but Henderson had released Scott, was grabbing at Schultz still bent over the natural.

"They're coming, c'mon, where are the horses! You brought the horses!"

"Horses–horses," Mrs. Schultz grasped that, abruptly. "Yes! Three horses."

"Three!"

"That's all!"

"C'mon." Henderson grabbed at Schultz again. "Two of us ride double, c'mon!"

Schultz hesitated an instant, heard the sounds approaching, and sprinted after the others; followed the sobs of his wife down to the nervous horses.

And so Lépine and his men brought those two innocents to us who had heard screams, running, and seen the distraught girl collapse in a huddle of women on the snow. Two soldiers carried Young Bertie between them; Elzéar followed, undraped Hughie Sutherland from his shoulder and laid him beside the natural on the dancing hides. There was a scream; Mrs. Sutherland broke through the horrified people and fell sobbing upon her son.

"Get Dr. Schultz," said Riel, "from the guardroom. Quick." The men could look nowhere, for shame.

"Schultz is," Delorme said finally, "he's...gone. They got away."

"What!" Riel swung to Lépine.

"Yes," Lépine said in his emotionless voice. "The guards were drunk. So was the guard at the gate."

The men stood humiliated before all the silent people. Gabriel, kneeling took his big hand away from Sutherland; there was nothing to be done there except let the mother cry. He turned to Bertie, touching his body here and there with great care, looking at the battered head, the froth that bubbled at the smashed lips. Then he bent closer, listening. He looked up at Riel.

"Something like...a Scot...Scot?"

Lépine said, Scott got away too...with Schultz and the others."

Riel stood, head down, watching Gabriel try gently to tie a woman's neckerchief around Bertie's head. It was impossible, of course; as impossible as trying to recapture any celebration in a night that had been destroyed. We people of Red River surrounded them, looking from the two bodies to Louis Riel. In complete silence.

2.

UNDER the dead blue sunlight of winter the white prairie always moved, its surface wandering like sand in search of obstacle; slipping over the glazed, or granular, or shadowed levels always forward, always steadily east. And the bell tolling, he might have been kneeling and ready to rise to go for prayers with the others, but the bell here sounded without echo from mountain or building, the snow hissed to itself while each toll moved as it seemed endlessly on and on into space. It might have been, it was so nearly the sound of the angelus tolling through the winter walls and his rising to go, already late and knowing the priest at the doorway would grimace, a new penance already piously in formulation, and her mother looking up from her embroidery, watching him move from the couch where they sat all evening playing stupid little games for her sake, both of them on the couch all evening like boards nailed together by planless children, that detestable woman saying with such supreme Christian commiseration, "O, is it your feet hurt again? They are so painful, your feet? Again?" and suddenly it burst in him like the agony of the humiliation exploding into vision at the altar, and he tore off the horrible shoes they forced him to wear–"Would you believe it, those poor children, nothing but buffalo hide on their feet!"–hurled them, it was his own voice screaming but merciful God be praised missed her head, even her immense, gaping mouth. And he spent two days plastering the hole in the wall, painting the entire room, Marie-Julie locked away silent somewhere while he smeared over the marks of his rage. Locked forever away—

He had been praying. He jerked his head away from the seduction of the snow, felt his knees cold and his own small blackness on the white platter of prairie, heard the cathedral bell across the distant river. There was his burden, and he hunched again into the weight of his prayer:

"...and Holy Spirit of God, our Father, hold them in your infinite power, and love. In your mercy grant them eternal rest, rest; in your mercy forgive them their sins; in your great mercy receive their marred and tangled innocence as the pure innocence of your Son, Who died for them. O my God, why these? Of all who wanted to do us evil, and did it, these two who were innocent of anything. I have sinned–too often–and have been forgiven, I feel I have your blessing now–but have I done wrong? O Spirit of God, O my God forgive my thoughts that wander, help me...."

He was slowly bending lower as if before the relentless wind, eyes closed, gradually probing the outlines of pain inside this necessary prayer. Suddenly, between the bell tolling, a bridle clinked; Riel looked up. Gabriel was sitting there on his horse. A motionless quiet surrounded man and animal as though they had materialized like hoarfrost out of the brilliant air, the shaggy horse and shaggy man hacked out in one lair of cold. Slowly Riel stood up.

"I like praying here," he said. "Out loud."

Gabriel grinned through rime. "Too much for me, kneeling in snow."

Riel leaned against the horse which breathed so strongly, steadily into the mocking sunlight; his hand rested against Gabriel's rifle butt.

"You have lots of time to pray, riding?"

"I have to keep my eyes open, where I ride." Abruptly the air seemed to ring with emptiness; their expectation hung on nothing and they both turned, stared across the blinding prairie to the Fort far down in the snow, the low huddle of Winnipeg, and found St. Boniface beyond the black edge of the river; smoke losing itself upward into blue light. The bell had stopped. Gabriel shifted, shrugged towards the sudden silence.

"You think that was...God?" he asked.

"'Shall there be evil in a city and the Lord has not done it?'"

"Who said that?"

"A prophet, Amos. In the Bible."

"What kinda God is that?"

"'What has come to pass unless the Lord ordained it?'" Riel said heavily.

"Yeah?" Gabriel rubbed a hide mitten through the ice in his whiskers. "The way I always thought it, it was people are sometimes so stupid they kill. Now Young Bertie, one of our people, he got hold of a gun and started it, a child really who never understood nothing."

"The guard was dead drunk."

"Sure, so it's his fault, like the priest would say, but Bertie needn't have come by just then, eh? One of God's unknowing little children."

"How could God have done it any clearer?" Riel asked.

"But...why?"

"Yes "

After a moment Gabriel said, "I never wanted to be nothing but a hunter." He leaned forward on the butt of the rifle stuck in the saddle before him. "Le Petit, I've worn out five of them. I live by killing things. Mostly animals, and I try to do it clean, fast so they don't suffer–but sometimes they do, suffer. I can't help it. And sometimes I have to kill people too, it...just has to be done. It's just part of God's system here, eh? You quoted the prophet yourself."

"No!" Riel's conviction burst from him, "God's system is life–beauty, love, life!"

"That'd be nice, yeah," Gabriel said, "but I don't see just that."

"We all see enough of it to know it's the best. Spring, flowers, mothers loving their children–that's what Eden is about: nothing would have had to die, ever, if man hadn't sinned against God. Sin–evil has messed up everything."

"Even the way plants and animals live?"

"Yes! You think man can sin against his Creator and not mess up the universe?"

"Well..." Gabriel began slowly, stopped. He stared down into Riel's intense face; I could have told him that delivering a scouting report to Riel was not necessarily a simple matter.

"You think there'll be death in heaven?" Riel continued relentlessly.

"The Indians have death in theirs...for animals and enemies anyway." Gabriel laughed a little. "Which don't make much sense, does it, unless you fix up separate heavens for Cree and Sarcees and Bloods–even then you'd have to make sure there were living *enemies* in each one so you could..." he stopped. "The priests, they say there won't be, in heaven, but..."

"How would it be heaven if there was agony and death?" said Riel."It'd be nothing better than earth, right here now. If I can think of a heaven to come where the good God allows no death, then I can think of such a heaven having been once, too...perhaps it is right now, but we aren't in it. Because this world, the one we stand in–and it can freeze us to death, painfully–is messed up by sin. My sin, too. That's why I pray."

"No priest ever told me anything as hard as that," Gabriel said slowly. "They just have it worked out, you've done that wrong, so you pray so much, that often. Finished, everything's cleaned up. You always know where you stand with the priest's God."

Riel's glance into the light at Gabriel flicked, 'Then get yourself a better priest,' but he said nothing; the mathematical legalism of a calculable God was not worth opening his mouth about. After a silence Gabriel said,

"Just two people...I figure you started this good here. You spoke for what our people wanted and they stand behind you with their guns."

But Riel would not move. "When I was in Montreal," he said, "seven years, I almost became a priest."

"Yeah," Gabriel said slowly, "that woulda been really good, one of us a priest."

"Yes," Riel's moccasins scuffed the dry snow, "and there isn't one yet. But then my father died here in Red River; I hadn't seen him in seven years...and there was a girl...I was only a half-breed, you know. In Montreal. I had been thinking I was French-Canadian. I actually wrote better Latin than any French-Canadian in the whole College and I thought...but...so suddenly I had nothing...no call, no vocation, nothing."

Riel said that to Gabriel, who had never spoken ten real words to him. He was a leader like that; he knew whom he could force with his confidence.

"And finally, out of nothing I said, 'Lord, give me ten years in this world, and then I will leave it to serve you. Forever.' That's what I said."

"You made a..." Gabriel's voice grew small in amazement, "a deal?"

Riel's head barely moved.

"When?" Gabriel asked finally.

"Five years ago."

Gabriel snorted in his nose. "And after this," he said, "maybe you don't want to go ahead with the next five eh?"

"The first four weren't...so good, either."

The horse stamped; Gabriel shifted, saddle and clothes groaning in the cold.

"I've never made no deal with God," he said. "I wouldn't touch that. Just with people."

"You've been captain of the hunt."

"Oh yeah, I know God has to bring the buffalo. I just make sure I've got the guns. Now you know what the people want here, and you've got the guns; you just talk it through with those elected delegates, and then tell Canada. They'll listen."

Riel stared across the wind-patterned prairie. Along the edge of the horizon, beyond the bumps of villages and fort, a fine haze like yellow cream was gathering.

"Because of your guns?" he said.

"Oh, anybody'll listen to good talk–but guns, guns always make them remember better."

"I don't like that."

"We aren't in heaven yet."

"Why not?" Riel wheeled around, face clenched with intensity. "Why aren't we? Why don't we make a heaven here in the North-West, where we can have peace between all people, no killing..."

"We've gotta kill buffalo."

"How long will they be there to kill," Riel asked heavily, "how long?"

Gabriel laughed and swung his huge arm west. "On the Saskatchewan there's plenty for everybody. Anyway, Lépine sent me to report."

Riel's eyes moved up Gabriel's frozen leather length and his face–except for a moustache it was clean-shaven then—broke in a happiness that charmed us whenever we saw it.

"I'm listening," he said, starting to walk. "I didn't think you rode out to pray with me...though," he laughed suddenly, "someday you might."

Gabriel laughed with him. "I've ridden for worse! Okay, three things. One, Schultz and his wife didn't run to St. Paul, the sleigh-drivers were lying; they're in Stone Fort."

"Stone Fort!"

"Yeah, and they're using McDougall's proclamation to talk the Scots over."

"And the Swampies and Saulteux will still back them?"

"Oh sure, those Canadian liars convinced them they'd be fighting for the Queen. Two, Boulton has just about got his big army together at Portage, to come and *'release* the prisoners' we got in the fort."

"How many men?"

"Baptiste thinks no more than fifty; that includes Henderson and Scott and Farmer."

Riel lunged so furiously ahead through the snow Gabriel had to nudge his horse to keep alongside. "That devil McDougall, he's ruined and running back to Macdonald like a whipped beggar and still he sends out that devilish proclamation—he wants Red River bloody, that's all."

"War isn't all bad," Gabriel said.

"People have words; they don't have to kill each other!"

"It sure sometimes cleans up a lot of shit fast," Gabriel muttered.

"What?"

"I was just..." Gabriel hesitated, staring at the low huddle of the fort ahead. "Three, Macdonald's new frontman is just about at Pembina, he's coming—"

Riel wheeled, seized the horse's bridle and jerked it to a halt, his face ecstatic.

"Who is it, who is it?"

"Just a guy named Smith," Gabriel said doubtfully; "every second Englishman they say is called that. I don't know if he's any good for—

"*Donald* Smith?"

"Yeah, maybe, it could be, those English names—"

Riel danced like a dervish; the horse swung its head aside, rearing as Gabriel controlled it with his knees.

"But *Donald* Smith is the head of the Hudson's Bay Company in Canada!" Riel shouted, laughing aloud. "If he's the Special Commissioner, it means Macdonald finally understands: we control Red River. That's the most powerful non-politician he could send."

"But if he's Company," Gabriel said doubtfully.

"The Company doesn't want to administer Red River; they want their money and a stable government, so they can—"

"Make money."

"Of course, so let Smith come and talk. If he just has the power to make decisions, we'll get what we want; you'll see, we'll get it. All I want to see is his papers from Macdonald."

"What's that Macdonald like?"

"I've never met him," Riel said. "Is your horse too tired to ride double?"

"No...c'mon," Gabriel offered his arm and a stiff foot; in one motion Riel was up, tanned buffalo in his nose. "He like Mactavish, you think?" The horse eased into a trot.

"Maybe...but he drinks more, and is three times smarter. Ah, Gabriel we can handle Sir John A. Macdonald if we can handle Mr. Donald Smith."

Handling Mr. Smith was a closer thing than Riel suspected when he cantered into Fort Garry holding easily to Gabriel's muscled gut; I could have told him as much if I'd been there, because Smith was of the Clan Grant and so Scots cousin to Cuthbert Grant and my wife Mary; we knew him well enough. His father was a Letheredie tradesman, so poor Donald could not study law as he wished and therefore at eighteen he was apprenticed to the Hudson's Bay Company. He married Factor Hardisty's half-breed daughter and used the Company, together with politics and banks and railroads, to become one of the richest, most powerful men in the British Empire. A penniless dour Scot who comes to sit in the House of Lords: that was what the North-West made of poor Donald Smith, though he worked hard and God ordained him nearly a century to arrange it, a small gaunt man who ate cold oatmeal every day he lived and never laughed a day's worth of laughter, total, in his ninety-four years. I once asked him if he kept account of that too, how often he laughed, if ever, and he stared at me from under those eyebrows like willows hoarfrosted along the Assiniboine on a February morning. Mary said, "Now father, stop your teasing my little Donald," but I could tell from his eyes, unblinking and no warmer than he liked his porridge, that about three o'clock some night his Presbyterian soul would wake to wrestle with those few miserable seconds of tempted levity, adding, multiplying them also into some sum of accurate, business-useful guilt.

Smith arrived at Red River, but he carefully left all his government commissions at the border and so Riel could not know how much power Smith had to negotiate until he agreed to let Smith present his case directly to the people. That was the first, private, round, and on January 19, 1870, we all gathered in the Fort square for the second, public, one. It was almost noon, the sun fiercely cold, when Smith and Riel came out on the little balcony above the officers' mess door—Riel had never spoken from there and Smith with his white face looked almost like a picture of English royalty waving a hand benign with limpness to people from some high palace, all we needed was a fat little woman—that Smith had carefully distributed at least five hundred pounds of Macdonald money; I could see the Nolins from Oak Point, and maybe my neighbours the Brelands too, were ready to cheer whatever he opened his mouth to say into the cold, the canny crook. We stood five hours in the snow, heard him say how he really was a Red River man—wasn't he a Grant, hadn't he married a Red River woman? —and he was ready to resign from the Hudson's Bay Company if the intentions of the

Canadian government weren't of the very best for this North-West. He waved letters and pledged himself to that, and after five hours I for one had enough of general good-will pledges. Riel loomed beside Smith but said nothing; just translated for him like a paid clerk. He seemed no more than a black shadow up there until the sun was almost down, and suddenly a voice yelled from the crowd,

"Release the Canadian prisoners! Now!"

And for a moment that spread across the cold square like fire leaping. Abruptly then Riel seemed alive; he was centred on the little balcony, Smith trying to push around from behind but quite out of sight, and the Métis guards at attention along every wall, their rifles carefully at ease. I was beginning to wonder if our 'little Donald's' money would manage what McDougall's stupidity could not–Charles Nolin was yelling as loud about prisoners as anyone–but Riel shouted suddenly, his arms up as if our flag only, not the Union Jack also, was flapping on a second, thank god shorter pole above us:

"Not yet! Those who signed the pledge not to raise arms have been released. But not the others; it is too early. Go home now, and come again tomorrow. We will talk more."

And the heckler–it was John Burke of St. James–was silenced by the cold men around him. We all left to find some place warmer, mostly the American saloons.

I didn't stay longer than one drink. Dutch George Emmerling now had a new attraction: Métis girls as bar-maids. It brings many settlement English into his hotel, but for the Americans women who work in bars are of one kind only. A lovely girl served our table, she had the skin and beautiful dark eyes of a Lagimodière, I thought; she was abused at other tables dreadfully, without ever a hand being raised to touch her. The world grows strange; I could not ask her name for I did not want to think so badly of her parents who allowed her to work in such a place.

Next day there were, I think, more of us in the square, about a thousand, and it was, if anything, colder. Twenty-five below zero at least, and I for one was not ready for another five hours of "Her Majesty's Government has only your good at heart." Maybe overnight some of us had begun to ponder whether a government ever has heart. As Riel raised his hand on the balcony, John Burke in the crowd asked for the floor and apologized for yelling yesterday; our Donald heard him and several others in an astonishment he could not quite hide and before he could begin again with his careful Ottawa confidences Riel intervened to propose that "the elected delegates from each parish consider Mr. Smith's commission and decide what would be best for the welfare of the country." The motion was carried with immediate, spontaneous, cheers. Smith was in a corner of the balcony and Riel centred above us, Louis Schmidt and Father Ritchot on either side; and suddenly he was no mere juggler of languages for the benefit of a leader; he was himself the leader, speaking.

"I step forward almost in fear," he said. "Our opponents had almost made us enemies again, but now we understand each other. We people of the North-West demand, all of us together, our just rights! Gentlemen, we will have no half-rights! We will have our rights in our own land, and we will decide what they are!"

Our caps were flying into the cold air, blown high by our hot cheers, which left nothing at all to be said by Donald Smith and his Macdonald letters, most of which he had not yet read aloud. But he did not try to interrupt us; from his balcony corner he could study Riel who had allowed him to hang himself in one long, cold day of Ottawa generalities. This round was clearly lost, and from below Smith's sour rectangle of a busy face betrayed that same strange mixture of respect, embarrassment–almost humiliation endured–it held when my Mary clasped him in greeting, her hands still grained with flour from mixing our noon bannock, her soft voice in his ear, "Little Donald, our little Donald." Through my cheers, I was laughing.

So we all drove or rode home over the hard snow and sent our forty delegates to examine Donald's Ottawa papers in the heated comfort of the Court House beside Fort Garry, and to debate what we should demand if we joined Canada's Confederation. McDougall had been routed, our Métis boys rode patrol to protect us from the Sioux and any stupidity Dr. Schultz at the Stone Fort or Boulton and Scott might be able to churn up in Portage about freeing Canadian prisoners. Besides, a snowdrift caught between the walls of the Court House and Fort Garry provided an excellent repository for bottles; winter is then surely the best time for thoughtful talk. James Ross loved it; he faced Riel across the wide long table of delegates where the chairman, Judge Black, sat at the head with Louis Schmidt and Thomas Bunn, the two language secretaries, and between them they translated every word that was said.

"It's not often," Ross said in French, smiling, "that men as young as we so determine their country's place in the world."

"They won't remember us for our age," Riel said in English, wrinkling his nose, sniffing elaborately.

Ross burst into laughter, "Nor if we drank!"

"My men know how to shovel," Riel began, "that snow bank'll be gone—"

"Order," Judge Black thumped the table. "After a fine dinner with which we all no doubt heartily agree (much table thumping) I call this Convention to order for the twenty-first session. I would ask our French secretary, Mr. Schmidt, to read the final three resolutions we have agreed upon to treat with Canada for the North-West."

Schmidt rose, hands full of paper. "The resolutions are numbers eighteen through twenty, and carried unanimously.

Eighteen: *That the English and French languages be common in the Legislature and the Courts, and that all public documents be published in both languages.*

Nineteen: *That all present properties and local customs
be fully respected, particularly as regards parishes and
river-lot land ownership.*

Twenty: *That every man in the North-West, except
uncivilized and unsettled Indians, who is over twenty-one,
a British subject, or who has resided here three years and is
a householder, shall have the right to vote."*

"Thank you," Black said after the translation. "I believe that
concludes our List of Rights. The final matter then is discussion
of how we are to present them to Ottawa, whether through Mr.
Smith or perhaps a delegation of– Mr. Riel."

"I gave notice last week," said Riel, standing, "that we have
one final resolution to consider: whether we should declare our
intention to be admitted to Canada, not as a territory but as a
province. I would like to raise that matter now."

Black was looking down the English side of the table; when
he was chosen chairman of the Convention the balance had been
upset, nineteen votes to twenty in favour of the French, unless it
was a matter of principle where the chairman might vote and
force a tie; fortunately, the resolutions until now had been much
more unanimous than that; but this matter...he could find no
help. James Ross seemed content to stare at his hands folded on
the table, his lips twitching slightly. "Well," Black said finally,
"yes, I believe this was set aside earlier, though raised briefly in
committee; it could properly be raised now. Yes." He took a deep
breath as Riel stood again.

"Mr. Chairman," Riel said, "and worthy Convention, it is
clear that as a territory we would escape some heavy responsi-
bilities, but I ask you to consider several critical matters. The
British North America Act..."

He shuffled among his papers, then raised a small brown
book. Ritchot, seated next to him, began drawing circles on his
agenda, looping numbers and words with tiny curlicues; Riel

bowed to Ross, who bent his head in sardonic acknowledgement, "...contained in this book which Mr. Ross has so kindly lent me, gives certain rights exclusively to the provinces. For instance, regarding education and the sale and control of public land. Do we want the right to determine how our children are to be educated? We have not spoken to that in our List, and the Act allows us to determine that only if we are a province. Do we want to make regulations about our land–land is the greatest resource of the North-West, we have more good land than Canada twice over–decide how our land beyond our present small tenancy is to be sold and administered? Then we must be a province. Further, as a territory we will be administered by Ottawa. Now Ottawa, as you know, gentlemen, is *very* far away; so far that it is barely a month ago that it sent us Commissioner Smith. Until then Ottawa apparently did not know that there were people in the North-West who must be talked with before they are disposed of."

All the French and many of the English drummed the table thunderously at that. Ross was rising even before Black could catch his eye, and Riel slowly seated himself; but tilted forward on the edge of his chair.

"Under the Hudson's Bay Company," said Ross in his thin, clear voice, "we have never had a single elected right; the representatives we had on the Council were appointed. They did well by us, but they were nevertheless appointed, by the Company. In other words, our people have never known one scrap of self-government." His tone was suddenly edged, sardonic: "For two weeks now we have contemplated, here and in various committees, the high plateau of becoming a 'New Territory.' For us that climb is a great one, but now, not content with that, it is proposed that we scale an even greater height, that of 'New Province.' When we have agreed to this, what will be suggested next? The ultimate mountain of 'New Nation,' perhaps?"

There was a moment of stunned silence; Black's face darkened with anger at Ross's perversely misplaced irony. One quick glance was enough to show that only O'Donoghue, of all the French delegates, accepted it for the debating point it was; the rest with Riel were lifted almost to their feet in quick fury. Ritchot placed his hand on Riel's arm as Ross said, steadily refusing to give way, "I can say that—"

"For shame, Mr. Ross," said Bannatyne from the English side, "for shame."

"I repeat, I can say that, Mr. Bannatyne, because though I am considered English, nevertheless I am as much mixed blood as anyone at this table."

"You were elected, not born, a delegate," said Riel thinly.

Uneasy laughter around the table; Ross bowed politely to Riel, smiling easily,

"True, true! That was simply to underline that despite an unfortunate Toronto education, my home and my family has been, and is, the North-West. Now Mr. Riel and I have discussed the British North America Act at length, and we quite agree on the advantages gained by being a province. But I fear the heavy burden of the Canadian public debt. I fear selling our lands cheaply now for the public improvement that our settlements must have. I say, let Ottawa pay for the massive surveys, for the roads, bridges, schools, courthouses we need. When we have these, and the larger population that will surely come with immigration, then is the time to speak of being a province."

Riel did not even rise, or glance at Black. "Why do you suppose," he said, "Macdonald wants the North-West?"

"That's self-evident," Ross gestured, "you've explained it—to complete 'dominion from sea to sea,' to dev—"

"To raise money from it! Don't you know Ontario?"

"Yes! And I know they'll have to pour money into here before they get one penny out! That's the crux: money. A province has a right to impose direct taxation and that's fine as long as you control the Legislature, but what about the massive immigration that has already begun? What about when we as a peculiar people find that the foreigners who don't even want to understand us and our customs–we've already seen enough–outnumber us? We have protected ourselves from that in our present List I believe, but if we are a province we will be outvoted. Also the Dominion will then appoint our judges and that power—"

"You have been to Toronto," Riel said. "You would be appointed."

Silence like a thin grey cloud covered the room. Of them all, only Judge Black perhaps had ever heard, or thought, of the questions the two were debating: the others had simply that good sense and maturity for which their people had elected them to interpret what these two alone could explain; and at the moment it seemed as if Riel, in silly anger, had thrown away his argument for pettiness. Ross turned to Black, his debater's face wiped clean.

"Mr. Chairman," he said very politely, "I base my argument on what is in the interest of all our people." He sat down.

Riel was on his feet, and he knew his temper had cost him, that he must now make his main thrust to carry the argument even with his French backers.

"I intended no disrespect to Mr. Ross; I merely emphasized that in regards to judges the matter of province or territory is of no consequence; in both they are Ottawa appointed. My basic desire for a province, and Mr. Ross avoided this, has to do with the Hudson's Bay Company. It has helped us at times, it has worked us to the raw bones at others, and it has always, let me remind you, for two hundred years made an immense profit on our labour to send to its lords living over the sea in a luxury none of us can imagine. To serve their ends, these lordly unknowns have tried to subvert ours by a quick sale of rights they have never controlled, not by any known charter signed by any drunken sot of a king. I therefore propose that we stop referring to them as 'The Honourable Company'; I find 'The Shameful Company' much more suitable."

O'Donoghue roared with laughter, and then they were all, even the English, laughing and thumping the table.

"This Company has reached an agreement with Canada to sell us for a sum of money, plus one-twentieth of the land in the North-West. That decision has been reached at a level we perhaps cannot touch, and we have no wish to destroy the Company, but we also do not wish for it to have the extraordinary influence over us it must if it owns– remember, it has never had title to any land before, simply held trading rights–if it now owns, by title, five out of every one hundred acres. That is too much!"

There was silence then, the silence of conviction and agreement. Riel's face hardened.

"For four months the English population of Red River has stood aloof. They have talked, yes, but done nothing. We French braved white men and Indians to achieve our present position of formulating rights, and this Convention, English and French together, by meeting here and drawing up our List of Rights has in effect accepted the Provisional Government we French alone formed, and whose soldiers riding patrol and standing guard at key places throughout Red River have so kept order that no one–except during the prison break–has suffered any harm. Now I believe the Provisional Government must represent *all* the people of Red River: I believe this Convention, tomorrow, should discuss a truly representative Provisional Government—"

"Mr. Riel," Bannatyne interrupted, "you are piling important matters too quickly on each other. From rights, to province, to Hudson's Bay Company, and now a new Provisional Government, what...?" It was obvious the storekeeper spoke for most of the delegates, at least those open enough to let their minds show on their faces.

"You have stated our decisions in exactly their right order." Riel continued, smiling, "Thank you. Once we agreed on the basics we all wanted from Ottawa, then we could discuss 'province or territory,' which related to the continuing status of the Company here. Then we must set our house firmly in order: form a truly representative provisional government which will not only control Fort Garry but deal with those Canadian riot instigators who are still at large, fomenting—"

"What," said Ross so indolently it would have been impossible to decide whether he was baiting Riel or providing him with a leading question, "what are your soldiers, under our worthy Mr. Lépine," Ross bowed across the table but Lépine moved not so much as an eyebrow, "doing about the Canadians at Portage and at Stone Fort who, we hear rumours, are gathering men and arms. Surely you know about them?"

"Yes," said Riel. "And we know as well as you all that a band of them tore Henri Coutu's house apart on Monday in Winnipeg because they thought I was sleeping there. Our French soldiers would have cleaned out Portage, and Stone Fort too, gladly, but neither Mr. Lépine nor myself want war, Mr. Ross. And I doubt whether you want a bullet in the head either."

"Oh no," Ross laughed, his hand flapping in mock terror, "I'm definitely a talk, not a bullet man."

"We must forget bullets, they never—" began Ritchot.

"Of course," said Riel. "That's why we're here. That's why we must agree that we the people must control all the lands of the North-West, and we can do that best as a province."

Suddenly, into the convinced silence, down the long table a deep Irish voice spoke: O'Donoghue.

"I still am not convinced that we should rush headlong into Confederation at all, under any terms. The North-West is rich, could we not do at least as well being an independent colony? Or consider the United States? When Texas joined the Union, it retained all land for its own jurisdiction and use. Why must we close with Canada at all? Independence, perhaps, or..." He stopped, his gesture as eloquent as his voice, no matter what it said.

"Gentlemen," said Judge Black. Everyone, except for the three who had spoken, sat as if the total confusion which had been piled between them when they first faced each other weeks before had bludgeoned them once more. "Gentlemen, we have here discussed very high politics. War is for us an understandable concept; we do not want it. But territorialism, provincialism, imperialism, annexationism—all these 'isms' are numbing and, for my part, if we wish to speculate, I would recognize any of you who advocated the reliability of aereal machines which might make our annexation to the mountains of the moon as feasible as our annexation to Texas. (Loud laughter.) That would at least permit us the luxury of breathing a properly lunatic atmosphere. (Laughter and cheers.) Regarding the land, I thought we—"

"Mr. Chairman," Riel interrupted, half standing, "laughter helps, thank you, but we all saw how the Canadians, the surveyors, behaved. And how they continue to gather guns to further their purposes. Once we *sign* away control of our land, we will certainly never get it back!"

Black stared at Riel steadily. There was 'young upstart' in that stare, almost as if he were looking through the judicial table where often he had handed down judgments upon Métis and was studying the moccasins on Riel's feet; a flush slowly soaked upward in Riel's face.

"Whatever you, Mr. Riel," Black said slowly, "might want this convention to do, or to be, it should be clear to anyone that it cannot be a Court of Revision on arrangements already reached by the Imperial Parliament in London. If you wish to discuss that, you may, but I must advise you it is beyond my reach. I thought this Convention had sufficiently safeguarded the land question in the approved List of Rights."

"I agree," said Charles Nolin down the table on our French side. Everyone looked at him, dressed more like an English gentleman even than Judge Black, if that were possible. "I feel that all of us have our minds made up about these issues. We have formulated a strong List of Rights for Ottawa, and I move that we enter the Canadian Confederation as a Territory."

"Second," said James Ross.

Throughout the Convention something had been simmering between Riel and his cousin; though the delegates could not know what, and though Nolin had consistently voted with the French, the feeling that existed between them might have been personal, or family; who can know the niceties of hate between two proud young men who see power beckoning? I would not say that power and pride were all that moved Nolin: he was much abused later for his stand, but I am certain he did not perceive that Riel was too committed on the issue ever to be moved from it; he could not grasp that Riel had too much power to lose the issue even if he lost the vote. For he did lose it: twenty-two for territory, seventeen against. The American saloon keeper Alfred Scott voted with Riel; and Nolin and his colleagues from Oak Point, Klyne and Harrison, voted against him. Riel, absolutely livid, was on his feet shouting, "You can all go to the devil, we shall have a province! No matter how you traitors vote!"

And our Charles was on his feet too: "I was not sent here to vote at your direction! I vote according to my conscience!"

Ritchot's hand and voice had quieted Riel somewhat by then; but not completely. His chair had tumbled aside, he began to pace between Schmidt scribbling and Black, who looked at him with a deepening glower but said nothing, made no move to his gavel; as if he had decided to allow Riel to hang himself as effectively as his uncontrollable temper could manage. Riel's voice gradually rose higher and thinner until he was literally foaming, his spittle spraying the men who now stared at him, some like Ross and Gunn in amazement, but Schmidt and Ritchot in consternation:

"The vote–the–I do not want to speak disrespectfully of this Convention, but I say this matter will be carried! You English were quite ready to let that Macdonald dog Muck-Dougall raise his leg over the four corners of this country but we—the French Métis of Red River—sent him yapping and *we* formed the Provisional Government and *we* forced Smith to agree to our elections and *we* will force him to agree to the rights you have all been very willing to talk and talk and talk about. Well, talk! I am still President of the Provisional Government and Mr. Lépine is still Adjutant-General and we control Fort Garry and *we will do whatever is needed* and yes Mr. Ross, we will be bullet men when necessary; since 1816 we have proven that time and again, and we will do everything necessary to make a province here despite your miserable small-mindedness, not to mention cowardice, which never lets any of you, educated as you may be, think bigger than the lint caught in your navels. We will have a province and we will *all* benefit, you miserable mice. And as for you, Charles Nolin, and you Klyne and Harrison, two of you my own relatives, you're finished! You'll never be elected to anything, not so much as a cattle herder, I swear to you, I'll finish you, you won't be—"

The two-week tension burst into uproar. Nolin's companions were wrestling with him, Black's gavel thudded on the table, and Schmidt and Ritchot on their feet, hissing, their hands out, "Louis...Louis...please Louis...!" while Bannatyne waved his hand to get the floor, "Mr. Chairman...Mr. Chairman!" and everyone shouted at Riel or his opposite facing him across the table in whatever language he pleased. Only James Ross sat imperturbable watching spit, foam, jerking arms and bodies with an ironic smile as if caught in the heavy beard of his long sharp face, gauntly ascetic for a man who within the year we would see on his bier, dead of drink. The only man in all Red River who could think with Riel. If it had not been for him, perhaps Riel's rage and the long evening and the Convention and the snow-bank bar could have raised all their dignities into a brawl; and a good thing that would have been. Men who have felt their fists meet each other's faces can often endure each other's ideas much better than before–at least so the Métis have always believed or, in any case, behaved. Who knows how the history of the North-West would have proceeded had the French seated around that table in February, 1870, firmly established their English counterparts in the Métis principle that any convention (or party) worth the name must end in a fight? A split nose, a burst knuckle given and received might have saved Nolin from his treachery when spring broke through the long winter on the Saskatchewan fifteen years later. Who can say? Doubtless our Father will tell us when it is truly right that we know. But as it was, through the uproar and the confusion of bodies struggling with each other in their indignation and good intention, there came a thunderous pounding on the door; and all the delegates froze.

"A message has come," said James Ross still seated; as if he had personally arranged for an archangel to arrive at that moment and hammer them to their eternal judgments.

However, it was Michel Dumas in the opening doorway, his fur cap pushed back and capote belted over furs glistening with frost. The loudness of his knock because he still was not used to doors, nor to frock-coated gentlemen with their hands at each others throats like any celebrating buffalo camp.

"Mr. Riel..." he said, "Mr. Lépine, there's something."

Riel's rage was as if wiped from his face; his transformations were always so complete when they had to be that I personally know people who insist he was always completely in control of himself even in his most livid or childish rages: that he staged everything for his audience.

And now, with everyone slowly seating themselves, jolted out of their emotion back to their gentlemanliness again, Black could acknowledge thoughtful Bannatyne:

"We have had a long day, and evening too; it's very cold outside, and I'm sure we'll be happy to get to our warm homes...after what we've accomplished."

Not even Black was listening; Riel and Lépine were bent to Michel's message, but the storekeeper's soothing voice was exactly right for the background they needed to concentrate on that shaggy figure, a pistol bulge at his belt.

"...we must decide on the important matter of how we are to present our List of Rights to Parliament in Ottawa, and so I propose that we adjourn until one tomorrow afternoon and in the meantime our executive contact Commissioner Smith to ascertain..."

He stopped, for Lépine had vanished with Michel while Riel had turned, was striding down the length of the table; Riel stopped behind his chair and slowly Bannatyne sat down, silent.

"Mr. Chairman," Riel said, perfectly controlled, "it is important that the Convention know of a certain matter. The Canadian belligerents from the Stone Fort are now gathered at Kildonan Church. They now number about five hundred armed men since being joined three days ago by the Portage Party led by Major Boulton."

"What!" exclaimed Black, astonished. "When did they...?"

"Eighty men passed through Winnipeg about midnight last Monday, while you were sleeping. That's when the party led by Thomas Scott ransacked my friends, trying to find me. We are now informed there will be a march on Fort Garry tonight, presumably to attempt a release of the remaining prisoners. Now everyone in Red River knows, and Boulton and Schultz certainly, that the only prisoners we still hold are those who refuse to swear to keep the peace—"

"But you have not fed them reasonably; they are freezing in those cells..." Bannatyne hesitated, stopped under Riel's glare.

"You may rest assured that our Métis soldiers," Riel bowed curtly to James Ross, "who are all bullet men, every one, will take whatever steps are necessary. Those of you in Winnipeg, if you hear guns, make sure your wives and children are in your cellars. Schultz's men fire a great deal, in any direction."

Ross said suddenly, "Is that why you wouldn't let Mrs. Schultz keep any clothes?"

"What..." Riel was jarred out of his rhetoric.

"When you raided Schultz's house Tuesday–because Thomas Scott raided your cousin Coutu?"

"Ours was no raid." O'Donoghue was on his feet. "I led four men in a legal confiscation of goods for all the debts Schultz owes even some of you, and that woman is—"

"Excuse me, Mr. O'Donoghue," Riel said sharply; "since this Convention has never yet spoken to the matter of our Provisional Government and as that Government has for months administered Red River in complete peace–except for two deaths caused by our opponents–and since Red River has been and will continue to be under martial law until this Convention decides to discuss our present circumstances in relation to ourselves, we need explain nothing here. However, to prove that we really do want all the people of Red River to cooperate in our government, and especially the English, we inform them if they ask that when women behave like men in raising conflict, we treat them like men in return. Soft voices and delicate hands, Mr. Ross, make no case for special treatment. I agree," Riel turned abruptly to Black, "with Mr. Bannatyne. By tomorrow noon these Canadians so eager to march will have been accommodated by Mr. Lépine and our men. I second the motion, adjourn till one o'clock tomorrow."

That was February 16, 1870; about eight o'clock. In the darkness outside, as various people recorded in their journals, the weather was clear and very cold.

$\mathcal{3}$

RIEL could hardly be so confident
about the morning. The Canadians at Kildonan Church had at
least six hundred men, maybe eight, including Henry Prince and
his very eager Saulteux, Presbyterians to a man, and plenty of
ammunition for four cannons; one of them was a rifled eighteen-
pounder excellent for grape; by god if the attack was well
executed Fort Garry could easily be blown to pieces; yes, and a
lot of good men with it; and bastards too; such were the considered conclusions of the saloons. And how could Lépine and his
captains, tough enough, sure but still basically buffalo hunters,
face Canadians trained by Boulton into those unstoppable
English formations? Hah! The deepest drinkers were the more
firmly committed to be on the winning side, no matter which;
Dutch George needed no drummer on a kettle, he simply
needed more girls to lug glasses as courage grew steadily with
noise and men braver than they had ever been, or might possibly be again, staggered home over the fierce dark snow to drag
their sleeping wives and children out of beds to cellar doors.
They were men who would carry on for Queen (or President)

and country even if the Métis and the Canadians, perhaps for everyone else's convenience, wiped each other out. And since most of the Americans lived in the hotels and had no cellar door to locate, they simply stayed in the bars until the fumes of cheap alcohol hid them in insensible safety.

While Lépine mustered his captains with their mounted companies of tens in the moonlit square, Riel was daring one of those brilliant manoeuvres which, like the shotless capture of Fort Garry, made him a legend with us forever. He ordered the prisoners–there were only thirty die-hards left who knew nothing of the intended attempt to free them by force–brought from their cold cells scattered among the fur huts of the Fort, past the sashed, blue-capoted Métis soldiers, and into the warmth of the officers' mess. After an unbelievable round of hot rum, he was about to address them when the door burst open: it was Bannatyne. The postmaster was the most trusted man in Red River and his long bearded face was grey: bloodshed must be prevented or the country would be destroyed. Riel shrugged suddenly, then let him address the men: "It is right that you sign Mr. Riel's conditions, for the good of us all. He does not ask you to take an oath to him personally, or to anyone. By signing you simply give your oath to keep the normal laws of any country, to keep the peace and not fight. That is what any law-abiding man wants, isn't it? You are not taking an oath *to* anyone." The prisoners muttered among themselves, their emaciated faces in the abrupt light of the hall underlining their three-month seemingly useless stubbornness; then they came forward, one by one, beginning with Robert Smith. They signed the oath as Riel's finger moved down the page, showing each his place. Many of them could do no more than form their X; Riel shook their hands and they pulled their filthy coats about them and walked out, free. But when James Farquharson, Anne Schultz's father stepped forward to pick up the pen, Riel suddenly started, jerked the paper away. Farquharson looked up, his eyes clean hatred, his mouth opening slowly in a curse and behind Riel Bannatyne gestured desperately, 'Keep quiet, keep quiet!', but Riel was smiling; talking almost cheerfully,

"Mr. Bannatyne, here is someone truly worthy of his wretched son-in-law. He has already twice broken his personal oath to me." His voice grated like ice: "Why should I demand this–thing–perjure itself again. Get it out of here. Get!"

Farquharson's freckled reddish face glazed speechless in fury; Bannatyne had him by the shoulders, had spun him around and out into the square. Whatever he screamed there was lost in the tramp of horses moving towards the North Gate.

The release of all the prisoners destroyed the Schultz-Boulton army's reason for being: when Schultz raged about the crowded Kildonan Church that the release meant nothing as long as Riel controlled Fort Garry, Boulton asked him loudly, where the men who would have to shoot and be shot at in turn could hear him, whether the worthy doctor was concerned about the citizens of the country or a private vendetta. The gathered Presbyterian and Anglican ministers supported the Major. So the march on Fort Garry did not occur early that morning; the Winnipeg celebrants gradually awoke to another silent, cold winter day little relieved by sunlight, and the Convention met at one o'clock–even Lépine was there. Riel immediately moved that they deal once and for all with a Provisional Government that should represent all the people of Red River alike.

"The Provisional Government is an actual fact, practically recognized by your acts so far in this Convention. Now help us make it strong and complete, all of you."

The English hesitated; perhaps Governor Mactavish... so a delegation of four (including Lépine to get them past the guard at the entrance) went to the sick old man. Mactavish muttered, "Leave me alone, I am a dead man with no authority," and when John Sutherland asked, "Would a Provisional Government be advisable," the old Governor whispered so quietly they could barely hear him leaning about his bed, "It is necessary, for God's sake, establish one. We must have peace." So the English of the Convention agreed: Riel was unanimously elected President; James Ross, Chief Justice; Bannatyne, Postmaster; Ambrose Lépine, Adjutant-General. But about that time another Métis messenger, John Norquay, arrived from Kildonan Church with a list of demands that had been hammered through all day there. The Canadians would lay down their arms

1. *if the prisoners were released;*
2. *if all now under arms were granted amnesty;*
3. *if everyone who desired it be free* not *to recognize any Provisional Government.*

Standing at the long, crowded table, Riel studied Norquay expressionlessly. Perhaps in that intelligent face he suddenly recognized that at best it would be such carefully neutral men as this, at worst the smart bigots who were born and married right, who would succeed at last in binding the North-West to the implacable faceless power of Macdonald's Ontario; perhaps he already recognized before him a future premier of Manitoba: I would certainly believe that of Riel's vision. Facing Norquay, however, he stated quietly that the prisoners were all released, as they no doubt knew, and that Mr. Mactavish (he was careful not to name him Governor) had asked them for God's sake to form an English-French Provisional Government, as they had. It did not seem to him an unjust demand that all honest men should recognize what had been done by properly elected delegates. Of amnesty he said nothing; and when Norquay returned to Kildonan the situation was clear. Schultz's army scattered despite his harangues, and Major Boulton ordered his men to prepare immediately to return to their homes in Portage.

The generally sober Scots of Red River must have been assuming by now that if a government was not soon settled upon, the country would in any case be utterly ruined for the night of the united Provisional Government declaration created a more resonating celebration than the girding for war the night before. Métis soldiers riding on alert about the town deterred no one; even Riel, it was heard, raised a private horn of brandy with Bannatyne when the fireworks–stored for six months in Schultz's basement in anticipation of McDougall ascending his throne, long since ashes–burst like flaming flowers over Fort Garry that February night.

Across the river in St. Boniface men and cannon were being set about the Cathedral; in the French settlements there was little noise and certainly some prayer. Would there had been more. The Portage Canadians felt their laborious trek to Kildonan less than useless—though the prisoners were freed, they had helped the English delegates decide for Riel's Provisional Government–and they refused Boulton's advice to disperse across the prairie to their homes. "We'd have nothing of that, not for no Riel," Murdock MacLeod told me. "We'd come down like brave men and we were going back the same, all together. It was early morning, February 18, still long dark, and we were on the trail back for Portage."

"That was the same road we rode in 1816, the other way," I said. "With Cuthbert Grant."

"It's just a few hundred yards off the Fort."

"That's the one."

He looked at me curiously for a moment, his calloused hand opening and closing on his cup.

"Then I guess we did," he said finally. "The other way. After sun-up it was too bright on the snow, we were almost blind and the Fort low in drifts–you know how distance on the flat land...pushes things...down–it's like a dream now, long ago–suddenly horsemen all around us as if the snow had exploded, them riding like devils burst from shining hell. Most of us were walking on the track between sleighs to keep warm, and our guns were piled in the sleighs, and these horsemen–it was Lépine and O'Donoghue we knew later, leading them–they were hauling their horses down, surrounding us, and men from the Fort were charging up in snow up to their waists, panting so hard you could barely see their heads but their rifles, some repeaters, were plain enough. My rifle was in the sleigh but I had a seven-shooting revolver and I jerked it out, swung around at the rider nearest me and yelled, 'Get back or I'll knock you down,' and he hauled his horse in fast, he didn't even have a gun, and behind I heard Boulton yell, 'Don't fire, I order you! No one fires!' and then I'm sure it was O'Donoghue on the horse in front of me, pale as snow under his fur cap, and sometimes I still wish I had just pulled the trigger on him. That pig American Fenian."

"He didn't have a gun?" I asked.

"That's what saved him, or all of us, just...sure, not Boulton yelling. I'd been drilling six weeks and all of that haggle in Kildonan Church and slogging home useless and cold, past orders. As it happened, not one shot was fired. Funny, I guess I come closest to it. Then there was just talk again, us frozen and half-blind, and Lépine said something about going into the Fort, the man next to me understood French said it was for ten minutes, and Boulton waved to us and we all plowed through the snow, sleighs, men, everything, your French riders and others all around but nobody saying much or even waving their rifles, right into the Fort, there must have been four hundred men on horses milling around in there, god we'd have been slaughtered. Somebody said Riel would talk so we waited for him to come from wherever he was, and talk. I'd never been inside the Fort before–it looked pretty strong, especially with seven or eight guns set high at the corners with maybe a hundred Métis standing on the wide walls–they're as thick as anything in Kingston, I'll tell you, or Fort George–and Tom Scott said to me, 'It's cold, goddammit, let's get a glass in town, who wants to hear that shit-head,' so he and I pushed through to the gate and were going out, I couldn't believe it but the gate was open and people were driving or running from all over to see what was happening and the gate just open. Scott laughed, his white, cold face–he always looked like a boy, you know, a kid till he opened his mouth and started swearing–laughed, and we walked out past everybody rushing in! There were even fancy Winnipeg women, long skirts in the snow, mincing along, then out of nowhere these big arms swung in front of us, it was this huge hairy Métis—Scott was tall but this guy was taller half a head, and wide, hands like grappling irons–and he had a half-twisted grin on that big face all white teeth and black beard. You must have known him, eh, biggest guy—"

"I did," I said. "Elzéar Goulet."

"Yeah, that's him, he got finished later, well, his hands on our shoulders, he just took us back through the crowd like we were kittens and Riel was there asking about Schultz or even Charles Mair, and O'Donoghue shaking his head, swearing under his breath, you could see that he couldn't let Riel hear a word, when Goulet brought us up and as Riel turned to us, a paper in his hand and not even dressed for outside, his hair all curly and his face pinched red, he was going to go in and Goulet stopped us so Riel could see who he'd brought, and without even hesitating Tom Scott leaned forward and spit in Riel's face. Pfui!"

I just sat motionless a moment; I suppose I was studying that turn of the Assiniboine River I have seen outside my window for half a century. The willows swaying on the sandy curve of floodplain.

"I won't deny it," MacLeod said, "nobody that ever knew him...Scott looked like a beautiful boy, but he was like one of them horses you never gentle. You touch them with a quiet hand, or whip, or club, it doesn't matter. Deep down bad. The summer before he started that strike on the Dawson Road and he—"

"It was food." I had to smile, "Our Charles Nolin had the food contract. It was probably worth striking about."

"Yeah," he laughed, and echoed the trail testimony. "Always good provision, though it might have happened it was badly cooked." He laughed again, "Yeah, but you don't knock the boss into the river and hold his head under, not even on a bad-food strike."

"No," I said, and no doubt Riel saw that murderous vicious-ness there, not moving so much as a hand to wipe himself, his look going from Scott's face to Elzéar's giant hand tightening around Scott's neck, the veins in it suddenly bulging, pulsing like single living things and Scott's mouth gaping, his face screwed into choked, bursting agony; perhaps he saw Scott's body dangling, stretched tiptoe for the ground as that huge arm lifted, or perhaps already saw Elzéar's enraged face washed into its ultimate distortion of river water and stones.

"Put him down," Riel said quickly. "Elzéar!"

Elzéar's arm fell, fist unclenching slowly. "Louis, it's that Scott, he...bust out and Young Bertie, he—"

"I know," said Riel in English. "And he was looking for me at Henri Coutu's."

"My God!" Scott gasped, choking, "if I...God I'da...."

They were the centre of the crowd before the Governor's Gate, pressed tight by the cold, smelly hide coats of Métis sol-diers, Canadians, townspeople, hundreds, with the men high on the walls at the guns. Scott's gut-tearing curses rattled against the buildings and at Riel's gesture Elzéar grabbed his arm and clamped it across his mouth.

"Get that—" the blasphemy affected Riel far more than the spitting, "that...beast into a cell. And all of them," he lifted his arm to Lépine and O'Donoghue. "They're to be searched, all posses-sions except clothing removed, and imprisoned. Immediately."

"We were returning to our homes," Boulton stated. "We had no intention of fighting anyone or any...."

"Oh," Riel said. "And the messengers you dispatched over the country from Kildonan Church, the Indians you raised?"

"That was before you released the prisoners, before the Provisional Government. There never was an 'army.'"

"Not even one led by Dr. Schultz?"

"That 'army,' as you call it, is also dispersed. There will be no fighting, I am certain."

"I am certain also," Riel said sardonically. "But the Doctor? Was he agreed with you on 'no intentions of fighting?'"

Major Boulton said nothing for a moment. He had never wanted to leave Portage, and every subsequent event had proven his apprehensions about the march to Kildonan Church only too correct; now he must defend a man he personally detested. Though a Canadian, he had been well trained in the British Army tradition: when all else fails, bad judgment must be brazened through. If possible.

"I cannot answer for Dr. Schultz. All I say is that I and my men, using a public road, were peacefully returning to our homes, and—"

"Very well," Riel said, turning, "we will let a court-martial decide."

That afternoon the Métis court-martial sentenced Boulton to be executed.

"While we were sitting around Kildonan Church," MacLeod told me, "and all the clergymen talking to keep us from fighting, Alex Murray wrote a song. It was all we had to do, sing, and we got it in good shape, barbershop style, fifty or sixty of us on the bass and it would have been great marching too, but Boulton wouldn't permit one note of it that morning. We were supposed to be walking peacefully home. I guess he was right, you could have heard it in St. Boniface if we'd have all let go, marching. They stuck us in those little rooms off the Company Officers' mess, it looked like they hadn't cleaned them out from the last Canadians, Boulton alone in one room and the rest of us jammed eight to twelve in the others, and I was in the room next to Boulton and we started humming Alex's tune, not singing because there were always Métis who knew English, especially big smart ones like Goulet, but we were everyone of us thinking the words, it was all we could do, we were so mad,

> *O hey Riel are you waking yet,*
> *Or are yer drums a'beating yet?*
> *If y're nae waking we'll nae wait,*
> *For we'll take the Fort this morning.*

That tune, 'Johnny Cope,' has a real swing; some of our feet got into it, and forty-seven of us along one side of that old Bay building marching on the spot we'd have collapsed it in a rubble, I think, marching outa there 'O hey Riel are you...' and we had the rhythm going, I was roaring without words but loud because they'd taken my revolver and about sixty pounds, my life's saving. I'd been stupid enough to take it along in case we needed some–what was there in Kildonan Church to buy, not being a RC to buy a few prayers just in case, say, and that O'Donoghue opened his eyes wide when the Métis stripped me of it, and he wrote it down on the list but I knew I'd never see that again–and I haven't to this day. With five per cent interest it should be worth–what?"

"How many RC prayers could you buy now?" I said. "Just in case."

"Yeah," he shook his head over his beer, thinking Scots money and not catching my tone. "But we never hummed through the chorus, leave alone tramped it out because Boulton knocked a knot-hole through the wall and said Riel had just told him 'You prepare to die tomorrow at twelve' and that Archdeacon McLean would be there soon, could we be a bit quieter? That shut us up all right, but we were cursing too for the Archdeacon was one of those who had persuaded us for peace and here was Boulton to be shot and us unable to raise a hand to defend him. Tom Scott was ready to chew bars, he was so mad.

"He was in our cell too. He had been in it before, exactly that one, and the window was still broken so the room was cold as the devil. The only heat came from the fireplace in the mess hall, and the door between was always locked so we were happy to be jammed ten in that room, but poor Boulton was alone, one blanket and a buffalo robe, it was enough to freeze. And he was chained, so well that when he tried to take off his soaking moccasins and socks the chains fell off and about seven guards rushed in because they thought he was escaping, but the Major just wrung out his socks and put them back on and then the irons too, so they went out again. That was strange, that prison, strange. Once when Riel was in the hall questioning us by turn, not me but we could hear most of it through the door, a woman come rushing in dressed like an advertisment and threw herself at his feet–actually, she was clutching his feet! Scott was at the keyhole and he described it, we couldn't get him away, the beautiful Miss Victoria McVicar newly arrived from Ontario and wanting so dreadfully to do her part to promote peace, her delicate white hand fondling Riel's dirty moccasins, looking up at him with luminous eyes and the front of her dress bulging, begging, 'Mercy, mercy, mercy!' We just about wet our pants, laughing so hard, and Scott's eyes nailed to the keyhole, he said she'd do more for peace if she came in the cells and knelt down for us in various positions, all that soft tit and ass wasted–shit– Riel sitting there like a monk, looking away from all that stuff staring open at him for god's sake, and the guards finally got her out. That night was unbelievable, so cold we could feel Boulton through the wall shivering where he was lying against it trying to get a bit of warmth from us. The Métis had put a guard in with him, I guess they were scared he'd escape, and all night the guard was praying those prayers, he wouldn't shut up so the poor Major could sleep, exhausted as he was and the firing squad coming next day, he kept on waking him up, kneeling beside him, praying, I don't know what..."

"That was old Parisien," I said. "Father of the natural that got killed."

"But in god's name why?"

"He was praying, for his soul."

"Boulton's?"

"Yes. He didn't want him shot any more than you, he was praying for him."

"Oh. Well, I figured the Major would rather have got a bit of sleep, he kept waking him up with these long prayers he couldn't understand anyway. Didn't the guy go off the deep end, after, go crazy?"

"Yes. His mind was not strong."

"Yeah. There was funny stuff going on there, and next morning about eleven Riel said sentence was delayed one more day and they put another man in Boulton's cell the next night and in the morning, did you know that, he was dead?"

"You heard he was dead?"

"Heard! I saw him carried!"

"Oh. I thought he was dead drunk."

"Don't you believe it! When they carried him past the key-hole he was stiff and dead as a rail. Boulton told us himself, he woke up when he heard the death rattle."

MacLeod would not have changed his mind if I had produced the three bottles Isidore drained; when Charles Boulton was nearly a Manitoba senator he told this story in a book where it can be read for all time. No doubt he suffered in that freezing room, and the staggering effect of his imprisonment upon his guards no doubt was a solace to him; we all need whatever help our interacting senses can supply. Whether he understood why Riel reversed his sentence and let him live so that he could finally shoot Métis fifteen years later is not so clear; probably the complicated politics of an emerging nation are beyond a man clear-headed and courageous enough to be an excellent soldier when a superior was available to give orders; but Schultz would have understood. Besides raising armies he had been sending fast messengers everywhere, so that while the Provisional Government had been celebrated in Winnipeg and Fort Garry, in the other English settlements it was as good as dead. When the English delegates who had voted for it returned home, they were treated as if they had sold out to the French, who were both half-breeds *and* Roman Catholics. James Ross, the new Provisional Government's chief justice and the best legal mind in the country, was forced to resign by his electors in St. John; that helped his addiction to the bottle nothing at all and destroyed his usefulness besides, when he should have been counselling Riel about Thomas Scott. For Riel was determined to use the shotless capture of the Portage men to solidify all the people of Red River behind him: if not willingly, then by destroying their active opposition.

"When he faced Sir John A.," I told MacLeod, "he was going to speak for *all* of Red River."

"So executing Boulton was a political trick?"

"Who knows? But Boulton had raised an army, he had marched to meet Schultz's men, he had helped stir up the Saulteux, even the Crees."

"But he had all our guns in the damn sleigh! He ordered me not to shoot O'Donoghue!"

"Of course. That's why Riel could reverse the sentence on Boulton. But not before Donald Smith, Government and Bay man both, agreed to support Riel in getting a province for Red River, agreed to a three-man delegation to Ottawa—no list of rights Smith alone would carry—agreed to travel to each English parish and convince them of the necessity of the united Provisional Government. That was what Riel got out of Boulton."

"He just used him!"

"Yes! He used the Métis guns to set up the North-West politically. Just like Gabriel said he should."

"But then he shot Tom Scott."

Yes. What the Métis guns did to Boulton to help create Manitoba, they also did to Scott to help destroy Riel. Since November Lépine had patrolled Red River and kept everything orderly with his men organized in companies of ten, each responsible to a captain. This was the way of the Métis buffalo hunt and when the prisoner Scott not only refused to swear to keep the peace so he could be released, but rather continually cursed, prodding his fellow prisoners to harrass the guards to the point where once he attacked them barehanded, once urinated on the doorway bellering they would not allow him out for that purpose, the captains, as they would have had they been in a hunting camp on the plains, at last called a court on the evening of March 3, to try Scott for insubordination. Ambroise Lépine of course was the presiding officer, and six captains heard the evidence. Scott was not present; that was not necessary in a hunters' court. Two guards testified against him: his armed escape with Dr. Schultz, his involvement with Young Bertie's death, his raising arms at Portage, his armed ransacking of Coutu's house, his spitting on Riel, his attack on three guards and his striking Riel when the latter ordered the guards not to beat him, his continual stirring up of prisoners with shouting and lewd songs–it was a heavy list. Finally Riel himself was called in to testify. He studied the faces one by one of the men who had given him their fealty; for such Métis their word to their chief was as good as their life–an echo of what Gabriel had said to him a moment before walking through the March snow across the Fort almost as familiar now as the slant-walled bedroom above his mother's kitchen where he had not slept in four months: 'He's white, to him we're just Catholic savages, something to spit on,' and the remembered Montreal and Chicago and Minnesota years, a world lived through the blur of youth and guilt so totally other than his own he never knew the right connections, the correct behaviour as even the most ignorant white did instinctively; he always had to laboriously puzzle things out, hold tight an uncommitted face while juggling off-balance in a world that would never be his; his people mere pemmican-eaters, not a word about them necessary anywhere in the libraries of the world, while their words crowded upwards in him until he felt his head would burst! He *must* write their words down, the persistent sound of their words rising, vanishing with the grass, the fading buffalo; and who would hear them if he did not speak, did not write, write? The dark steady eyes of those six men, only two of whom could have written the letters of his own name:

"It is the cursing," he said. "It is Thomas Scott's terrible cursing."

The men of the court stared at him as at a revelation.

"Yes," said Captain Elzéar Goulet. "The few French words aren't so bad, but to understand English, it's so...at home I soak my head in cold water, in snow, but the blasphemy..."

"Shoot a man for telling you to go to hell!" MacLeod burst out.

"If you really know..." but how do you explain the eternal annihilation of your soul to someone who doesn't want to know he has one?

After Riel's testimony, Gabriel led Scott into the room and Riel translated the accusations against him. Scott stood sullen in his chains, saying nothing, glaring from one to the other; but as Riel talked slowly the expression loosened on his pale, vivid face. Finally he was broadly smiling; it appeared that except for Gabriel like a wall behind him he might have laughed out loud. The captains leaned forward slightly, curious, waiting. But Scott said nothing; he explained, asked nothing. There was nothing worth his asking of these men.

After waiting a moment Janvier Ritchot said, "We have heard enough then, from the three witnesses. I move the death penalty."

"I second that," said André Nault.

Baptiste Lépine looked from Scott to his brother at the head of the court. "No," he said slowly, "that is too much."

"I agree with Baptiste," Elzéar Lagimodière said. "Permanent exile would be enough."

Joseph Delorme, the main prison officer said, "Death."

Elzéar Goulet sat with his head bowed for some time; staring perhaps at his huge clenched hands. "Death," he said.

"The majority then is clear," Ambroise Lépine said heavily. "The accused stands convicted, and the penalty is death."

Riel looked around at them. They all faced him steadily; slowly Elzéar's eyes lifted too. Riel turned to Scott, Gabriel tense behind him.

"Mr. Thomas Scott, you have been tried, convicted, and sentenced to death."

Scott jerked but his expression remained inert; Riel might have been speaking French. Then suddenly his face cracked.

"You call that a trial? A trial! I never even had a lawyer–a jury of nothing but Pope ass-lickers, holy jes–ugh!"

Gabriel had his arm twisted up behind him, he was doubled forward in wordless agony. Lépine said quickly,

"Get him out of here. Sentence carried out tomorrow, twelve noon."

"Give him pen and ink," Riel called after them. "And a minister, if he wants one."

If Riel slept that night, no one noticed; visitors flowed into Fort Garry as if the sun had stood still. The Reverend George Young pleading for Scott; a Métis scout reporting that Dr. Schultz and his wife had fled, south maybe; James Ross slightly tipsy but all the better for a 'what-if-you-do-this' session; O'Donoghue reporting that the Company fur warehouse contained 18,500 marten alone, and more beaver, they hadn't audited them yet; Delorme reporting that Scott was hammering on the walls so loud they had to lock him in short irons; Robert Tait coming for the order that would permit him to get his flour mill grinding again.

And Gabriel, just before he returned to his quarters. Beyond the walls of Fort Garry he could hear singing, a solitary man's voice wailing something in English–perhaps Jimmy from Cork again having taken the wrong turn at the saloon door and wandering between Winnipeg and Fort Garry, his lyric tenor no guide in the darkness through the flat, deep snow. For a moment Gabriel stood, looked at the cold stars; thought of Madeleine so warm and round in his arms, sleeping alone in their cabin above the Saskatchewan. The houses here, walls, the dirty sounds of barracks and prison–Scott who made you swallow rage, made you chew it until you felt nothing but gall when you so much as opened the door of the building that held him–the open air, campfire smoke, the sweet pointed softness of his wife hard holding him, dear god he was turning to dirty stone behind dirty stones; there was no happiness here any more, that blasphemous rage grinding itself into filth.

"Let's give him a gun and boot him out, then I trail him, let him try any soldier stuff he's got, and finish him, clean. This...." Gabriel gestured, both his hands empty of even the small comfort of drink, let alone smoke. "It's no good, Louis."

Three in the morning and the sheets of paper Riel had covered with writing were stacked about Mactavish's dining-room table.

"I've never seen this done in a camp," Gabriel said.

"He has nothing," Riel said. "Only his body."

"Lépine won't get anybody to do it...who? That's not our way, standing lined up against a man tied up, staring from in front of a wall."

"He'll be blindfolded."

"That's worse. I couldn't shoot a man flat-footed, you know, just lift my gun...no matter who said I should."

"You need a horse, a half a mile run?"

Gabriel laughed slapping his leather knee, "Yeah, yeah, or whisky! Just drunk enough so I could stand, see enough so I might just hit him..." he broke off abruptly. "God, I'd never use that gun again, I'd... Louis, I'm going back to the Saskatchewan."

"Now, when we've almost done it? You'll let someone like that chase you away?"

"There was joy here when I came, happiness, people singing, dancing...it's...have you heard the men? They were happy when you pardoned Boulton."

"Yes. And they want Scott dead."

"I know," said Gabriel heavily. "They know he deserves to be shot, but they're not happy that they know it."

"You think I am?" asked Riel. "How many men have you killed?"

"What?"

"Men, shot with all your Petits?"

"It was always in good clean fights, Louis, they had a chance to get me.

"I've never so much as fired a gun in anger. You think I'm *happy*? Good Lord Jesus."

And when he faced Mrs. Sutherland across the cluttered table in the early sunlight he was unhappier still. She could not seem to speak for a moment, her strong hands working over a balled handkerchief. Finally he said,

"Is it anything to do with Hughie?"

"No, no...John and I we, just miss him so much..."

"We can only pray, and I do that, every day, so that his death and Young Bertie's aren't useless, aren't..."

She wheeled to him as he hesitated.

"Then don't do it, Mr. Riel, don't shoot Thomas Scott! Those two dying, maybe it was–a–accident, who can say, but it's enough. We don't need any more blood."

Riel got up, wiping his arm across his eyes. Then reached down, took the crying woman's hand so she had to stand, had to look into his eyes.

"Mrs. Sutherland, do you know anything about a Métis court?"

"You pardoned Major Boulton."

"Yes! And I'm glad, glad that was possible. But for Scott it was a captains' court, set up as they are in the buffalo camps."

"But this–isn't a hunt–a..."

"Those are men, with some pride," Riel said slowly, his voice so brittle now he might have been speaking for himself. "They have been laughed at, ridiculed, their kindness to prisoners about visitors abused by knives, ropes smuggled in for escapes–cursed, day after day. If those men heard one word like that from a man on the street, they would gut him."

He could not say that if he forced the men now the best of them would simply go, return to their neglected families the way Gabriel had finally thought aloud, the way Norbert had gone three days before: "I don't need such–it's shit, Louis, shit they throw...I'm covered with–I don't need anything that bad," and no fast words about freedom, about land for his children stopped him from riding out the North Gate. Nor could Riel say to Donald Smith, who was waiting with Father Ritchot to see him next, what the Reverend George Young was discovering in the guard room.

"But Jesus Christ Rev," Scott exclaimed, "I just escaped like any fucking prisoner will if he gets—"

"Will you stop blaspheming!"

"Oh yeah, excuse me, but I—"

"For once in your life, listen!" Young leaned forward, his closed Bible curled like a black stubby club in his large hands. "They mean business. I just talked to Riel for almost an hour, have you ever used your eyes, the guards, how they look at you? They mean business, and you will swear yourself right into your grave. Have you written those letters? Your mother?"

"But Holy H. Jes—" Scott stopped himself abruptly. "Rev, nobody gets shot for swearing, not even in cuckooland. That fart wouldn't dare shoot an Orangeman!"

"Tommy, please," Young glanced at his watch, almost distraught, "I tried to get a twenty-four-hour delay from Riel, but Lépine wouldn't do it. He wouldn't even talk about it; he just got up and left the room. Now will you listen?"

Donald Smith was listening to Riel at that moment, very carefully, and he certainly heard more than literal words. No expression was crossing his gaunt Scots gambler's face; he had succinctly declared that so summary a sentence was really too monstrous to be possible, the young man was in no way prepared to die, and he heard Riel speak words which, despite the fact that they not once mentioned Ontario, really told him what he himself absolutely believed: he will not dare shoot an Orangeman.

"...and if I had not arrived to stop the guards three nights ago," Riel concluded, "he would have been dead without any benefit whatever of clergy. They were taking him out to beat him and I had to talk like a madman to get them to take Scott back in his cell, they were so–can't you understand what that blasphemer does to my men? And he kicked me for my pains, as hard as he could in socks. If Elzéar hadn't grabbed Joseph Delorme, he'd have strangled Scott with his bare hands. Métis men do not allow anyone to kick their chief, you understand?"

"Mr. Riel," Smith said slowly, "everyone knows Scott is a stupid fool. I am trying to point out how Ottawa will see this, Mr. Macdonald and Mr. Cartier, who sent me as their Special Commissioner. I agreed to talk to the English parishes and did; I agreed to support your List of Rights and your delegates to Ottawa, and—"

"Mr. Smith, you had no choice. The Métis have run this country by martial law for four months."

"But Canadian law does not—"

"Canadian law!" Riel burst into laughter so completely that the small room echoed. Smith was momentarily staggered out of his expressionlessness and even Father Ritchot, who had not yet said a word, almost smiled. He had not heard Riel laugh for weeks but now Riel's face slid into rage before he could appreciate the thought.

"Canadian law! You think Canada bought us from your Company? You know as well as I you never had anything here except permission to trade. So, let Canada trade! But if Canadians come here and defy us, we will punish them under *our* law."

"Scott isn't worth it," Smith said softly, "not when everyone knows you've kept the peace so well."

"Does Macdonald know that? Eh?"

"Yes! He knows. I have written him, and so have others."

Ritchot spoke for the first time. "Yes, he certainly knows that."

"Don't ruin what you have done," Smith said, his voice as close to pleading as it would ever get, "not for this one thoughtless man. To k–shoot him is the worst possible political blunder; he is a Canadian citizen, and if you—"

"Thomas Scott is an implacable devil."

"Then exile him!" cried Smith. "Don't make a martyr of a bigot."

"They weren't unanimous about him," Ritchot said; "the vote for death was only four to two..." His voice trailed off, because Lépine was standing in the open door, his bearded face dark as usual, heavy, so profoundly immovable. None of the men in the room knew how long he had been standing there and they all slowly stiffened as, one by one, they became aware. Riel glanced at his watch; he said in French,

"It is God's truth then, they are really taking him down."

"It has gone too far," said Lépine. "It's time now." And he turned, and went.

After a moment Riel walked slowly to the window overlooking the Fort square. Men milled about there, crowds, as if waiting in front of the mess hall. Below him Lépine emerged, strode through them.

"You should know English history, Father," Riel said, not

turning. "The vote to behead Charles I was carried forty-one to forty."

Ritchot studied his back a moment, hesitated, then turned into the bedroom and knelt beside the bed; slowly he raised the crucifix from his belt. Smith remained unmoved beside the chair, his short stocky body almost formally erect as if he were waiting for a procession, or at least a state entry. He said, at last, "You are the leader here, and you alone will be remembered for this."

Riel leaned at the window, his voice like iron, as if he were bracing himself more and more rigidly against the wall.

"God knows I don't want that miserable life. But we will make the Canadians, Canada, respect us."

A beginning flicker of comprehension, and suddenly fear, crossed Thomas Scott's face when Elzéar opened the cell door; armed guards stood behind him but the big Métis had no weapon, only a key and a winter coat on his arm. He bent to the irons.

"Sorry, Reverend Young," he said. "It's time now."

Young could not close his Bible, could not seem to move. "But–but he's not...ready, he is not nearly..."

"All night, all morning–put this on–it's more than most of us will get, sir," Elzéar straightened up. Scott had jerked himself against the wall, freed arms clenched behind him.

"You bastards, I'll see you in hell first!"

Elzéar gestured; an armed guard behind Gabriel at the door entered, took the coat. The captain deliberately peeled Scott from the wall, broke his grip on himself, bent first one arm and then the other while the guard tugged the coat on.

"It's cold outside," Elzéar said, expressionlessly, "almost thirty below."

"I'll kill that son of a bitch Riel with my bare—"

"You shut your mouth," Elzéar's fingers caught a few buttons, "or you go out with it stuffed." He tugged a wide white cloth from his pocket, tied it tightly about Scott's forehead; and the sudden whiteness in the shadows cast by sunlight on the cell floor suddenly reflected the prisoner's pale face as if a fearful comprehension was finally dawning there.

"All right," Elzéar said, "let's go."

Young glanced again at the guards in the doorway, standing aside; he reached for Scott's arm. "Come, Tommy, you...must prepare your heart now, come..."

The prisoners were crowded at the keyholes or tiny windows of their doors; as the small procession moved through the dark hall past Métis soldiers clustered about the fireplace, Scott looked along the gloomy length of doors, each with a guard holding himself rigidly at attention; and he almost grinned, dreadfully, tried to lift one arm to them as he walked while Young clutched the other, the guards all about him.

"So long, boys," he said.

And he seemed about to say more, but the attempted derision of his tone did not quite catch. The prisoners, straining at their small holes, saw the white cloth bound about his head disappear behind the dark guards through the door and vanish into the sunlight in total, terror-struck silence.

The snow squealed under their feet in the brilliant cold. Men stood everywhere, at the tiny windows of the buildings, lined along the tops of the walls, but not seeing the white curves of the Red and Assiniboine rivers or the huddles of Winnipeg and St. Boniface and St. Vital sending thick smoke into the blue sky, their eyes intent upon a black cluster of men moving under the limp buffalo flag and steadily on towards the small gate near the middle bastion of the long eastern wall, the head of one bound by a white cloth. They could almost hear Young's uncertain murmur, his eyes trying to concentrate on the open Bible he clutched in one hand, his steps so wavering they could not tell who supported whom across the square. The small sounds swam like their shadows in the hard crystals of the air:

"...I am the Resurrection...Life; he who believes...though he...yet shall he..."

Suddenly the men in the square began to move, forward, following; and very quickly then the procession was through the small gate and Elzéar had stopped, gestured against the wall.

"Over there. Stand there."

A group of men stood away from the wall, as if waiting. Scott stared about, a terrified wildness leaping into his body, twitching it as if he were mechanical, spastic, jerking him to face Lépine standing alone with a white handkerchief in his hand beside the men with rifles butted in the snow, and beyond that a long wooden box, almost hidden by blanket-wrapped legs, rifle butts, it's cover half slid aside, and tilted.

"My God, Rev...good God..." His legs as if cut from under him.

"Yes, yes, my son, that's right," Young knelt swiftly beside Scott, their knees in the hard sleigh tracks leading to the gate, clasping his hands in his own, shaping them together, "Kneel, just kneel, don't move, kneel and say the Lord's...prayer...you know it...begin, just begin 'Our Father who art...'"

Scott's eyes were closed, slowly his mouth found those solid words. Young glanced up frantically as Elzéar–just one more minute, just–implacable, leaned over, tugged the blindfold down. Under that arm the minister could see Lépine's hand raised and the rifles of the six men, lifted now in a wobbly line. Muzzles facing him. Then hands on his shoulder, pulling him loose, up; he had to stand and turn, move his legs, away from the sleigh tracks, his entire body shuddering and shuddering, it would not stop.

Riel stood at the window, head down on his arms. The room behind him was empty but from the bedroom still rose the steady murmur of Father Ritchot's prayer. When the rifle volley stuttered outside, Riel's head did not move in the brilliant sunlight.

Lépine had picked up the white handkerchief he had dropped and was looking down at Scott; fallen on his left side, his coat torn at three not very large spots across his shoulders and chest. He twitched, jerked, then suddenly writhed on the snow, gruesomely. Lépine straightened, looked at Elzéar standing beside him now. His face clenched upon itself, his voice thin with fury:

"Finish him."

Elzéar was as tall as Lépine; for an instant he looked his chief in the eye, then in one motion he had jerked Lépine's pistol from his belt, swept it down to Scott's face outlined tight, contorted behind the white bandage; and fired. Red exploded on the flashing snow.

Sir John A. Macdonald heard that shot in his panelled office in Ottawa. He leaned back into his chair, stunned; and Sir George Etienne Cartier reached over, picked up the telegram.

"Now he's gone and shot a man."

"Dear God," Cartier said. "An Ontario Presbyterian. Crony of Dr. Schultz."

Macdonald studied his tented fingers. "Just when Smith reported their list of rights was not unreasonable."

"Ontario will howl."

"And Quebec?"

I always wanted to write a song about those two, the slickest–there is no other word–political operators Canada would ever see, actually forging the second largest nation in the world out of a small complex of confronting hatreds rebalanced at every election with infinite care. They had sufficient earthly reward for their work, I think. And when they went on to whatever they truly deserved, in Ottawa they each received a statue at either end of Parliament Hill–larger-than-life anchors, the Canadian Parliament as it were balanced on their shoulders–or perhaps forever keeping them apart. They were Canada's greatest statesmen and her greatest rogues: Macdonald the unequalled giant because he had twenty years more than Cartier, but between them they juggled the first Canadian chances into such a mess that the impossibilities of bilingual Confederation were shaken down into the practical manipulations of staying in power forever, if possible.

Macdonald suddenly chuckled, his eyes gleaming as at an election.

"If we handle this right," he said, "Riel's a gone coon."

After a long moment Cartier replied, "And if we don't, we are."

Any opposition to Riel and the Provisional Government that remained in Red River after Thomas Scott's death seemed content to wear itself out in the saloons. The prisoners, even MacLeod who had come close to being tried with Scott, signed agreements to keep the peace and trudged back to their neglected farms, though not before some had spent an evening in Winnipeg gathering the latest rumour and their resolution together. At The Red Saloon, across from Dutch George's, they heard that Riel was sick, really sick, and no wonder the upstart son of–but they kept that to themselves and drank. Alfred Scott, the bar-keeper elected a delegate to carry the List of Rights to Ottawa–he was still denying he would actually go, but didn't he have to keep some godless balance straight between Father Ritchot's papist logic and Judge Black's Presbyterian dourness, eh?–moved about behind the bar, efficient as usual.

"Hell, nothing'll get done at all if none of you can drink with old Mac!" someone yelled from a rear table.

"And when you're out, you can go find that hot lay you're always yapping about. Her in that New York."

Scott filled a shot glass, "Oh yeah," he said, "yeah."

"At our expense! Bull!"

But through the usual saloon uproar ran the most savage rumours: coffin stories. That pistol shot hadn't finished Scott, don't you believe it, even Elzéar was too drunk like all the rest of the squad, too drunk to shoot straight with only three of six guns even firing and how many of them had had a ball in them, tell me that, eh? And who ever seen a Métis even hit a wall standing flat on his feet, shooting, leave alone a man standing–he was on his knees, kneeling–they'd have had to take a half-mile run at him at a dead gallop, everybody knew that and drunk as they all were, all that bloody snow just a flesh wound? All right, maybe two. May you cut Moses, that Scott had been butchered, they'd just rolled him into the pine box he wasn't even dead, stunned maybe and starting to groan when they hammered the lid nailed down and Lépine chased everybody, even off the wall, scram, but Scott talked in there! Yessir, his voice while they were carrying it in through the east gate and into the bastion and some of them were digging, chopping through the ground solid as ice in the southwest of the fort, "O Lord, O Lord," that's what was heard coming out of the box, "O Lord, O Lord." And when they shoved it into the bastion and the hole wasn't ready, there were people standing there guarding it, and Scott's voice said, "For God's sake, kill me, or let me out of this, O Lord," so they tore the lid off and shot him again! Just like that, and that time they were sure because there wasn't much head left. Somebody could name names, somebody stood inside that bastion and heard the voice and heard that shot. God that guy was tough, unkillable Irish. And where was the body, eh? You think in that box they stuck in the shallow hole and tramped the frozen ground down? You bet your last damn dollar there was nothing in there but rags and rocks. Otherwise why dig the hole *inside* the fort where at least two gate sentries are always looking at it? And why not let Young have it to send to Ontario so his mother could bury it proper? Why not? If Riel was such a fucking Christian like he is always yelling, so kind and uniting everybody, always praying in the Cathedral over there with those nuns, sure as hell he's always praying, my God I'd be on my knees too night and day if I had a sister looked like that Sara but not in front of no bleeding altar, holy Jesus no, "for God's sake let me out," there's nothing in that box they buried, if they buried it. Who saw them, eh?

Heard of anybody? He's chained to rocks at the bottom of the river, they stuffed him through that hole where they water their horses. There was men working on the ice the night of March 4, I know what I know, they'd never let nobody see what they done to him before they finally got the poor bugger ki—

Elzéar Goulet and Gabriel Dumont were in the doorway, coming in, and the evening darkness behind them pushed them up perhaps a little larger than they really were, though they both were large enough even in ordinary light. The whole room was floating with silence; as if a big hand had wiped over all the men and not one could remember the word just taken out of his mouth.

4

DR. John Christian Schultz was standing tall on a table in St. Lawrence Hall. Very short beside him but with one arm most comradely up on his shoulder, stood His Worship the Mayor of Toronto the Orange Good, and strained together, shoulder to shoulder before them and all about the platform, on the balcony and in the very niches and cornices of the walls the blue gas light of the crystal chandelier shone o'er the fair women and brave men of Toronto, Canadians all and already half hoarse with cheering. For His Worship had assured them that the names of those gallant men who had upheld British honour at Red River would be handed down side by side in history with those who had led the gallant charge at Balaclava; that the same courage that had sufficed at Lucknow and Delhi would suffice to put down that miserable creature (*cheers*) who attempted to usurp the glory of the Union Jack at Fort Garry; that this meeting was purely non-political, called to express admiration for those who had given of themselves to the cause of law and order, to uphold British supremacy on this continent and in that cause had been subjected to–he dared to give it its rightful name–murder (*CHEERS*).

For Schultz the hall bristled with even louder applause, and with placards, banners waving: "RED RIVER OUTRAGE," "A ROPE FOR THE MURDERER RIEL." At his feet young men looked up his long slim length to his handsome jaw, chiselled as it seemed out of weathered white granite, and saw honour, glory personified. Young John Kerr, two days away from Perth and his parents at last, felt his strong Irish blood rumble even as his neck was kinked, staring up.

"...and that's why we came to Toronto tonight, to tell you. That gallant band of men who marched from Portage to join us and almost took Riel hostage–they marched to overthrow tyranny. They marched to rescue Canadians who had stood up for their British rights, jailed for months because they would not swear to keep the peace of that miserable half-caste (*Cheers*). And Thomas Scott..." Schultz's voice dropped and John Kerr at his feet shrank into himself, the intensity so overwhelming. "I was in the same cell last December with Tom Scott. Held by that tyrant. And we escaped together, because my beautiful wife God bless her, who is on the platform here with me..." Schultz turned, and cheers rang for the slim beauty of Mrs. Schultz that could be better imagined than seen from the gloved arm waving out of the press on the platform, "...because my wife smuggled a knife past the guards, she brought us the horses–Tom Scott, I say, was a Hastings County boy; his brother Hugh is with us tonight. Tom was a little wild sometimes, I admit that, Hugh admits that–as young men are when their blood is up. And who would want it otherwise, eh? A Canadian he was, through and through. They were *all* steady, loyal Canadians in that half-breed jail and for trying to get them out our Canadian brother Tommy Scott was most foully and unnaturally murdered! Murdered!"

St. Lawrence Hall exploded, the yells and the currents from the waving placards– "HANG RIEL," "REVENGE TOM SCOTT," "A ROPE FOR THE PAPIST" –threatening to extinguish the chandelier. John Kerr's blood roared; he wanted to break something, to rip apart—but pinched in tight by other rocking bodies, all he could do was beller.

Schultz raised his hands high; after the humiliations we had forced upon him this was sweet, so unbelievably sweet. Finally the roar fell to a murmur. "It was here in Ontario," he cried, "that the movement to add the North-West to Canada was first begun. It is to Ontario that the North-West properly belongs, because the sons of Ontario have died to gain possession of it. And we'll have it!"

His "Thank you" was drowned in cheers that threatened to burst the hall. He stood above them, slim and tall and broad shouldered, the perfect son of Ontario—didn't they say he had snowshoed over two thousand miles often with his wife on his back, oh! to bring them this message about a land just waiting to be taken, his hands clasped above his head in a victory salute. Then he bent down, handed up his wife out of the crowd to the table-top with him; it is doubtful whether in all Canada a more perfect couple—such strength, such beauty—could have been found. Beside him, hand in his, Anne Campbell Farquharson Schultz raised her gloved arms above her gleaming bare shoulders; in a moment they were rocking together to the rhythmic cheer of the crowd, laughing, smiling into each other's eyes, they would certainly have kissed on the table-top if that had been publically viable. Then Schultz dropped his hands, in one smooth, outdoorsman motion he stepped down and she stood alone, her arms appealing to them and her lips moving. Silence immediately, the very gas flames leaned towards this tried and true and beautiful woman, towards her mouth opening, her gentle words:

"Those brave Canadians marching on Fort Garry," she cried, her voice high, brilliantly hard, "they sang their own marching song. I'd like us all to sing it tonight here in Toronto, in their honour (Yes! Yes!). It's to the familiar tune 'Johnny Cope,' and you have the chorus on the sheets you were given at the door, all right? (*WE'LL SING IT, YES! WE WILL!*) Right. I'll sing the verse, and you all join me on the chorus."

She gestured to the faces below her on the platform and a drummer, then a piper, squeezed forward there; in an instant they had begun the rhythm, then the tune. Anne Schultz sang, her voice sweetly lyric over the violence growing in her words, over the crowd's growl gradually gathering into tune with her:

Riel sits in his chamber o' state,
With his stolen silver forks and his stolen silver plate,
Listing more Canadians to send on to their fate;
But he'll not breakfast alone this morning!

She conducted with her body snapping, sharp on the beat; as the crowd's bearish voice rose she caught her husband's eye and the gleam in hers repaid him forever for her then seemingly perverse adamance that he turn Roman Catholic, that Bishop Taché marry them in St. Boniface Cathedral: you big dolt, race and politics are always thicker than religion, I told you. And rocking with her now, the crowd attacked the chorus:

O hey, Riel, are you wakin' yet?
Your stolen cannon well primed yet?
If you're not wakin', we'll not wait,
For we'll take the Fort this morning!

She was marching the three strides across, then back on the table, oh, if she only had a flaming torch to hurl, her long dress flaring at her boot tops to the swing of her arms! In the roar of the last repeated line she certainly saw beneath her husband's rumpled hair and excellent long nose below her a heavy tropical overlay of gold braid, the stiff whorled gold of the standing collar under the bearded chin of Lieutenant-Governor Sir J. C. Schultz, his mouth open and roaring to her rhythm, as she had always known her own beautiful shoulders were destined to curtsey before the Queen herself into nothing less than a Ladyship. Her heels drummed the table as hollow as a coffin, and she did not care in the least whose it might be since it most certainly was not her own.

Bellowing "We'll take the Fort this morning!" his eyes level with her unbelievably delicate buttoned boots, John Kerr was beside himself, beyond any imaginable Methodist heaven.

Outside the gable window, bright snow was sinking into itself under the March sun. Between stark poplars and beyond the long sloping fields a first thin blackness of water gleamed in the Red River. Sara Riel heard a bunting chirp, saw the glitter of shrinking drifts, the wavery glass swimming a possible spring to her like a smudged dream framed in bits of rag stuffed around the cold unevenness of a window. She had stood there, praying perhaps, she must have been praying certainly because she never stood thoughtlessly now without prayer, even for a moment, it was adoration she now effortlessly and eternally lived, until that sunlight world had become part of her prayer and she felt a distant happiness begin to stir, hope, which was the divine moving of prayer within her that when she lifted her head from her arms leaning in the window, her eyes open to what wavered like heat outside, and turned, she would find Louis breathing openly in sleep, quietly toward healing at last; but when she turned now, certain in her renewed expectation, he twisted under the blanket so violently she nearly cried aloud as if her very turning had convulsed him again. Their mother watched by his side, and Joseph coming at the corner of the staircase, another pan of snow in his hands. Mrs. Riel took the pan, whispered and the boy stood a moment staring at his awesome, suffering brother, and then turned, the stairway creaking after him into the silence of the small kitchen below. Abruptly Sara tugged the curtain over the sunlight, came to her mother folding snow into a striped towel.

"I think the light bothers him," she whispered. "Let me do that."

"The doctor said only five minutes at a time. Here."

Sara took the snow pack, laid it to his white forehead gently to give the cold, gently without any weight, and he squirmed away groaning, the towel dragging across his face that dipped, spread out like dough rolled she could not find it so thin under her hands; she was clutching a long stripe too far away, beyond her in a distortion of water perhaps, unconnected to her, gigantic bloated hands swimming by themselves...

"There is a time to cry," Mrs. Riel said reaching to take the pack from her, but Sara found him then; held him quiet with her hand along his burning cheek. "They may have to let blood, he said, the doctor."

"I'll manage, Mama," she said, "I will."

Mrs. Riel watched a moment, then silently turned and the stairs creaked down. Sara concentrated on her right hand holding his left cheek, the sharp prick of beard stubble more vivid than the growing cold, as if she would draw the fever out, cleanse him into herself with the power of her prayer and her serene beauty bent to him, draw out the fire that raged in double spires, bits floating away in flames, a cathedral blazing to its two gigantic crosses tilting toward each other in the relentless slow motion of melting into themselves though their bells tolled on, closer and closer, as if the fire intensified their thunder, and through their tolling the flames spoke to him in a voice he had heard, o he had heard

You have a call, my son...Are you so proud?...
My son, you have a call

The crosses themselves ablaze now, leaning upon each other like numinous, gaunt old men until the spires crashed down into the cathedral while the bells and the voice tolled on in indistinguishable thunder. He tore his aching bones away, flames burst like flowers over his body and he roared with them, a rolling sun of fire—

"Louis! O my beloved, Louis!"

Her face swung past him like a candle in wind, again, and then he could wrench himself, wrench himself out of the ache soaked into his marrow to clutch, hold her. And finally he lay still, panting; but she was there, bent to him.

"What did you see?" she said.

He could even speak, he knew it, his head almost a coolness. "You...always know."

She nodded, her eyes alight at his consciousness. "Tell me."

"It was a...fire." He hesitated. The corners of the bed seemed almost cool–he had never spoken to anyone of what he really saw. "Like two steeples, burning together but the bells still rang and..."

"The old cathedral?"

"Yes," he said in wonder, "of course. Here, St. Boniface, you wrote when it burned."

"We were little girls melting tallow for the Christmas altar candles, and it boiled over."

"I saw that, now, but the bells kept tolling even when the steeples crashed into the nave, and a voice, 'Why...do you rebel, why?'"

He stopped suddenly, aware of her face almost touching his, and he saw its purity brushed by cold against the new cathedral with the other Grey Sisters of the Cross coming from prayer the February morning Boulton was to have been shot and she had touched his hand, nothing of her visible under grey except love in the precise oval of her face. That picture tore across his mind now, the agony in her face as she bent down, held him close.

"O Louis, Louis, if only my love were strong enough to help you carry your suffering, o dear God, if only..."

Her head was in his blankets, shaking with sobs; her long

black hair, uncovered but braided into such painful severity he had to look up to the uneven corners of the gabled ceiling, the angles an awkward mark always crossed over him when he awoke but never in his sleep for then he knew his body was not there; in sleep he was only soul returned to that heavenly shelf once more where it rested eternally before he was born and God Himself again told them the stories of the creation and of the fall, of the glory of shaping soil touched with water and His breath, the strange three-pronged angle that every waking moment pointed him away into his own beginningless and endless immortality.

"You are so beautiful, Sara," he could say finally, "so good, and I am so bad."

"You are the best man I know."

"My conscience, if you knew...and across the river, all that across the river."

"You are good!" she said fiercely. "Good! Those terrible men hounding you, cursing, trying to—" she broke off suddenly, her tone abruptly gentle. "The night you visited us at the convent and Mother Superior insisted it was too dangerous to go back to Fort Garry?"

"That was the night Scott raided Henri Coutu's."

"Yes, and you were in the convent," she nodded. "The sure and perfect hand of God, and you slept there; there was only a thin wall between us."

"Ahh," for he remembered exactly that, again and again, and the memory was a happy agony. "I saw you that night, as I have so often."

"You did?"

"When I fall asleep with the lamp still burning, sometimes people who love me come to me."

Sara's face was brilliant with happiness. "And you know what I felt that night?" she said. "Your goodness. It was like...water surging through the convent, through every wall and room like a flood and I thought they will all awake, it is too strong for them to sleep, and those who are praying at this moment will adore God in blessedness forever. Your goodness like I felt it when I was a girl, there in my little room and you were in here studying so hard to please Bishop Taché so he could send you to the seminary. I felt it right through the wall, here. Your love for our family, and all our people who are so few and nothing, just nothing, the Canadians look at us like...even in the convent—" she caught herself, horrified at her own thought, and suddenly she tore herself from it, gripping him fiercely by the shoulders. "Oh Louis, God will reward your terrible sacrifices, for He has called you. To a great calling, He has! Now is the time for you, and for me. Let us make a pact with God, right now! That in all our sufferings God will guide us to—"

"Sara!" Louis was staring up at her, "Sara! Don't you know what you're—"

"I do know! I would sacrifice, I have prayed to God to take me into exile and I would go for your sake, forever, if God saw me worthy. I would gladly, so gladly—"

"No," he pinched his eyes shut like a spasm of fever driving through him again. "No pledges, no vows, no!"

But she saw only the incomprehensible beauty of holiness.

"Louis," she said, "when you left that morning I followed you with my eyes across the river until you were hidden by trees, and I hated those Portage men. I hated them, I could not have prayed for one of them if he had been shot at noon. Do you know that? Oh the long nights I agonized to get past that hatred, and how you have helped me, you Louis yes, I pray and pray for Thomas Scott, every day, every evening and morning that he may be saved as a brand from–o my brother," she stopped the words stumbling from her, her eyes quiet, locked on his. "Let us be saints, we two, together."

He had to close his eyes to her terrifying intensity, and his words came at last like a groan. "The feelings boil up in me, I can't stop them, I can't pray them into control like you, yet, I can't pray that much now, never enough. There is all that Fort business, all that—" he clutched his hair as he would tear it out by the roots.

"Sara." It was Mrs. Riel behind them.

Sara leaned back, her face all contrition. "Please Louis, forgive me."

"You shouldn't vow anything," he said, and she looked steadily at him, standing up, her eyes not leaving his and he was forced to continue. "Or be very...careful, what. Without you I am lost."

She bent swiftly, kissed him and was gone. Mrs. Riel began wiping his shoulders, arms, face with a towel,

"There was someone at the door," he murmured. "Have they brought the Ontario papers?"

Mrs. Riel straightened the blanket, the buffalo robe over his feet; none of us needed to read English, to read at all to know what the Ontario papers said in blood-thick red headlines, but now she had one small happiness at least:

"No, no papers today. That was Gabriel. Bishop Taché is on the steamer from St. Paul. No, don't," as he jerked up in excitement, "there is just that, nothing else, and Lépine has everything ready, Gabriel said, as you planned. Whatever you planned–" her tone turning slightly, as if any Lépine connection with the Bishop was at the very least strange.

"He has been six months in Rome." Riel lay staring up at the corner of the walls. "And twice in Ottawa, going and coming."

"The Holy Father, he will have talked to him."

"You think the Holy Father knows we exist?"

"The Holy Father knows everything." Mrs. Riel laid the pack on his head again. "There?"

"Yes. Yes."

"His Worship will have said what has to be said in Rome, and in Ottawa. He is always so good."

Riel stirred, answered nothing; I don't think anyone in Red

River suspected what Riel was beginning to think about Rome, or Taché, or why. The mention of our bishop now gradually hunched his face together as if the agony in his head were twisting tight again. Mrs. Riel watched him, sadly.

"Do you remember the last time you saw your father?"

"Last night...I saw him."

Mrs. Riel hesitated; his eyes were covered with the striped pack and she held the sudden surge of her tears stiffly out of her voice.

"I meant, before he died."

"Just past Pembina, on the prairie, I was being taken to ...Montreal, we could hear their carts, they were just a speck. He was bringing more machinery."

"'Weaver of Red River,'" Mrs. Riel murmured. "He was such a dreamer."

For an instant Riel's face smoothed under the pack, "That machinery is still in the shed, why should they make all our cloth in Ontario? When I have time I'll get a mechanic and set—" he clutched the pack to his head.

"Louis," Mrs. Riel said, "I have a treasure from him for you."

"After...six years?"

"Some day I knew you would need it, especially, so I kept it for you. When he was dying he blessed us all and then asked a particular blessing for his oldest son, special, far away in Quebec...what?"

For Riel had thrust the pack aside, stared at her. His face seemed transfixed; he struggled suddenly, powerfully to sit up.

"I must Mama, please, I must."

"But Louis!"

"Yes, I must, please," he had hoisted himself to the edge of the bed, and as she looked on in dread he turned, rolled to kneel beside it. Slowly Mrs. Riel knelt with him.

"He prayed," she said slowly, "he couldn't speak much then, but it was almost as if he...he knew what you would have to do...our merciful Lord Jesus told him something in his dying moment and gave him a special blessing for what you have to bear. 'O God, most holy Lord Jesus, strengthen my son Louis, his faith and his courage. Help him to love his people.'"

The thick pungent underfur of the robe like silk against his burning face, his mother's blessed hand, her voice over him filled with his father's prayer. His father's voice was barely there, thin as a cart's smudged wavering out of prairie heat, but his pale face and long flared nose and hard, implacable eyes in the bristle of hair and beard–that face he had seen again and again rising like a mountain from its open bier, flesh folded into white rocks laced and pitted with grey now giving him this final blessedness as of an immense field of golden flowers, he might have been running there. The flowers dusting him with effortless sunlight and his happiness leaping like love in his body it was impossible to touch the ground through their very brightness, or perhaps it was the girl's hand holding him, carrying him like a waterdrop, a feather caught aloft in a wind of adoration. He could, he could almost see the face of the girl, it might have been Sara...or Marie-Julie...it was...her hand danced them together as if they were clouds in blue, golden sunlight, but the flowers were already gone and they were plunging perhaps down an overgrown mountain, it was so steep the gaping valley below disappeared and the girl was gone, he was struggling in steep thorns, under-brush, groping for her perhaps beyond the spined and silky leaves, the white rocks which slipped under his fingers like blood, he was calling frantically and he did not know what name was snared between his teeth and tongue, there was no sound, nothing though he screamed and screamed, terrified by the very terror of his soundlessness, the distant, falling clatter of rocks. And the bell thundered; he had to lift his head. Its toll so doom-struck his heart stopped dead to the steel clasped about his chest

My son, you have a call, My son

he wrapped his arms about his head to hide himself from the small, gentle voice speaking through the bell with the precision of needles: it was the high shriek of cartwheels, the thick dust of their turn choking him and he could not so much as cry in agony, only twist, burrow down into the cool tender earth and the field was there golden about him, nothing else, no sound or girl, the golden field stretched beyond his seeing and words rose in him like his complete body moving through flowers,

"O my God, it is too beautiful. Give me ten years in the world, and I will serve you forever."

His mother was holding him; on their knees side by side in the gabled bedroom where he had been born under the strange corner angle. Her strong arm clasped his shoulder, her left hand wiping sweat from his face; she held him like a child, tenderly wiping his face. When he was calm again she helped him into the bed, covered him. He lay so limp and still he might have been dead.

"When did you vow that?" she said at last.

"On the Feast of the Immaculate Conception," he said. "The year father died."

"Do you need this?" Mrs. Riel lifted the snow pack. "I'll get Joseph to..."

"No," he said, "the fever is broken, I think." Still in the voice thin as grass.

Mrs. Riel began to laugh, gently, gradually more and more, until her large, solid body shook; she might have been totally happy. After a moment Riel was caught in it too, the deadness on his face gone as if wiped away.

"Gabriel and Lépine," she could say finally, between laughter, "it's providential; they won't have to face the Bishop alone."

"I told them to take ten men," Louis laughed.

"That's even worse than alone."

And they laughed harder. Sara was at the stair corner, peering at them in amazement.

✳

Surrounded by the carved walnut dignity of the Privy Council Chambers in Ottawa, deliberations regarding the List of Rights and what was already known as the "The Manitoba Act" had been at last completed. Aides cleared the tables, handshakes were in order: Macdonald gave the full, official double-handed pump to Father Ritchot who, no more than ever during the three-week talks, allowed himself a small smile.

"And so you have what you came for, Father," Macdonald said, his long face crumpled in cordiality, "not only your List of Rights, but—"

"With a few changes," Ritchot responded soberly.

Macdonald laughed aloud, "Well, not many! And presumably only God can have *everything* His way...and you have the province now too. A fine, euphonious name that, 'Manitoba'–the God who speaks, the speaking God–an excellent choice."

"Yes," Ritchot said and, as always when the enthusiasm around him seemed to be rising to unnecessarily political levels, he took his hand away and folded it with the other across his stomach. "Yes, Mr. Riel was particularly clear on the name."

Macdonald did not so much as blink at the name Ritchot deliberately pronounced into the echoing room; he turned to Judge Black whose handshake with Cartier had just been completed, and beyond him Alfred Scott smiling wordlessly as he had throughout their stay in Ottawa. And, as so often during the negotiations, Cartier's soft French eased around the eddy, his warmth that of one Quebec son to another:

"My dear Ritchot, without you to speak for Red River we would never have agreed to what we did! Your Convention will surely accept our proposals."

Ritchot's eyebrows moved slightly against the shining expanse of his forehead; when he and Scott had arrived together in Ottawa they were immediately arrested on charges of complicity in the murder of Thomas Scott. It took a night in jail to straighten out that ridiculous charge and Macdonald's official expression of regret at such regrettable behaviour–just Scott relatives and friends, you understand–had not soothed the priest when after a single short meeting it became apparent that the acquiescent Black and uselessly impressionable Scott would say yes to any government proposal. You did a fine job then, Ritchot, all alone forcing Macdonald to Métis land rights, to separate schools, to province, and you can be proud of that List basically untouched; but there were two matters rooted somehow in parliaments over oceans that could not be gotten at except through Macdonald, who always had endless imperial impossibilities at his fingertips. So Ritchot spoke to Cartier now, as he had at the best of the deliberations, when Macdonald was too sick–or hung over–to be there, and I, who had seen enough of such friendly politicians, would have told him, Careful, careful now. Especially when he smiles so brilliantly.

"Our Convention will agree," Ritchot said, "if that military expedition doesn't—"

"Be easy about that," Cartier said hastily, hand to his shoulder; "be easy, reassure them Colonel Wolseley is ordered by the British government, and they—"

"Your word on that?"

Cartier was caught a moment. "On what?"

"The conditions of the expedition?"

Cartier pushed aside papers on the long table, found his sheet, "My dear Father, this will be the Governor General's statement, we have already agreed on it: 'Her Majesty's troops go forth on an errand of peace, and will serve as an assurance to the inhabitants of the Red River Settlement and the numerous Indian tribes that they have a place in the regard and counsels of England...impartial British protection...' you saw that? It is clear."

"I saw that, of course; officially it is clear." Ritchot did not alter his expression. "What I and you also see is Schultz and

Mair cheered across Ontario. A lot of Ontario boys have joined that expedition."

"Wolseley is British; over half his men are drilled British regulars."

"And only a quarter of the Quebec volunteers so far speak French."

"The Quebec battalion isn't full yet, perhaps," Cartier stopped suddenly, laughing. "You really have contacts, don't you!"

"There are few enough advantages to being born in Quebec," Ritchot said drily.

Cartier's laughter roared. "And from what I have seen you do here," he gestured, "it's clear where some of Riel's best advice came from."

"My friend..." Ritchot leaned his bald, bearded head toward him, rigid with abrupt intensity; "if you do not help us here, if we do not have your good heart, we French are lost in the North-West, lost."

Cartier shifted uneasily; Macdonald, his arms linked with Scott and Black, was almost at the door.

"I remember Riel. He sent me verses when he was at Collège de Montréal."

"Verses?"

"Yes, he was asking for a job," Cartier smiled. "A very impractical young man."

"He is that no longer, I assure you."

"Of course, of course, and surely he and his—" Cartier covered his momentary hesitation with a cough, "the present council will maintain law and order in Red River until the new Governor Archibald gets there?"

"I'm sure Riel will be happy to, if you ask him officially."

"This is official, yes, yes."

"As long as the Governor arrives *before* Wolseley's army."

"It is *not* an army! And I'm certain he will, he will leave as soon as the Act is passed. So..." Cartier crooked his arm, turning the priest towards the door, already walking. "A good piece of work, the keystone to Confederation built on our French people, it will give us an influence in history which—"

"And a general amnesty," Ritchot continued relentlessly. "I've mentioned that so often. A general amnesty proclaimed for *all* persons involved in the problems of the North-West."

"As far as Canada is concerned, the slate is clean."

"I should have that in writing."

"My dear Father, Bishop Taché already took a letter. It is understood." Cartier seemed mildly exasperated, as with a child; they were at the door. "Come."

For a moment Ritchot hesitated, looked back into the magnificent Chamber he would never see again; it was empty now, seeming to echo still with Cartier's very hearty assurance. Push him, push him, the letter. And three weeks later, facing Riel and Lépine and Schmidt and O'Donoghue and his Bishop Taché in the spare chamber of the Courthouse outside the walls of Fort Garry, he wished again he had not only that echo but the words in hand, written, signed. There were words everywhere, spread in thick newspapers over the table between them as the five men looked at him expressionlessly. Riel said,

"And that's the way Cartier left it?"

"Yes," Ritchot said. "'It's official,' he said; 'it's not necessary to dot every i twice.' And the Governor General told me he would send the signed general amnesty the day after the Act was—"

"Then where is it?" Riel asked.

"It hasn't come?" Ritchot said dully.

O'Donoghue snorted, seized the newspapers on the table.

"And look at these: 'A Rope for Murderer Riel,' 'Revenge for Thomas Scott,' 'Belleville Boys Marching, to bring justice to the North-West.' Huh!"

"Both Cartier and the Governor General assured me—"

"And Macdonald?"

Ritchot hesitated. "No," he said finally. "Macdonald never said anything in so many words."

"My god, don't you see what he—" O'Donoghue caught himself, then said more quietly, "You did wonders, Father, but your mind's far too clean. Macdonald's a politician, he lets Cartier say it, and when Ontario yells the tricky bastard'll say, '*I* never said that.' You'll see, they're slick as snakes, your nice Cartier'll say that's what he understood at the time and they *won't* write it now, not when all Ontario knows why their boys are coming up the lakes."

Lépine rumbled suddenly into the silence, "Those eastern devils tricked you."

The silence was so long that the echo of birds gathering beyond the opened windows, their shadows moving across the oblongs of sunshine on the table thick with headlines, moved like thunderous footsteps in their heads. Riel had been looking at Taché for a long moment before the bishop looked up, met his eye. Taché had been very unpleasantly astonished when, on his return to Red River after six months in Rome and two arduous sessions in Ottawa hammering single-handedly, as he always thought, for the rights of the North-West people, he was met at the river wharf not by the usual immense crowd of cheering parishioners but rather by four very diffident Métis soldiers who guided him to his Bishop's Palace in respectful, solemn silence. The letters of special commission from Macdonald had weighed heavily in his pockets, especially when Father Dugas visited him that first long evening alone and informed him Riel had watched his arrival from a window in Fort Garry and as the bishop had been driven by had muttered to Lépine, with a wry twist, Dugas had noted that particularly, "It is not Bishop Taché who is passing, it is Canada." The child for whom he had had so much hope, returned to Red River an unemployed, over-educated and mostly unemployable young man, now in uneasy control of the country and setting guards at his Residence door. Doubting him. Asking, when he came to see him at last, "What does the Holy

Father say to us?" and, "What is the point of being 'Holy Father' if he does not know us? He sounds like 'The Great Mother' in England. Who needs all this greatness, this holiness far away and ignorant across oceans? We are ourselves, people living here." And though he had come to the Great Service on Sunday, March 15, in St. Boniface Cathedral and had sat in the front centre aisle with the hundreds crowded to hear the sermon, had tears of happiness in his eyes at the proclamation of the Word, had sat there with his great curly head so erectly proud among the bowing Métis–as if nothing had ever happened outside the walls of Fort Garry, as if his Provisional Government were organized so efficiently it needed not a word of advice–Riel was asking advice now. Clearly, and Taché knew suddenly he had so little to offer...but he must again become the trusted advisor. He must.

"Yes," he said, "O'Donoghue is, I think..." and he had to stop, for the letter he had brought from Macdonald had smelled faintly of a unilateral collusion between church and state which ignored all that the delegates of the people had decided in four months. But he had to try that again; he knew Macdonald better than Ritchot did, thank heaven. "In the letter I brought, Macdonald does refer specifically to 'there will be a general amnesty granted to all who—'"

Riel interrupted, "That was on the condition that Company Government be restored?"

"Yes," said Taché slowly.

"Have you seen any Company Government here to restore?"

"And that letter," O'Donoghue muttered, "was written before Thomas Scott. Let's not fool ourselves again."

Riel did not seem to hear; he looked at Ritchot whose brilliant achievement in Ottawa now registered like consternation on his face, then back to Taché; weighing things.

Down the table Schmidt said, "But if we don't accept The Manitoba Act, what?"

"We accept The Manitoba Act," Riel said suddenly. "And that is one of the conditions under which we accept it...a general amnesty. The Act comes into effect July 15?"

"If the House passes it," Ritchot's confidence was gone.

"The Conservative majority will pass it," Riel said. "And after July 15 we continue to administer Red River until this Archibald comes?"

"So Cartier said."

"In any case, there is no one else who can." Riel looked at Taché, and suddenly he smiled. "My good Bishop, are you willing to do a job for us?"

Where did you get this Machiavellian shrewdness, Taché was thinking; you are worthy of a cardinal at least. And laughing within himself that this prodigy he had once, almost unwitting, nudged forward should so easily give him back the power he seemed inexplicably to have lost by a simple eight-months absence, a power that for fifteen years he had known to be his by divine and irreplaceable right.

"Certainly," and Taché smiled. "My travel callouses are still hard."

"Good. Then you carry our reply to Ottawa, and the condition of the amnesty." Riel looked about his council; there was no question he would not have his way again for he knew what he wanted while they simply had their doubts. "We've run this country for six months. Our people were voiceless, unheard of until we took for them the right to elect representatives, conventions, delegates. We'd never had so much as an election, and now we have a province! Do you know what that means?"

His face glistened with happiness.

"Don't worry about that Wolseley," he said to the glum Lépine. "English colonels just obey orders."

O'Donoghue said sardonically, "They've been obeying them in Ireland for two hundred years."

Riel stood up, laughing, "Sweet William, the name of this

place is Man-i-to-ba! Call the Convention together, I've got to see the hunters."

No one ever saw him go through the small East Gate now; below the River Gate three York boats bulged bottoms-up against the gleaming Assiniboine, where others already rocked. The bright air floated with the smell of pitch and pine and oak planking, the sounds of men working. Bales of goods lay stacked at the wharfs. As he turned the corner of the east wall, the whole length of it, boats and canvas and baling burst upon him, our people intent at what they loved, their hands shaping and mending. The June sunlight was a benediction and he paused, almost staggered at how mercifully it had begun to emerge, how the air stood in his nostrils like sharp incense. He could hardly believe himself, that out of his often fumbling insecurity dreamed like a nightmare staggering in the agonies of brain fever, that out of these decisions which sometimes burst with the clarity of an explosion into his rages–there is no other way and the devil do what he will this will happen–this goodness had happened. All of it in this glorious hunting sun, province and peace possible even for the buffalo hunters; he looked at his hand, moved it joint and thumb, fingers. The tight skin stretched: it was real. He saw, felt, smelt it. Real, and he waved suddenly, ecstatic as a child laughing while the working men near him looked up and waved, laughing, but he was signalling to horsemen clustered far below near the ferry on the Red River. Someone there, it looked like Gabriel, waved back and then they all ran, had mounted and were galloping up between the boats and workmen in one deep blue wave, their beautiful horses washing them up against the river and the far roofs and spires of St. Boniface.

"I hope your carts are in shape," he greeted them. "I've got good news."

The riders cheered to their horses' rearing and the workmen began to crowd about. To their shouts he was being hoisted up, laughing, the immense rounded curve of a York boat under him; he could feel the ridged planking through his moccasins.

"All right, now listen," he shouted; they were craning up at him, the horsemen above them, all brown faces in the early summer sun. "Ottawa has agreed to everything we said, everything, and we'll have a—"

The cheers echoed the length of the wall, and around along the two river flats; from everywhere more men came running. He knew the Convention should have heard this first, but he no more wanted to resist these cheering faces than the immense joy in himself.

"We're not just a territory; we're a province called Manitoba! And we keep our river property, just as it is. We keep our farms and our grazing lots, everything!" The air rang. "And a new governor is coming–a *good* one this time who—"

"Does he speak French?" yelled a voice.

"Not like you," Riel shouted back, "*good* French!"

The young man who remembered this to me a year later could hardly speak then for crying.

"All right!" Riel waved them quiet at last, the brown, hard faces gleaming below him like water in spring. "We have work to do. The Company has to get its goods out; you're almost ready with the boats. Robert has his windmill turning again as you can see, the grasshoppers may be bad, they could be as bad as last summer so you have to take good care of your cattle, and all you hunters..." he gestured to the riders, "you get your people out on the plains for buffalo. Lots of dull police-work, lots of politics but now we need pemmican."

The hunters cheered, were wheeling their nervous horses but several held steady, watching him. Elzéar shouted, "What about the soldiers, we heard they're coming?"

"That's a police force, so no more guard duty for you. Half the men and all the officers are English regulars. And they won't be here before the new governor, so get your people and carts together, and let me know when you start. Now, everybody, back to work."

Through cheers the men scattered. Riel jumped from the boat, the ground so solid under him, but three horsemen remained: the remaining three–Isidore Dumont had ridden back in spring–"savages" from the Saskatchewan country, looking as wild as if seven months in the settlement had simply settled them in their difference. Riel said to Gabriel, "You have further to ride than anyone," gesturing to the whooping riders by the river's glare, but Gabriel's expression did not soften in the least.

"I don't like this," he said.

"We have to have food; all the inland trade, everything depends on pemm—"

"I know that, I know." Gabriel leaned forward; his horse jerked its head against the summer flies. "It's them eight hundred greenhorns; we could pick them off anywhere on the Winnipeg River like—"

Riel gripped his leg. "We've just made the biggest country in the world. Without killing anyone!"

"Ontario doesn't think so."

"One, necessary, *execution*. You know how many people were killed, in anger, to make the United States?"

"Who cares, now?" Gabriel said very softly, and suddenly he was off his horse, nose to nose with Riel. "Let me tell you something, my fine politician, you've made the 'biggest country in the world' because of our guns! That's why every settler and stupid Canadian here and that Ontario guzzler and whoever in England listens to you. This nice little gun right here that can pick you off a man at two hundred paces. They know power. And now they're sending their guns up our lakes and rivers and you're sending yours away? What's the matter with you?"

"Listen Gabriel, I know what—"

"I know Red River needs meat, everything inland needs it, but the Saskatchewan winterers had pretty good hunting, I can get you five hundred men for the summer, as good as these; we'll—"

"No."

"There'd still be enough on the plains to—"

"No! I don't want any 'army' around here to provoke any other 'army.' We must trust them, Cartier...show we trust their word. That, that's the only way..."

Riel's voice trailed off; he broke away from the big hunter glaring so overpoweringly at him. Across the molten river ducks flew north over St. Boniface and the trees lay like soft green froth among the houses.

"That's the only way different peoples can live together," he said.

"Okay," Gabriel said finally, though his tone remained unconvinced. "You trust. But I'd rather trust Indians; I know them."

"If we're going to be part of Canada, we have to."

"Well, that's a thing all right." Gabriel elaborately rearranged the tangles of his horse's mane. "You were too far into it when I came, and I've kept my mouth shut, all this elections and papers..."

"Gabriel," Riel reached out, both his hands on the wide shoulders, "you have been a great strength to me, a pillar for our people, not only here but in the West. Our people...I have not thanked you enough. But I love you for what you've done."

"It's been some fun," Gabriel grinned suddenly. "Lots of action, sure, though my Madeleine..." he shrugged, "we understand each other. If I hadn't wanted to, I wouldn't have stayed. They've heard about us now; they won't forget. But...why don't we just go West to all that country, Louis you don't know how big it is, the Saskatchewan country all the way to the mountains covered with snow, so high they're frozen, and beautiful...from the Missouri way up into the forests everything open, we lived near Fort Edmonton when I was small and the river valleys, the buffalo herds, my god we could have our own *nation*, by the blood none of this begging Ottawa for a province! You'd be our captain or president or king, whatever you wanted and all that land and water and air—"

"And the Indians dying of smallpox, the Blackfoot and Cree and Sioux killing each other, the buffalo just about—"

"There's millions of buffalo out there!"

"It's too late," Riel said. "You're dreaming too late."

Gabriel glared at him an instant; then with an abrupt, violent gesture leaped onto his horse. He leaned down, his mouth trying to lift into a grin.

"Five hundred men," he said. "We'd still have the fall hunt, that's enough for any good savage."

Riel stared at the ground beside his moccasins.

"Michel and Moïse are staying here," Gabriel muttered finally. "At least they'll give you some warning."

Riel looked up quickly; his hand gripped Gabriel's leg, the finger bent against the long Winchester tied to the saddle.

"Okay, my good friend, okay. And thank you for...staying." He laughed a little, "We have never had enough time to talk, always this with you sitting on a horse, ready to gallop off."

"I live on horses."

"Will you come back this fall? Wouldn't Madeleine like a winter here?"

"Maybe. I guess that'll depend what's...going on here," Gabriel suddenly clamped his huge hard hand over Riel's hand, crushing it against his leg and the round, tight belly of his horse. "God bless you, keep you," and he wheeled about, was galloping between the workmen towards the river trail, the strength of his emotion ringing in Riel's numb fingers like a bell of premonition. But neither of them would have believed they would not meet again for fourteen years. Neither would have believed that.

When Riel found his eyes again, he saw Michel Dumas and Moïse Ouellette on their horses. Waiting for him with the endless patience of our people.

And day after day we all waited that summer. Every morning as the sun rose over the flat, hot prairie to smudge the horizon with heat Michel watched the river north, Moïse the river south. Taché did not return; Archibald did not come; all they heard were the messages from the Indians arriving from the canoe route north and east. Wolseley has left Fort William; he has crossed the height of land to the Winnipeg River; he was at the three-mile portage two days ago. Michel's short finger pointed the route on the huge North-West map spread over the cluttered table in the council room, the inevitable progress, and Louis Schmidt marked another "X" and O'Donoghue wheeled from the table, cursing under his breath. James Ross and Thomas Bunn, as members of the executive council, now often joined them but they said little; there seemed so little to do, Red River almost empty and running itself. Dutch George said he was going broke and Alfred Scott had not returned, was still in New York perhaps where Ritchot had said he had gone after Ottawa, so O'Lone's Red Saloon did not even have gossip to recommend it in the long hot evenings. Only the whining mosquitoes, the inevitable saw of grasshoppers busy in the tall grass along the dried hollows of Winnipeg streets, beside the wooden side-walks. It was a summer when an old man would pray to die, but Louis Riel was only twenty-six.

"Why doesn't Taché at least write," Bunn said finally. "Then we'd know something."

"He has nothing to write," O'Donoghue said. "He's finding that out." Ross's raised eyebrow exasperated him. "What're you looking at me like that for, you—"

"Keep quiet," Lépine rose. "I'll check with Moïse again," he said to Riel, going.

Riel nodded, staring at the map. There was an inevitability about Schmidt's marks which even a child could interpret. He said, contemplating that staggering trail,

"Schultz is coming back, he's already in Fort William."

"What!"

"A letter in today's mail."

"Well, then we know—" O'Donoghue began, but Ross interrupted him,

"What do we know?"

"For sure what Canada wants, we've been played for suckers, that bastard would never leave Ontario if he wasn't sure of his backing."

"We wrote to Bishop Taché," Riel said as slowly as if he were reciting in his sleep, "on July 23 that we would welcome and receive the new Governor Archibald. No harm can come to us while God is with us.

"And that's what we'll do? Sit and wait?"

That is what they did. Riel seemed to have lost his decision, another one of those strange cycles in his life which would repeat itself on the Saskatchewan fifteen years later, and without his resolution to batter themselves against and move them, his council performed its small duties as directionlessly as the grasshoppers rising in clouds against a hard sun so brutal that sometimes on a July or August afternoon I couldn't see the willows across the Assiniboine for solid, layered heat. That strange deadness of soul: night will follow day, nothing catastrophic has happened, what...? Our people were far out on the plains beyond Wood Mountain and to the Cypress Hills looking for the buffalo, and perhaps they would have to go south and dare the Sioux beyond the Black Hills to the Missouri or even the Platte if they were to find enough to fill their carts in that long summer. I knew; day upon day on the empty blazing plain, water alkaline and children sick and crying for hunger; in such a summer in 1852 we had to go so far south the Sioux surrounded us on the Missouri Couteau. I made a song there, and we tried to sing it lying in the terrible heat of the sandy hill while they rode circles around us just out of rifle range, charged and charged again, and we shot very carefully, towards the end praying to God for nothing but

just a little rain, we did not care about death, only for rain on
that hill laid open to the blazing sky, and after three days Father
de Smet marched around our outer circle with a cross made of
two cart poles, chanting Latin; and the Sioux fled before the
Black Spirit-maker, as they thought, just as a dark cloud of the
Thunderbird came over, the Plains Cree with us said, and
blessed us with pounding rain as if we had been singing the
thirst dance instead of crying on our bellies in the dust. We
caught the rain in hides, drank it running in mud, not caring then
whether the holy St. Joseph or the Thunderbird had heard our
desperation. That's just how it is, a people with two heritages so
rich that often one alone is more than you want, when you feel
one of them move in you like a living beast and the other whis-
pers, sings between your ears with a beauty you would gladly
sell your soul to hear until you die. Such doubleness, such sometimes half-and-half richness of nothing. It would be hard to say
who was not praying for rain that burning August at Red River,
1870, but the fact is that Bishop Taché returned at last from
Ottawa on the second day of a rain that had already turned the
valley into floating mud, and into the blackness of that rain
which in its way was as fierce as the sun– this country is only
extremes. Who can be moderate in the North-West when he is
alternately fried or frozen or drowned with nothing but tiny bits
of autumn or spring to remember of either beauty or comfort, o,
that's not completely true but that summer was enough to annihilate saints–it was into storm that Taché returned. On August 23.
And told Riel that Macdonald would not talk to him; that Cartier
could not so much as travel about Ontario without a clamour of
armed rebellion to "put him in his place"; that Macdonald now
stated, by letter, that Canada had no jurisdiction over the North-
West before The Manitoba Act and that anything which had
occurred before May 15 must be decided by the Imperial
Government in London; that Governor General Sir John Young
refused to add a word to what he had written on December 6,

1869; that in effect, no one in Ottawa would say, leave alone write, anything concerning events at Red River between December 6 and May 15. There was no such thing as "general amnesty."

And while Riel stared, finally stuttered that his Provisional Government's acceptance of The Manitoba Act had been conditional upon a blanket amnesty for "all the parties who had to meet the difficulties with which the Provisional Government had to deal," a Provisional Government that was at this moment running the country at Ottawa's request until the new governor arrived–Taché had to admit that Orange Ontario had roared murder at him for daring to bring such conditions: that there had been demonstrations asking rhetorical questions like, "Is the Governor General to receive the North-West Territories from Bishop Taché?" and bellowed answers, "No! There are men from Ontario under Colonel Wolseley who will place the Queen's representative in power without any Bishop's assistance!"

Into the silence which followed that, Taché spoke his gentle assurance that whatever individual Orange Ontario thought, Wolseley took his orders from the cabinet and his orders were for police action only, as his published "Proclamation to Red River" had confirmed; there could be no question of anyone's personal safety. Taché was exhausted; in the darkening evening, candles guttered in the wind from the open windows where the rain drummed on the porch roof, the entire driveway of the palace awash to the river. He repeated, Louis, there can be no question of your, personal, safety. That cannot be in question. Archibald is coming, he left before I did, isn't he here? It's incredible; how can he take so long? But there is no question about anyone's safety. Especially not...

A horse was splashing up the driveway; the shape of the rider moved across the porch, his tread soft as moccasins. It was Michel, buckskin black with rain. The one Indian messenger had got caught in the mud, but the second hadn't let that stop him. Wolseley was moving almost night and day now; the first Indian said the troops were at Red River mouth on Lake Winnipeg but the second had already seen them passing Stone Fort. Twenty miles away. They had carried their cannon, dry, around the last of the rapids.

Taché stood in the open doorway and could not believe it. Michel said these messengers had always been right so far. Go to the kitchen and dry out, the Bishop said finally; feed your horse in our stable. There's room. But the hunter did not move; he was watching Riel who said suddenly as if awaking, ride over and tell Schmidt to call the council, and then the Bishop began closing the door, a haze of grey over his round, well-cared face, a glint of something beyond the spectacles shielding his eyes. My son, I have failed, o my poor Louis, I have failed. But aloud he said nothing; the face before him in the hallway so fresh now in the washed smell of rain was not that of the small, pious boy he had been searching for all evening, the one he had remembered with a vividness like pain for thirteen years; it was a bearded face now, broad but strangely sharp like a hatchet, unlined, a face wiped so blankly clean. A face that told him as clearly as his cathedral bells tolling that it had all been impossible, right from the beginning. Hopeless.

"Have you ever met...Macdonald?"

"What?" For a moment the Bishop could not comprehend.

"Macdonald, you have shaken his hand?"

"Of course...I sat in his office, with Cartier and, alone too...we even had a light lunch together, once, just we two, the last..." he knew he had been startled into silliness somehow, but the erased face facing him forced him to–this is for the best, his priest's mind told him, his careful lifelong training to be the complete churchman, because you are really sorry you have failed, not really sorry for him, for the people of–o my God you know my heart, you know I—

"Did he really say," Riel said again, "'they are nothing but pemmican-eaters'?"

The bishop wrestled with himself; there was so much here he was suddenly stranger to, that he must be precise, answer exactly, barely what was asked.

"He is a man of vivid speech, like yourself...he said McDougall had 'made a most inglorious fiasco at Red River,' like yourself, his speech...he probably did."

Riel turned, picked up his sodden capote. "So Father Ritchot said too, yes," coming to the still half-open door. "I've seen Schultz and Boulton and...often enough, but Macdonald and Cartier, I wonder sometimes if they actually...you think they ever have headaches?"

He was standing in the doorway against the totally black summer rain, and now Taché could say nothing. So Riel turned, went. "Perhaps I can see Wolseley at least."

The long room where the council had met so often steamed in the candlelight, a haze rising from their wet clothes. The word "Seven Oaks" had silenced them all thin as though they were cardboard. I could have told them again how we once rode to Semple there in the true, straight line of the Bois-brûlés but none of them needed to hear that while the rain pounded on; they looked at Riel; who stared at the streaming windows. Finally James Ross leaned back, moved his slack body against the table.

"They camped at Seven Oaks," he said. "They've got Red River guides?"

Lépine said, "Since Rat Portage."

"Who are they?"

"From Stone Fort, sent by that St. Andrew's minister."

"The Reverend Joseph Phelps Gardiner," Ross said as if he were calling a witness to the box. "No wonder they move so fast. Now, if we had only been able to decide what to do before they were here, just in case Archibald didn't come first..."

O'Donoghue exploded from his chair, "You know goddam well they won't touch your fat gut you son of—"

Schmidt, Bunn, Elzéar Goulet, Father Ritchot, Bannatyne were all on their feet, remonstrating; Elzéar's huge hands opened and closed as if he would have gladly strangled both Ross and O'Donoghue; but Ross simply smiled.

"That's enough," Riel said. "Sit down, all of you."

"It's true," he continued. "Until now we...I just haven't been able to decide what to do. But now we know a number of things: the troops are here, Archibald is not–Moïse hasn't been in?"

Lépine said, "Nothing south on the river, or the Dawson Road. Nothing."

"They lied to me," Ritchot said.

"Yes, they lied," Riel said. "They've decided that politically they couldn't afford—"

"Let Vickie do it, the goddam buck-passers," O'Donoghue muttered.

"And they're loading their political problems on the West; it won't be the last time. Now," Riel's voice grew warm, almost nostalgic, "gentlemen, we have argued and worked together, and we have nothing to be ashamed of. I thank you for the way you have stood with me during these long months since January and we started together to make..." he stopped, as if he had caught himself beginning a speech he must now refuse. "Mr. Ross, Mr. Bannatyne, thank you for your advice, I suggest you go to your homes. It's late enough. Mr. Bunn and Mr. O'Donoghue, make certain that all the accounts we have agreed upon are in order. Mr. Schmidt," the secretary was nipping at his flask but Riel's expression did not change as he noticed, "you have, I think, some papers to destroy. And after you have done that, ride to St. Vital and tell my mother...tell her what I'm doing. Mr. Lépine, how many soldiers are in the settlement?"

"With Elzéar and me, thirty-seven. Plus the scouts."

"All right. The scouts stay where they are, but the rest are all to come to the Fort. The flags up and the guns in order."

They all stared at him, aghast. Finally Bannatyne said, "You want to face Wolseley with thirty-five men?"

Riel was studying him with a hard, long look. "The only possible integrity Canada has left is the integrity of that British officer and his soldiers. We must now discover whether or not we have been totally deceived."

"But, how?" Ross began, and stopped.

Riel said, "I'll ride out to Colonel Wolseley."

"Not alone you're not," Elzéar said.

"No, I'll need Michel to show me where he is."

"I'm going with you," Elzéar said.

Michel was shaking his head, "It's really pouring out there."

Riel laughed slightly, stood up. "We won't melt."

Father Ritchot reached for his shoulder. For a moment it seemed the priest would embrace him, but he did not; he did not even make a gesture for prayer. He merely said, very slowly as was his wont,

"My son, no matter what happens, you have assured the rights of our people in The Manitoba Act. That they cannot change now."

"I pray not," Riel said, and went.

The rain was harder than when he crossed the river from St. Boniface; it ran over them in walls of wind and blackness, the very sounds of the horse's feet under him like fish swimming. The warm barrelled body was between his legs, but past the few windows of Winnipeg there was only black as though he were balled up tight in the storm's fist: when he raised his hand it was only there when he touched his nose. For a time he prayed, not knowing what while the horse moved with the others, and then suddenly he felt he was coiled in wool, a kind of cold shapelessness that could be nothing less than the enormous wormlike fingers of hell working themselves around to clutch him forever, the next step of the horse would hurl him over into the abyss: he jerked back suddenly,

"Michel?" His horse had stopped. "Michel!"

"Here, sir," Michel said beside him. "You're right, we should stop, about here..."

"It's so...where's Elzéar?"

"Here," directly behind him.

Suddenly Riel laughed a little. "I seem to be sitting in a puddle." The wind tossed his words away. "It's just as dark...wet for them, I guess.

"That's their fires, I think," Michel said, "there."

As if they were looking into a black lake, the points of light flickered, it was impossible to say how far away. They might have been sparks before their faces, or houses burning in St. Andrews.

"The master race," Riel said. "The English are always right."

"Yeah, that's their fires." Elzéar's deep voice said behind him. "They didn't cross the ravine; they're just beyond the bridge. You know it, Michel?"

"Yeah. Wolseley will have a sentry there. We better walk."

"Can you find the horses again?" Riel said.

Elzéar's voice was muffled, as if he were wiping his face. "He can always find horses!"

"Sometimes even my own," Michel chuckled. "Come on."

The ground felt so good, softly wet but solid when his weight fell, settled; walking was better and in a moment Michel hissed: there was a peeled spruce railing of a bridge before them, and the distant lights beyond had leaped out of the wet as if they were fires, flaring up. Against that, suddenly, for the first time he sensed Michel's shape moving beside him, and then Elzéar's too; they were not just voice, and when he moved his hands he touched them. Both.

"It's a short bridge," Michel whispered. "Don't touch it, I think..."

A shadow moved against the flaring firelight and in a small quiet of the rain they heard a throat being cleared. The light, apprehensive sound of youth: John Kerr staring against the darkness of the creek ravine he had never seen in daylight and so could only fill with skulking Indians and half-breeds, he would not have time to make so much as a squeak; the twigs were too wet to snap, if there were any twigs, before an arm would clamp around his throat, a–jumping Judas, no half-breeds would ever overrun Wolseley, sentry throat-slitters though they might be, he would face the ravine and then even if they had Indians to stalk–he jerked his mind away from that, warmed himself once again on the flame of Anne Schultz's long legs marching, shaping her skirt he could almost see where her legs joined her hips, formed the vee that had led him all across the Canadian Shield raised over him like a constellation—

A sound! He whirled, rifle lifting, "Who–who goes there–halt or I'll..." His finger twitched; he could hardly control himself not to fire, but he couldn't until he saw for certain where the–to the right, a blur; he wheeled—

"Balaclava," an English voice said sharply, "Balaclava is the watchword, private."

"Oh," Kerr let out his breath slowly, "it's you sir," hardly breathing for having almost shot his commanding officer.

"I expected you would see my light coming."

"I was facing forward, to the ravine, sir, I..."

"Oh yes, of course," Wolseley's tone shifted. He was struggling with his storm lantern. "This confounded wind, I've been on four continents and it's never blown out, there." The light caught, lifted to Kerr's wet face now capturing some pale confidence. "All well here? Nothing on the bridge?"

"All fine sir, no movement."

"Just a bit more, Kerr, and it'll all be over. That Canadian Shield, I've never seen a tougher trail, I can assure you; I doubt if there's a worse one in the world, water and rock and mosquitoes. But you chaps have been splendid, just splendid. And," he chuckled suddenly, bending forward into the enormous darkness, his hard face with its Crimean scar like a livid thunderbolt, "think of it, lots of fine Métis girls sleeping just over there."

Kerr said nothing, and Wolseley smiled; a commander was always commander of course, but that Winnipeg River had made them a team; he knew what soldiers dreamed of, even shy Canadians. Their shyness was charming, really.

"A bit of the brown?" He chuckled. "Wild meat?"

Kerr laughed a little, but stopped suddenly.

"You expect some hard fighting tomorrow, sir?"

"What?" Wolseley said. "Oh no, no. Those half-castes...a standing fight isn't their meat. But I do hope there's enough of them about to give us some practice. Man against man you know, we've come so far now."

"You think, sir, Riel might...well, surrender?"

"My heavens!" Wolseley was the complete, jolly soldier, "I hope not! If he doesn't surrender then we won't have to hang him, now will we?"

"We won't have to..." Kerr began, puzzled, and then suddenly he burst into laughter, Wolseley with him.

Behind them the firelight leaped so high the heavy trunks and branches of the oaks stood black out of the total darkness, the rows of white tents gathered under them like drifted snow. Across the bridge Elzéar and Michel instinctively hunkered lower, the light so clear now they could see water gleam and roll along the bridge rail where the wind had driven away the rain. They both looked at Riel, between them, their hands coming up to pull him down with them, but he remained erect, perhaps frozen in his attitude of listening to the words they had heard with such dreadful clarity in the rain-washed air that the laughter of the two men in the lantern's swing seemed simply to repeat, repeat them into unalterable echo.

"What's that English," Michel whispered, "what?"

Riel's rain-draggled head moved, his eyes found Elzéar's. The big captain stared up at him. They were so close they could feel each other breathe. And they saw in the bits of firelight leaping in each other's eyes themselves already running. Desperately. It was only a question of whether they would be able to run far, or fast, enough. Ever.

Between the squared tents and the oaks the campfire exploded, the heavy dark spraying the light upward like a celebration. Poles upon poles crashed down into the flames, the firelight writhing there as the dripping soldiers warmed their hard, mud-creased hands against it. Somewhere a voice began,

"O hey, Riel, are you wakin' yet..."

and, before the line was finished, a long soldier emerged with a pole over his shoulder from which dangled a half-human-sized figure. Loud cheers greeted the effigy swinging above their heads and as the second line came thundering,

"Your stolen cannon well-primed yet?"

the soldier was pushed forward to the edge of the light where he could dangle his figure above the fire. Suddenly Wolseley was there, clapping, and the sound rose to shouts, the figure swinging just beyond the flames that licked its straw feet for a moment, then burst upward into dark.

If you're not wakin', we'll not wait,
For we'll take the Fort this morning!

The short rope had snapped the figure's neck aside as if it were broken.

2

Wilderness

"Having so long held this country as its masters and so often defended it against the Indians at the price of our blood, we consider it not asking too much to request that the Government allow us to occupy our lands in peace."

— Gabriel Dumont, 1882

$\mathcal{1}$

THE English believe it is not manly to run. I saw Robert Semple wiped out in the English manly tradition. An English marching line will often break its opponents simply by its unalterable advance–which becomes, as your rifle grows hotter jolting against your shoulder and the powder burns in your nose, a kind of inevitability, the ranks of the falling being filled immediately by others leaping forward over their comrades, so that the advancing line appears solid and coming on to an unstoppable music, forever larger. Perhaps they wear the red coats not to betray their blood, the line a solid red wall and only when one small unit of it collapses totally–a rare occurrence in the nineteenth century–is it possible to see that your own firing has had any effect, or even that the wall coming upon you consists of individual men. One of the many military advantages of uniform; we never had those. English officers of course march at the very head with the colours, bravest of the brave, and it is an awesome way of fighting, certain to break the courage of any ordinary human being. For me it is impossible to imagine how many superb Englishmen–by that I mean Welsh and Scots and

Irishmen too, especially the latter who can become perfect mar-
tinets when their stomachs are filled every day and they hear a
martial tune played through a refrain of five pounds a year–how
many men have been used to form those advancing red walls
blown apart all over the world; the wives and sweethearts and
children, the possible children and the love...in this, the finest
tradition of white aggression, a man never runs.

The repeater rifle and the Gatling gun of course would
reduce such fighting to pemmican but the Indians and we Métis
after them never held such peculiar courage to be useful. There
was great personal glory in advancing alone against a worthy
enemy when your medicine was strong and you knew it was a
good day to die–a warrior could pray for nothing better–but you
could never demand, much less order, anyone else to follow you
for we believe that humiliation is the greatest possible defeat of
an enemy of character, and humiliation cannot be achieved by
walking forward steadily into his bullets. So we run. Louis Riel,
Ambroise Lépine, William O'Donoghue – they ran, while the
rest of the Council and the few Métis soldiers went home, and
until Adams George Archibald arrived we all pretended the
Provisional Government had never existed.

Wolseley's men slogging forward with Red River gumbo
clodded to their boots, came upon Fort Garry out of the grey
rain on the morning of August 24: its limestone walls loomed
gigantic above the river bank. A sodden rag clung about the flagpole, they could not tell what its colour might be; gun muzzles
protruded here and there from bastions; gates hung crookedly
open. Nothing. They might have been walking into a haunted
fortress heaved up overnight from mud into stony rain: the walls
and roofs were black with dripping, the rusted gate machinery,
the dirty guns shone water. There was nothing alive in the buildings except a scurry of asthmatic grasshoppers in corners, a few
rats under the floors of fur sheds. Inside what their fort plan said
was the Governor of Assiniboia's Mansion the once-sumptuous

furniture in embroidered Victorian damask sat dust-covered, the fourposter uncurtained; the worn table ringed by chairs in the dining room held two half-emptied tea cups with a third fallen on its side in its saucer. Tea the colour of urine.

Gradually the soldiers emerged, gathered cursing in the square; someone jerked the flag down; they discovered it was the Union Jack but they ran up their own, cleaner and with sewn edges, while a scattered twenty-one-gun salute rattled from the corners; someone threw debris together, began a fire that smouldered smokily in the sodden air but grew as more and more cart shafts, straw, planking were thrown into it. Soon they could warm their hard, mud-slimed hands, clear their throats and begin their favourite song. Toward evening they tried a burning effigy again but there was no anticipation in it; the flames at its sodden trousers frizzled into smoke. They'd got the job done and what a shit job of bull work walking and walking it had been. Was there nothing to drink, no fucking women?

Riel reached St. Vital very early that morning; there was no time to see Sara at the Grey Sisters in St. Boniface and Lépine and O'Donoghue arrived with the horses while Mrs. Riel was tying up a package of oat cakes and pemmican. Her face was soft as the dry grey cloths she bunched in her fist; the watching children stood about her at the door as Louis mounted: Marie, Octavie, Eulalie, Charles, Joseph, and Henriette with little Alexandre, born the year his father died, standing against her, her hands kneading his shoulders. Riel lifted his empty hands in blessing; for them and himself he had planned ahead so badly that their cow he had sold to support himself that summer was still not paid for; he had naïvely assumed Macdonald would pay him a salary for administering Red River. But as they rode down the avenue of trees they could hear a gun, then another and another boom, north beyond the curve of the river; so they nudged the horses into the drizzle facing them from the south.

That night as they slept in a haystack their horses disappeared. They kicked themselves across the Red River on rails pulled from a Métis fence; Riel's moccasin loosened, vanished in the muddy water. Exhausted, they later watched from willows as a troop of men in British uniforms bounced clumsily south on horseback; not even O'Donoghue had the energy to swear. He said almost wistfully,

"I have to be dreaming this, Louis, really, I lived it all in Ireland."

Lépine said, "That last horse was André Nault's."

Riel looked up from bandaging his bare foot again. He could still feel Lépine's arm under him as he sank, lifting him alive and powerful out of the grey cold suck of the river.

"It was his horses that worried André," he said, "when the Canadians surveyed across his pasture."

"I'll kill them yet," O'Donoghue said. "We've gotta make someplace clean of English pigs."

Between willows Lépine was watching the soldiers jog on. "That poor little pig won't make the border," he said. "Not on André's spavined plug."

Suddenly Riel laughed. "That's better revenge than killing, Will, make them ride Métis horses!"

"Only if they bust their balls," O'Donoghue was on his feet. "Trust the Queen, oh yes, trust that old bitch."

They crossed the border that night, Lépine said west of where they had run McDougall back, and O'Donoghue went muttering east to Pembina while Riel and Lépine stayed with Father LeFloch in St. Joseph. LeFloch had once prepared Riel for confirmation; everywhere Riel met people who had known him only a few years before and they stared at him now as if they would analyse this prodigy who had so unbelievably created Manitoba, found him depressed and unspeaking, and wondered that they had not immediately noticed the strange power in his eyes. He lay on the cot in the room behind the chapel, heard furtive sounds rub the log corners, perhaps village dogs; stared up into the board darkness; read Taché's letter that even Schultz arrived in Red River before Archibald; dreamt of Manitoba, of each Métis secure on his two hundred and forty acres of river land; wrote and wrote to explain to himself again why and how everything had been done, almost as if he were already preparing his defense for the public trial he dimly recognized the rest of his life must be; and did not hear about Elzéar Goulet until he rode back to St. Norbert at the pleading of the Métis and on September 17, just before O'Donoghue presented his new plan for annexing Manitoba to the United States, Riel met Sara in Father Ritchot's rectory and she told him.

"I didn't know Elzéar could swim," Riel said. "He told me once that's what horses were for."

"Right there on the river, the street past Dr. Bird's house, that's where he ran," Sara said. "He had come into The Red Saloon and some Canadian soldiers were behind the bar. There was only Mr. O'Lone there, and they were tearing up the bar, and he couldn't get at the shotgun they say he always has there. There were so many of them, and Elzéar bellowed and started throwing them aside, and somebody yelled, 'He led Scott out!' and somebody else, 'That's him, he finished Tommy,' and then they turned ...Louis?"

"What did they do?"

"Is that true, did Elzéar 'finish' Scott?"

"I'll tell you about that, but what did they...Sara!"

"They turned on him, perhaps thirty of them, and he was running, knocking them aside and running out down the street towards the river, they were after him and they say his clothes were so torn, he was bleeding everywhere from the knives and fists and he ran down to the river but there they were coming from both directions and behind him so he took the river, sliding down the mud and waded towards the cathedral spires over the river but the water was so deep and swift from all the rain—"

"But he couldn't even swim."

"He was so strong and tall, Louis, he was wading, on his feet in the current and only his shoulders and head, he might have made it, there were no boats there, but then they found the rocks."

"Rocks?"

"The rocks Dr. Bird has around his flowers, the white-washed rocks."

Riel could only stare at her in horror.

"They were bellowing like beasts, people said. At the funeral the coffin couldn't be opened."

Riel took her in his arms; she was crying softly against his shoulder, her tears like a kiss on his neck and he felt this enormous tenderness move in him like a wave, he was crying with her for all the great goodness of a good, faithful man now utterly broken, destroyed by water and white rocks and his fingers, hands felt her frail bones through the coarse fabric of her habit, the slip of her skin there where her heart beat and her warm love was so overwhelming after running and long dreary days listen; is that something! lying empty and sleepless on a long autumn day not moving, waiting for the late dark to go out and stare at the stars perhaps, or at the moon peering through clouds red as a vicious face: her warmth overwhelmed him and he held her at arm's length or he would have crushed her, such terrifying shudders gripped his body.

But her face was abstracted; her body simply caged her heart and her emotion was somewhere quite different.

"You must," he was almost chattering, "tell me. Everything!"

"Louis." She would have buried her face on his shoulder again but he kept her distant; for a moment she cupped her face in her hands. Then slowly, through her fingers,

"At the funeral Mrs. Goulet and the children knelt...by the coffin, as we do...and they prayed."

"But?" he insisted at her tone.

Sara's narrow face, a faint shimmer of summer freckles bridging her nose, was turned to the tightly curtained window; as if she would see something beyond it in the darkness.

"It's Sister Agnes Goulet."

"Elzéar's sister?"

"Yes, she had just completed her vows."

"Oh. He said something once, about her."

"She knows herself so full of sin, now, but...she cannot pray."

"What?"

"She has confessed to me, she cannot pray. Because of you."

Riel's mouth opened in amazement. His hands fell from Sara's shoulders and she reached forward quickly, touching his neck, her fingers in his hair.

"Oh Louis, I have to tell you, you are suffering enough, as if all the sins of our people, forgive me, you carry them like a scapegoat, oh I have so cried to our Heavenly Father until I am half-crazy, but she..."

"Sara," he said, "you must tell me everything they say. Our people."

"I will," she said with that abrupt, fearsomely direct voice of her childhood standing in the blue turning summer dusts of the mill. "I will say everything, before God the truth. They say you hated Scott because of what he did to Lucille when she was in O'Lone's bar, that you wanted her when you came from the East; and that would have been all right, but her brothers should have beaten Scott; that was all such a girl deserved."

He had expected–this was such ridiculous gossip–but what were our people? For us such thoughts of daughter, of family decency were not ridiculous, and after a furious moment he could mutter, "When I came back I talked to her; you know that, she's our cousin but she was a silly girl. Her parents couldn't keep her from working in that saloon–surely no one believes that!"

"Perhaps not, no, but they talk, and that you sold Mamma's cow and she and the children had so little to eat Joseph once went to Paul's and begged, just for a little soup. I know," she added hastily, "I know why you did that, we all know and the children believe in you, every one, you should hear them pray at the table and evening prayers, 'God bless our beloved brother Louis and keep him safe.' Even little Alexandre," she continued, a little panic creeping into her tone, "when he goes home after school he knocks on the door and Mamma says, 'Come in,' and bows to him because he will not come in the open door until she does; and then he makes a deep bow and says, 'Mamma, am I like little Louis now?' And he goes out and comes in again and again until Mamma says yes, yes he is."

"Sara," Riel said softly. "Tell me about Sister Goulet."

"She cannot pray. Because you made the men execute Scott, and for that her brother is now dead."

"And Guillette killed now too, and André Nault stabbed, left for dead on the prairie?"

"Yes."

"And what about Hugh O'Lone," he went on, still softly, "why did he die in his saloon, or James Tanner in the dark, and Thomas Spence, and Father Kavanaugh, why, why all of them?"

"One terrible sin is enough, if you have always believed in—" suddenly she clasped him to her, murmuring down into his hair, "O Louis, I am not blaming you, don't believe that, when the soldiers broke into Mamma's house they all just stood aside, Marie and Eulalie, everyone, all the children, and let them tear what—"

"The soldiers broke into our house!"

"But no one was hurt, they stood aside and they broke a few things but nothing—"

"What were they looking for?"

Sara looked at him, dazed. "You," she said finally.

They had been sitting for so long on Father Ritchot's worn couch, face to face and now a silence stretched between them, staring at each other's hands as if they could not endure eyes any longer. Sara's words came so softly they might have been the whisper of his memory: "In the mill, upstairs the sunlight came a blue line through the cracks and you turned sideways and it was a sheet, the dust turning blue..." and he heard the slow groan of wheels, wooden cogs grinding upon themselves and the drive shaft from the waterwheel turning perpendicular up into the enormous darkness where the pigeons cooed along the beams and little Sara dancing as if held in the sheer distance of clouds, he could not see her for peering so intently the muscles of his face ached to see, impossibly, her pale arms wings and her tiny body bluely beautiful as a naked angel, the empty space of her movement holding her in the smell of crushed grain like the flaming heart of Jesus torn open for all the world, his father's voice through the floors beside the running water roaring the "Te Deum."

"For me to be a saint," he said to her now, "God would have to work—" he stopped, stunned at the impossibility of living his memory and his body into holiness. "But I can't live if you don't believe in me, Sara. You must know that," he clutched her hand so hard she winced. "I can never prove now why Thomas Scott was shot, no one will believe anything about that now if they don't already want to. And perhaps I and Lépine, and others, will have to pay what Elzéar paid, but you at least must believe me. It became necessary, though I saved Scott's life once, to do—"

"When?" she asked. "You saved his life?"

"When he and MacLeod started the riot in prison, on March second, and the guards were dragging him out into the snow."

"And you stopped them?"

"That was when we agreed he must stand trial before the captains."

Sara was contemplating him as though she had seen a vision she had despaired of seeing; the voices of men gathered in the church behind them but she did not move for a moment. Then she bent forward, kissed him on the lips.

"I will help Sister Agnes to pray again." Her hands emerged from the folds of her habit. "Here, I brought this for you."

He held the book of prayers in his hands; just the right size, he thought, to fit into a breast pocket when I'm running.

"When Mother Clapin gave me permission to come to you, here, I wanted to...Oh, I have nothing and I prayed for a gift, some gift, and I opened my eyes and saw the little book."

"It's the book from your Perpetual Vows." He looked at her happy face in awe.

"Yes."

Inside she had written: Louis David Riel.

"'David'?" Strangeness passing like premonition behind his eyes.

"Yes," Sara said. "You are our singer-king."

The strength of the words she had thought and written before she could even voice her doubt to him, that sustained him in what was left of the five years. When she left, her trust led him like a light to outface O'Donoghue that night about petitioning President Grant to annex Manitoba to the United States. It sustained him during the long months he was sick at St. Joseph, and when first his sister Marie and then his mother with little Alexandre had to come and nurse him; when they told him of the Métis winter hard from weather and arrogant Canadians and the families starting to leave west, not bothering with the land scrip The Manitoba Act should have given them, the titles to lands they had lived on for generations. When his friends in Red River urged him to run for the Manitoba legislature, and he refused while Charles Nolin ran and won and became Minister of Agriculture–for all he knew about farming–for three months. And when he could finally come back quietly to St. Vital in September, 1871, and live with his family and pray again in the cathedral and walk by the river, thinking, and hear of O'Donoghue gathering a Fenian "army" of thirty-five Irishmen in Minnesota that crossed the border to conquer Manitoba for the United States on October 5 and a company of American soldiers shooed them back before they saw so much as a gopher to shoot at or the Métis hunters who had gathered at Riel's request to repel them could be issued supplies; when Lieutenant-Governor Archibald shook hands with him, though no one dared mention his name as he stood at the head of the Métis who had been willing to shoot it out with the foreign Fenians if necessary to keep Manitoba Canadian. For her faith in him as she nursed the sick at St. Boniface Hospital helped him believe in the rightness of his original vision of the North-West as part of Canada; and then on the howling March day when the Government of Ontario under Liberal Premier Edward Blake proclaimed a five-thousand-dollar reward "to such person or persons as may be instrumental in bringing the said murderers" of Thomas Scott to trial, everyone in the North-West knew Riel's head in a sack would suffice.

That was a black time. In April more Métis than ever started for the Saskatchewan country where the buffalo still grazed and no Canadian speculators pushed them about land, or bullied them or plied them with whisky, and Riel decided he had had enough of sitting behind curtained windows and moving unexpectedly to other friends' houses: that he would run for Parliament and defy them all. During the summer campaign in Provencher, which everyone already accepted he had won, came the news of Cartier's defeat in Montreal and with it Prime Minister Macdonald's letter to Manitoba Conservatives, the same Macdonald who had once suggested to Quebec supporters and twice to Archbishop Taché that perhaps the best thing Riel could do to relieve them of the political embarrassment of amnesty was to go into five or ten years voluntary exile with perhaps a certain arrangement of cash in hand, Macdonald let it be known that perhaps a certain person might resign his sure election in Provencher to allow Cartier to run in the seat. After all, a powerful Cabinet Minister would be much more useful to Manitoba than to be represented by someone who was considered, perhaps wrongly but nevertheless it was hard to convince *every* voter, by some to be a criminal. And Riel, argued at, bullied like a scrip-holder, let Cartier's name be placed alone on the ballot, and while the election was being rigged the North-West heard not a whisper that Cartier was sick, that he most certainly would never come nearer St. Boniface than the Ottawa River. And a few days after Cartier's election five pioneering Canadians just arrived from Ontario who had found the long trip more expensive than they'd anticipated, concluded they could build some very comfortable homes in the west with the five thousand dollars Blake (now elected to Parliament with Cartier) still offered; they approached William Farmer who from his cell window had watched Scott being led across the Fort square to the east wall and he swore out the warrant to arrest Riel and Lépine. Riel was warned by Bannatyne listening in his post office and ran for his life to the woods, the hayfields south of St. Norbert and there Michel Dumas came to him one sullen winter day–found him filthy in a haystack though he had papers with him and was still writing, writing desperately to give his people a voice until some bullet found him and presented his head to the Canadians who would never forget that one Irishman whose pathetic cursing face sometimes appeared to him in the grey clouds that trundled snow over the earth like judgement–the faithful Michel Dumas now told him Cartier was dead, that he was elected by acclamation to represent them, no man in the constituency would dare run against him even though no ten people in it knew where he was, and almost in the same breath, as if he had to tell everything or nothing immediately, while Riel was still thinking of food for his family and travelling to Ottawa and of clean clothes and warm water on his face in bedrooms with sheets clean as altar cloths which for the first time in his life he would have money to pay for, Michel added, "I've had enough, whatever you do. I'm going to Saskatchewan to Gabriel."

Four years of messages, of keeping watch, of careful and uncaring love. Riel reached and held Michel close, that hard horseman's body warm against him like nothing he had felt, dear

God since when? And then remembered, "What about Lépine?" And Michel cleared his throat, heavily, crouched with him in the hollowed haystack.

"They got him, three Canadians. He was bouncing his kid on his knee after breakfast and he could have just bust all three in half, if he'd just lifted his hands, just opened and closed them on them...but he said, 'Three years is enough,' and got up and walked out. They didn't have to touch him."

They sat in a long silence.

"And I'm elected?" Riel whispered, finally. "Ottawa?"

"If the police don't find you, and arrest you, sure. So Ross says."

That incredible contradiction left him for a time with nothing but tears, though that might have been more the letter Michel also brought; which he was pulling out of his hide pocket, gingerly, like a thin white explosive already burned down to its fuse:

I have made my bargain with God; you cannot take your cross and forbid one to me. I have dedicated my life to the Indian mission at Ile-â-la-Cross, and when you read this I will have begun the two-month journey to the Saskatchewan and far, far north. Dear Louis, when will I see you again? Perhaps some beautiful May when the crocuses bloom and we can kneel with them at the altar of the Holy Virgin as we once did. I go weeping, but with great joy in my heart for now I share your exile, my brother whom I love more than I can say. Perhaps God will accept what I offer; I pray every day that He will accept. From your sister who loves you.

Sara Riel

A year later, March 30, 1874, Riel did at last see Macdonald. By then Sir John had been relegated to Leader of the Opposition by the railway dollars he had thought would ease all of his Canada's bits unobtrusively together. In the new election Riel had again been elected Member of Parliament for Provencher and as the carriage crossed the bridge from Hull into Ottawa he could not resist looking between its curtains at the towers built on the cliffs above the river; unbelievably immense, like rocks piled together by giants above the rapids, higher and higher, into thin black spires, finally cobwebs. They stood there like power, solid, secure in themselves like the arched gothic of windows set into the East Block, the magnificent swirl of crushed-stone drive with bits of snow caught at the borders of the black flowerbeds, the human order of mortared stone and iron which wandered through his dreams sometimes like nightmares of bars and steel-laced doors and dreadful marches echoing, sometimes like the perfect ordered cleanliness of singing heaven. Our log shacks, buffalo hunts, moccasins–he recognized what he saw on his own feet and almost laughed aloud. What was he doing here, fingernails clean, cloth moving on his body like silk? If he stepped out here and some sweet Orangeman shot him against this wall, more than half of Canada would praise God.

"We'll go in from the back," Roderique Masson said beside him. "The Library at the back. It's safest."

They turned their collars to touch their hats and got out. Above them the arches and circles and spires of stone reached up, turned round upon themselves by flying buttresses into a steep copper slope, a peak. A weather vane pointed north, blue against the lead sky as the enamel of his mother's basin.

"It's the most perfect building I've ever seen," said Masson.

"The North-West has nothing like this," Riel said in wonder, "though Gabriel might think a mountain..."

Masson chuckled with him and then they were through the small door; and suddenly the entire centre opened upwards as if they had entered the shell of an enormous egg of white oak and stone, arched windows curved like lace to a perfect flower groined together by iron sprays at the top. It was unbelievable.

"Wait here a minute," Masson whispered, and the small sound moved from them like air upwards in water. "I'll make sure about the corridors, the clerk. Just wait."

His friend was gone, silent on the floor laid out in wood as intricately as snowdrifts, the white oak...those tiers were book-shelves built in slender double-chapels about the room, books upon books, the entire circle rounded by books and white oak...at the centre, like a white flame a stone woman draped to her toes; one word cut deep at the base: Victoria. She was not short, dumpy as we had always heard, here she had been dreamed into a shape slender like a column holding aloft her headed tiara, her body draped as it seemed in cloth. He stepped down under her, looked up past her name and the looped fold of her robe: her right arm was curved away from her body by the power mace she held in her bent hand and beyond her marble chin, nose, rested the perfect white sixteen-petalled flower of the dome in its nest of iron lace. He stared up; the world turned like roaring in his head and he might have been staring down into some perfection, into a stone-polished symmetry that horrified him as nothing he had ever felt before. He reached down–up–he could barely touch the irrevocable ordered marble of her name: cold like rot in his nostrils.

But the books: immediately his perception flipped as if a fever had galloped through him; he was surrounded by books, the thoughts of all the wisest men who had ever lived, the poets and popes and philosophers and giants of men, if he could only stay here dearest gracious God he would read and read until the greatest thoughts of all mankind stood before him like living people, singing praises to the Almighty; he would cram this beautiful room full to its top with the white living beauty of magnificent thoughts and create a country men would sing for-ever of its freedom and love, and knowledge. The greatest men of history stood around him like sentinels. Before the ethereal beauty of this white queen he would melt away the ignorance of his people like snow in spring and he would see wisdom come with horsemen along the hills of prairie sky, sing hal-lelujah great merciful God.

There was a step behind him and he wheeled; but at the same instant a movement up in an upper tier, as if a shadow had moved past books: an old man going there, already gone with only a spray of grey hair over an ear, the shadow of a long, angled nose gone against a brown sheen of books.

"Was he in here all the time?" Masson's voice whispered at his elbow.

"I don't know, who...?"

"Did he see you?"

"Who was that?" Though he suddenly knew as certainly as a premonition who that gaunt man, bent forward as if into authority, was; and in the small chamber down the hall where he tonelessly repeated the words at the head of a scribbled paper proffered by a fat hand, "I do swear that I will be faithful and bear true allegiance to Her Majesty Queen Victoria, *So help me God*" with his hand resting, it was certainly his own hand, resting such an enormous distance from him on a black Bible so crisp it could never have been opened; and the hand aiming a pen point to where a fat finger pointed on the sixth row, almost at the bottom below a fancy "E.A. Richards," and this distant hand was shaping the name of our "Louis" and with a jolt caught the hand already in gesture, hesitated, and bent the letter around to an even more undeniable "R...iel" then suddenly the fat whitely whiskered jowls of the man, there was a man before him robed in squarish white collars like a judge, the blank front of the face rose to him and eyes staring in amazement and mouth sagging open; he felt Masson's hand on his shoulder and backed away, at the door his body moving into a deep, sardonic bow at all that rotund dignity sitting there so slack-mouthed, small rubber eyes bulging: none of this as the carriage wheeled around the corner and down the drive towards the bridge and Hull, Quebec, and the small safety of a room with Dr. E.P. Lachapelle, like Masson, his friend since their days when Riel like I decades before was supported at school as any Métis must always be by some kind, charitable French-Canadian, nothing could really disturb his knowledge that, standing under white Victoria, he had seen a glimpse of Sir John A. Macdonald.

So he like we all had to read of the furor in Ottawa; how, before a gallery packed with visitors which included the Governor General's lady and at least a hundred men with pistols in their pockets, a Mackenzie Bowell, Grand Master of the Orange Lodge and now a Member of Parliament for Belleville Ontario, but later to become Prime Minister of Canada, moved that the Member for Provencher be expelled from the House of Commons, and Dr. John Schultz, Member of Parliament for Lisgar but later to become Lieutenant-Governor of Manitoba, seconded the motion;

how after acrimonious debate during which the former prime minister refused to admit or deny that his now dead lieutenant Cartier had ever agreed to any amnesty or that he personally had ever recognized such a thing as a "Provisional Government" led by anyone in the North-West, leave alone received delegates from it, the great House of Commons passed the motion 123 to 68. Masson told Riel this, told him of Wilfrid Laurier's first great speech in his defence; Riel stared out of the window. The words of exile were written on the thick April river, grinding its near bank steadily into mud; he would never come closer to Macdonald than that one glimpse which, before he had actually seen it, it had already been gone.

3

WHEN he was in the cells the North-West Mounted Police built especially for him in 1885, Riel told a newspaperman, "Let me tell you that if I am mad, I have been so since the eighth of December, 1875." By that time he had been elected four different times to represent our people in the House of Commons of Canada and yet had never dared to appear openly in Ontario where Parliament sat because of the five-thousand-dollar reward still hanging over his head. Ambroise Lépine had been tried for "the murder of Thomas Scott" in Winnipeg in November, 1874; and when the jury brought in a verdict of "guilty with a recommendation for mercy," the judge sentenced him to death by hanging. We all deduced the justice of this verdict when the new Governor General Lord Dufferin reduced sentence to "two years in prison and permanent forfeiture of political rights"; when I heard that, I went down my path to the Assiniboine and laughed to the frozen river until my tears froze in my white beard. We Métis were certainly being taught the true value of political rights in Canada. Finally on February 12, 1875, Liberal Prime Minister Mackenzie moved in the House of Commons that:

a full amnesty should be granted to all persons [a fine plural generality which I suppose also granted pardon to Sir John for all his lies] concerned in the North-West troubles save only L. Riel, A.D. Lépine and W.B. O'Donoghue. That a like amnesty should be granted to L. Riel and A.D. Lépine conditional on five years' banishment from Her Majesty's Dominions.

Lépine was then in jail, of course, and O'Donoghue died in Minnesota on March 26, 1878 so poor the farmers whose children he had been teaching collected for his gravestone, but on its inscription they caught the best of his sometimes intractable spirit: "He loved liberty and hated oppression, therefore he died in exile"; he was thirty-five years old.

And Riel, barely thirty in February, 1875, heard his sentence while living with Father Barnabé and his sister Evelina and their aged mother in the rectory at Keeseville, New York.

It was fitting that Roderique Masson, whose mother's charity had once sponsored Riel in seminary, should bring the news direct from Ottawa and tell him in the Barnabé living room where Evelina had just placed their tea. She looked at Riel, tears starting in her large eyes, but she saw only a kind of stolid resignation. "Being an outlaw," he said, "is at least something definite." The months of flight, the dependence on charitable friends created by letters from other charitable friends down to his very clothes and food, the interminable movement from an acquaintance in Suncook, New Hampshire to another in Worchester, Massachusetts to Woonsocket, Rhode Island to a sympathizer in charitable Washington, D.C., and then back, penniless and unemployable, most thankful for priests who left him to the stillness of small gloomy churches: the vanity of power gradually overwhelmed him. Answers to his long letters to Archbishop Bourget in Montreal found him here and there, carefully general responses to his growing belief that the faithful believers of the North-West could still, if God be pleased, build a Christian nation there. Then in June the Archbishop's letter came again to Keeseville; for a long time Riel contemplated it like the plaster images above the altar of St. John's Church until he at last reached a conviction about it which even in the moment of his death he could never doubt. He kept that letter next to his heart when he was awake and under his head when he slept. In it the venerable Archbishop at last committed himself, gave Riel the text from which he would one day on the Saskatchewan preach his most powerful sermon:

> *I have the deep conviction that you will receive in this world, and sooner than you think, the reward for all your mental sacrifices, a thousand times more crushing than the sacrifices of material and visible life. But God, who has always led you and assisted you up to the present time, will not abandon you in the darkest hours of your life. For He has given you a mission which you must fulfil in every respect. May the grace of God keep you.*

For he knew his ten years "in the world" were almost completed, the success of the world like ashes in his mouth; and he was waiting. The weight of necessary commitment tolled him like bells and often drenched him with happiness at St. John's altar, especially after mass, or exhausted from sitting, waiting, or terrified too when he let himself wander through the awesome writings of the Jewish prophets: abruptly he left Keeseville for Washington, D.C., again, taking with him little but Bourget's letter and the memory of Evelina's small, longing face. He sat in the gallery at the opening of the House of Representatives and was moved to tears that the legislators of such a powerful nation a hundred years old should begin their day's work with prayer. December 8, 1875, was the Feast of the Immaculate Conception; the sixth anniversary of the Provisional Government of the North-West.

Let me tell you that if I am mad, I have been so since the eighth day of December, 1875. On that day I partook of the Grand Mass of the Immaculate Conception at Saint Patrick's Cathedral, in the capital of the United States of America. At the very moment when the priest, having completed his sermon, began the Credo, and while the people were all standing, I with them, suddenly it seemed I stood alone on a mountain top and the same spirit that appeared to Moses in the midst of a burning bush appeared in flames before me. The kingdoms of this world were a map at my feet; I was dumbfounded. I felt to the depths of my heart the swift terror of holiness. I fell to my knees, but a voice of infinite gentleness spoke from the flame: "Rise, Louis David Riel. You have a mission to complete for which all mankind will call you blessed." And then I felt in my heart a joy so overpowering that in order to hide the ecstacy from my neighbours I had to spread my handkerchief to its full size, hold it against my face with my hands, like that, and I could have laughed aloud, the immense cathedral would have rung for me like a bell, and despite my handkerchief a boy in the next pew noticed my overwhelming joy.

But as swiftly as it had come, while the voices of the people rolled with their undying faith—while I still heard that gentle voice in my ear—an immense grief of spirit seized me. Though my joy had been great, the noise of my sobs, my cries and my weeping now would have overwhelmed the organ affirming the Credo. I could not have felt deeper sorrow if God himself had declared that my sister Sara had sold herself for all eternity to the Devil. I sank into my pew, stifling my grief in my heart, trying to contain it in my handkerchief, and the terrible sorrow passed quickly, as quickly as the joy that had been there only an instant before. The joys and sorrows of man on earth, so short, oh, so short! But deeds of faith are not com-

*pleted in a few hours, or a few days. A century is but a
spoke in the wheel of everlasting time.*

*Not long after, only a few days in fact, they began to
call me a madman.*

I have used Louis Riel's words for what happened to him in
St. Patrick's; ten years later to the day his broken body would be
brought back to St. Vital to lie in state in his mother's house where
he had been born. During my lifetime I was given many songs,
and I have often prayed to the Good Father who made the world
and us all, who are to tune ourselves to love here so that we may
adore Him in all eternity: I have prayed, give me to make this
song of Riel. You gave me so many songs of people, of Cuthbert
Grant and Lépine and Gabriel hunting McDougall, even of silly
Dickson. Give me this song too so that when in the century to
come our people lie in the miserable trenches of poverty and
humiliation and disease and perhaps despair, when troubles surround them like automatic rifles they can sing a song of faith, of
belief in vision for which the mud on their feet gives them no
evidence. I prayed for that for some years, and that song of Riel
was not given me until I lay on my deathbed. So even his vision
I can only offer in the words which he so clearly borrowed from
the Bible he read both in Latin and French: and sometimes, desperately, in English. He once even told a reporter the voice from
the flames spoke to him in Latin, that he received his "divine
affirmation notification with uplifted hands and bowed head";
like Moses praying for the children of Israel. For the violent and
silly acts of our people I received songs; for this, our greatest
vision and commitment to a hard road, nothing. I must leave the
words to stand in all their unmemorable bareness: their
unearthly power will have to be seen in the effect they had on
Riel, on our people, and on Canada during those *last* ten years.
And most of all, I suppose, in their impossibility.

4

IN June the prairie seems never dark; as our mothers told us, Sun never sleeps in summer. Before the last light has gone from the north-west there is already the barest shimmer of...I know that's impossible, but the farther north you go the clearer the line of light grows all around the northern edge of the world until the sun is surely always there below the red glowing out of that deep blue, just beyond the pale mist that rises from the mounds of the buffalo, the warmth of their breath rounding in vapour small mounds of what may be drifting wool which the first level light will cut through, rainbow over the black, wet, stones of their sleeping bodies. The buffalo birds stir first, chirp, hop immediately to their endless search in dew-matted wool, and the dun calves are moving, shakily up and butting the cows, rubbing their heads against sleeping noses until the cows rise, the bulls groan and blast long sighs like explosions; their joints crack as they heave up, and up again, the sunlight outlining their black heads and shoulders and massive humps like waves breaking. Our mothers told us they were the gift of the Great Spirit, together with the land and the water and the air: all gifts too perfect for the white man not to destroy. We too, who are half white.

When Michel Dumas galloped into Gabriel's small hunting camp, the eight men in it ran together around him before he could slide from his heaving horse.

"They're there," he yelled, down on his knees and already drawing on the ground, "the buffalo, now in that plain south of the elbow."

"I know that place," said Gabriel as the men cheered. "How many?"

"I was up the ridge behind them; they're grazing easy, about twenty-five, maybe thirty, and good calves too."

"Bless God," and a murmur circled them; when we see buffalo, we know where they come from. "That's more than we've seen this spring." Gabriel was scratching ridges and valley, fast. "We'll ride up-wind through here, Isidore and Moïse you'll take the far wings, and stay in front of us, we've got to get them running straight and not let one get outside you. I'll be centre, here, and the rest of you spread between us. Not one gets through."

They were all leaning in a tight circle to the ground, and Isidore Dumont said doubtfully, "Those'll be real small calves."

"We need everything," Gabriel said. "C'mon."

Moïse Ouellette said, "What about that Ballendine and Whitford?"

"Sacré!" Gabriel didn't break stride, "Where in hell are they?"

"They rode off, I think south."

"What? Why'd you let them go, together, they—"

"I thought they'd talked to you."

"I said they could come because if they run around alone they'll just mess up—" Gabriel swore, walking faster, his short broad body blazing in the early sun. "We can't wait; we'll give them a share." He stopped suddenly and turned to Moïse's father, Old Ouellette who, though eighty, had insisted on one more hunt. "Will you pray."

The scattering men came together in a tight circle, bowed their heads.

"Holy God," Old Ouellette murmured in his voice soft as leather, "in the name of Jesus and Mary and Joseph we thank you for the buffalo that Michel saw. You know our families have nothing to eat. Protect us and help us bring them meat. Amen."

The men crossed themselves, ran for the horses jogging their heads against the summer flies.

For the three generations of our Métis nation, riding to buffalo was a man's occupation; for Gabriel, who was the greatest hunter of us all, the three-mile canter to loosen the horses for the long run was a slow drum roll that would gradually gather tempo, the horses smelling something, the wide plateau sweeping out to the crest of the cliff where the North Saskatchewan spread out of sight below them on the right, the drums not holding steady as they did in the Thirst Dance but gradually, gradually beating faster and faster as the horses' heads lifted higher under stiff rein until suddenly Gabriel shouted, hauled his horse back to a halt and was on his knees beside it, ear to the ground. But he didn't need his ear, his flat palm told him as much and cursing he hurled himself on his rearing horse, waving his arm with a scream toward the height of land where a blue haze was already forming. Michel galloped beside him, the wind in their teeth so hard they had no breath for curses, and as they topped the rise they both saw the small herd a cloud of dust far up the valley, and two horsemen riding hard but losing ground.

"It's them two white bastards," Michel yelled, "coming downwind!"

"God *damn* them!" Gabriel screamed, "Ride!"

His rage seemed to hurl his horse down the slope, the other plunging after him; but on the flat he was the perfect horseman, bent low against the lunging shoulder, eyes ahead, anticipating long tangled grass and the sharp rip of spring water and gopher mounds with his hand light but steady as the unswerving sun:

his grey ran as on a levelled path, no hesitation or shift anywhere to break his strength from the necessity of speed for the man rode easy, lifted him over stones with his hard legs clamped around his belly. They passed the two whites, their horses staggering now, heaving but Gabriel wasted no glance at them: he was riding with the last desperate hope of that dust-cloud rolling away at the end of the valley.

But it was impossible; the lead was too great. He knew his grey would run till he fell but a dead runner was even worse than no meat. He jerked out Le Petit, tried an impossible running shot, balancing his shot again, and then again, on that delicate instant when the horse hung between hoofbeats and suddenly a bull staggered at the nearest edge of the herd vanishing down a far slope. It could only be an accident, he knew, but he pulled the grey back and thanked God, galloping more easily. Perhaps they could trail the herd, perhaps, but spooked like that they would run for twenty miles and then graze warily on the widest stretch of plain, be so completely unapproachable that only a two-day crawl behind a tumble weed, if you could keep up...the old bull was stopped, facing him. Trying, for his left front leg was shattered, it might have been a badger hole and not his shot but there he was, blood flaring at his nostrils, lunging to keep his massive head up over his one front leg, his back legs churning his small haunches in a circle while the gigantic humped shoulders threatened to topple him like sand: Gabriel shot him quick, before that final humiliation.

He stood for a moment, head bowed and waiting out the long, bloody snore. His runner coughed a little behind him; that had been very, very close. And a pure gift here. He rubbed the grey's forehead, the living animal nuzzling him, and he felt better, good for the gifts of life given and taken. Then he stuck Le Petit back in the scabbard, untied the blood-sack from behind the saddle. He leaned over the bull. Its gigantic head–from the horns he must be eight, maybe ten years, a good life and long enough–lay tilted right; his skinning knife found the jugular under the thick hide and he watched the blood pour into his sack. Through the ground he felt riders approaching.

When Gabriel looked up they were there, the two English half-breeds on their exhausted horses in the centre of eight Métis. He tied up the heavy blood bag, keeping his movements slow while his rage roused again. Whitford looked ashamed and scared; Ballendine would be defiant as soon as he got pushed.

"You guys said you hunt for a living?" Gabriel said in Cree, and then, "Get off," before they could answer. He squatted in the lee of the buffalo; two vultures, three, hung like sailing ash in the sky.

"I declare this a court," he said. "Michel, Isidore, you're the witnesses, the rest of you the jury, I'm president."

The six men of the jury squatted; the witnesses moved aside and left the two looking from one to the other, alone in the centre. "Listen Gabriel," Ballendine said, "we weren't—"

"Not now. You explain everything to the court."

"I've got every right," Ballendine said, voice rising, "to run buffalo."

"Keep quiet!" Old Ouellette said sharply. "You knew the hunt laws before we started."

"What did you see?" Gabriel asked Michel.

"I got up after midnight like we agreed and rode along the river and found this small herd, about thirty including calves, just after sunrise, it was a good time to find them, on the flat about four miles back. They were well bunched, like they are for night."

"How far away were they from you?"

"About two miles."

"Did they notice you?"

"No, I was up wind and they were just getting up for the first graze."

"Any other hunters around?"

"I watched a bit but I didn't see nobody."

"And they were still grazing when you rode to get us?"

"Yeah."

"And when you came back?"

"The herd was a cloud of dust and these two shits," Michel gestured violently, "chasing them a mile and half *down-wind*, by god I'd—"

"That's enough," Gabriel said. "Isidore."

"Yeah, these two had come at them down-wind, and then they tried to run them anyway."

"You saw these two trying to run that herd?"

"Oh yeah, they were trying."

"What's your explanation," Gabriel asked the sullen pair.

"I, I don't talk Cree so good," Ballendine began.

Gabriel glared. "That's the first time I've heard that. Whitford, you talk."

"We rode south about dawn," Whitford started uneasily, "Moïse saw us, right?" Moïse in the jury nodded.

"You never reported to me," Gabriel said.

"Well, but when Michel went north..."

"Did you report to me?"

"No...we thought, we'd go south and there was nothing so we figured there'd be some herds near the river, you know they'd have been down late in the evening to drink and come up, so we made a big loop west and north—"

"And rode with the wind?" Gabriel asked.

"There was almost nothing—" Ballendine interrupted and Gabriel snapped,

"Whitford's talking!"

"The breeze was south-west," Whitford said, "and the river was north."

"Okay," Gabriel said, "you can't always hunt into the wind; so the herd had already smelled you when you topped the rise?"

"Yeah," said Whitford, sweating now, "yeah."

"But the herd didn't break," Gabriel said softly, "did it?"

Ballendine half-shouted in English, "It sure as hell did, as soon—"

"Whitford!" Gabriel roared.

"They, the bulls started milling around, pawing like they do, and the cows..." Whitford stopped at the circle of leathery faces staring at him, waiting, knowing so perfectly the animals they had always lived with.

"The cows broke," Gabriel suggested, "when you started riding at them dead with the wind?" The horses snuffled, jogging their heads in the silence. Gabriel looked at the jury.

"I move," Old Ouellette said, "they are guilty of not reporting a herd, of going alone, of starting a buffalo run without report or the captain's signal."

One by one the jurors right hands went up.

"Unanimous vote, guilty," Gabriel said. "You got something to say before sentence?"

"I'm riding straight to Fort Carlton." Ballendine was livid. "Lawrence Clarke will hear about—"

Gabriel had leaped to his feet even as Whitford grabbed Ballendine, hissing, "Shut up, you fool!" but the Métis chief controlled himself; the only sign of his fury was his huge hands clenching and opening, slowly.

"You ride wherever you want," he growled, "but when you ride in our country, you obey our law. Clarke better know that. I sentence you to a fine of twenty-five dollars each."

"What?" Whitford gasped. "A month's wages? You can search me!"

Ballendine just glared.

"You can't pay?" Gabriel asked.

"Who'd have twenty-five..."

"Okay," Gabriel gestured to Isidore and Michel. "Break their saddles and rifles."

"Now by god, Dumont!" Ballendine burst out, "that's too much, I'll—"

Gabriel stood like a rock, defying him to come, but Whitford clamped his arms around Ballendine and held him.

"You can thank our law I didn't break your neck," Gabriel said, turning. "Our children haven't eaten meat for a month."

Behind him the sound of leather ripped, of wood and iron breaking on stone. He rubbed the dried blood on his skinning knife off against his leg, found the skin fold under the huge neck and notched it with two quick twists, then started to draw the long clean line down the belly of their one buffalo.

In late August when ducks were beginning to cluster on the reedy loops of the South Saskatchewan River below his cabin, Gabriel saddled his grey in the afternoon sunlight. Yellow, splotches of red already touched the valley but the clouds were those of summer, white puffs outlined by black that might coil into thunderheads. In the lee of the cabin Madeleine swung the handle of her washing machine and looked at Gabriel in moccasins and leather pants, his naked chest gnarled with wounds like an old tree-trunk.

"You're riding off like an Indian?" she said.

"Annie," he called, "Annie!" The little girl came blinking out of the cabin into the sunlight. "Get my shirt off the line, hey."

"It won't be dry yet," Madeleine said as Annie ran behind the cabin. "So show your manliness."

"You want the Widow Tourond to see me like this?" he was suddenly advancing on her, huge arms wide and fingers clawed but she swung her washer as if he did not exist.

"She wouldn't mind," was what she said, but then he had seized her in his great naked hands and hoisted her up, was whirling her as easily as if she were a flag for signalling over his head and she screamed to an echo ringing down the valley, round and round with laughter, "Gaby! Gaby! Put me down you ugly brute!"

"Ugly, eh? Eh?" He dropped her abruptly, held her eye to his eye with her feet just off the ground. "I'm taking those hides, they're too raw to roll in yet."

"Ever tried?" she stared back at him, her eyes green as lake water in spring.

"If you'd ever stop pushing that silly washer," he hissed.

"You'll be the cleanest biggest man west of Red River," she hissed back into his teeth.

"And who used to grab me so stinking all horse and sweat and buffalo blood after the hunt that they stood outside our tent, listening to us, who was that?"

She flicked her tongue across his open mouth and brushed him away as though he were a feather. "Mature women," she said, "get over smells. There comes a time, a time."

"Bullshit!" His huge hands were gentle as rain on her body, he was using her washer rhythm to move her close into him, when they heard Annie.

"Daddy!" she rounded the corner, the half-wet shirt flaring behind her. "There's some men, two with bright red coats!"

"What?" He grabbed for the shirt.

"On the trail, by the ford."

Gabriel shrugged into the shirt; behind him, above the rub of her washer, Madeleine was laughing. "A man shining like that sneaks up on the greatest hunter west of Red River!"

Gabriel laughed, watching the three riders come up the trail. "I got my scouts," he said, nubbling Annie's warm little head.

One was Joe McKay but the two in coats...they were certainly strangers, whites who sat their horses like riders but their clothes, they'd need more than one small washing machine wherever they were going. So he was grinning when the lead rider raised his hand in greeting, when their horses, legs and bellies still black from the ford brought them up on the flat and they dismounted. Gabriel was watching McKay but the biggest white was pulling off his– jesus–white gauntlets.

"Good morning," he said. "I'm Inspector Crozier of the North-West Mounted Police."

"Police?" and suddenly Gabriel knew. "Oh yeah, we heard something about that, police last summer, from Canada." He smiled, stuck out his hand. "Welcome to Saskatchewan country."

"Thank you." Crozier's hand was big and hard enough. "You know Joe McKay, and this is Constable Blank."

"Lucky for you," Gabriel said to McKay, shaking hands, "the river's low or you'd have got your nice clothes dirty."

But it was Crozier who answered that, too.

"Then we would have waited for your ferry, Mr. Dumont."

Gabriel studied him then; he was half a head taller than himself, the kind of white reddish skin that only gets redder, as it was now, in a summer of sun; droopy moustache and hooked nose that any Cree warrior would have danced four days for. Under the slightly dusty scarlet coat, the silly round box tied under his chin with a blue ribbon, he still looked tough as a spruce.

"Anybody that knows me," he said, "I'm just Gabriel."

"And you are President of the Batoche, ahh...Métis community?"

"That's me. You just travelling through, Joe just taking you around?"

"No, we're stationed at Fort Carlton now, fifteen men, permanent detachment."

"At Carlton? You working with the Company, and Lawrence Clarke?"

"No, no," Crozier said hastily; "we have nothing to do with the Hudson's Bay, we just rent some buildings. We're here in the name of the Queen and the Government of Canada, to protect everyone under Canadian law."

"Oh," said Gabriel, slowly, "oh yeah."

Crozier turned his patrician face: the woman stood now at the cabin corner with the little girl against her, both watching him intently and, oddly, not dropping their glance like Métis women did. The cabin, the saddled horse, the yard run to weeds quite untrampled and green hides piled everywhere–they must have been on the hunt all summer–looked no better or worse than any Métis shack...that was really all they were...he had seen along the river. The girl was adopted, McKay had said: such a full, vivid woman and such a man, yet no children: the leader of the immense Dumont clan childless. A nice...prophetic?...irony?

"Actually, Mr. Du–Gabriel, we came on a particular matter," he hesitated. The Métis chief's eyes were on him as calmly intent as if he had been transparent water. Crozier signalled to the constable, who began to untie a sack from his saddle.

"Ballendine and Whitford?"

"It's them, yes. They swore out a complaint before Magistrate Clarke against you for destroying their hunting outfits." Crozier was reaching into his jacket for the paper, but Gabriel's eyes had not wavered.

"They didn't say anything, about why we did it?"

"They didn't, no," Crozier said, "but Joe here got it out of them."

"Yeah, Gabriel," McKay finally spoke at Gabriel's glance, "I explained to the inspector about the hunt rules you have, and how you and Father André set things up here at Batoche."

"It was all of us together," said Gabriel, "we have a council meets every month and regular elections every Christmas, you tell him?" "Yeah, I did."

"Then what," Gabriel's foot swung at the sack the stiff constable was dropping on the ground between them; it clunked half-open on the smashed barrel of a rifle, "what did you bring that for?"

"Like I said," Crozier cut in, "we represent the Queen's law here. This country is part of Canada, and you cannot simply take the law into your own hands."

"Would you tell me," Gabriel said very slowly, "what Lawrence Clark has to do with the Queen's law?"

"Mr. Clarke has been named the Queen's magistrate; he interprets the law in this district and if anyone has a complaint he—"

"Yeah?" Gabriel interrupted. "And he talks just English, and most people around here talk only French or Cree."

"Well, it has to be someone that can—" Crozier stopped, his red face slightly redder, and the corner of Gabriel's mouth lifted.

"Father André can read and write," he said. "So can our elected secretary, Ambroise Fisher."

"Well, I don't have anything to do—"

"Sure their English isn't so good, but there's a few others too I could tell you about."

There was a moment of silence, but when Crozier opened his mouth Gabriel drawled deliberately,

"Lawrence Clarke gets excited fast, and he has to make money for his company; he hired those two to hunt buffalo for him, that's the kind of judgement he has of people."

"Okay, okay," Crozier was laughing a little, his hands up. "I may agree with you about certain things but I have nothing to do with decis—"

"You have to know what you're doing now, to live here and hunt buffalo. We had to go all the way south to the Forks on the Red Deer, Blackfoot country, to get our carts half full this summer. The fat life's over."

"But you realize that this is all part of Canada; you cannot take the law into your own hands. The Queen's law—"

"The Queen's got no law for men wrecking a hunt, so children starve? Then she better get one, fast!"

"No, no," Crozier was laughing a little, "I'm not saying that, I—"

"You got here yesterday with the Queen's law," Gabriel said more calmly, but then his huge voice exploded again, "Well goddam good for you! I've been on the plains all my life and I've hunted buffalo and protected my family from Indians and white skinflints and before we ever heard about the Queen we needed laws and we made them and we enforced them and—" suddenly he broke off, and then he was laughing, not loudly as he could, but a deep thoughtful laugh as of a remembrance that came again like a discovery. "That's a human right," he said, "for people to organize themselves for their own protection and better life. Louis Riel told us that six years ago, a fundamental human right."

Gabriel was peering forward into Crozier's immovable face, shirt still open on his gnarled chest. Slowly Crozier smiled, a warm open smile.

"Yes. It is a human right." After a moment, "Louis Riel told you that?"

"You heard of him?"

Gabriel's tone was faintly sardonic and Crozier's smile shifted to grin. "Oh yes," he said, "yes. Listen, the Ballendine and Whitford business is straightened out. Since they knew your Batoche hunt laws, they got what they deserved and that's the end of that."

"For Clarke too?"

"Yes. But things have changed now. The North-West Mounted Police now represent the Queen's law; you cannot hold your–courts. You have to report to me now."

"The Métis law is dead?"

"There can be only one law at a time," Crozier said. "Nobody needs more."

"Dead like the buffalo here," Gabriel said as if speaking to himself, remembering the words Riel had told him on the snow across the river from St. Boniface, had told us all later, listening. Heaven. "You know that one small herd was all we saw within ten days riding of here, between the two rivers all summer? Thirty, and we lost them! What will we eat?"

Crozier shook his head. "Maybe grow something, like at Red River. Or work for wages."

Gabriel had turned away; perhaps he was looking at the

ruined rifle beside his moccasined feet. They were surprisingly small, Crozier thought, for the bulk of the man; with those rider's legs and that chest he must weigh two hundred; and a straight head too.

"Will you stay for tea?"

A woman's voice; Crozier turned in amazement: Dumont's wife had obviously asked the question. For a moment the inspector was not clear which was the more surprising, that she spoke unaccented English or that she dared open her mouth to a white. A surprising couple indeed. To prove much more so than he would wish.

5

"Yes, Mother Thérèse, you are right, of course," said stolid John Lee. "It is Louis Riel, my wife's nephew."

"You have brought him back into Canada?" The heavy eyebrows grey as the habit lifted slightly on the otherwise immobile face. "We cannot admit an outlaw into our hospital."

"He is not an outlaw, Reverend Mother," said Father Barnabé. "He is a destitute political exile, which is—"

"Which is no different here, Father."

"We had arranged to see Dr. Lachapelle, Mother Thérèse," John Lee said in his clearest alderman-of-Montreal tone.

"You understand," she rose slowly, "that though Dr. Lachapelle is our resident physician, the hospital belongs to The Grey Sisters of the Cross."

"I understand."

She went. Father Barnabé took a fast turn around the tiny office, soutane swishing.

"I'd never have...how'd she recognize him?"

John Lee laughed abruptly without humour. "Maybe she smokes cigars."

"What?"

"The biggest tobacco company in Canada has a promotion, they give away Louis's picture as their first premium."

"Good heavens!"

"The poor bugger," Lee muttered. "He's famous, face worth a fortune and he goes nuts because he has no job, nothing to do."

Barnabé stopped, looked at the stout businessman staring at his folded hands. "You believe that's what has made him sick?" he asked finally.

"Well, I guess visions and prayers are your line of business, but he never seemed to have them when he was running Red River; at least nobody noticed. You think it would've happened if they'd let him be an MP? If I was sitting around on my hands for months and years—"

"And a possible assassin in every footstep you heard."

"Sure, sure, I'm not saying he isn't sensitive, tabern–you should have seen him in '64 when he heard his father died. He mooned around for eight months, oh, he's sensitive all right, and some people have to be more sensitive than me, who wants everybody a contractor hammering up houses," he laughed a little, more easily. "I like Louis; we'd gladly keep him, but three weeks is enough. We can't keep any servants, he's just too much. Heavenly Father, that moaning, all night long..."

"That was too much, for us too. My mother, and Evelina..."

"Sometimes my wife says it sounds like his soul is coming out by the roots!" Lee shook his head in wonder. "He should have been a priest, all this politics, he's a priest really."

"I don't think that would have changed—"

"His mother really wanted to be a nun you know. And Sara is one, Grey Sister like these."

"I wish we could care for him." Barnabé was pacing again, "He has such...greatness, such a feeling of..." he was searching for a word, a phrase to contain his overwhelming feeling but Lee had heard something else.

"We'd keep him, the cost's nothing to me, he's my relative and I'd gladly keep him. But it's become impossible. Henri, who was driving the coach coming here, said he couldn't—"

"Mr. Lee," Barnabé said quietly. "I'm not sure if you understand what a *good* man Louis is; he will never lack friends who want to take care of him, who will love him because he is...money is nothing, I wanted to care for him, but I had to call you when it became impossible for my ill mother, and for my sister..."

Lee looked up at him sharply. "How is your sister now?"

"Her health is better; she can care for mother again. And she waits, now."

Lee shook his head. "She'll have a long wait."

Rapid footsteps approached, the door swung open into the middle of Dr. Lachapelle's big, confident voice which had obviously mastered crises before they arrived. "...there can be no question about it. After all, Louis and I were at the Collège de Montréal together. Ah, Mr. Lee, and you must be Father Barnabé."

Mother Thérèse watched grimly as they greeted each other; than she asked, "Does he know where you have brought him?"

"What does that matter?" Lachapelle wafted his hand as if to clear a tone away from the two men watching him somewhat uneasily. "If he cannot help himself, and I have no doubt of Mr. Lee's ability to decide that, and Father Barnabé too, then his friends must help him. Now, if you will admit him under that assumed name, I will clear the details with these gentlemen, and," he gestured to her continued question, "I will regulate matters, of course, every proper form. Never fear, never fear."

"If the Government–or Orangemen learn he is here, how will—"

"Mr. Chapleau, the Provincial Secretary. He was also with us in college; now please."

Her Orange question unanswered, Mother Thérèse walked down the short corridor to the waiting room; I have seen the afflicted mad, and the horror of their life pales before the horror of the way they were handled–not even the Sisters cared for them–in Quebec in 1876. Through the soles of her feet Mother Thérèse could feel like a distant endless roll of subterranean thunder the ceaseless hand and foot and head and body pounding of the violently insane locked in their stone vaults far below. When she opened the door, saw again the pale handsome face, much gaunter than the picture but with the same wavy black hair and delicate feathered sideburns, the strong clean chin, so obviously a gentleman, still sitting with the same patience at the window; here among madmen, how would he....fortunately William was in his place at the door, and Jean-Baptiste entering with a leather suitcase. She smiled as he looked about at her, rising immediately.

"I am happy to see you, Mr. David," she said. "I am your Mother Superior and in a moment Dr. Lachap—"

"What? What did you call me?"

The attendants had moved imperceptibly at his tone, but she continued to smile, raising the blank file in her hand as if studying it.

"Mr. David, that is what...we have here—"

He was reaching into his breast pocket, his handsome face tightening. "Excuse me, my name is not David, my name is—"

"Fine, fine," she interrupted hastily, "your friends have told me you are Mr. David and if you—"

Her habit was like Sara's and he could so easily, he wanted to love her for that despite her lumpish face; but her voice held that thoughtless superiority of all whites, infinite churchmen...as if they were something sacred, chosen, so special he would be forever obeying, peeping about their legs like a child that might need to be petted, slapped, beaten, or praised or allowed to babble at their untouchably superior indulgence or as conveniently placed out of sight when not wanted: an icy calm was growing, growing in him and if Mother Thérèse had known him as we did she would have already been terrified.

"My friends," he said, "should know better. I am Louis David Riel, here." He thrust the prayerbook under her nose. "Look! 'To Louis David Riel, from your sister who loves you, Sara Riel.' Sara is a Grey—"

Her claw leaped, snatched the book; the title page ripped out like a scream.

"Here your name is Mr. David, you are nothing here but—"

And it burst in him like a roar, he had torn the little book from her hand, the paper linking Sara's name with his broken and crumpled, the place where she had shaped his name torn as if he had been crushed out of existence; the pieces were changing like jelly before his eyes, the very shape and feel of that great comfort which had guided him six years, he felt himself explode, "God confound you, you grey sack!" and he was moving upon her, the arms of clutching attendants flying off like chaff, he had raised the mutilated book above her cowering, the words rolled like walls breaking, "From Sara, who gives her life in exile! You are damned to blistering hell, devils fry you the burning pinc—" Choked; he couldn't breathe, his arms twisted back into scream while curses flamed on inside him and his teeth dug for an opening through the arm that choked him, his body to throw off the mountain crushing him down, the squares of the tile floor rising slowly, slowly until suddenly they crashed against his face.

Through the sounds of bodies falling, groans, running feet, there were words...a word drifting, caught in the web of a face that squinted in a desperate struggle with a Latin verse, between pieces of sleep a face beside him, his own body not there in a long, numb slackness, but a voice and gradually bits of face "Louis...Louis...it's Emmanuel..." and he knew some recent violence had steadied into breathing, and it was that little rich boy too bright to work hard until the midnight he would need the translation for morning, "Louis, please..." If the proctor in the next bed heard him this time it was expulsion, flogging at home, they might even hang him like a dedication flag from the high crosses blessing the barns of their seigneury, begging a Latin verse into French "...please, will you..." and he smiled, his body powerful and living again, quite rested and he could move mountains, could stand up and declare who he was and the anxious face rose waveringly with him as things broke away, were scraped off, clutching, and he was very nearly erect, almost on his feet and laughing behind his two hands in his great secret joy.

When they left him alone in his cell where the late afternoon sunlight crossed the bars over his leather suitcase on the floor in a pattern he would remember very very well nine years later in Regina, he knelt down, unlocked the case, took out paper, pen, and ink bottle. He placed the mutilated book in the sunlight, open at the torn page. And wrote very carefully, as he always wrote every word for he knew that if he wrote enough of them, even if they were taken from him and someday he vanished like vapour drifting up from fire, what words he had made would be there to prove him, defy his forced disappearance:

"I am Louis David Riel."

He looked at that a moment, kneeling on the stone floor, and then he dipped his pen in the ink again and underlined *David*.

"I am."

It is now seven years that I have been dying, and six since I passed into the fire. Monseigneur, you cannot know how your letter has strengthened me in my sad hour. Last December I dedicated myself to the Holy Spirit for the rest of my life and, however useless I may be as a servant, I have begged your Grace to witness this consecration so that your testimony would be for my happiness in this world, and the next. Your great heart deigned to answer me: 'Therefore be blessed by God and men!' I prayed to God: how is this blessing possible? How can I truly be blessed by God and by men if I am not able, in the name of God, to give men what they most desperately need: salvation? And how can I give

*men salvation if I cannot absolve them of their sins, cannot
give them the nourishment of the blood and body of Jesus
Christ? Monseigneur, the Holy Spirit said to me: Build up
the small number of good men; edify the unnumbered who
long for righteousness but still hesitate before the altars of
the world; give liberty to those who languish in chains;
show the right paths to those far from their homeland. And I
understood at last that with your great blessing, you had
reclothed me in the priesthood of our Lord....*

He was battering the door with the sides of his fists, echoing the
rumble that lived in the walls of the building like a spirit forever
groaning there, and he shouted through the peephole in the
door where he could never tell if anyone was watching him or
not, shouted until his own ears drummed with the reverbera-
tions in the tiny stone room,

"Get Dr. Lachapelle! I want him, right now! Dr. Lachapelle,
or I'll break the door down, you hear me!"

The door rattled, Lachapelle's voice was there as it opened
on Jean-Baptiste, the bald dome of his forehead glinting with the
lantern from the corridor gloomy even in the early morning.

"Louis, Louis, I'm here, such a racket...the whole corridor,
now really."

"It's your attendants," Riel said calmly, turning; "they never
listen unless I beller." Lachapelle stood in the doorway, watching
for an instant. "If you gave them the proper orders, I wouldn't
have to."

"Well. What's the matter now?"

"Look here," Riel bent to his suitcase, "look!" There were
tiny triangles impressed in the leather, scratches about the lock.

"Is the lock broken?"

"No."

"Well?"

"Those are knife-marks. Somebody's been prying here, I

noticed when I woke up, they've been at my letters, they were in a different order."

"Now really," Lachapelle smiled almost as if he were uncomfortable, "while you slept? You'd have woken up with all the noise that would make, right here by your head."

"Not if I slept heavily, not if I had something in my milk last night that tasted a little sweet."

After a moment the doctor looked away, but suddenly Riel gripped him with both hands to his shoulders, pulling him around. "Listen to me! Whatever you think of me sometimes, right now I am Half-breed Louis who can still think circles around you the way I did in philosophy class. All you have left me is in that suitcase, everything I've written to give my people a voice, everything you have left me of my friends–the letters they send me. You want to know who my friends are? Well, ask! My sister Sara on her Indian mission two months walking beyond Red River...Masson in Ottawa...the Barnabés in New York...and Archbishop Bourget here across the river. This letter," he scooped up a worn envelope lying on the bed, "you will never find unless you search me bodily every night! If you take it, you may as well kill me. Quick."

Slowly Lachapelle put his clean, competent doctor hands up to cover Riel's still gripping his shoulders.

"All right, Louis," he murmured, "all right now."

"I'm sure this will never happen again," Riel said glaring steadily into his eyes. "You will please tell Father Bolduc that I am to be allowed to pray, alone, once every day in the chapel."

now...and the Holy Spirit has revealed to me, Monseigneur, that the savages of North America are Jews of the purest blood of Abraham with the exception of the Eskimos, who come from Morocco. For while Moses was exposed on the waters of the Nile in order to save him, an Egyptian boat containing twenty-seven Egyptians and seventeen

Jews was lost at sea. This ship was tossed about for months,
and they abandoned all hope until one evening the four-
year-old daughter of Agareon the Jew, who had been
praying to the God of his Fathers, took him gently by the
hand. My father, she said, you are still looking for the land
of the Egyptians. And pointing to the sun which just then
touched the horizon, she said, Let us reach that fire there.
Then the father knew that God was speaking to him; the
ship's company had faith in him, and so they changed
direction. And, though they experienced great storms,
eventually islands did appear, the strait between Haiti and
Cuba, and finally the mainland of Mexico. Nineteen days
after the vision, on the thirteenth day of April in the year
after the birth of Moses they reached the happy shore, found
through the faith of a virgin. The Egyptians went south
into Mexico, the Jews north....

Before the altar of St. Jean de Dieu chapel Riel knelt in his long,
grey hospital clothes, his hands clasped in prayer, his eyes lifted
to the picture of The Abused Christ that had hung over the altar
for decades, its red heart weeping over pathetic sinners. He had
begun in silent meditation, murmuring rote Latin prayers, but
then in great happiness he had found words rising to his lips,
the unbelievable mercy of unwatched prayer, alone before the
lacerated figure:

"...and you have given me to be persecuted and pur-
sued; you have given me to be exiled and my people to drift
leaderless, oh grant my mother health that she can bless my
family that has no father, no brother to lead, provide for it.
You have given me visions of wonder and terror I cannot
voice to anyone, I am torn by fiends. O grant Sara holiness
in her every thought, O my God and me also when I am
alone, the shining eyes of my jailors at the door, what would

you have me do? Your holy Bourget assures me you will never abandon me in my great troubles, O God my God in this place where I am tied up and locked behind walls that shiver night and day with devils roaring, do not abandon me! I am yours, I will serve you through my worst temptations, yes, to the last temptation of my life, in your unending and measureless mercy do not cut me off...."

His words had stopped, staggered by what his eyes tried to tell him of the altar, but he jarred himself back,

"I wish to hold nothing back, no humiliation as long I understand it is from you...but, sometimes, I am terrified. What shall I do? I am torn by fiends, I am cut off by those who say they love me...I feel in my soul I must fly to the aid of my Métis people, that this is your call for me, and yet for that vision I am chained here, imprisoned. O my God where have I sinned? Where has my zeal been too small, my humiliation too—"

His prayer broke, his fingers black from the dirty altar-cloth. He felt his body lift like the rage in him, saw his arms go forth, his fingers like talons hook in the cloth and suddenly it was slashed away across his sight, the candelabra and utensils crashing to the floor, shattering, and the almighty words of the prophets were sounding like thunder through the chapel:

"The zeal for Thy House has consumed me! And the insults of those who insult thee have fallen on me!"

There were shouts behind him, feet thudding closer, but he found the kneeling bench in his hand; it was smashing down on the bare altar, candles and wood splinters flying.

"Filthy! The altar of The Abused Christ filthy, neglected! You will low, you will bellow with my rage, you will destroy the filth of this—"

Grey attendants were hurtling aside, the black skirts of Father Bolduc, and the white space of a strait-jacket clouded over and flapped away, the long board from the kneeling-bench crashing holy pictures from side-altars, candles falling in lighted arcs like rainbows through the dust and gloom of their recesses until it was all smashed, smoking and splintered, only The Abused Christ hanging intact and dripping his bright-red motionless blood from his perfect heart, gathering it red like a fountain for washing, a cleansing flood.

"Those who insult thee have fallen on me, I have become a shame for my brethren, drunkards make songs about me in the streets O Lord" and a rush overwhelmed him, carried him and while his body convulsed, tore and was torn, he felt his self like an easy gull riding waves that crumpled, hurled him about yet the violence went slipping under him like water and even when he opened his eyes for a moment and saw hurtling up at him the white staring eyes of madmen in their stone vaults, their fists and misshapen heads hard calloused blurs drumming on the walls, their mouths and matted hair gleaming like naked flowers, their teeth poised petals opening in a scream of happiness that their long anticipation was over, ah come, come, he experienced only the perfect rest, the absolute white beauty of peace; falling to them.

...in your first youth you threw yourself into the arms of Jesus and Mary and because you experienced long and terrible anguish, because by your faith in God once torn from you, you became the greatest of sinners, the holy Mother of God has prayed for you; she has drawn you back from the abyss of your sins until you will appear before men's eyes as the standard of divine mercy. Therefore the Lord said to me: In your misfortune you invoked Abraham and the prophets, and above all the holy King David as the patron of statesmen. In your particular devotion to the prophet-king you were given his name, to honour him before men. And now I will use your enemies to make you resemble David, for it is your pretended friends who have given your

*secret name to the world to add to the lovely name of Louis
the sainted king of France. For by the savage blood which
runs in your veins, you are Jewish, and by your paternal
great-grandmother you belong to the Jewish nation just as
the first David belonged to the Gentile by his paternal
great-grandmother; as David belonged to the Jews in all his
other ancestors, so you belong to the Gentiles. You are the
David of Christian times, for whom the ancient David is
the perfect pattern, the spiritual and temporal king of all
nations....*

The silent darkness of his cell opened over him. He could move
his head: the walls still murmured in their rolling ceaseless
thunder. Distant, he was not buried in it; his arms were folded
over his chest, tight about his body a white column stretched
down his narrow bed. The window shone orangish yellow;
evening light, the light of the coming angelus.

"I will bless the Lord, His praise shall forever be in my
mouth."

He sat up, he knew how not to fall when he began to stand,
his legs moved well though hesitantly, rusty. The barred light
rested against the wall and he backed into it, took the light on
his crossed chest and rubbed the wall until something hooked,
ripped. When one arm was free he tore the rest of the strait-jacket
through, dropped it at his naked feet. The air was cool over his
body, his skin seemed to hum faintly in the orangish light, and he
rested there, let his breathing quiet a moment, leaning head back
against the wall. Then he went to his bed, pulled out the sheet,
tore it lengthwise into one long narrow strip which he hung
about his neck like a scapular. They had left his prayerbook in
his suitcase; he took his crucifixion medal and hung it by its long
chain about his neck. He went to the peep-hole in the door.

"Jean-Baptiste. Jean-Baptiste!"

He covered the hole with his left hand when he heard footsteps; there were words outside, a name perhaps but he knocked steadily with his right until finally the door rattled, clanked open, and the words gagged on themselves as he stepped through the door into the corridor, the Agnus Dei a spot of heat on his chest, his prayerbook in his hand, knowing himself a white naked flame in the gloomy corridor as prayer lifted in him like music:

> I love thee, o Lord my strength.
> The Lord is my rock and my fortress,
>   of whom shall I be afraid?
> The cords of death encompassed me,
>   the torrents of hell rolled over me;
> In my despair I called on the Lord,
>   and He heard my voice,
>   my cry came up to him.

The thunder of the words rolled before him down the long hall, returned, and he felt the glory of God over his naked body like the sacred fire raining on Mount Sinai. O blessed king, O prophet of the Métis!

> ....the divine voice said to me, Take off those clothes which have been forced on you; and I obeyed. My lord, your word is a treasure; it seems like one of those great iron ships I see skirting along the river to seek the depths of the sea, and so I have meditated with the fire of the seven gifts of the Holy Spirit on what you have written to me: you must always keep yourself well clothed. And as I meditated on these words, the strong voice said, Is it not written of the singer King David that he danced and sang before the ark of God girded only in a linen ephod? And further, O man, why do you wear clothes? It is to hide the nakedness of the sinner, the shameful weight of arrogance which marks his flesh. O man, O woman who hide your living bodies under what is

*left of dead animals, by what vestige of Satan have you
come to make these shameful coverings a means of pride?
By what madness have you made them an element for your
vanity? Arise, the hour of worship is here....*

"I would really prefer two glasses of white wine to this milk,
and perhaps a bit of meat."

"But we are in the middle of Lent."

"Have you never read that David ate the shewbread of the
tabernacle, which it was forbidden to do on pain of death, when
he was hungry and fleeing from Saul?"

"You insist you are David?"

"To you I must insist nothing, but you call yourself my
doctor; you invite me to your house again, you allow me to walk
in your beautiful garden, and so—"

"Aren't the flowers beautiful?"

"Of course, and the air so fresh, your dining room beautiful.
But then for dinner you set before me boiled eggs and this
undrinkable milk."

"Undrinkable?"

"Like Father Bolduc in theological debate, you continually
contradict yourself. You prescribe that I walk several miles every
day so I will be tired, and sleep better. But the hospital yard is so
tiny I can hardly turn there, and at night they lock chains on my
feet and hands. How can I sleep?"

"That was only when you were violent."

"The chains are still there."

"What? There have been no chains since—"

"How would you know what I am forced to wear at night."

"Well. True, true. But the milk, now really, I am drinking it
too, and it tastes perfectly good to me."

"You can taste nothing?"

"No. If it tastes bad to you, perhaps, ha, ha, that is one more
penance you have to accept in this very fallible world!"

"How could it be a penance for me, Emmanuel, that you are willing daily to drink dirty milk? I am called to a great mission."

"Oh, I know, you are a prophet."

"Even the son of a prophet would detect this overpowering taste of cowshit."

...the mission entrusted to the French-Canadians, as children of the eldest daughter of the Church, is to continue the great works of France on this side of the ocean: the salvation of all unfortunate infidels through our Holy Mother, the Church. When the French-Canadians become afflicted with the infirmities of old age, their mission must pass on to other hands. The voice of God said to me, In my hands the earth is no bigger than a robin's egg; if I let it fall, it will be lost; if I shake it near my ear, I can hear whether it is empty. Therefore I am working to make the French-Canadian Métis people worthy to receive the heritage of Quebec.

The visions of Louis David Riel: a heavy hammer. And I said, Lord, what does this mean? And the Lord answered me, Take this heavy hammer in your right hand and hurl it against Ottawa.

The visions of Louis David Riel: I was lying on my bed and suddenly my legs and body started to bounce, as if I were riding. And I said, Lord, what does this mean? And the Lord answered me, By following the path of obedience, as you are, you are returning to your people. They will come for you on trotting horses, and a great company of riders will bear you back.

The lights of civilization move through the ages from the east to the west: man born on the banks of the Euphrates,

Christ in Palestine, the Papacy established for a time in Rome. A new order is coming.

Monseigneur, the Holy Spirit trembled within me at these awesome words....

Riel stood rigid, pointing. He was so clearly terrified that for a moment Lachapelle could not even notice what he was pointing at.

"There, there, you see that? You always say I'm seeing and hearing things. Well, look, look!"

It was the window, Lachapelle finally comprehended, the window with its glass intact, as usual, nothing...the bars had been cut out, the steel frame was gone.

"Louis! How did you—" Lachapelle exploded, then controlled himself. "We'll have to chain you again."

"With my teeth?' Riel shouted. "That was cut from *outside*, during the night!"

"What are you—"

Riel at his collar had jerked Lachapelle so close he saw his own bulging reflection in those terrified black eyes.

"Will you believe now what the guards whisper? Whoever did that wanted me *out there. They* know I'm in here!"

"What have you heard, about guards?"

"That the Orange Lodge of Montreal will burn this place down. That's why you have a night patrol now."

The walls might have been singing to him: no newspapers, only a few letters, but he knew everything; Lachapelle could only shake his head and turn to the window. Obviously it had been cut from the outside, a single person must have got past...the exact cell? God.

"But, what's the point?" He turned; after the spot of morning light, he could barely see Louis in the dark, only his pale face begging as he had never seen it, ever; even as a boy crying in a weed-grown corner of the Sulpician Gardens.

"They want me out so they can kill me."

"Louis, you—"

"For the love of God, Emmanuel, let me go. Let me go."

"Louis, your visions, your prophecies, your...how can I?"

"You talk like Father Bolduc: only the Pope can declare divine truth."

"But your prophecies are, so impossible..."

Riel's face changed, sunlight breaking through clouds. "Tell my servant David, I took you from the pasture that you should be prince over my people, and I have tried you as a blacksmith tries iron in the forge and I have been with you and I will appoint a place for my people and plant them there. The vast British Empire shall have but one sail left in the port of London, Rome shall sink to the bottom of the sea and I will give you rest from all your enemies, thus says the Lord, your strength and your Salvation."

The doctor was suddenly overwhelmed with tenderness. Such a clear case of megalomania, of messianic paranoia; overheated on Bible-reading and persecution, the world in the clutch of evil, take the flaming sword of God and destroy it in judgement. Father Bolduc saw too much religious problem here; Riel's political ambitions on earth finished forever, and now clearly he was making himself a role so unreal that actual events would never prove him wrong; destroy Protestant London, papal Rome. Oh, poor Louis! Lachapelle placed his arm carefully around his patient's shoulder; a brilliant mind, a charismatic personality destroyed, destroyed. The doctor could have wept, if that would have helped; but never believed the way we would.

"'David' was just a name, a convenient name," he said finally.

"And I should just...forget what I see, and hear?"

"You can be so perfectly rational; you can explain so perfectly why you do these mad things."

"You'll never believe me, will you."

Lachapelle had to look away a moment. "If you heard everything we hear from the patients in this place," but stopped. There was something horrible about equating such things; and yet, and yet. Megalomania? Messiah complex? If he were asked to declare himself under oath, what would be the truth?

"Two years," Riel was saying, perhaps to himself. "That's long enough. If you write to Chapleau, to get me out, you won't hear anything more about visions. Not from me."

I thank God with you that I have passed my worst time of suffering; I bless God that He humiliated me. He has made me understand so well the extent of human glory, how quickly it passes, and how empty for him who, having attracted the attention of men a little while, suddenly feels the weight of God's hand upon him. Patient Evelina, I had seen the lights of civilization move through the ages from east to west and it came to me that the papacy ought to leave the worm-eaten soil of Europe for a younger world; it seemed to me that I had an important role in this new order. By pen and the spoken word I tried to make proselytes, and in all the disappointments I experienced, I remembered our Lord was also misunderstood by his own. But one day a light dawned in my mind: why struggle with those who refuse, and refuse? God will provide the fruit, and ripen it for the picking. Today I feel better; I laugh at some of my arrogant hallucinations, and my spirit is free, as my body will be soon. I will come to the United States and till the soil God gives me there, unknown, far from Canadian affairs and their excitement. I will build up the small number of good men and women, and if anyone speaks to me of the Métis, those poor people in their land clean and beautiful as paradise hounded by Orange fanaticism, of those brave hunters they call savages who are of my bone, of my faith, who again and again chose me as their leader, who love me and whom I will love forever...Evelina, if the sacred cause of the Métis reclaims me, could I, their brother, refuse them my life, my blood?

Remember us, Louis, remember your Métis people. For we will never forget you.

THE May blizzard roared out of the south over them as they rode through the long gap between the Cypress Hills; its grey had been piling above them like a pall for two days since the South Saskatchewan Crossing. They rode single file, the wagon last of all, and the horses floundered through a draw, the wind howling wet spring snow: Gabriel breathed frost into the air. Behind him the storm whirled; he could see nothing of The-Old-Man-Lying-On-His-Back. He looked south through the snow coming in splotches against his clothes, his steaming horse, and he could see the far shoulders of Milk River Ridge. It would not last long, already beyond the Sweetgrass Hills like burial mounds on the horizon shafts of sun were almost breaking through. He nudged his horse ahead; in two hours the white ground shone here and there with green, water gurgled in draws, and beside a spring creek running through snow they camped where the last evening light outlined willows and still-grey cottonwoods. He hunkered beside the fire, steaming a little, glad for the heat of cooking while Moïse Ouellette and James Isbister rubbed down the horses. He turned

199

the gophers carefully on his spit, laying the driest sticks just right in the fire. Suddenly Michel Dumas was there beside him, squatting down, placing four more gophers in a row at his feet, each with its head cleanly shot off.

"They won't believe it's winter either," Michel said.

"It's ready," Gabriel said. "C'mon."

He lifted the spit, held it out to them, and each stripped a roasted gopher off on the point of his knife.

"Salt would help," Ouellette said.

"One mouthful of gopher in four days," Michel said, "and he wants salt. Salt."

"Well if you want small enough," Isbister said, "you might get it."

"I never have."

Gabriel was trying to skin another gopher with the tip of his long skinning-knife, and suddenly Michel jerked; stared across the creek into the darkness. Shadows moved there; the firelight glinted on eyes.

"They've been there all evening." Gabriel did not raise his head. "Blackfeet."

"You think," Isbister said slowly, "there's a camp?"

"If any men were alive, they'da been here already."

After a moment Ouellette got up, walked toward the trickling water, and for an instant he saw the goggle-eyed face of a starving child before it turned away, slowly, towards the stir of bodies already gone; but its gaunt hand was there open, closing around the tiny gopher leg he put into it. Gabriel would not look up; his knife-point continued to pick, pick the gutted body almost lost in the grip of his huge, barely bloody hand; his face clenched tight between rage and tears.

THE knobby hills, like seven sen-
tinels marching to the mountains, were dappled with the May
snow, but the evening sunlight came in level under the heavy
storm-clouds, washed the room all over as with gold. He had
been writing verses, practising English and trying to make the
rhyme mirror the accent; but that was the hardest thing about
English, the accent; he could so rarely be sure:

> You play the most criminal role
> The love of Power makes you cold
> As the seas of the Northern Pole
>
> It is not that from the Frontiers
> Of Mexico to the Sweetgrass Hills
> Thousands of Half-breeds live in tears
> Kept down like Indians with their

If he could finish it, it would sound a little better, but not much.
The letter was lying there, and letters are dangerous; I never knew

a Métis except Riel who liked them, though I wrote a number myself. The words crouch black on pale paper, unchangeable and deadly. This one from his brother Joseph in St. Vital. Thinking of that, some words began to form again, and he let them, as they wished:

Born in the 23rd of October 1844
in the morning, a beautiful day, said to
me my dear mother.
 Went to confession when seven years
old, to Reverend Father Bermond.
 Made my first communion twenty-fifth
of March of 1856. Began my Latin studies
at the Boniface on the 1st of September 57.

"Louis," Marguerite said, leaning almost against his shoulder, "what have you written?"

"The words write themselves," Riel said, bending his head back and looking up for her thin, dark face. He could not recognize her upside-down, the yellow light catching her black hair in a cloud; she had untied it, she was like Sara might have been for a man had she not married Jesus, but even the strong sun could not bleach her hair blond, her skin to that diaphanous ivory of Evelina above him, eyes blue with–her lips were on his, the tip of her tongue. In the wonder of this he lifted his arms around her, held her gently beside her breasts.

"They don't for me," she said.

"I'll teach you; then they will," between her open lips. "They will say 'Marguerite' and 'Montana' and 'Missouri' and 'Marguerite-Marie'..."

"Why will they stop when they say 'Marguerite-Marie'?"

"Because that was Sara's name. The name she took after she died the first time. Her lungs hemorrhaged, and they gave her Extreme Unction and the Plenary Indulgence and the Benediction with the Ciborium and she said, 'Goodbye, God of the Eucharist, dearest companion of my exile. Welcome, my judge, and grant me your mercy.

"And she died?"

"Yes. But the sisters did not know it and they prayed to the Blessed Marguerite-Marie who is their special devotion at Ile à la Crosse, using her Litany of the Sacred Heart. And suddenly Sara's lips moved, and she was praying the Litany also, and she had returned from the dead. As soon as she could breathe, she asked for her clothes. The sisters hesitated, but she insisted and got up and walked steadily to the chapel and knelt at God's feet. 'My judge has become my guarantor,' she prayed. 'I now dedicate my life to the Divine Prisoner of Love at the altar."

"Who is that?" Marguerite asked him, her soft body resting on his right shoulder, breathing lightly as a child. She always accepted perfectly, without question, everything he told her, and in this she was to him the perfection of our people.

"The Blessed Marguerite-Marie of France. Her devotion had created the miracle of resurrection in Sara, the first Métis missionary.

"We should go to her grave now, and pray for our sins."

"It's over two months from here, and what sins do you have?"

"Many."

"Many?" The quiet movement of her ribs under his hands filled him, as it always did, with the amazement of a living person he could feel there without sin, the sensations of that miracle drenching him like water. "You are nothing but goodness, work and goodness."

"I do good things, but my thoughts...."

"Thoughts are...very hard. They go, anywhere. But your thoughts are pure and good." He tried to concentrate on her feelings only; "You are always so good."

"I think so much of you."

"That's a sin?"

"I think, the way I think, sometimes."

"What do you think, of me?"

Past his face her hair like a fall of black water, the long cate-chism of his questions abstracting her voice more and more as if she were reaching back into the recesses of herself to satisfy him perfectly with a perfect unflinching honesty; no matter what he would dare ask, she was bound to answer as though she were on her knees.

"What?" he asked again, and felt his body stir like a subter-ranean animal.

"Pride," she said against his cheek. "I am so proud when you speak for our people, write against the crooked politicians. We are so small and you...give us bigness. We know nothing, they do what they want with us."

"Were you so proud when I was in Fort Benton jail?"

"Yes!" Her hands clamped on his chest, fiercely. "The sheriff was bad; to be arrested when you have done good is like our Lord Jesus who died—"

Riel was laughing against her hair, at her innocence of a Democratic sheriff arresting someone who could deliver all the Métis vote to the Republicans, laughing because if such action in Montana were criminal he would have been convicted; sadly, because even conviction would have further confirmed his purity in her eyes. She gave him such faith, words rose in him like memories of ancient prayers, he could almost see again our white cheers wisp upward into the cold blackness of Fort Garry.

"Speak to me, conscience," he recited into the wispy black-ness covering his face, "speak to me, who are in truth the Christ of my confidence, the Christ of my love."

"Sing," she said.

And the final sunlight of the day came golden through her black hair, through the tiny window as words came again, sounds of running water under cottonwoods:

Sing to me, mountains,
Sing to me, everlasting hills,
For my God has not forsaken me,
He has graven my name in the palm
Of His right hand.

Sing to me, hands,
Sing, rise high against the Gentiles,
For my people will come
Bringing their sons in their arms;
Their daughters shall be carried upon their shoulders.

"It isn't just my pride that becomes sin," she whispered. "In you."

"What? What other terrible sin?" He could feel her breasts, usually so bound and hidden against her chest by coarse dresses, swing down, almost as it seemed heavy against his hands. "Terrible sin, eh?"

"You are, such a man, so...big and you..."

"When I want you?" he said, and his mind leaped to a sudden fury for he heard his own guilt in her hesitations, the sounds of nuns whispering, of priests clenching themselves in confessionals; and he sprang up, swinging her aside almost cruelly to find her glance in the last of the evening sun. "Look at me," he said through clenched teeth. "Look at me! We are man and wife, married before God and Church!"

"But only after eleven months...."

"Marguerite, what are you saying? Before your parents, there was no priest in the Missouri brakes! I love you, we have a son and daughter, we...what is this, sin?"

"Nothing," she said, her voice moving into that dead usualness it always contained, the tone of our people most of their lives because they can expect nothing and so they hunker down under their blanket and think of nothing, feel nothing, drink themselves senseless if they can. I have seen that all too often; or just exist like dormant animals in a long, long winter. Riel heard that all-too-familiar sound and he shook her, his mind leaping now in rage.

"Marguerite!"

"You will wake Jean, the baby...Louis, please."

He could control himself. For four years now her calm voice had often led him out of the rages he felt less and less frequently—there was so little among schoolchildren that could thrust him into fury: they were all the poorest, most helpless children who sat daily, listening patiently for what he told them, memorized the words, memorized, memorized; and if they ever thought their unending routine dreadful they never revealed a flicker of it to him; what was there to be incensed about now, teaching the helpless poor children of our people fled to Montana?

"Listen to me." He lifted her head with his right hand, so her eyes could not avoid him. "Father Taché told me long ago, love is the sacrament between a man and a woman. Whatever they feel, whatever they do to make themselves happy, that is pure, that is holy. You understand."

Her eyes were hugely black in the fading light. "I want to be holy for you. Like Sara was."

"Sara?"

He had to blink his eyes at her voice; they felt seeded with dust, like the carts bending their long squeal across the heat-swimming prairie. "Sara was holy, and she is with God. And you are holy too. For me, you are and will be my pure Marguerite. Anything we feel toward each other is holy."

"Anything?"

"Yes," he said, and the dust was washed away; his hand could move to her shoulders again. "Anything. I want to undress you."

"Yes," she said, calm but a trace of brilliance at the edge of the single word; she stood motionless while he unbuttoned her dress so coarsely heavy against her incredible skin shining now in the silvered light, bending a little one way and then the other as to a secret tune while his fingers stumbled with buttons, until she stood outlined against half silver and black in curves and roundness, everywhere, the pointed loops of her breasts so strangely full, the line between her legs so beautifully curved in its straightness that he felt a jolt of agony to clutch her to himself, the black hair of her groin like damask against him; he would have fallen on his knees but she said, watching him look at her completely,

"No."

"What?"

"I want to undress you too."

"What!"

Her smooth, easy hands held his amazement, the evening air suddenly cool on his chest and back and arms and he could not quite believe what she was doing. They had always lain under blankets beside so many others, in tents or cabins or under wagons and the brilliant secretless stars, listening, keeping his body surges silent against other sleeping sounds, she silent and motionless under him but breathing softly, gasping once when he found her too deep, too quickly, but both of them with their eyes clenched shut under blankets and feeling only with those strange parts of their bodies which their hands would not touch, now suddenly unexpected as rain he could study her nakedness, the dark circles of her hanging breasts and his hand came up, his finger touched one as she opened the buttons of his trousers and she looked up at him, her eyes crinkling in a smile, and he almost shuddered aloud remembering in one livid blaze André Nault's stallion in the pasture beside the Seine, gigantic white-and-purple-ringed penis rising like some violent rooted lever between the stallion's powerful legs and then swinging over the small mare as he reared over, onto her, the mare's scream while her legs almost buckled under the stallion's drive, his terrible, machine-like thrusts, and Pierre yelling in his ear, "How's that for making babies, you like that, you like it too!" And he had stared in horror at the older boy, knowing babies came only as sweet gifts from God, knowing nothing so terrible could ever happen between a man and a woman—how would they ever dare face each other again, such shame, viciously personal violence so unbearable and unforgettable—even as his own body shook with a sickening conviction, even as Pierre laughed, mouth open, crouched forward to see the stallion now so completely hammered into the mare there seemed nothing left of her but her white stockings, a foam-splattered neck and head leaping back and forth in a kind of torture between the stallion's yellow teeth. "Someday your little Sara, I'll stick your pretty little Sara like—" and he had smashed his fist sideways across Pierre's open teeth as he leaped up, ran, still feeling teeth break against his bones, hearing another scream, human, somewhere, running in terror at what he was being made to think and at her white body ground down, at what his own thudded into him as he ran achingly. But he could not run out of his body, not then, nor would he now watching Marguerite push down his open trousers and he stepped out of them, stood in bare feet and the underpants she had sewn that winter from a flour-sack.

"Marguerite," he began, but she laughed a little, as unobtrusive as always but also with a certainty he could not quite fathom, her hands inside the underpants pushing them down so that the inside of her arm brushed him; he could not look anywhere, he did not know what he saw—the darkness of the small cabin they no longer had to share with another family, the darkness where in a corner at the foot of their blankets Jean slept in his box, the baby, what if they awoke... "Jean," he said and Marguerite smiled in his face.

"Come." And she touched him, deliberately, as if to lead him. And for the first time in her presence he felt himself naked, the evening air so cool and good all over himself he might have been swimming in some river of heaven, his apprehension washed from him and he suddenly felt that long root growing inside him, strength like a tree that wanted only this naked woman smiling in shadows made by the last of the window light, her hand on his hip now, welcoming him.

So at the corner blankets he would have helped her lie down, would have dared to kneel over her naked, perhaps even dared to kiss her and known he could have looked steadily into her eyes the next day in the full glare of the mountain sun. But she said to him,

"Lie down."

"What?"

She stood beside him, hand insistent. "On your back. Yes."

It was only when she was kneeling over him and not touching him anywhere except at his hips with the inside of her knees and her long black hair–loosened now, yes, she had had it unbraided right from the beginning, hair drawing him up to her as through a curtained oval–that he began to give himself over to her. For she would not let him pull her down; she barely kissed him until he surrendered his insistence, then her breasts came against his, her knees widened until she lay on him fully but she was too short, he could not reach her and he tried to push her lower, curl himself up against her and she whispered into his teeth, her breath rising a little, "No, no," until he lay still, feeling a flicker of anger that threatened to shrink his tension but she moved down slightly, chuckling in his ear and instantly he was taut as a bow, ready to drive upward, forward, but she would not let him, held his shoulders tight and his hips down, outlining his lips with her tongue.

"You said it," she whispered. "You said it."

Whatever it was. For he was strangely angry at her, and also amazed at doing things he had always driven past or thoughtlessly through; they were both naked, yet she would not let him lunge ahead but guided him slowly, she spoke to him. How could you speak, teeth to teeth, while these terrifying feelings grew to tear you up at the very roots? But she did now, and he knew he had bungled past some impasse he had never admitted, she whispering words like breath in his ear, or was it just one word; it seemed to him he grew immensely beyond what he had ever known even in his most overwhelming dreams, his whole body could reach to the four corners of the world as she gave him her centre and circled down lower and lower, her slim body covering him with a delicate, searching lightness that held him rigid, gyring down like furry animals dancing, he was suddenly finding out the giant hollows of earth, and he thrust against her let her feel it and scream but she thrust back as hard as he, they were hammered down together like sheet metal, springing together in one rhythm against the naked spring night and what they heard were each other's great shuddering groans as if death had found them out; both.

"Did you love Evelina?"

"Yes."

"Very much?"

He knew then more precisely than he ever had, or would, how naked was good; to feel love all over his body forever groaning for redemption. Marguerite's warm length enclosing him, the cool evening and the warm earth on which they lay: there is nothing on earth like such emptiness, such fullness, he could say anything. A wall broken which no one had ever touched within him; words could come, so much forbidden could now speak, face to face, in awesome nakedness.

"Not like this, love," the mound of his body holding hers and for an instant the memory, so quickly memory, of her body's groaning with his own leaped through him like the shudder of his embrace, her rich body beautiful and giving: "I don't know if you can understand; you were always in a good close family, and your father—"

"But so poor," she said.

"There are no rich Métis. They're rich only in family, and

I was too till thirteen, and then I was sent off alone just when I began to comprehend the ranges of love, and took cold showers and prayed half the night on the stone floor of the chapel to forget a girl whose family would not have me but who had shown me I could never be a celibate priest, and I—"

"What is that, 'celibate'?"

"A person who can't marry."

"Are there other kinds of priests?" she asked.

"Not in the Roman Catholic Church. But for me there was only Sara, my perfect sister like a perfect star to follow, so pure and perfect and holy and untouchable in her love, there was no woman on earth like I remembered her, and sometimes I dreamt I was her knight carrying her beauty I didn't have to see like a shield against the world, I could never touch her as a man does a woman, but she was a...like..."

His words stopped with the comprehension of where their nakedness had led his thought, with the letter of her death lying on his table, and a woman, his wife, lying so completely in his arms: the memories of his life abruptly were so purposeless, his certainties so small, for at that moment he could not think of anyone other than his mother and brothers and sisters–and per-haps Evelina still–who cared where or what he was except this woman in his arms, the children sleeping so deadly silent through their groans: he who had contemplated bringing heaven to earth and had set all Canada on its ear, Washington and London singing with telegrams about him, but now he could not even groan for that call which seemed at this instant so small, not even to matter O dearest God...he felt himself hollow and simply huge as if his fingers and hands, all his limbs, were no recognizable part of himself, mere somethings connected dimly to him beyond some far edge of the world, by strings perhaps, all so...empty...if he would at least ache.

"What's a 'knight'?"

"Uhh."

"You were Sara's 'knight'?" Marguerite was talking into his mouth, her tongue delicate as cobweb at the edges of his lips.

"Oh," and she was there so fully naked in his arms again he rolled her onto her side, laughing, and she was tight against him in the warm damp of his groin. "Knights were men long ago, on horses searching for monsters they could kill to help people, or the Holy Cup of Jesus to help them be pure, and they sometimes had ladies—"

"Of Jesus?" she whispered, wonderingly, "the Holy Cup."

"The cup they drank from at the Last Supper, Jesus and the disciples, and they knew it was somewhere, the purest most faithful man in all the world would be blessed of God to find it and while they looked they often remembered ladies whom they loved as purely and without sin as any man would love the Mother of God–ladies they never touched, they might have seen each other only once, but that inspired a knight with holy thoughts those long years they rode, looking for the Cup, or monsters for their good deeds."

"There is so much beautiful in the world," she said. "The Holy Cup of Jesus."

Her wonder had moved him the first time he saw her sitting in her father's Red River cart, and her black eyes from under her shawl had caught him as he propped his thick, white notebook on the edge of the cart and began listing her father's trade-goods: seven buffalo hides, two cougar–she was brushing his curls back from his neck, her lips at his ear.

"It would be a cup all of gold," she whispered, "shining like the sun."

"That's what they say but Jesus never had any gold, he was as poor as we."

"But he was Jesus, when he died on the cruel cross every-thing he had ever touched turned to silk and gold."

He lunged up on his elbow, "Who told you that?"

"Father Damiani, one Sunday he–Louis!"

He had knocked her back, was leaning over her and his eyes glared like fire in the darkness; he could have strangled her, he was so strangled with rage,

"God damn those priests!" His voice was rocketing about the tiny room—and he was, in some recess of himself, amazed for he had not felt this for so long, and never where she would have heard him, but along the terrifying wilderness of Montana where kites sailed over the last plains of rotting bones and offal and he could have cursed God, had he dared, at the horror visited on people who had done nothing except live where they had always lived and were now so totally destroyed—"Damn them changing his holy poverty for a lie to the poor, 'Suffer on earth, suffer, you'll have everything silk and gold when you die, you'll eat nothing but meat and sugar there, accept your starving here.' God damn them all to stinking hell!"

A child's voice, Jean wailing in terror; Marguerite's light shape knelt at the foot of the bed. He found himself standing, he must have been hammering the rafter above his head for his fist ached; when he put it in his mouth there was the taste of fresh spruce pitch still, like a Manitoba morning in his mouth.

"Shoooo, shooo," she crooned, her arms curled around dark, rocking.

He could see only her body bent, curved down into a whiteness. He gnawed the ache in his fist; God had preserved him from ever cursing the priests the long, crowded year they lived with the Swans—surely he had?—God save him before schoolchildren. He knelt, his legs bending slow as iron, pulled the blanket aside and stretched out under it. When Marguerite turned at last, he whispered, "Come."

"My clothes."

"You need nothing, come."

She did then, but with that set physical reticence, almost a kind of clenched hopelessness—he knew as she lay down and lifted the blanket across her that she would have lain perfectly still, accepted like snow opening and closing to a hand if he had mounted her; not making a single living sound. He had known this for years, he suddenly realized. And now knew it was all so different.

"That's why we are always...poor," he whispered straight up into the darkness. "Be quiet and obey; you'll get so much more for it all in heaven. That's why."

She said nothing. The night window sat in the corner of his eye.

"Only priests can speak for God," he said bitterly. "And they always say what has always been said. They're like doctors, or politicians of one party, alone they can be sometimes human and good but you want them to do something public for people and there it's finished; they all say exactly the same old thing. Do you think God has had nothing new to say to anyone in two thousand years?"

"Then why do you teach for priests?"

Her voice was so thinly odd in its question that only later would he hear it.

"Father Ritchot was different. We could talk, and laugh; he once said, 'If priests and nuns know so much, how come they can't have children?' He was feeding his fat pig then, it was summer and he just wore old Métis pants. Pouring slop into a trough without a shirt on".

"Our women stagger around," her voice sounded as if she were dead, "the saloons in Carroll and their children cry for hunger."

"God knows," the misery of our people like a groan in him, the world so changed it seemed impossible for them ever to do anything but try to forget; how many years did I feel like that, Louis. "God knows."

And the joy they had found in each other that evening, this nakedness that would have allowed him to speak aloud at last to another human being–of how he loved Sara beyond her exile death and Evelina also though he would never answer her last letter: 'It will soon be five years since you wrote, I could not believe my eyes...how could you be capable of such infamy...you have destroyed...' now over two years old in his coat pocket—that was all now turned into a strange, quiet rest as he lay staring into darkness. The rage of his wildness for heaven and earth still lived in him, slumbering until the moment another voice he now knew certainly would say, "Come," and he would go, his sure vision his guide.

Sunday June 4, 1884 he was in church hearing again the inevitable sequence of the Mass. The terrible winter was past but the Mass: once it had been his only solace; in Washington he had spent entire days walking from one church to the next to take it five and six times, but during the gathering years in Montana people began to disturb him beyond rite. They knelt with such awesome longing in their bent bodies, what would bits of flesh and blood matter to—he was past terror at his thought, and a woman in the next bench, her winter-pale body heavy with child and her face clenched in prayer, roused a distant, almost dispassionate, anger in him at the incomprehensible suffering of the poor. They knew the why of nothing; the simple stupid acts of leaders in capitals were unknown to them: why force them with a killing winter? There was a hand on his shoulder and he turned eagerly, half expecting the angel of judgement; and he would have blazed questions even as the long sword fell, but it was merely one of the boys from the school. Four strangers were outside, asking for Mr. Louis Riel.

In the churchyard, the seven-fanned pattern of Bird Tail Rock brilliant in sunlight beyond them, four riders on worn horses. Buffalo-hide jackets: Métis hunters, rifles strapped to saddles for a long ride. He stood on the log step a moment, the bright world turning into premonition as though he had looked beyond the transparent blue-and-orange-rimmed globe behind his own eyelids; but one broad rider had swung down, was coming toward him in the wide-legged roll of a horseman, and his heart leaped before his mind could name this man, this giant opening his arms, mouth agape as though he would bellow for joy but having that very joy silence him beyond sound.

"Gabriel," he could say then, stumbling forward, "my good brother, Gabriel Dumont!"

He had never felt such a hug, man and horse sweat like a power raging about in his head, crushing his chest; the boys from the school ran together, staring. Two of the riders jerked out their rifles and shots rolled crashing over the valley. He pushed back, looked at that long-remembered hard face, older and grizzled and it seemed smudged by water. He had to turn away; and Gabriel too, face contorted, not able to say a word.

"Fourteen years, this month, almost the day."

"You had made Manitoba, and I offered you five hundred men."

Riel nodded; those eyes he had never forgotten. He could read their wonder at his patched suit–the one his friends had given him when he walked out of the hospital–at the small cabins, the ragged children, and he could only smile, let his fingers brush Gabriel's own worn jacket.

"That's all. This is the empire God has given me."

"But there are more than five hundred men waiting for you on the Saskatchewan, right now."

"What?"

"Not just Métis, whites and Indians too, English, everyone. Help us Louis, come home, to the Saskatchewan."

Riel stared at him.

"Our Montana children, they must be taught," he said finally.

"Somebody else can teach them." Gabriel's huge hands were on his shoulders. "Louis, we need you to teach that Macdonald."

Riel saw before him both revelation and sentence.

The frogs sang in the patches of water caught like sky between hills brushed green by melting snow; the trail wound around the sentinel buttes of the Sun River valley. Jean was perched on blankets beside James Isbister in the front seat of the buggy, Marguerite with the baby sat beside Riel in the seat behind; he had his leather suitcase between his legs, was reading letters, and listening.

"Right now," Gabriel nudged his horse near the buggy, "we have fewer rights than the Indians. They at least have the treaties and the reserves, but with the buffalo all gone we don't—"

Riel looked up. "When did you last hunt?"

Gabriel looked across the buggy to Ouellette, "When would you say, Moïse ?"

"The year Dewdney come Governor, about four, five...it's five years."

"But the Blackfeet still hunted in Montana last summer!" Riel exclaimed.

"Yeah, a little, but they starved this winter."

"Yes," said Riel. "Almost half their people died."

"Our Cree had salt bacon and flour, some of them."

"Five years." Riel stared across the small river where, over marshes, ducks whistled into the air. "How do you live?"

"I've got a bit of a ferry on the South Saskatchewan," said Gabriel. "There's some freighting from the CPR, and some trying to farm."

Isbister leaned back, "Last year we had grasshoppers, this year drought."

"That's for the good farmers," Gabriel said; "but me, I don't know a thing about farming. I've got no money for machinery, nothing."

Riel said slowly, contemplating the letter with its pages of signatures–God in heaven over seven hundred–"Macdonald can't make it rain."

"Sure as the devil he could give us title to our land!" Michel Dumas' words sat so fiercely on his face, Riel could not see there that scout forever riding, the silent guide, face washed with rain. Something was happening on the Saskatchewan; perhaps, perhaps.

"That's it." Gabriel leaned forward. "Land. We've lived on our river lots at Batoche over fifteen years– I had my cabin on the bank before I met you–and now there's settlers coming from Manitoba or Ontario or Minnesota, on the railroad, and they like river land too, they—"

"Hell," Isbister interrupted, "there's no survey, on our lots or nowhere else. These Canadians and Americans come in with machinery and just squat anywhere, on our land it doesn't matter, nobody's got any titles, nobody knows where boundries are gonna go, they just—"

"These crooks jump our best land," said Ouellette. "After fifteen years!"

"But surely you did things, you tried something."

"Oh sure!" Gabriel snorted. "Before Dewdney came Father André and I sent a petition to Ottawa for machinery and a survey. Nothing. Then we sent another petition about the buffalo being gone, and machinery and survey. Nothing. The year after that and last year again all of us, St. Laurent Métis, English Halfbreeds, whites, everybody, a petition to settle the land boundaries. But nothing, nothing!"

"This Governor Dewdney," Riel said, "what's the matter with him?"

"Nothin' a bullet in his fat ass wouldn't fix!"

That was Michel Dumas. Ouellette reached over, whacked Michel's horse with the flat of his hand.

"Get up front, go on!"

Michel jumped his horse out of its jog, was galloping ahead where the trail bent up between hills topped with rocks and spruce.

"He's really mad," Gabriel said to Riel; "you'll have to forgive him."

But Riel was listening to Marguerite; she had sat silent, the baby at her breast now, but he had felt her tense beside him.

"Ask him," Riel said to her, "you want to."

"What?" Gabriel bent across his saddle.

"It...it sounds so much," she began, glanced at him swiftly and then down at her sucking child, "like you want, almost war."

"In our North-West," Gabriel said slowly, "we've never had Indian wars, like in Montana, we've never needed them, but..." He glanced at Riel, and the memory of Red River was vivid as lightning to them both. "We've reached for guns before."

Marguerite would not lift her head; but Isbister, half-turned, saw the fear working in her face.

"Mrs. Riel, it's not just a few of us," he said gently. "That Ottawa government just *won't* do anything; they're all fumbled up with building their railroad, nothing but that railroad matters to them, and lots of settlers like Frank Oliver in his *Edmonton Bulletin* say if we can't get our rights the west will just have to pick up guns. That's all."

"Their railroad's complete?" asked Riel.

"Just on the prairie, yeah. We have to cross it," said Gabriel. "They've nailed it down right across."

"It's Red River all over," Riel said. The mounds of the hills so impervious, themselves only; and in his breast pocket the prayerbook with Bishop Bourget's letter folded inside, whose words he could read on the sky: "You have a mission which you must fulfil in every respect." Mission...it was there perhaps, now. The mission. Did he have the courage, the strength to face...? Out of the depths have we cried...land, abuse of human rights, and hunger–it was all 1869, but somehow–he could not seem quite to remember now for all these running years–he had felt so strong then; everything had been so clear, inevitable, so obvious what had to be done. What–the depths have we–time was needed, for the people to talk and say everything over again and again until they found their deepest, unknown, feelings. The land, titles–that was obvious, but what was beyond that? Did they care anything for a New Nation? For the call of God? Were they like Montana Métis, already hammered into the uncaring mud of drunkenness, dirt, prostitution, eat today what we can grab, who can think about tomorrow? Out of the depths O Lord have we cried—

The wagon jolted violently, the trotting horses veered too late to avoid a badger mound; Jean, leaning aside and watching the wheels spin against the ground, bounced, almost flew. Isbister grabbed his shirt as Marguerite lunged forward.

"Jean!" she gasped, "you can't lean...."

"That's okay," Isbister said. "We won't lose him."

The little boy was laughing, face streaked with dust and mouth open.

"There is a Territories Council," Riel said to Gabriel. "Who represents you?"

"He's appointed–Lawrence Clarke," Gabriel said in disgust. "Big Boss of the Company at Fort Carlton."

Donald Smith again: everything fit, everything fit, all standard Macdonald stupidities. My god, the instant he saw him he should have run and strangled him for the good of–dearest god by the rivers of Babylon there we sat down, we sat down and wept when we remembered....and then beyond Michel riding in the distance he saw a round hill between two others, curved against the sky, and he stared. When we remembered...the hill stood before him like a vision forming out of his prayer to be kept from hatred, somehow; and he sat so tense, held rigid, that after a time Marguerite's voice in his ear came softly, broke what he saw but in very gentleness nailed down its memory forever...remember O Lord, remember.

"Louis, is something...?"

Ouellette, Isbister, finally even little Jean turned, looked at him, as if fear had brushed them like a whiff from the wolf-willow blooming gold and silvered along the river's edge under the cottonwoods. But Gabriel was studying the hill ahead of them also.

"I thought," Riel said slowly, "I thought I saw...I want to stop at Fort Benton, the church please."

"It's seven hundred miles," Isbister began.

"Then an hour for another prayer means little."

Gabriel sat so silently motionless on his horse Riel suddenly felt happy. "Gabriel, would you come and pray with me," he said, "will you?"

The whitewashed walls of the little church shone greyly in the afternoon sunlight; the benches were raw wood. After a time Gabriel sat down hat in hand; waited. The worn soles of Riel's moccasins pointed downward at the altar in the corner of his eye, but he could not look there. He was still trying to understand what had happened to this man, this Master of Red River who had known what he was about and had run Macdonald to bay in Manitoba and been elected four times–oh, they had never let him near Parliament but he had powerful friends; he had scared the greatest in the land: he now had one patched suit, two boxes of clothes and some bedding for his wife and children, and nothing else. Except a leather case full of papers. He had been running, he had been sick; after fourteen years they could put everything in one wagon and still have room enough for three people. And not even decision; hesitation, almost fear, though he was clearly happy they had come. This man who should still be boss of Red River with land, cattle, a rich family...but there seemed nothing left of that. Isbister grunted by the evening fire, "What do we want with him, what can he do, he stutters, has nothing." And Moïse, glaring across the firelight, "What do you want for a leader, a grabber? Riel believes in us, he's lived himself sick and poor because he believes in us!" And Gabriel himself wondered, where is the man we rode all this way to find? Hesitant, surrounded by children, kneeling so small and worn.

The ways of God on earth are mysterious to us, and contradictory beyond our earthly knowledge; but rest content in faith, as I did: His ways are best. If Gabriel had not known Riel at Red River he would certainly have had more doubts than Isbister; if he had not been with him that June day in the small, mostly unused church at Fort Benton, Montana, almost everything they lived through together in the next year would not have happened. And why did it? I have asked myself. You have my word, I could not have made a song about it even had I been there, for I was never given songs out of misery; I could never make easily memorable old men and young men and children remorselessly killed. For in that church, as Gabriel sat turning his broad-brimmed hat slowly in his hands and not daring to look at Riel crouched in prayer—wondering indeed if he dared slip away quietly and wait with the others in the sunlight for prayers and priests were never much in his way of—what in god's name had ever nudged him to—suddenly he found himself on his feet, listening, hearing the man he had remembered all those years like a distant echo of confidence and power praying so pathetically,

"And all these years, Holy Spirit of God, you have led me through exile and exaltation and humiliation, again and again, alone and friendless, I need courage...I am afraid..."

It seemed gradually to Gabriel that there was nothing pathetic or even very personal about this prayer; he was apparently some steps nearer then, could see that Riel faced an altar—perhaps hastily cleared for this very occasion by some back-handed swipe that knocked the usual furniture clanging out of sight somewhere in a corner and left nothing but the faintly grey cloth draped crooked, the wall above it so blank any possible prayer would have to come from the invisible alone; arise from the self in such blank, wooden emptiness.

"...I have been ground into nothing, and now they would raise me again...of us who were carried away captive is required a song, they that wasted us say sing us one of the songs of...precious God whom I have loved and served and who has called me, the decisions, the pain, the hatred, the terrible hatred will come again, give me courage..."

Riel's head was hidden in his arms; he was doubled on his knees like a baby being born, a mound on that splintery floor.

And Gabriel was almost at his shoulder, stooping as though he would touch him, perhaps lift and hold him up again–or kneel with him too. And suddenly Riel's head moved, rose high; he clenched a small prayer book in his hands and his voice grew like a chant in the sounding church:

"If I forget thee, O Jerusalem, let my right hand forget her cunning. If I do not remember thee, let my tongue cleave to the roof of my mouth. O God my God, make me holy that I have the courage for glory, and for agony...for decision."

He was almost erect on his knees now, the prayer book held like a talisman or sword, high in both hands before his eyes, his voice like thunder:

"Remember O Lord the children of Babylon in the day of Jerusalem; who cried, Raze it, raze it to the ground! O daughter of Babylon, who will be destroyed; happy shall he be who rewards you as you have served us. Happy! Happy shall he be who takes your little ones and dashes them against the stones!"

The silence rang with that terrible cry. Riel's face streamed sweat, or tears, his body rigid like steel driven into rock; and yet it shifted into something else, almost softer, and his voice and expression were those of a penitent prostrate before a shrine: Gabriel found no strength in his legs, he had to kneel, he was kneeling with the ragged edge of altar-cloth a line across his eyes before he clenched them shut, heard Riel's resonant voice now quiet beside him.

"O most holy Lord Jesus, strengthen my faith. Help me to love my people according to your mercy, which is beautiful beyond measure. Amen."

And in that silence shivering still of hatred and mercy, Gabriel found his own rough voice. So strongly reduced from its usual size that he could not recognize it as his own, nor that the words moved farther than the strange, contradictory...saint?...he could not know for he had never met one, and the very notion rising in his head was like the words so strangely searching out something he had never prayed, he had been to confessional or given a thought to faith he could not remember when:

"Lord, strengthen my courage, my honour...."

And the words stopped there, though he felt them pushing up in him, demanding his voice but for a moment he could only remember Madeleine praying, like Riel her self completely committed as if she had hurled herself from a cliff, and he felt his muscled body like a cask holding him, a shell that rattled his "...faith," he could say then, and he knew longing like the ache for a woman to the very roots of himself; he had to move his shoulders, arms, and felt himself gigantically strong and small at the same time, as if he were nothing and everything at the very tips of his clasped fingers far away before an unreachable altar; he hurled himself:

"My courage, my honour, and my faith," he said aloud, "that I may profit all my life, from the blessing I have, received, in this holy place."

The two men kneeling side by side saw reflected in each other's eyes their own peculiar surrender, and wonder. The church glistened with it, to the splintery floor. Riel placed his hand on Gabriel's shoulder, stood up, and offered his other hand: Gabriel took it, and stood also. Then they were walking down the short aisle together, hearing their common footpads where their commitment surrounded them like a sounding echo, their minds blank with the wonder of it as Riel opened the door and they stepped out together, and beyond the horses and wagons and people patiently waiting for them they saw that hill again and in a glance knew they had both seen that revelation: a gallows there and a man swinging from that gallows. Vision and certainty. Though it might have been no more than a heat mirage bending a dead or stunted cottonwood up near the edge of the river, the wavering blackness a momentary crow perhaps struggling in a downdraft against the open sky, struggling upward.

When you see that, you know.

3

Gabriel's Army

"I yielded to Riel's judgement although I was convinced that, from a humane standpoint, mine was the better plan. But I had confidence in his faith, and his prayers, that God would listen to him."

— Gabriel Dumont, 1888

Y EARS later when Gabriel Dumont rebuilt his burned cabin above the South Saskatchewan, as large as he needed it for himself, he often remembered that long journey back from Montana and the summer that shaded into autumn and the talk, the talk. French or English, Riel magnificently tireless with talk. Briefly it had seemed then a miracle could perhaps blossom at long miserable last out of Macdonald's immovable Ottawa, but Gabriel knew, later, that the horses at the railroad had felt it truer than the people gathered at Fish Creek to greet them on July 1, 1884; he should have remembered the horses, not been so impressed with fifty or sixty wagons clumped above the ravine on the Widow Tourond's farm, waiting, leather-and-rags people, their gaunt faces expecting—he should have asked them what? An army marching with flags, a vision at the very least, and seeing—past the four men they had sent and a dark woman with children that looked very like their own—a bearded man in a worn wool suit too thick for prairie summer but with a bronzed, sharp face and quick eyes that laughed at recognized faces now so much older, so worn, that laughed or cried for very happiness when they saw him.

And the young people riding. No cross-breed stallions tip-toeing about like girdled ladies but riding: Napoléon Nault, André's son, on one of Gabriel's gambled greys that would certainly have been a buffalo runner but now would never have to learn to twist, pursue one animal through the bellow and dust of a running herd, never stand steady against the stench of blood and spilling guts. Or Patrice Tourond who when he was no more than ten stood beside me and heard that now unbelievable declaration in Fort Garry, Patrice breaking from his mother and her cluster of sons to circle the wagon twice at full gallop, now erect, now down at his horse's belly, to present Marguerite with a fistful of prairie flowers. Or Annie herself, gone in those later years, not quite like Madeleine or the days of the buffalo hunt and the all-night gambling and the races and the confident tension of something enemy perhaps riding just below the crest of that hill, but just gone; throwing her life away as if she had a thousand to scatter like flowers, his Annie so beautiful then in the first days of her young tangled love galloping between Napoléon and Patrice to present Riel with an immense saskatoon bough clustered thick with purple–royal indeed he was laughing!–berries. And tiny Jean picking, his solemn mouth purple while Riel laughed as they reached the flat above the ravine and the people shouted for happiness, though some cried at the memory of that December in Fort Garry. The disappointment of The Manitoba Act, the retreat to an empty land hoping for something better than the overwhelming whites that now at Red River hemmed them in against language, attitude, such impossibilities of majority rule that made old custom suddenly illegal; here French and English together might still make words against the divisiveness of both opportunists and Ottawa:

We the French and English natives of the North-West,

knowing that Louis Riel made a bargain with the Govern-
ment of Canada in 1870... have thought it advisable to send
to said Louis Riel and have his assistance to bring all mat-
ters... in a proper shape before the Government of Canada,
so that our just demands be granted....

If they only had Louis once again, and he was there at last, certainly. For there was no more retreat; the railroad had forever
destroyed any space west.

Gabriel remembered years later as he watched the sun fall
behind the hills still spruce-black across the river: the horses
with their ears pricked to the waving people and to cheers–endlessly swinging their heads at July flies, but not shivering, not
lunging sideways in some exploding terror neither Isbister at the
reins nor Moïse nor Michel riding beside them was prepared for.
The wagon would have tipped off the raw bank into the ditch
but for Riel leaping out with Jean in his arms, dust swirling.

"Down, Papa, down!" Jean cried.

"Quiet, it's—"

"The iron, see the iron!" The little boy scrambled up through
the dust, he was on the ties staring in amazement at the parallel
iron laid straight and level out of sight. As if he could already see
his truncated destiny there hovering over CPR steel and wire.

Marguerite still clung to the baby, braced rigid in the tilting
wagon; when Isbister and the riders had the horses controlled
the wagon was well back on the prairie again. They held the
horses tightly talking, talking; but heads jerked, feet sprang up
again and again as if the prairie under hoofs smoked. Gabriel
dismounted, talking too.

"Were they like that when you came?" Riel asked, standing
in the grass.

"No, nothing." Gabriel rubbed their foreheads gently, their
nostrils flaring red.

"What's the matter?" Riel asked.

Gabriel said nothing; he mounted his grey again and nudged it forward into the smooth, sloping ditch sheered out of the prairie but when the horse had minced across that and faced the higher grade, the steel rails almost level with its eyes, it stopped, shuddering. Gabriel had been speaking softly as you do when your horse hesitates in the dark and you accept what it alone can sense and try to take it through whatever that may be while wanting to avoid it too, if it's better avoided: I was riding home one night to White Horse Plains, and my horse suddenly stopped as if it had hit a wall. The frogs were loud as bells in the loops of the Assiniboine where the trail led through willows; I had ridden there a hundred times and now a balk barely half a mile from my house. I must have been feeling happy, singing so I gave the horse its head and it circled that copse and we came home through the back pasture, our cows standing up nervous as we sang past. I never knew why: all I know is that years later an Indian told me those willows grew on the place where Sioux arrows killed the Cree warrior and the beautiful Sioux woman he had won riding his white stallion; the horse betrayed them with its colour as they fled in the darkness. I knew the story but had never known the spot where the two lovers were killed together; and my horse, no white certainly but a dappled bay, balked there once in fifty years.

On the level above Gabriel tiny Jean stood between the rails, happily bending to throw one stone and then another; occasionally they pinged a small, solid sound of iron bolted to earth. But Gabriel's horse stood shuddering now, snoring as if deep in its lungs something rattled, held only by Gabriel's implacable hand. For a moment the five watchers thought he could force it, heave it off the scarred ground and over the track with one spring of its coiled body, but suddenly he relaxed; instantly the horse wheeled, in one leap was back on the prairie again.

"We'll have to try it somewhere else," was all Gabriel said.

The wagon and riders moved east parallel with the tracks,

Riel and Jean walking between them. Tired soon, the boy rode his father's shoulders and as the wagon and riders dipped, vanished for a moment behind a hill, the immensity of carving out and tying down this long double steel rested like rocks on Rids shoulders. The innumerable iron spikes, the plates on each tie, the bolts clenching the rails together; he could not fathom such numbers, the weight of people somewhere working to belt this over the North-West. A meadowlark sang on a telegraph pole with its two wires. The same monolith that could produce this must be moved for the North-West people: he felt so gaspingly small; it was impossible to walk either these cindered stones or axe-trimmed wood or the smooth narrow steel. Especially carrying a child. And there, beside this incredible human effort and the smell of grease and cinders (perhaps like brimstone, he thought suddenly) lay as it seemed unaffected prairie and sky, the sun hidden an instant by turreted clouds with their bottoms scraped flat against the earth. Untouchable, as if the buffalo still grazed here and the land were not yet white with their rotting skeletons, as if the giant grizzlies he had never seen but remembered from the hunting stories his father told about his father, north and west where the rivers broke through the mountains, the grizzlies still stalked the herds whenever they felt within their usually grass-filled recesses the terrifying urge for bloody meat. Dearest Saviour of the World, if he could only tear apart this incontrovertible steel!

It was almost noon before they found a spot where ditch and grade were no more noticeable than prairie: they piled rocks and dirt against the rails for the wagon wheels and when the fire they began had burned itself out against the cut they led the horses across blindfolded. Finally, black with ashes and dust, they were over. The horses seemed totally exhausted; the fifty-foot cut had taken them longer than the snow-swollen Milk River. Then at last they were moving slowly north again to find the trail, and they heard the far shriek of a coming train. The horses did not so much as shift an ear at that unbelievable sound. Only Jean said,

"What, Papa?"

Riel tousled the boy's hair and said nothing. Years later Gabriel remembered Riel's black curly hair bounding against his forehead; that and the deep shudder of his grey horse, dead then too, facing the railroad as if something in its very roots were being torn apart steadily, and very, very, slowly.

In his old age Gabriel felt still that physical shudder between his legs; he was mounted before the railroad still, cast there forever in the steel of his own will. Why had he not then understood that moment as premonition? I might have told him, but the sometime clairvoyance of the aged usually comes when it is of no earthly use to anyone, especially those still able to do things beyond understanding. In my lifetime I thought about "understanding" a great deal, about "moments" that are telling you the essence of things: I had a little longer than Gabriel to do so, though he had the wider river valley and the more dreadfully clear picture of our people destroyed to push him in his thought. During much of his own slow ending he refused to think altogether: he watched the clouds move across the sky, the light in patterns on the water where he had once worked his ferry, the rain drop square streaked blackness over one loop of the river while the sun shone brilliant in rainbows just beyond; if he thought of Riel then it was to remember the spire of St. Anthony's pointing out of the gnarled poplars where the Saskatchewan far below bent left through rapids and then north again like a silver arm crooked around Batoche; and the roof of the rectory beside the church unpainted, as Major General Middleton would notice less than a year later. It was the jagged memory of Middleton everywhere that made Gabriel avoid those thoughts; he would hate forever that English soldier who had destroyed the memory of so many places along the river for him. Or Charles Nolin: he should have shot the bastard the day he arrived from Manitoba, just ridden over when Patrice Tourond told him, shot him and thrown him and his endless government money into the river; Crozier could never have proved anything. But our Charles had come, all big smile and papers carefully written in English, built the biggest house in the settlement complete with carved white posts on a veranda, always a government contract–interpreter, justice of the peace, telegraph poles, spy–to furnish it and make people envy him until he could ride out dressed in white like a trader for parade and welcome his dear cousin, invite him to stay in his house, there were plenty of beds of course they would be staying at his house there was more than enough room. And Riel said, "Thank you, Charles. Marguerite and the children will be grateful."

Riel who was forced all his life to depend on his acquaintances for a bed to sleep in, for food to put in his mouth, for money to get away from his enemies–that too Gabriel understood only later when he had travelled the world. It was always the way of our people that as long as one of us had something to eat, we all ate; in Montana, Riel did not ask Gabriel what or if he would be paid. In Batoche his family ate and slept with whatever family invited them and it was Louis Schmidt who first gave him another suit. Not quite new, but better than what he wore. Gabriel had not thought of clothes in Fort Benton and there were none between the Missouri and Prince Albert where Schmidt now worked.

"It's for the government," he said, turning his hat in his hand. The crowd waiting to hear Riel speak spread far across the hollow trail that was Batoche's main street. "The land office. I got temporary leave but I want to quit, I want to work for you again."

"No," Riel said, "not yet. You work in Prince Albert, faithfully, and write for the papers about what we're doing. We have to reach public opinion."

"*The Prince Albert Times* is just so Conservative it—"

"This has to be heard about. If not the *Times* then some paper in Winnipeg, or Edmonton. I need you to report."

Young William Henry Jackson, organizer of the Settlers' Union had finished his welcome speech, "...freedom of the people of the North-West!", and James Isbister was shaking his hand to applause. Gabriel saw old men who understood no English clapping as loudly as anyone. Then Charles Nolin waving from the centre of his veranda, shouting first in French, then in English, "...and now the man who has come home from Montana, the founder of Manitoba, who will speak for us to the Government of Canada, the man we love, Louis Riel!"

The crowd burst into cheers, Gabriel himself roaring as Nolin shook Riel's hand in the shade of the roof and Riel stepped forward, raised both his hands open-palmed to the crowd. For a moment he stood, arms wide against the white post, the welcome of his people washing over him in the hot, bright sun. And as Gabriel looked about at the peoples' response, suddenly over their cheering heads he saw two white helmets. Unmistakable! And he was moving towards them: Lief Crozier, now stationed at Battleford as Senior Superintendent of the North-West Mounted Police and, it was rumoured, soon to be Commissioner in Regina, smiled his easy Irish smile beside the inevitable, expressionless constable. Did they hire them all for that, or make a plaster mold of them in training?

"Quite a return for your friend," Crozier said, and the thin edge of his next words made Gabriel lose forever Riel's first public words to our people on the Saskatchewan, "from exile."

Temper leaped in Gabriel, almost burst, but instantly he held it; on Poundmaker's Reserve just two weeks before Crozier had arrested Kah-wee-chet-way-mot from among five hundred of Big Bear's and Little Pine's and Poundmaker's warriors riding circles around him on the slopes of Cutknife Hill and singing their war songs, an arrest made without a shot, using nothing but eighty motionless men and unbelievable nerve. That confidence in himself haloed Crozier, like his immaculate uniform; when it became necessary to touch this man, Gabriel knew he would need something harder than Saskatchewan dust or temper.

"...the coming of your messengers to me was a blessing amongst the blessings of my fortieth year. I thank you, it is one of the gratifications of my life...."

Crozier listened intently to Riel repeat himself in English, that tiny lift of his lip-corners remaining. Gabriel said, easily,

"I am still chief here. We asked him to come, all French and English, to be our political advisor."

"Oh." Then, "There's nothing illegal in that, I'm sure."

"...though I am a son of the North-West, I know also that I and my family are your guests; though a most respectable body of men signed your invitation to me, I must urge you again that neither I nor anyone can accomplish anything unless we all stand together, unless we speak with one voice too loud to be...."

"Whatever he did," Gabriel said, "if he did anything, he served fourteen years for it. That's enough."

Crozier looked at him then; in the crowd cheering Riel's every word, they might have been blocks of stone.

"...by petitioning the Government with you," Riel shouted, "perhaps we will all obtain our just rights, and then I can return to Montana again, to my home there, in early fall. For our people are there also who...."

Crozier's glance shifted over Gabriel's shoulder, past the constable; as if he looked over the roofs of the houses, the poplars, past the spruce and pine of the west bank of the South Saskatchewan to Fort Carlton beside the North Saskatchewan, its walls too close to the valley hills to have been any possible defence even before rifles. The police committed so long to that Hudson's Bay place in that lovely valley tight as a picture drawn in the palm of his hand; Gabriel had to grin at Crozier, he very nearly laughed aloud. To warm Lawrence Clarke's ass there!

"That's interesting," Crozier said. "Fall."

"If he *wants* to," Gabriel said, and his rage flared like fire. "No army's gonna chase him away from us, not again."

Two priests had stood at one edge of the crowd, watching expressionlessly as priests do; we never had any Métis priests and so, like the police, they are always above things, but they can also fold their hands across their crosses and inside their sleeves. Riel saw one clapping now, the taller one, and when they came through the press he knew that the tall one, who must be Fourmond, did not matter at all.

"Lovely, lovely," said Fourmond, pumping his hand. "The people have needed a leader, Gabriel is good, oh, very good, but he cannot read, his—"

"I was very happy," squarish Father André interrupted quietly, "for your moderation, your call for unity and peaceful pressure. There has been too much careless talk already of force to gain our rights."

Riel was smiling, reaching for his strong hand, broad and calloused as he remembered Ritchot's long ago; perhaps here too—"I am no longer twenty-six, Father," he said. "Nor is this Red River." Perhaps. O let it please God, this bearded stolid Breton priest.

All that long, hot summer Gabriel watched Riel work to build the agreement he himself had already built among the Métis but could never have achieved with the English. On July 8 the Métis leaders gathered in Nolin's house at Batoche, on July 11 they drove to Lindsay School at Red Deer Hill and met three hundred members of William Jackson's Settlers' Union; on July 19, after being invited twice and receiving a written invitation signed by eighty-four townspeople, they met with seven hundred in Prince Albert. Whether in French or English, Riel said the same things: he stood for peace, they must have free title for their land, the districts of the North-West must be made independent provinces, and the land laws must be amended to encourage settlement. And it was in Prince Albert that he first mentioned the Indians. Big Bear's thirst dance and council at Poundmaker's had been broken by Crozier's stunning arrest, but they were now gathering near Fort Carlton: all the northern bands including Star Blanket, Big Child, Beardy, Broken Arrow, John Smith and it was rumoured, Gabriel told Riel as they whirled along on the wagon, that Big Bear was coming to speak, the only Plains Cree chief who had refused to sign treaty until the buffalo were gone, and who still refused to accept a reserve. He was the only unbent Plains Cree left, and he had a band of over three hundred warriors they said were as unbendable as he. It was in Treston Hall, Prince Albert, that Riel declared the Indian nations had been robbed of their living by the advance of white civilization; and that they, like the half-breeds who could not compete in the white world, must be compensated by the federal Government; that rotten flour and salt pork and rocky land were *not* compensation; that begging from their white neighbours, who often had nothing themselves, was *not* the proper rights and privileges due every human being who lived under the British Crown with such a motto as "God and my Right." The hall rang with clapping, and Gabriel had the satisfaction of getting a hand on Richard Deacon who suddenly stood up in the middle of the crowd, waving his fist and yelling that Riel was nothing but a killer, that he personally had marched to Red River in '70 with Wolseley to—and heaving him bodily out the door. There were plenty to help him, so many in fact that it was easier to grab hands than the captain, and as that plump cursing body was hoisted from the hall steps into the tall weeds they could see in the long, slanting northern evening, Gabriel wished suddenly he were young and sitting in the circle of an Indian fire, smoking, the smooth invitation of a leather-skirted thigh already waiting for him. This endless repetition; they were so much worse than Indians, who would talk even longer but at least knew what they wanted and mostly talked to find out if they had the nerve to try getting it. Whites never

knew anything, not even what they wanted–unless it was something for nothing, and then they were sure.

The sun was a prickly line of red over the spruce on the
north shore, the bellies of the clouds over him faintly orange,
bulging. Sometimes he let Patrice drive Riel about; always there
were Charles Nolin and Will Jackson "discussing strategy," as
Nolin called it. How would this sound to Protestants? To
farmers? To storekeepers? Would Dewdney get mad at this?
What had that policeman been asking about near St. Catherine's
School? Would Lawrence Clarke support them if they said it this
way? How many white signatures could Jackson get if they said
that? And Riel listened, tirelessly, though sometimes he studied
the dust rising from the trail to the spinning wheels and it
seemed to Gabriel he was not listening at all; praying perhaps,
or searching far away in some land where only his soul could
walk for something that he had not yet found though the circle
where it might be, if it existed at all, was growing smaller and
smaller, and then suddenly he would say a word. Gabriel had
no such patience, had no wish to have it; sometimes he took a
quick run ahead on his grey, studied the willows where they hid
sloughs squawking with ducks and ducklings and sometimes
caught himself thinking that somewhere, someday, he would
again surprise a buffalo, a bull too old to follow the herd, and
mean, he wanted to feel the muscles in his neck and haunches
strain again, tear something apart once more before he died of
painful age, some old bull with a good tongue and blood and
hide not too bad, maybe even some meat edible if boiled long
enough. But the known thud of the running horse would drum
him into his forty-six years, he hadn't seen so much as a stray
buffalo east of the rivers since he was forty and the last small
herd three hundred miles south-west, where Big Bear and his
Cree had kept them at the Forks of the Red Deer and South
Saskatchewan the winter before Dewdney came. 1879. When
half the people of Batoche wintered on the plains for the last

time, and when Big Bear had sent tobacco to him—come, smoke with me in my lodge, and when he got there, he found Crowfoot of the Blackfeet and Sitting Bull of the Sioux sitting across the fire from Big Bear, all smoking already. Talking: chase the police off, take land for people from the mountains to the Souris River, from the Medicine Line to the North Saskatchewan or maybe the Beaver, where not a white will ever dare set foot unless invited. Big Bear's talk; with whom Gabriel had once quarreled in that time gone now forever like a stone falling into a river, when there were still buffalo to quarrel over.

They had not met again since that winter day, but the memory of it was in their faces when Big Bear rode into Prince Albert from his Carlton councils on August 10 and they greeted each other in Jackson's house. In five years Big Bear had hardly changed appearance; but Gabriel thought the muscles of his giant chest seemed wasted, his face peaked as if he had been peering too long into some endless distance where he could never quite see what he was looking for. But the chief smiled, drew his finger with its huge moonless nail across his opened mouth.

"I still have teeth," Big Bear said, his voice too deep for the room and Gabriel smiled a little; knowing that in the summer of the Indian treaties a dying badger had told him he would not die until his teeth were worn to his gums.

"The railroad will wear everything down," Gabriel answered. "Hard as it would have been then, it was still easier then than now with the railroad."

And Big Bear nodded. Riel looked from one to the other, understanding the words but not their meaning; Jackson, understanding neither, brought tea, gestured for them to sit down.

Father André later offered them no tea; his rectory in Prince Albert was as bare as the log hut at St. Laurent where Gabriel had first met him almost twenty years before, but the square beard that covered his lower face was almost grey now, his brown eyes so piercingly intent on Riel that Gabriel could not understand what he meant. Nor Riel, pleading in a voice Gabriel had not yet heard that summer,

"But Father, we need the support of the Church; our people need you..." he gestured; it was so self-evident.

"And I have promised you," André replied in his church voice, "and I have so instructed the priests of the district, we do not interfere with your activities as long as you remain peaceable, you work within the constitution."

"'Interfere'? We want your support!"

"What do you mean?"

"What do I...?" Riel looked at Gabriel; neither of them could quite believe it. "I mean," he said quietly then, "support, like when you helped Gabriel set up the St. Laurent council, like when you petitioned Macdonald in 1879 and again in '82, '83. I mean that you declare publicly and to all officials our cause is your cause because we are in the right."

"I cannot," said André heavily. "Not if you continue to encourage the Indians in their demands."

"What!"

"You met Big Bear, here in Prince Albert?"

"That's no secret, we haven't tried to hide—"

"Don't you know his reputation?"

"Yes," Gabriel said very loudly. "That he's the head and soul of the plains Indians because for ten years he's said the whites robbed them with those fast treaties."

André sighed, his stocky body shrinking a little inside its wide soutane. "I know, Gabriel, I know, but his warriors are wild, no chief can control them. You of all people know that once Indian warriors start, how terrible...all the white women, children, scattered on farms in the bush."

Gabriel's mouth hung open. This squarish face hunched together in – this was not the man who had once lifted his hand high to the cheering people on the steps of the St. Laurent

Church, whispering in his ear, "God be praised Gabriel, we will build community here, community!"

"The Indians are our brothers," Riel said thin and quiet. "They are starving on those useless reserves."

"I have given them the food off my plate," cried André, "the clo—"

"They don't want the food off your plate!" said Riel. "Can priests no longer understand a simple human right?"

"Once they begin," André said more calmly, "Indians cannot be controlled; an Indian war—"

"And the Church of course must control everything," said Riel. It was early afternoon but the light in the small room was turning grey, almost sinister. "Dear children, be obedient. Be simple and content with anything on earth, because God will give you perfect happiness in heaven. If the Company pays you ten cents for a ratskin and later sells it for a dollar, don't complain. Your reward is in heaven. When speculators get you drunk and take your land scrip for ten dollars, don't beat them up when you're sober. Vengeance is mine, I will repay says the Lord, perhaps on earth but more likely in hell, that's where I'll really repay those with their bellies so tight full on earth every day. I've heard all that Father, and I hate it."

"I'm a fighter too! But you cannot mix religion and politics, you cannot—"

"But Lawrence Clarke can mix business and politics, of course?"

"What?"

"If we are whole people, we mix everything we are. How can anyone pray in your church if he has nothing to eat when he gets home? You do not believe, do you, in the mission of the French Métis.

"The mission of all believers is to serve God and do His will."

"And our people could serve God here in a way that–you

and Gabriel started it when there were no eastern laws to mess you up, we could serve God here in a way that would be a miracle...." Riel stopped, his face almost radiant in the noon darkness of the tiny room, his hand in his breast pocket, fumbling. "Where is your christly daring? Can't you believe in the North-West mission of the French Métis, a mission to create a paradise they will by the grace of God complete in every respect!"

He had the worn prayerbook with its frayed letter closed within both his hands before his eyes, as if he prayed. But in a moment he faced André again, his eyes hard as diamonds shining while the wind rattled the house in long, shuddering gusts. Rain dashed over the roof again, and again.

"I love the Church, it has given me salvation," Riel said slowly. "Wherever I ran in my years of exile I found the Church and in it there was peace, rest; the Mass gave me strength to believe I was still a human being, worthy in the sight of God. In the Church I have seen visions of God sweeter than the flesh of Jesus on my tongue after confession. And when you priests went with our people on the hunts, prayed and starved with them when they faced no water and the Sioux and no buffalo, you were God's good love to us. We are in great need now, much greater than when a herd over the next ridge could save us. If you have nothing to do or say now but 'Obedience, quiet obedience,'" he shrugged suddenly. "What good is the pope, vicar of God, if he doesn't know we exist?"

Gabriel knew. Father André was profoundly wrong; he was trying to reason through Riel's words when he should have heard their emotion. Riel was hard to face. Without benefit of ordination he lived a harder, holier, life than any priest. And having been near him all summer, sometimes Gabriel himself felt a nudging – what was it – Riel could not be confronted physically and overcome – he had first felt it when he knelt with Riel – he sometimes could not explain to himself how he had come to be kneeling there; he had sat turning his sweaty hat – why had he gone into that church – it was the tree on the hill; and the strangeness of this man moving him towards a possible happiness. Yes, he thought, watching the wordless André while the rain drummed roof and window, a possible happiness so great he was suddenly afraid.

"If you mix everything together," André said abruptly, ponderously, "our political situation, the whites, settlers, your mission, and the 'mission' of the French Métis, as you claim, and the Indians, then you must be m—"

The priest stopped himself; Riel ignored the word he had been about to use as judgement.

"You do not believe in the Archbishop of Montreal?"

"I have as much faith in Monseigneur Bourget as you," said André, "but his general blessing cannot give you licence to threaten the country with Indian war."

"Unlike you," Riel said, and then he added, "Father," in a long, Montana drawl, "both Gabriel and I are also Indian. Now, we must be quite clear: I have been called, and the people of my blood have called me in turn. We want your help, but if you cannot understand that, then we cannot worry about it any longer, can we?"

Slowly André straightened in his chair; his large hands rose, crossed together over the brass-and-wood cross hanging at his waist, found the wide sleeves of his soutane, vanished. A black, upright figure.

Lieutenant-Governor Edgar Dewdney could reach Ottawa from Regina by railroad via Winnipeg and St. Paul and Chicago and Toronto in four gritty days and nights but despite that, and the telegraph lines strung five years before to Carlton, Prince Albert, Battleford, and Edmonton, the Saskatchewan country remained as far from Ottawa as our Red River had been. For Sir John A. Macdonald, now very aged, still roosted there, and that without benefit of any strong Quebec lieutenant.

"Haven't you got a French-speaking assistant?" Sir John leaned back in his leather chair and swallowed his favourite afternoon drink; and another. "Anyone?"

"Of course." Dewdney had an English engineer's accent he would never lose. "Amédée Forget; he's perfectly reliable."

"Well send him up there then, look around, take two weeks, three, tell them we're looking into it. You're doing that with the Indians already, eh?"

"Yes. Hayter Reed has gone up—"

"Good. I'm suddenly getting these personal letters not just from Clarke at Carlton but even from Crozier – he's supposed to be very level-headed?"

"Outstanding. He'd make a better commissioner than Irvine; at least he'd know which way to vote."

"Aha." Macdonald drained the second glass. "That's always important, yes; it you don't know how to vote, you soon won't recognize the door to your own bedroom!"

Dewdney laughed but Colonel John Dennis, now the Deputy Minister of the Interior, did not so much as chuckle. He noisily shifted papers, the thick file of petitions from the North-West he had inherited in 1878 from his Mackenzie cabinet counterparts, to which he had been adding every year. Macdonald's slightly clouded eye caught his, winked.

"Crozier says, and I quote – correct me, John – 'Do not in any case be too economical with the Indians all at once, for such a policy will be far the most expensive in the end; and there's only one other policy, that is to fight them, by doing so, the country could no doubt get rid of all troublesome Indian questions in a comparatively short time' – right?"

"Substantially, sir." Dennis did not raise his head.

"Our police officers," said Macdonald, "operate by sarcasm now?"

"Crozier's an excellent man, but, perhaps impulsive," ventured Dewdney. "Lawrence Clarke eggs him on at Carlton and maybe he now thinks Reed's investigation—"

"I understand," Dennis interrupted sardonically, "Crozier had just outfaced five hundred Cree warriors on a bad hill and perhaps he feels another Reed report isn't quite enough."

"He could hardly leave the North-West," Dewdney bit back, "disguised, like some, as a squaw."

"That libel," Dennis began, but Macdonald interrupted,

"Now now." He tilted himself away from Dennis' furious face toward the decanter. "We do what we have to do. I'm sure you've got it under control, Edgar, and if he's good – let it ride. Now Riel, he's getting lots of publicity, lots of followers?"

"Yes," Dewdney had swallowed some of his anger. "And the Liberal papers love him."

"Of course, of course. Isn't the *Prince Albert Times* one of ours?"

"It was, but in May it talked of armed rebellion, and it's supported Riel, more or less, since he came."

"Well put a little in that pot then; a newspaper always needs something. And Charles Nolin, don't you need another batch of telegraph poles, timber, maybe something he can organize, good for the country, good for him? Don't you need translators? If there's one or two of those young hot-bloods that can write, get them into Indian Affairs. And your North-West Council, you should have a half-breed on it."

"I do," said Dewdney. "Pascal Breland."

"He never supported Riel at Red River," Dennis said. "Pierre Falcon made a verse about him the Métis sang, it called him a 'cochon.'"

"Well?" Macdonald demanded.

"A very small pig."

Macdonald's head and hand might be shaky, and he forgot about petitions, but as long as he lived the Prime Minister would

245

smell a political blemish. Dewdney caught his look and said slowly,

"That's true. The Brelands have traded in Cypress Hills for fifteen years, Pascal hasn't much influence with the Saskatchewan people."

"Has he ever introduced a motion?"

"While I've chaired the..." Dewdney hesitated. "I can't really remember."

"When you send Forget up there," Macdonald poured himself another shot, "have him sound Riel about a seat on Council."

"Riel on my Council!"

Under Macdonald's guffaw Dennis almost hid his laughter, but he wasn't at all amused. He was trying to put the words together while Macdonald gestured.

"Just to give him a position and a thousand a year; he has nothing. You can always handle his talk."

"Easier said here than in Regina," Dewdney muttered into his mutton chops.

"Their problems are really very basic." Dennis hefted the petition file at Macdonald. "Sir, we've been collecting this since 1873, when Gabriel Dumont and that priest formed the St. Laurent council. In eleven years surely something straightforward, to meet their just demands—"

"No man," Macdonald reached wearily for the stack of budget files, "will ever thank you for giving him his just demands. Or even vote for you, as you would know if you had to try and get elected every four years. No, a good crop, an early winter with the roads closed, we're all right till spring. They won't fight, it would just be messy."

"The question is, sir, why should they have to want to fight?"

Macdonald shifted his heavy eyebrows. "Edgar will handle it," was all his growl admitted, and Dennis knew he had gone one, perhaps two sentences too far.

Gabriel of course did not know how John Dennis, whom he

had once very nearly thrown out of McDougall's sled onto his ass in the snow, was speaking for our Saskatchewan people. He let Patrice Tourond do all the driving now: it gave that young man something to do besides staring after Napoléon Nault and Annie, and he needed whatever money the ferry brought for himself; despite saskatoons like clustered grapes (too bad we're not birds, Madeleine said) it was going to be a hard winter. His crop was so drought-eaten it would not be enough for his hunters, let alone his ferry horses. He watched, and listened. He heard Isbister tell Riel that the white settlers thought he was too moderate, too slow in his demands for them; that Clarke had the Protestants worried about the priests now doing their damnedest to break up the agreement between French and English. Gabriel stacked his oats, nothing but dry feed, along his field by the trail and the travellers there asked him how they could get even two cows through the winter when their crops were poorer than his. Use whatever money you've got, he said swinging his pitchfork steadily, buy bullets for hunting. He smiled when he watched the jewelled mitre of Bishop Vital-Justin Grandin of St. Albert bend again and again over the bell at St. Anthony's Church above Batoche, the Latin blessing drifting in incense past the people bowed under a September sky pale blue as river ice; and Riel loomed at the edge of the crowd waiting to tell the Bishop about his priests, who spoke so much about authority, so little about justice; for Michel Dumas had just told Gabriel that M. Amédée Forget, travelling in the Bishop's party, had offered him, person-ally, a job with the Indian Department. Three hundred a year.

"To do what?" Gabriel said from the side of his mouth. "Spoon out flour full of mouse shit?"

"Nothing big like that," Michel said, very sober. "I'm just a has-been hunter."

"Yeah, but you can really pick off gophers."

"Didn't I tell you?" Michel whispered, "I met a big bunch of gophers packed up and going south so I asked what was up and they said it's just too tough in Saskatchewan. They're all heading for the States."

The Bishop's incomprehensible prayer drifted over the valley willows and trees almost blotchy, yellow with autumn; the tactics were always the same, whether he talked about Red River or the Indians' treaties or here: divide them, offer them crumbs. Gabriel was hunting alone in the Minetchinass Hills east of One Arrow's reserve when he thought of that, and of Riel laughing aloud in the Bishop's face when Forget said perhaps a seat on the Territorial Council could be arranged. Laughed in Grandin's face! If that had been said to him, he would have thrown that dapper French-Canadian sell-out to the Conservatives out the window, not ignored him and laughed in the Bishop's face. And yet...he nudged his horse, the whole north slope of the hills motionless, that very laughter when Grandin had just agreed to help found a national Métis association and even suggested St. Joseph as patron saint, that telling Grandin that for an American citizen, as he was, to sit on the North-West Council would have questionable legality – legality, by god Gabriel had been ready to roar pay-off – the laughter while Grandin's plump face curdled red; that controlled devastation of that slick Forget, who sure as hell would become governor after Dewdney, or like Schultz ride his hatred of Riel all the way into the Senate: he was messing his mind, thinking of them. He snuffed the dry, cold air; he needed a clean deer loafing through the trees, now almost striped of yellow leaves. But he found none, as he had not the day before, and that night he rode into One Arrow's camp and shared the old chief's small meal of coyote thigh. Coyote wasn't so bad, if you smoked enough.

"Our crops are nothing," he said when the pipe was nearly empty. "We will be hungry too. I am saying to people, use all the money you have now to buy bullets."

"If there are no animals," One Arrow said, "what is the good of bullets?"

"One can never be certain," Gabriel contemplated the small fire; smoke rose through the lodge like a delicate, wavering tree – "when one will find something good to hunt."

September 24. St. Anthony's was packed with our people. Father André celebrated mass and preached the sermon at the founding celebration of the Métis Union of St. Joseph. Gabriel listened, heard Father Fourmond sing the canticle he had composed for the occasion, a canticle no one would ever sing after him; he was Breton priest, like most of the Oblates, and his honest enough enthusiasm could never reach the heart of our people as I did with my silly songs. If nothing else you need a simple tune, and a few lines any fool can remember. Then Riel addressed them from the steps of the church, not the pulpit, and Gabriel knew here was what they had really come to hear, as he had. There was nothing about temperance in Riel's mouth, nothing of humility as the eternally blessed St. Joseph had meekly lived to the last breath of his life: Riel acclaimed the Pope, the bishops, the priests sun-blinded on the porch beside him, her majesty Queen Victoria, but the greatest cheer rolled across the last gold and orange of the valley when he cried,

"Our patron is St. Joseph; today we are established as a Nation!"

Innocent Fourmond cheered, but André flinched. Charles Nolin stood in the crowd as black-faced as a rock; the day before Riel had moved his family into Moïse Ouellette's small house.

Fall hunting was no better in the sandy hills south-east; in October he rode that way with young Napoléon Nault and alternating set and riding circle, they scoured the country. After a week they gave up and rode into White Cap's camp on the Sioux reserve. His shacks and patched canvas lodges were down in the shelter of a creek valley where the tops of the tall trees soughed in wind running high above over the prairie.

"We do not have even the miserable blanket of a treaty," White Cap said. "'You Sioux have no claim on us,' they say once or twice a year, that is, whenever we ask them for food. Even though our people always hunted north into what they now call call Canada," The old chief paused, chuckled a little, his mouth black with broken teeth. "That is, whenever your Red River hunters would let us!"

Gabriel answered carefully; it was a long time since he had talked this language and Napoléon squatting across the fire could do nothing but watch faces. "At least they did give you land, not like Sitting Bull whose men now are getting shot year by year in Dakota. And they will shoot him too, when they find a good excuse."

"True," said White Cap, thoughtfully. "Though it is always better that a man die properly, better than that he starve."

Next day the sky was leaden; as they rode home trailing their packless horses, Gabriel could already see the streaks of snow caught under the gnarled trees and in the gutted, sheer grey cliffs below them and across the river. Young Napoléon rode beside him, pretty well considering he had hardly been on a horse before he came to Batoche the summer before; there probably was more to him than the scribbling meeting organizer; there was doubtless some sense to Annie tottering between him and Patrice.

"I'd never have thought he was saying that," Napoléon said suddenly. "He looked so cheerful."

"He still thinks Indian," Gabriel said. "They believe in places, times. I've seen them ride into a fight singing, 'This is a good day to die.' There are things a man has to do, and when you know that why shouldn't you be really happy about it?"

"When you were with them like that, did you have to do things too?"

"O yeah. Yeah."

"Did you ever have to kill a man?"

Gabriel laughed so loud the pack horses almost spooked. "You always ask that, every kid that grows up behind a school desk, always." He stopped. Napoléon was looking at him, swaying easily in the rhythm of his horse, saying nothing.

"Yeah," he said slowly, feeling suddenly he wanted to explain to this youth how things had been, how they might still be. "Yeah, you have to do things, sometimes, when you start them they're just what you've done all the time and then somewhere they turn you don't notice where, and...I wasn't that much older than you now, south near the Forks with the Plains Cree, that's really Blood country and six or seven of our tents were with them and one day when I was out scouting for buffalo the Cree decide to raid the Bloods they've found coming north up the Belly and when I come in that night they're already dancing and one of them's taken my buffalo runner. That's the best horse in the camp—"

"They just took it?" Napoléon was incredulous.

"They considered us one camp, and when they ride to fight, anyone who doesn't want to ride will lend the other their horses. They always want the best in case they have to leave fast."

"Had they asked you whether you—"

"No! And that's why I was mad, they hadn't even waited to ask me whether I wanted to, so I went to the dance and sat at the back among the women and toward morning when they were all about hot enough to go, I yelled and jumped into their circle and started telling them. They were all sweaty and painted, wild as stampeding buffalo, but I told them how warriors were scared of me, how I could ride and shoot, the bragging that's necessary for Indians, and I wouldn't accept the offense they had offered me by taking my runner. So the raid leader got up and explained everything but I was still mad, I was such a hot-head, and all night them bragging and dancing and me quiet among the women hadn't helped, I said I was going out to show them some fighting if that's what they wanted. Sweet Moses," Gabriel paused, laughed a little. "I could boil for days, then."

"So you rode with them?"

"All us Dumonts were hot-heads, especially my oldest uncle, Gabriel. They knew us, you mess around with a Dumont you'll get back more than you gave. When we met those Bloods they all stopped, then two of them trotted towards us and I was still mad, I give a yell and charged them. The two split, riding back hammering their horses but I picked one and my runner was so fast I was near him in a minute and fired from the hip, just like I was running a buffalo and he went flying in front of me my horse almost threw me trying not to trip over him. I caught his horse and rode back to the Crees singing for me, and when I got back where that Blood was still lying I saw he was dead."

"Jesus," Napoléon said.

"He was just young, younger than me, and he'd done nothing to me. I'd never seen him before. He wore a little bunch of hair on a string around his neck, I don't know what it meant to him but I keep remembering that, and...funny." Gabriel stopped; the strangeness of what had happened twenty-five years before on the Belly River welled again in him, making him suddenly explain to this educated young man who had come from Red River to follow Riel and had entered his house mostly because of his daughter and was now staring at him as if he too wanted to become a bloody Dumont, riding the prairie like any thunderstorm, the long line of sky and land drawn out of the red sunrise and the black herd snuffling, heaving up one by one until the whole earth had bumbled up black outlined in hairy red, if only that were left sweetest sweetest Jesus....

"What was that?" Napoléon asked. Gently through the saddles creaking.

If only. To see this earth sown black with living meat again, he would gladly walk to Ottawa on his knees.

"I, I was really mad then," he said aloud. "But mad...different. They lived their life, okay, but they'd pushed me so I had to do what they did and I liked them too, and so I, I rode straight back to the Cree who'd taken my horse, right up close his eyes bulged but he didn't dare move and I said, 'Here next time you want something, just look for me,' and I cut the reins of that Blood's horse right across his war paint so hard his face bust open –squitch!–and I rode away."

When they arrived home next day they found the river frozen almost thick enough to carry horses, and snow clouds moving over steadily. Soon Patrice was driving Riel and Will Jackson from Prince Albert to Halcro to Fort à la Corne to Saskatoon in a covered sleigh, and finally in December the petition was ready, both the Settlers' Union and the Métis Union of St. Joseph had approved it, so the united executive committee could finally meet at Batoche for signing. Jackson was everywhere; he declared the covering letter Riel had written set an excellent, bold tone:

> You will perceive that the petition is an extremely moderate one, I may say in fact that to the Canadian and English wings of the movement a more searching exposition of the situation would have been much more satisfactory. The opinion has been freely expressed that our appeal should be directed to the Privy Council of England and to the general public rather than to the federal authorities since...all our previous petitions would appear to have gone astray....

"That will stick them!" Jackson said, signing the letter with a flourish, "right where it stings most."

He and Andrew Spence, as secretary and chairman of the executive committee, then signed the petition; Father Fourmond stood watching, glowing with enthusiasm; and young Napoléon Nault, James Isbister and Albert Monkman looked on confidently but Charles Nolin was glum, saying nothing. Maxime Lépine, Michel Dumas and Moïse Ouellette stood with Gabriel at the back of the room, wordless and motionless as our people always are before the mystery of words written. I have seen them stare at my written words of verdict in court as at a talisman, a numinous stone. Riel sat at the head of the table. For some reason he had brought Jean with him to the meeting; he had never done so, even when they still lived at Batoche with Nolin, and the little boy absolutely quiet sat in his lap endlessly crossing over, back and forth, the thin tails of the bow tie that hung below Riel's heavy beard. Nothing, not even the pounding of Jackson's fist as he ceremonially sealed the envelope, could jar the boy from his singular motion, as if his small body were humming somewhere under his breath; nor Riel from his untouchable, staring preoccupation. But Jackson seemed not to notice. He offered the envelope to Father Fourmond, who blessed it, then Patrice Tourond stepped forward, accepted it, thrust it inside his coat as he ran out the door. The hoof-beats of his horse faded quickly: he would catch the mail at the Humboldt telegraph station.

That's that, Gabriel thought; finally. Now we can wait. Except for Jackson chattering to Spence in English, the room was silent; little Jean was humming something, yes, he could almost hear it, that small childish tune. Riel is somewhere already, Gabriel thought, far ahead of us. Waiting already.

The silence that winter lay like a thin, impenetrable sheet of cold over the Saskatchewan country. When Riel walked, as he did every morning, above Batoche the wood smoke from the houses stood between the bare poplars, the green-black spruce against the sullen sky; sometimes the far cliffs of the river vanished in grey, or glistened as if the depthless air set upright on edge like dull, almost transparent paper were sprayed misty silver. Dogs barked somewhere, ravens perched on black branches, calling; the snow was hard and granular as driven rock. Nothing but his shadow came near him as he walked. Except Gabriel, once, late in February when the sun cut them in pitiless white silence.

"An Italian writer," Riel said, "once wrote the pit of hell was a lake of ice, not fire. The Devil sits there frozen in a lake of ice."

Gabriel laughed a little, white puffing out of his long rimed beard. "He musta heard of Saskatchewan."

"The priests made it hot for him, changing things like that."

Gabriel's laughter rolled across the valley. "Hell, I bet! But fire or ice is better than nothing at all."

After a moment Riel said, "You came alone?"

"Napoléon too. Patrice rode to the telegraph." Riel glanced sideways at him quickly, and Gabriel added, "He just wanted to, we heard nothing."

"Is Annie deciding, with her two young men?"

"Aw, she's such a... woman, she...."

"What else should she be?" Riel smiled faintly.

"Maybe it's not woman so much, young. She wants a man, sure, and the trouble is they're both good. I wouldn't want to decide between those two. Would you?"

"I've never been so lucky," Riel said; but Gabriel was too much in his own thoughts to catch his tone just then.

"A man who has a farm, or one—well you know him; he followed you here to learn—and Annie if she had two dresses she'd stand there all day naked, not knowing what to wear. I don't know, I don't know nothing about women that can't make up their minds. Madeleine always knew, right from the start when I bust the guy's arm who was chasing her, what she wanted."

"You've only known one woman?" Riel grinned.

"Huh!" Gabriel snorted, the sun-blackened skin over his nose crinkling. "I wouldn't lie about that, just every woman I've ever had knew what she wanted. In the buffalo camps on the prairie you live while you're alive, tomorrow you can bust your neck, get run down, shot...what are you walking out here for, in this cold?"

"The house, it's so full, people."

"A winter like this you curl up and sleep, like bears. Just sleep."

"I get so tired of sleeping, and the smells, everything...it's silly," Riel's arm swept about the gigantic river valley, the distances circling them on the blazing snow. "Crazy really, all this space and we're stuffed in cabins so dark with one or two tiny windows; half the year we're crushed inside them!"

"This cold sun can fool you; it'll kill you as quick as a storm. No," Gabriel turned. The smoke of Batoche lay ahead of them down the valley, "You're thinking wrong, to live here you have to think bear or Indian: come out when it's warm enough, get the sun then, breathe all you want, otherwise sleep and store it up so in spring and summer you don't have to sleep at all."

"If we had houses with windows, a whole wall facing south, there's so much sun we could—"

But Gabriel was laughing in disbelief. "A whole wall of glass!"

"In the east, in the cities where there's nothing even to see."

"I can just see all that glass coming here on a bumping cart!"

They both laughed then, the sound of their footsteps like one on the squeaking snow.

"Madeleine was Jean-Baptiste Wilkie's daughter."

"My father hunted with him in the forties. But people sometimes are sure of themselves, because they don't know, or think. A woman...." Riel hesitated, then suddenly plunged on, "I knew one once, very well then, a gentle woman, so quiet and thoughtful of others; she lived with her brother, a priest. She hated English Canadians so much when I told her what they were doing in the North-West she wanted me to lead an Indian movement, get all the tribes together and fight, spare nobody, 'massacre them all until there are no more of that infamous race left in your country.' That's what she wrote, and she nearly fainted once when I cut my finger. Just a nick."

"You wrote letters like that?"

"She wrote them to—"

"About Indian wars?"

"In exile, yes, and later when I was coming to Montana."

Riel frowned, remembering confrontations, personal impossibilities. "Far away things seem easier than they are when you get to a place. The Indians wouldn't agree with me."

"You talked to them?"

"The Cree, they were hunting along the Missouri, and the Assiniboines and the Blackfeet; they were all down there then."

"No," said Gabriel slowly. "Those together wouldn't."

"And when I thought of it myself, sitting in their camps and actually riding and talking with them, I was always praying, 'God, there has to be some other way.'"

"You think so?"

"What?"

"Some other way?"

Riel walked, head bowed. Dogs were barking below them among the trees of the village, and the shouts of a boy running horses to water snapped like branches in the bright, frigid air.

"I have prayed all these months," he said finally, "when we came and worked, and especially since we sent the petition, and I...nothing. Nothing comes to me. I walk, and pray, I kneel at the altar...."

Gabriel walked beside him wordlessly.

"Brass," Riel said; "heaven is sealed over, frozen brass. Gabriel, there was a time when everything spoke to me. Angels walked with me at night showing me the wonders of God's plan, in a garden I would see a flower or a spray of them in some wild place and know I was to leave there. The whole world opened like a book I could read and understand, wherever I looked in it and whatever I explained in long letters to Bishop Bourget; he read it all and gave me his blessing, confirmed my faith and my vision; everything was God's voice. Once just before you called me in Montana, when my wife came to me I knew a mystery, hidden till then; when she put her arms around me I heard as clearly as your voice talks in this frozen air, what I would do, should do, very soon. But here–once I thought I heard it again; you were there, in Prince Albert when we talked to Father André."

"Yes."

"Once, just once there I heard God's voice as clearly as the thunder; and it said: the priests help destroy the way for our people. And that held me clear and strong till Bishop Grandin came, but...I hear nothing. People's voices yelling, screaming, wanting things, nothing ever right or fast enough or talked over enough; the smallest decisions take months, nothing moves, I have no joy, the world is smeared over blank, and heaven and earth...as if God had—"

He stopped talking suddenly and stood still. Gabriel followed his glance, hope suddenly leaping in him; but there was nothing; only the blank level folds of the white valley, the sun smeared as high as it would rise in the winter day.

"I have to go away, back to Montana," Riel said. "It cannot be here, there is nothing here."

"No," Gabriel said. "Don't go away."

"One petition in eight months, and they don't even answer it! All they do is give Crozier thirty more police in Carlton, try their miserable bribes– Forget says maybe a council seat, Clarke tells André tells me there are maybe five thousand dollars or twelve if I–for the people, they set the English–Gabriel, there is less unity now than before I came! Can that be God's way?"

"Maybe, maybe."

"But I haven't felt...." Riel was looking at Gabriel now, pleading. "Since before we sent that petition, I cannot pray; the priests are noth—"

"You will be your own perfect priest."

"Don't you understand?" Riel cried. "I am cut off!"

"No," Gabriel said, "that is not possible."

"You don't know how I can lose God's presence; everything goes black with—"

"It's not possible now," said Gabriel remorselessly, "because when we knelt in that church I got a prayer just like you, the same prayer and I pray mine every day. That was our prayer, Louis, and we are right, here!"

"What?"

"It's my prayer too. What do you think I've been doing all these months?"

Riel stared at him. They stood beside a clump of willows and spruce thrusting out of snow; a fold of the land driven over level in hard whiteness.

"You have a vision here bigger than at Red River. Heaven and earth—show us, help us to see!"

Our world turns on small events, sometimes on things no person does consciously. Past Gabriel's head was the small spruce, barely green as it seemed in the fierce cold because granular snow had driven between its needles; it appeared hoared with dying age. They had not spoken alone since that June prayer together and they would not have spoken now but for Gabriel finding him out: Riel had never known anyone who had the faith to find him in his godless reaches of silence and he did not yet grasp that this man had given him his commitment of fealty before an altar and he would never retract it even after the name Riel meant at best madman, at worst pathetic child; such evidenceless faith was still too much for Riel to believe he could inspire and Gabriel might have gained nothing beyond that momentary hesitation before the spruce when suddenly, coming up from their watering, the horses broke past Nolin's house and swarmed into the fields. Though they crashed through the snow's hard crust at every plunge, they seemed to fly effortlessly, their heads stretched level, mouths gaping, their legs reaching in great lunges that whirled the snow about them like a gigantic devil-wind funnelling over the fields, the mist of snow rolling in the steam of their hot, driving bodies. The two men stood transfixed; the horses spread, split, going down instantaneously, rolling in the snow that hurled clods high into the air;

their hoofs and legs struggled, swung momentarily and nearly over, caught, and down again, their pale shaggy bellies rolling back and forth, their heads lunging up, their front legs leaping and the backs driving up too, they were all standing for an instant, shuddering in the cold as the snow sprayed from their black bodies like beauty flying. And abruptly, as if pulled about by a string they turned their heads towards the two men beside the spruce at the willow clump, stood motionless, ears cocked above their long, slender faces at Riel and Gabriel.

A whistle. One by one the horses' heads turned; one by one they neighed, trotted away to the boy at the edge of the houses. In a moment nothing was left but the trampled snow, the faint smell of animal heat vanishing in the sparkling, frigid air. Gabriel looked at Riel; he could only see the side of his mackinaw, his black beard bristling with frost over his collar.

So Riel was at Batoche when the telegram from Lieutenant-Governor Dewdney finally arrived regarding the petition whose receipt in Ottawa had been acknowledged by a letter as early as January 5 but which within a few months the Prime Minister would find it convenient, and politically necessary, to deny ever having received, seen, or even known about. In this regard the petition of December, 1884 was exactly parallel to the so-called amnesty of 1870. Bishop Taché could have stated about the one what he did about the other: "The Right Honourable John A. Macdonald lied in his teeth like a trooper." When people naively presume that their country at least is run by honesty, what happens when leaders lie to save their necks? No one has ever accused me of being a cynic, but the story of our people versus Ottawa tells one that if a leader seems forthright, definite, and very lucky his lie may work long enough to break his opponent's neck and then, of course, his own is safe until the next election. Nevertheless, I believe a certain breakage always takes place, somewhere; that is in the very nature of lies.

Dewdney sent the telegram, not to Spencer or Jackson who

had signed the petition, nor of course to Riel who everyone knew had written it, but to Charles Nolin then submitting tender to construct a telegraph line between Edmonton and Duck Lake. On his own Dewdney could never have been so stupid; after all he was well aware of his own neck, but Dennis was gone (by July, 1885, he would be dead), and Dewdney had orders from a Prime Minister who had grown old in power using particular methods to keep what he thought were small people in their small place. The very general telegram to the minor committee member merely stated that the "Government has decided to investigate the claims of half-breeds", and that it would "soon appoint a commission of three members to make a census of such in the North-West." Nothing about Indians, survey, land, province, loan assistance, nothing at all really; and Riel roared in rage when Nolin showed it to him. So did the people when they packed into St. Anthony's, from which Father Fourmond had hastily removed the Blessed Sacrament.

"I am a foreigner here now," Riel told the hundreds of faces lifted to him on the platform. "This Government will never deal with me as your leader. They have said what they will do, and it is no more and no less than what they always promised–nothing. But I will return to Montana. I am of no use to you."

"No! Never!" The shouts rang in the small building, and Nolin and Fourmond were shouting loudest of all. "No!"

Old Ouellette, ninety-two years old who had ridden with Cuthbert Grant seventy years before: I remember how he sang the song of the Bois-brûlés at Frog Plains, his face so broad and homely shining for happiness; he was on his feet, arms high, shouting, "If you leave, nephew, we will go with you!"

And Pierre Parenteau beside him, seventy-three, and thundering in his hoarse voice: "Stay, stay!"

"But what of the consequences?" Riel said quietly, and Parenteau looked at Ouellette beside him, around the church filled with faces they knew, every one.

"We have moved enough," said the old man who had sat with Riel at the 1870 Convention in Red River. "We will do here what we have to do. But you stay."

So cried they all, including Jackson and Spence from Prince Albert; and Father André, hastily come to Batoche to prevent the worst as he of course felt he could, for a moment saw Riel standing before them as the people saw him: his bearded face and black curly hair so shiningly handsome he might have been an angel newly come to earth, his eyes, his beautiful words, his brilliant mind bowed before this altar in this church, reading, writing, going to confession, living penniless with his wife and children on the small charity possible in their tiny packed cabins; accepting them with a gentleness they had never known it was possible for a man to have and, even if it existed, could never have been directed towards them. A touch of...grace?...in the sodden round of their lives. Bishop Grandin, André suddenly knew, had been right. "For them he is a saint; I would say rather a kind of god."

And the English settlers, Andrew Spence and James Isbister who had observed him three weeks on the trail and certainly Will Jackson, his mouth fallen open and eyes fixed as before the beatific vision, felt his power. Such adoration was wrong, André knew; even Charles Nolin, whose wife had been healed miraculously of an unknown terrifying disease just a month before as they prayed, properly, to Notre Dame de Lourdes at St. Laurent, seemed caught: adoration must be returned to where it belonged. André rose, called upon all who loved the Blessed Saviour to make a novena here at St. Anthony's so that in nine days of public prayers, confession and communion they might together and individually consult their conscience before God as to what should be done.

Nine days of prayers; the priests attending. Riel studied the short, heavy man for a moment. His long grey-bearded face gave him a special status with the Indians, his careful eyes hid his sharp thoughts: an immovable rock; everything must eddy about him. But he would have to return to Prince Albert and Fourmond, Vegreville from St. Laurent....

"Yes," Riel said for he saw it sudden as a light blazing. "Yes. A novena is an excellent suggestion, for we must do everything necessary to save our souls, to fight for the love of God in all things and in all places so that we will save our country from an evil government. We have been robbed by a company or by a government for two hundred years; we must now pray for the courage to pay the price to save ourselves. The novena will begin on Tuesday, March 10, and conclude on March 19, the feast of our most blessed St. Joseph, patron saint of our New Nation."

In a surge the meeting agreed; André could not now trust his own proposal, since it had been so quickly accepted by Riel, and he certainly did not like "paying the price" or "our New Nation." Or "fighting for the love of God." He would have liked it even less had he heard Gabriel saying to the men as they left,

"When you come to pray, bring your guns."

At the corner of his eye Gabriel could see Inspector Gagnon, whom he had ordered out of the church before the meeting began, waiting implacably alone in the rotten snow of the churchyard. No Métis went near him, but Gabriel knew he would report to Crozier that they were collecting arms for certainly among the hungry people they had paid informers; the very fact that the only officer in the area who spoke French was stationed at Duck Lake and came so openly to their meeting proved their spies, proved how little they needed to hear anything directly in order to put up such a transparent front. And Crozier wired Dewdney; André wired Dewdney; Lawrence Clarke, signing for both Company and North-West Council, wired both Dewdney and Macdonald directly; to Dewdney's fourth wire in two days, the old prime minister, perhaps waving a weary hand to an assistant as he rests on the couch now installed beside his desk, replies, "You have the police and the responsibility to keep peace in the

North-West." To which Dewdney promptly answers, "The sooner the Half-breeds are put down the better. They are like Indians, when they gather and get excited it is difficult to handle them, but if taken unawares there is little difficulty in arresting the leader." On Sunday, March 15, when Riel for the first time attended the novena at St. Anthony's, North-West Mounted Police Commissioner Irvine was ordered to take all men available at headquarters in Regina and proceed north to Carlton. With all the horses and, of course, the cannon.

Riel was at prayer now almost continuously: when Napoléon drove him to Prince Albert, when he rode a wide loop south and stayed at the Touronds for the night while talking to the people about their cause, their commitment to total action whatever it would have to be he could not yet be sure exactly what but had they lived this enough; were they ready to bare their teeth?–even in the saddle he prayed, so that the spring sun soaking snow on the hillside warmed him unawares; or blessed him into thought-less happiness, into trust for the vacancy before him which then held no fear, nor even apprehension, only anticipation. Then he felt as if poised on the trigger-tip of discovery, in the seemingly and only momentarily motionless vortex of a devil-wind; but at other times rage possessed him, or despair. When Gagnon and his man rode up to Moïse Ouellette's house and with his uniform terrified Marguerite–though Rosalie Ouellette as befit a Dumont came around the corner of the house and told the policeman there were only two women and seven children in the house and they had better ride out the gate faster than they had ridden in–then momentarily he would have laughed to see every police post in the country rising in black smoke. When Louis Schmidt came from Prince Albert, hesitant, finally asked how a provisional government could possibly be set up when there already was a government, complete with council, magistrates, and police, running the country however badly, not like Red River, where–then he was staggered momentarily, his mind blocked as if God himself had closed a door in his head. Heaven on earth, he must see God's direction; whatever was done must catch the people's spirit as directly as the taking of Fort Garry in 1869. Often when they rode and his talking with the people opened his thoughts like a path through bush, he would awake at night rigid, the blanket he had been given stuffed into his mouth, cramming back his terror against vacant, dreamless sleep; at home Marguerite was there, rocking his emptiness in her thin, strong arms, her breathing soothing him, the warmth of her breasts sweet as fire against his mouth open on the edge of screaming. Then he could have lain with her forever in the fetid cabin darkness, O the thoughtless bliss. But immediately he could not endure it: the night an endless surround of snores and hacking, would the sun ever rise, would there be something clear as light to...O Son of God, I must fulfil this completely, in every...completely...respect....

On Sunday, March 15, he drove up the hill from Batoche to St. Anthony's with his family and the Ouellettes; the five young men Gabriel had ordered to go with him everywhere now beside them. Father Vegreville gave the sermon. Charles Nolin sat at the front of the church; Will Jackson was there too: he had declared his break with the Methodist Church into which he had been helplessly born and his adult longing was to be baptized a Roman Catholic. In the church words fell in the air, one, then another, and another. Not even the winter-blackened faces changed those detached, dead sounds; Riel went out. The five riders waiting there leaned toward him, the rifles on their backs leaning with them.

"I need a horse, Patrice," he said, and smiled as young Tourond immediately swung down. "Anyway, Annie is here."

The young men laughed softly in the spring sunlight.

On the Feast Day of St. Joseph, March 19, Riel and Gabriel rode up the hill to St. Anthony's with seventy riders. The bell was tolling as they entered the yard; those riders who could find no place in the crowded church remained outside with the horses, listening at the opened door and windows. Father Fourmond's voice rang with fervour; above the people he was a black pillar bristling thunderous words:

"... and St. Joseph, like the Blessed Virgin with whom he lived in untouchable holiness all their earthly days, knew only of his utter worthlessness in the sight of God. We must be small, like the blessed Joseph! We must sacrifice our smallness to God and then He will regard our lowliness, 'for He that is mighty hath *exalted* me, and Holy is His name.' Pride is wrong! To want to be someone is wrong! Obedience! Obedience to God and to the authorities He has set over you, the powers He has placed above...."

The eternal silence of the people before the declaiming priest; I heard it all my life and sometimes wondered, sometimes knew though I said nothing aloud. Father André sitting below Fourmond sensed something in St. Anthony's, a murmur perhaps, or the gradual waver of a beginning keen; he could not say he heard it but he looked at Vegreville beside him and the other was already looking at him, eyes arched in question. Beyond him Nolin stirred as if he sat on a burr. Something wrong. André glanced at the window, half open to the chilly spring air: as of bees, swarming. That was much too early, if only Fourmond would not get carried away; his musical voice rolling, he sometimes got a little past his knowledge; certainly discretion:

"... to rebel against the properly constituted civil authorities is as great a crime against God as to rebel against the Holy Mother Church, or the Holy Father! For God proclaims it the duty of all Christian people to render to Caesar the things that are Caesar's and to God the things that are God's. All rebellion is mortal s—"

"Yes!" Behind them, and it tore Fourmond's incantation in midword. Riel was standing there among the men, shouting in a tremendous voice, his eyes caught upwards as if something wraithed above them in the peaked vault of the church.

"Yes!" he thundered again, the congregation turned and open-mouthed about him. "Render to God glory, honour and adoration, and to the tyrants of this world render what is due them: defiance! Sling back their authority, which they have torn from the people, in their teeth! Tear them down from power, that is what God orders! For the glory of His Name!"

The sound was the sound of the men, André suddenly realized with a jolt he would only later recognize to have been fear.

"It is a crime," Fourmond roared, "to deceive and mislead these poor people into destruction, despair, dea—"

"Listen to this priest," Riel's arms slashed up, "who dares to call you 'poor', 'misguided' because you have had enough of such 'obedience' to tyrants, because you see the truth of my divine mission which calls us together in the sacred cause of our rights and our God-given liberties. Obedience–to Ottawa, to Rome, to every policeman, every priest, every wandering Canadian who wants something we have, every Hudson's Bay pimp! Obedience!"

The roar of the men now drowned Riel's voice also and André was about to leap up, to break this dreadful shouting over the people before something truly horrible happened, when a movement rippled the men nearest the door. A head was shoving through there, face redly wind-whipped as of a rider who had ridden far, hard: Michel Dumas. In the sudden silence of that movement everyone heard him:

"Gabriel, Gabriel."

His square shape pushed past Riel and stopped, for Gabriel was there; and all the people staring. He should not have rushed in here–but Gabriel said, abruptly loud,

"You have a report?"

"Yes."

Gabriel's glance flickered to Riel; there was Red River rain and leaping firelight in that rapt face; and Michel's already told him–this is the moment, there is no turning back.

"We are all together here," Gabriel said. "Say it."

"Lawrence Clarke says five hundred police are coming from Regina. Isidore Dumont confirms, police left Regina yesterday. With cannon, to arrest Louis."

On the day he died in his small house above the river, Gabriel remembered that moment; how his body felt like an empty cask, gigantic as if he were all one sphere of muscle poised to tear, rend, utterly destroy. But in the absolute silence of our people waiting, breath caught like a cry in their throats, it was the explosion of vision on Riel's face that he remembered most clearly, the light he had prayed to break there at last into ecstasy. And the words more devastating than he could quite grasp even as he lay dying:

"Rome is fallen, is fallen; it has fallen to the ground! The place where it stood shall know it no more, the Spirit of God has left the Pope of Rome, who has never known our names, nor felt our sorrows!"

It was chant, echoing in the church and Riel moving forward through the people, arms lifted; and they sank to their knees as he passed, almost singing, "The Spirit of God fell upon the sainted Bourget of Montreal, blesséd be his name, who knew us and knew our prayers, who told me my grand commission for our people of the North-West, and hear his words: 'You have a great mission to fulfil, which you must complete in every respect'. And God's glory has broken like lightning from the vaulted domes of golden cathedrals, his voice has rolled thunder to us in a wooden church: 'Hear me! My son, why do you fight against me? Have I not called you, Louis David Riel? To the great mission of the Métis people? Rise! Call your people to that mission with which I will bless the earth!'"

Riel was on the platform; before his hand and the sound of the people Fourmond faded like wax at the entrance of the pulpit, the tall figure in a darned suit, the terrifying voice:

"O Lord my God! I cried unto Thee, and Thou has healed me! O God my God, Thou hast damned the evil and Thou wilt destroy the wicked for the old Rome is fallen; it is fallen forever."

And then he was smiling at them, face above them beaming in incredible beauty, arms high as in praise. The moan of the people sank into silence at his voice almost laughing,

"Will those police marching with their cannon take me prisoner? Will those police in their shining red uniforms abuse our daughters and our wives? Will they say to us 'Thus says Sir John A. Macdonald?'"

"No!" roared Gabriel and the people exploded, "God help us, no!" Inside and out the church rang as if it were hoisted from its foundations on the sound.

"I hereby declare," Riel pronounced slowly, "the formation of a Provisional Government for the North-West. This government will fight for our sacred rights, the liberties and lives of our wives and children. It will fill our great land with God-fearing men and women from the poor of the world, from Poland and Bavaria and Italy and Ireland and France, everywhere. It will give the same freedom and honour to our Indian brothers as is right in the sight of God and men, and we shall live in peace. Have you all heard?"

"Yes," the men roared all in unison now with Gabriel, the back of the church one bristle of immovable clenched hands reaching up; the very windows small rectangles of fists reaching. Then the Widow Tourond was standing also, her great arms heaving as it seemed woman after woman to stand beside her, "Yes! Yes!" The entire church stood chanting, "Yes!" Only in front the three priests with Charles Nolin as if nailed down, rigid.

"Louis, Louis!" Out of the din crept a pleading voice. "I have to be baptized, I have to be baptized!"

Will Jackson knelt below the platform, hands stretched up, and suddenly Riel laughed with an immense happiness that rang about the thundering church. He swung to Fourmond,

"You are the first priest of our new faith!" he declared. "Baptize this man!"

Fourmond stared at him in horror.

"He has asked for baptism!" Riel began to move toward the priest, his eyes holding his and suddenly the church was silent. "Now."

If Fourmond's eyes could have found André's, if he could have so much as moved his head–but he might have been trans-fixed by those incredible black eyes, bound, and slowly he came as soft iron bending. Gabriel saw him bend, his fingers in the font and his eyes fixed by Riel, leaning, heard words like weights falling "... in...the...name...of...the Father"- O God, it was rising in Gabriel, for between people motionless as stone he saw the water glisten on Jackson's hair; it will be done, O dearest Lord my God–and only much later did he comprehend that this unknown worship which had moved for the second time so completely within him–strengthen my courage, my honour, my faith, that I may profit all my life from the blessing I have received in this holy place–had freed him completely into his most certain bondage.

Riel had leaned down past the bent priest, and he spoke as his hand touched Jackson's clasped in prayer:

"Rise, my son! From this day on you are Henri Joseph Jaxon, new son of the New Nation."

Sixty-seven years later Jaxon would die a pauper on the side-walk in front of the New York hotel that had expelled him; stacked around him would be his blankets and books and papers and rotting memoirs, words written and rewritten over each other which no one had ever or would ever read. Sometimes, when I think of him and the happiness that this moment on his knees gave him in a life much too long with sickness and rejec-tion, I believe I could accept losing my family and all those years far from my place and people, perhaps even accept to hear myself pronounced legally insane in a public courtroom and having to escape from a barred madhouse if I had one such memory: of kneeling in St. Anthony's Church on the South Saskatchewan with the dampness of baptism on my head and looking up, seeing that hand, that ecstatic face, reach for me in welcome. One revelation. I must count Henri Joseph Jaxon happy.

"This afternoon," Riel straightened, turned, left Fourmond standing by the font and André and Vegreville and Nolin, at whose very knees the baptism had taken place, still immobilized by that unstoppable roar of the people in answer to a new voice, "we will choose those twelve who will lead us. They will be 'Exovedate', chosen out of the flock, and we will give them Charles Nolin's big house for their headquarters. Our work must be done quickly; the police are at Carlton, and hundreds more on the trail. To those who will not listen to words, guns must speak. Be it on their heads. We will pray for God's blessed guidance."

He was in the pulpit, hands lifted, and our people easily found their knees in one long sigh of bodies.

"Out of the depths have we cried unto thee; O Lord, hear our cry. Beside the rivers of our land we have wept; O Lord, deliver us...."

It's begun, Gabriel thought, beyond stopping. A little early in the season, some haven't been able to feed their horses right and they'll be slow; but we'll kill cows for meat now, there'll be enough feed for the horses, the spring so early it's God's blessing and the sun almost warm on the hills.

"...give us hearts of steel, that our knives may find their bones; when they would tear our daughters from us, tear out their hearts, rot them in the sun of your wrath, let beasts swarm in the strings of their intestines...."

Packed down together, kneeling, Gabriel could see only the broad bony shoulders of his brother Isidore before him, smell old Emmanuel Champagne; and Michel was beside him too, solid and certain, and from those shoulders pressed against his he felt the fierce joy he had not known in five years, happy tension of spring buffalo.

"...execute vengeance on the heathen, steel us in hatred, your divine and perfect hatred...."

André, knelt in his bench, unable to counter his personal devastation here with prayer, thought suddenly he heard the death keen beginning among the women; for a moment of emotionless stasis his mind almost grasped that he would have to...Gabriel...the world they had built here in '72...but at that moment he had nothing left, no coherence, no strength. The death keen harrowed him.

$\mathcal{2}$

FROM the veranda of Nolin's
house that afternoon, Riel and Gabriel alternately called out the
names they had agreed upon; the Métis shouted their approval
of each "Exovedate." Pierre Parenteau was President, Phillipe
Garnot French and Henri Jaxon English Secretaries; Gabriel
Dumont Adjutant-General. Riel himself had no formal position;
he needed none and when Nolin objected not only to the expro-
priation of his house but to the Provisional Government as a
whole and the seemingly military direction of the Exovedate in
particular, Riel accused him of treason and called for trial next
day; Nolin was locked in his former bedroom, a guard at the
door. Gabriel organized his captains and sent them off to recruit
men; daily now he heard reports on the progress of Irvine's
column; he had cut the telegraph at Humboldt and was expro-
priating supplies in all the stores on the east side of the river.
Riel sent a long letter to the English half-breeds, and on the day
of Nolin's trial "Gentleman Joe" McKay arrived from Crozier
now commanding at Carlton; for a time Riel lost his temper.
McKay was exactly the kind of half-breed the Saskatchewan did

not need: a man who used his Cree wits and his Cree body to
carry about negotiation demands for the police. The Exovedate
fed McKay, let him sleep off his long ride, and sent him back;
when Nolin, outfaced by Riel's accusations and sentenced by the
twelve to be shot, quickly recanted, he was given the chance to
prove his loyalty by carrying a message to Crozier:

*The councillors of the Provisional Government of the
Saskatchewan...require you to give up completely the situation which the Canadian Government have placed you in,
together with all government properties. In case of non-
acceptance, we will attack you, a war of extermination
upon all those who have shown themselves hostile to our
rights. Major, we respect you. Let the cause of humanity be
a consolation to you for the reverses which governmental
misconduct has brought upon you.*

Nothing but a white proclamation came of that: Crozier called
on everyone who remained loyal to the Queen to come into
Carlton and receive police protection; but Riel had decided they
should take the Fort. Gabriel agreed.

"It's like Fort Garry, it means Company and Government
both," Riel said.

"I wish it was Fort Garry," Gabriel said. "Stone walls with
bastions and cannon on the corners. But here I could sit on the
river bank with my rifle and not a rat could crawl across the
square without losing its head."

"It's what it means to the people, Clarke and Crozier!"

"I know, I know, but for headquarters it's useless."

"There was no Crozier in Fort Garry," Charles Nolin said,
"with policemen and Prince Albert volunteers."

"We'll take the Fort without spilling blood," Riel said curtly.
Nolin rode silently between them in the cold morning;

Napoléon Nault was nudging his horse forward on the narrow trail when Riel twisted in his saddle.

"You think we won't do that?" Riel barked at Nolin. "There are two curses on this country, the Company and the Government, and you're still thinking about the third–the Roman priests!"

"Louis, I'm not thinking about anything," said Nolin hastily, "like that...but you've seen Crozier's proclamation, do you really think he'll give up Carlton?"

He was looking at Gabriel; who shrugged.

"What does it matter? We'll take it."

"I don't want any bloodshed," Riel said fiercely. Between the bare trees and willows of the creek valley they could see horsemen flicker on either side; behind them, sleighs filled with men. "We take Carlton, and Macdonald will give in as he did in Manitoba. A threat, that's all he needs."

"You know Macdonald," Gabriel said. "I know Crozier. He'll give up nothing."

"We have established the threat," Riel said, "and we must push it until they have no way out. Here..." he was groping in his inner pocket: "four hundred and fifty-five signatures from the English half-breeds say either the Government agrees with us, or there's war!"

"That paper's okay." said Gabriel, "okay, but I want those guys who write so good to pick up their rifles and ride with us."

"They'll ride," Riel said. "It's just they're English and Protestant; they catch on slower."

Gabriel and Napoléon roared; even our Charles grimaced in what might have been amusement.

"It's that Irvine coming," said Napoléon after a moment. "If they get those Ninetieth Rifles marching out of Winnipeg—"

"We just keep them in small groups," said Gabriel. "Who can't handle ninety men and sixty-six horses? Irvine didn't dare come through us to join Crozier, did he?"

"But he got around us to Prince Albert, and he'll just come down the river to Carlton from the north."

"What does that matter?" Gabriel said, and suddenly laughed at Napoléon's dogged argument written on his young face still stiff in the morning cold. "You got too impressed at that Winnipeg parade grounds. jerking a rifle around, shoulder, ground, shoulder, snap! snap! that don't mean nothing in savage country."

Saddles creaked, and behind them in the sleighs a voice began an old French marching song. They would be singing mine before the first ducks whistled north.

"Anyway, who knows?" Gabriel said. "Right now we're between them, and we've got to stay there till we get the Duck Lake and Carlton supplies. If we start shooting..." he shrugged. "They're both here anyway, there's not that many left anywhere else."

On that cold thought they emerged into the wider cold of the open prairie, where the sun was just breaking through clouds on the horizon. And a horse galloping towards them. "Isidore," Gabriel said instantly, and so it was, with a scouting report: Inspector Gagnon and Gentleman Joe McKay with twenty men and sleighs from Fort Carlton were heading for Duck Lake as well, probably to get the provisions at Mitchell's store. Gabriel swore and signalled out four companies of ten and followed Isidore to intercept. The police sleighs huddled immediately when they appeared on the trail. Soon McKay rode forward.

"We thought we were meeting men," Gabriel yelled at him. "Where are they? You're only a blockhead who won't listen to advice."

After shouting and threats, McKay returned to the sleighs and in a moment the entire group turned on their soggy trail and trotted back, to the derisive laughter of our Métis boys. Having set scouts again, Gabriel and troop rode to join Riel at the Duck Lake store. Hillyard Mitchell had refused to accept that Riel could commandeer his huge stock and so the Métis helped themselves, taking knives, rifles, ammunition, bullets, flour, salt, pork, lard, even thin muskrat spears none of them would have any time to use properly that spring and stowing them in their sleighs or saddle bags while Mitchell and his partner watched, sullenly enraged.

"We'll pay you when we succeed," Riel told them, touching nothing. "And if we don't, send Sir John the bill."

"Right now," Gabriel said, waving his men in, "you're our prisoners."

"God damned if we are." Mitchell glared from one to the other.

"Sure. We're the Provisional Government here." Gabriel was already turning away. "Either you're with us or you're against us."

They were feeding the horses in the deserted livery stable yard when a galloping horse interrupted them; and a shout, "The police are coming!"

It was Isidore again. "Gagnon sent a fast rider back, and Crozier's coming now, about a hundred men mostly in sleighs."

"How many left in Carlton?" Gabriel asked.

"Maybe fifty, sixty, with Gagnon. They've got about eighty volunteer whites from Prince Albert."

"We've got the supplies here," Riel said, "if we could circle these we could take Carlton."

Gabriel shook his head. "If we had enough horsemen, but forty's nowhere enough."

"They're bringing a seven-pounder gun on one sleigh," Isidore said.

"By god no!" Gabriel laughed, incredulous. "We can take that damn Carlton any time, but Crozier's come out with his horses and gun—he's stupid! We'll pick our spot and take them all."

Within moments they were moving west, the scouts already ahead, the forty riders clustered up front near Gabriel and Isidore, and the sleighs filled with men in a long straggling line behind.

The empty cabins of Duck Lake echoed; the small vacant windows caught their blurred shadows an instant. Riel looked at the deserted church and Gabriel thought, This is all too cold for him: the chance of blood, he's within a minute of saying no, we won't do this. Complete surprise and he would be completely in it but now...Riel was looking at him, face bunched up almost in pain and he swung his horse close so that whatever it was he alone would hear it, argue that they all had known it would come to something like this, how once they talked of "Provisional Government" and "war of extermination" there was nothing but push ahead and—

"We should have brought a priest," Riel said very quietly. "Paquette here ran away with the rest of the whites."

In his surprise Gabriel could say nothing for a moment, then Napoléon Nault came crashing through the crusted snow along the line of sleighs, plowing up to them. He offered Riel a long cross, a tiny twisted Jesus nailed to its brown wood.

"It's from the church," Napoléon said. "I was going to ask the priest, but he isn't there now, so I took this, for you."

Riel silently studied the cross in his hand but Gabriel could have laughed aloud, kissed Napoléon for joy. Then he said very clearly, for he knew the men around him were listening,

"You are our priest. There's your blessed cross, big enough to see. When we fought the Sioux on the Missouri Couteau Father de Smet made a huge cross out of wagon poles; he could hardly lift it, and he walked behind us in the trenches praying aloud, back and forth and the Sioux got so scared of him they ran away."

"I don't think," Isidore said, "Gentleman Joe prays much."

"Then today we'll make him!" Gabriel laughed, and the men laughed with him. But not as easily as he would have liked; they were so young some had never hunted buffalo, leave alone been shot at. They needed something, a sign to help them know, like we needed so badly riding with Cuthbert Grant–and Riel was not yet giving it. When would the Spirit catch him again? He looked so bleak, still in the warm air hazed grey. And then as they had crossed the frozen marsh north of the lake and the trail bent between the first stunted poplars they saw riders. Gabriel twisted to Isidore,

"What?"

"It's Patrice; he's with them," Isidore said, "with Indians."

Beside young Tourond rode Chief Beardy; and behind them about thirty-five horses, some carrying double riders all armed with carbines or shotguns or clubs or sticks, anything; Gabriel almost laughed.

"We heard the police ran back to the fort when you stopped them," Beardy smiled through his tremendous paint. "That made your tobacco even sweeter. Now they have more coming, so we want to help you make them run back faster."

Gabriel roared, "Good brother! We have all the Duck Lake supplies and maybe we can use your land to set our trap?"

Beardy's few straggly whiskers shook with laughter. "We would be very, very happy," he said, "to see Hardass Crozier run off our land."

"You are welcome," Riel said slowly after the laughter was over, and whether his tone was simply the dignity appropriate between two chiefs or his apprehension Gabriel could not decide. "Gabriel is our general, and we have agreed we will not shoot first."

Beardy looked steadily from one to the other, then at his oldest councillor, Aseeyewin; who nodded. So they all rode forward together with the sleighs crunching behind until in a few moments that seemed like hours stretching into the ever-brightening day the trail bent down over a low hill with a rotting cabin on the far left and Gabriel said to Isidore,

"Here?"

"Yes."

"Good, this is good, stop here."

For Gabriel and Isidore knew this place, could see like a bird flying what was past the spot where the trail bent away into the trees, and the land hidden so featurelessly as it seemed in snow. The sleighs would stay behind this small hill and Crozier would never know how many there were; the snow was too deep and crusted soggy to manoeuvre horses, they and the riders could be held in reserve in the shallow ravine behind and the men on foot sent forward on either side, the best shots with their buffalo guns into the empty cabin on the left and strung out in a line beyond that through the hollow and the sparse trees on that side; the ones with poorer weapons along the better hollow and denser bush to the right, where they could get in close. Gabriel sat motionless, concentrated; and he saw how the grouped police must come, their scouts ahead and the loaded sleighs behind riders and if his men stayed low in the snow and worked ahead there on both wings they could have them surrounded; Crozier would be forced to...but he did not think beyond that, or he would destroy himself by hemming himself into what should happen but might not, on the snow beginning to glitter in grey sunlight, the men and horses behind him, waiting. He could see the trail though, already run over twice that day and fourteen miles of it hard on winter-fed horses, as clearly as if he were a raven winging over the white and spidery brush. There they would come, and stop, so he gave his orders: Moïse Ouellette to command the sharpshooters and advance on the left, his younger brother Edouard Dumont on the left, and when these promptly started to move forward, a flurry among the rear sleighs brought Michel Dumas galloping through the snow, brandishing his rifle in his right hand above an exhausted horse: he had heard of the police trying for Duck Lake that morning, and had brought a hundred and fifty men and fifty-four horses; was anything happening? One Arrow was with him, come in from his reserve with forty men. Gabriel greeted him with a hug and sent some to the wings immediately, the tension settling tighter and tighter into him like a steel trap being slowly spread for bear. The men moved swiftly now and the emptied sleighs stretched out of sight behind him on the hill; he could not care now that if he had known Michel was coming, he would have sent him around to Carlton, for he had over three hundred men now and he was certain Crozier could be destroyed. Crozier must be made certain of it too.

"Remember," he said as his captains passed, "we do *not* shoot first. But if we have to, shoot as fast as you can, and keep it *low*. You'll be down in the snow and you'll want to shoot high so keep it low; legs we want, legs."

"I want them to surrender," Riel repeated, his eyes gleaming with sudden excitement, "I want them to surrender, without bloodshed, Gabriel."

"Yes, yes!" Gabriel said, and saw Riel would be all right, that was clear as lightning in the cold air. "When they come around that bend and see us here, they'll stop. That's when I ride forward with a white flag, to parley. They have to surrender, we've got them sur—"

"Not you," Riel said. "No."

Into the sudden silence Charles Nolin spoke, who had said nothing at all since Duck Lake.

"Why not?" Nolin's voice sounded unfamiliar, thin on that little hill. "A parley's no good unless the men are trustworthy, and Crozier knows Gabriel."

Nolin had helped himself efficiently enough at the store but he did not look very happy; Gabriel knew immediately for him to ride forward was bad.

"No," Isidore said, "I'll go. If something happens to you right away we're in trouble."

"I'm old," the soft Cree voice of Aseeyewin said behind them. "I have no weapon, I can carry a white flag well."

They did not have long to wait; really, it was barely enough time for half the men to get in position on the wings but it seemed long to Gabriel, as it always did though he could and had waited endlessly, motionless so often when it was necessary, hunt or battle. Soldiers spend nearly all their lives waiting; since the police came in 1875 he had had no battles whatever and strangely enough now the first policeman he had ever met ten years before was the first he would confront with a gun. But he felt only a tense happiness; this was inevitable; between Wolseley's betrayal at Red River and the police coming he had known that somewhere in his bones and had said so three times in five years of useless petitions to Macdonald:

"Having so long held this country as its masters and so often defended..."

André's writing but his own words; the fleeting thought of the priest, once so good to our people, meant nothing to Gabriel at that moment on the small hill on Duck Lake–Fort Carlton trail, and in this he was like Cuthbert Grant. Perhaps that was one reason they were our great generals: the priests had no hold over them. Not that they were irreligious, certainly not, but they had a kind of religious distance from priests. I never knew Grant to find the complete happiness before the altar that I did: he went because it was a part of all our lives, and so did Gabriel, but a hunt or a battle or a woman or a dance or a long ride over prairie reached deeper, held them in a total tension as no mass or contemplation of the Lacerated Christ could. The story of how Grant placed us along the willows at the Qu'Appelle Rapids in 1816 and how we neatly captured the Hudson's Bay pemmican crews as the long steep curve of the rapids ran their boats against our bank one after the other, that story told so often by old Ouellette on winter evenings moved Gabriel more deeply than any priest's eloquence about angels scaring sheep or shepherds; the clever unravelling of a practical problem, the look on that English face when, after sending down boat-load after boat-load at exactly ten-minute intervals, his officership stepped into his personal canoe and his personal crew ran him down between foaming rocks majestic under umbrella, and there around the bend were our still unfired guns, Cuthbert Grant waiting on the black sand of the eddy beside all the beached, empty boats. O long-nosed bastards reading Shakespeare while half-whites, maybe a son you never knew and certainly never acknowledged, heave you up the endless rivers of the North-West for a handful of corn and pemmican a day!

Riel was praying. He held the cross high, facing first right, then left, then to the horsemen and the men on foot beside the forward sleighs all waiting, spread out on their knees and praying perhaps too as they tried to peer between the riders clustered on the small hill with Gabriel at the centre. Perhaps it was Riel who made Gabriel Dumont a greater general than Cuthbert Grant; perhaps those moments at Fort Benton or Batoche; perhaps it was the cause of the battles they fought, here rooted in the necessities of our people and not beaver and London economics; but Gabriel turned now, said quietly to Riel,

"That's good," in the tone of 'enough,' and loudly, so the men behind him could hear; "they're here, the police. Down now, and quiet."

Two scouts had come around the bend of the trail and stopped; immediately one wheeled, rode back and in a moment the lead party was there. The tall fur hats, the bright colours of the police sparkled under fur coats opened to the noon sun. Crozier sat on a bay horse; come forward, but Crozier erect as a tree would not move another inch. The sleighs were crowding up behind him, that was good, and Gabriel leaned forward, rubbed down his horse's forehead between its ears, again and again: move Edouard, move Moïse; if they won't come any more you get around them, all the way round, yes, but Crozier was signalling now and quickly the police were piling forward, fanning to their right across the bare snow toward the cabin; their horse sleighs were pulling up into a long barricade on their left. It was incredible, Crozier drawing more and more men forward and in nothing but another few minutes Edouard and Moïse would have their wings opposite the centre of his position.

"That's Lawrence Clarke," Napoléon said, "the wildcat hat with the tail."

"Isidore," Gabriel said between his teeth, "if there's shooting either you or I kill him. For sure."

"There's the gun," Isidore said and Gabriel laughed aloud, not because he was amused but because the men around him were staring so intently; none of them had ever seen such a monstrous iron.

"All you do is get to the gunner," he said loudly, "that thing doesn't shoot by itself. Isidore...."

"When?" Isidore said.

"Now, I think now, and slow as you can. Let them see you, think a little; it'll give us more time."

Their right line was extending nicely, no uniforms, that must be the Prince Albert volunteers, skirmish position, the men wallowing after the officer in the snow; the police were unhitching horses from bunched sleighs: Crozier's tried and true bluff tactics. He'll come forward now, demand the supplies, maybe Riel.

Gabriel said over his shoulder to Nolin, "Give Aseeyewin your white handkerchief." Nolin's fat face is grey mud, he thought, scared shitless, but he had no time to look around and laugh in the coward's face. There's no government contract here.

"God protect you, my brothers," Gabriel said.

Riel was praying, lifting his cross over the two as they rode at a walk down the slope towards the police. The old Indian holding the handkerchief high, Isidore empty-handed, his Winchester stuck in his saddle.

When a rifle is taken from the wall and loaded deliberately, eventually it will have to be fired; Gabriel had always known that, and so did Riel though now he was praying fervently against it. Nevertheless, the first deaths are always the worst: until that point there is always hope despite rage and hatred and the furious momentary joy of an anticipated destruction of enemies. Now as Gabriel had known he would, Crozier rode forward alone, stopped, then gestured back. "Gentleman Joe" McKay moved his horse beside him.

"McKay's on a fresh horse," Gabriel said. "He's been riding for two days, he'll be jumpy."

Crozier was looking to his right, suddenly shouted something in. English, and then McKay yelled at Isidore and Aseeyewin in Cree so loud they understood him on the hill.

"Get those men back! Back! "

They've seen Moïse's men advancing, Gabriel thought. Now he knows we're no Cree at Cutknife Hill or Blackfeet at the Crossing, he can't bluff us with his uniform and gun, we've got him and we'll take him, we're the People here, tell him Isidore, tell him so he never forgets.

The four riders were very close now in the blank centre of the sparkling snow; McKay was nudging Crozier over so that old Aseeyewin with the handkerchief was between them and Isidore who held both his empty hands high though his rifle butt stuck up in front of him. That was bad, bad, and Gabriel standing rigid in his stirrups now concentrating himself completely on those four men shifting on horses throwing their heads violently, hardly controllable by the nervous shouting men–Gabriel understood with a jolt he had sent his wings too far forward; Crozier and McKay would not permit themselves to be surrounded and Isidore, Aseeyewin were...

For an instant everything happened at once: old Aseeyewin leaned across McKay towards Crozier, the handkerchief extended in his hands a white splotch against Crozier's scarlet uniform and McKay suddenly jerked as if he snatched something, jerked and a pistol fired and Crozier spun so fast Gabriel's heart leaped but the policeman was enraged, screaming at McKay and it was Isidore on the outside who was sinking, clearly gut-shot, Isidore get out your rifle, Isidore!

Gabriel had Le Petit up, his horse under him steady as a rock, but old Aseeyewin was blocking the centre there, wrestling for McKay's pistol and Crozier wheeled around, his arm high and smoke puffed here and there behind the sleighs, a bullet shrieked high over the hill. Isidore slid dead to the snow, his horse wheeling frantic and the rifles across the brow of the hill behind Gabriel burst into roar as Riel screamed there,

"In the name of God, return their fire!" but Gabriel had already fired. The instant Crozier's head was clear of the two still held together as in a bending, swaying weld and then the Indian was hurled from his horse as if clubbed and in that instant Le Petit's sights caught Crozier's head and he fired, fired again and saw Crozier's right hand leap to his face–jesus he was galloping, two inches and he'd have no face–the police bullets were too close now and the gun muzzle rising ponderously. Gabriel hauled his horse back among his men, leaped off, threw Napoléon the reins.

"Get Crozier, McKay," he yelled, "and low, shoot low!"

The centre was empty now except for the two bodies; and the two horses lunging, hurling themselves about the snow in terrified circles. As he waded back to the front of his line, Gabriel saw the gun puff smoke for the first time and Isidore's horse arching itself in another desperate lunge seemed to explode into spray, its head and withers one enormous splotch of brownish red while its hindquarters still erect in the snow gathered themselves as if to leap for a long moment and the thunder of the gun rumbled over the hills.

"God," Gabriel muttered, "they're using shrapnel." He yelled to Lépine, Carrière, old Ouellette on the ridge right, their long buffalo guns curling smoke in the cold air. "Get the gunners, those gunners!"

Clarke had disappeared but Crozier was very conspicuous on his bay among the overturned sleighs. The police there were firing steadily but the skirmish line of volunteers extending far right had almost bogged down in the snow, unprotected against our boys' fire there. Especially Captain Morton still untouched apparently, still waving his men ahead with his sword though none of them moved. Crozier swung to his gun captain.

"Howe!" he shouted. "Take out the cabin, a shell on the right! Shell!"

A bullet pinged on the gun barrel, sang away as all the crew except Howe flung themselves in the snow.

"Our men are extended there, sir," Howe said. "I may fire into them."

"What do you think's happening to them now? Shoot through them, or they'll all be killed!"

"Your orders sir," the captain said. "Load with shell, boys, c'mon." The men scrambled up again as Howe began cranking the gun around. "If you hear a Sharps bullet like that," he explained to his powderman, "you can be sure it hasn't hit you."

"Gabriel," Riel rode up on the hill, "this is useless. We should advance, forward."

Gabriel was reloading swiftly, "No, no, we're no English square, and not half of us would get to their sleighs." He put his hand up on the horse's withers.

"You're kinda high up there," he grinned, "fur hat and all."

"They won't hit me," Riel said.

"Just carry your cross, high so the men can see it. But you're right, we should move, they've got Moïse pinned—"

The gun sounded again, but strangely, and the men on the hill cheered. Napoléon yelled,

"It exploded, the gun's finished, finished!"

"What?" Gabriel wheeled toward the sleighs, the grey smoke drifting up there. Like the fireworks in Fort Garry, the February night of the Provisional Government.

"It exploded!"

"God be praised! We have to get around them, right, through that draw, right!"

Crozier was bending over Howe and cursing under his breath. "Are you hit bad?" he asked.

"Right leg's numb, I don't...." Howe grunted in pain. "A Métis bullet, not the gun."

"What the hell happened?"

"They rammed in the ball, before, the powder,"

"Can you fix it?"

"It'd take, a day," Howe grimaced.

Crozier wheeled away, wiping his still bleeding face, cursing; McKay galloped up. "How far are they?"

"They're starting around on the left again," McKay reported. "Down that draw, riders now too."

"How many?"

"At least two hundred there, sixty, seventy horses."

"Christ. If they circle us..."

"Should we pull the Volunteers back on the right? There're seven to ten dead, I think."

Crozier hauled his horse around on its haunches, "Get the teams hitched!" he yelled. "Retreat. Watch the left flank. Officers, orderly retreat, all the wounded and killed on the sleighs! Retreat."

Gabriel had led the riders at a plunging gallop right through the belly-deep snow, wide around the copse where Edouard and the men on foot still struggled forward, firing, but the police sleighs were already retreating across the next clearing when he arrived, their blazing rifles protruding over the sides of the boxes. The ride was violent, beautiful, Gabriel's horse leaping through the crusted drifts and the riders behind him hallooing like a run for buffalo down in snow and he charged straight for the frantic sleighs, roaring,

"Come on! We'll make the red coats jump!"

Firing two shots each time his horse hung momentarily solid between leaps forward, stationary they would have been easier picking than squirrels off a spruce tree, never more than one bullet for a head shot, but suddenly his head! As if a hammer had smashed him, the snow lunged up into his face and his horse's heels, its belly torn one long red, an axe-chop through it and guts about to burst, over him Joseph Delorme's worn face, his mouth open, screaming,

"Gabriel, Gabriel!"

"Shut up Joe!" Gabriel blinked. The world washed red, the snow red diamonds, and he sat up, "I've still got my head, I can't be dead yet! Feel it."

But his hand slid aside warm as grease, the snow tilted up black over him, a sheet; and then a crucifix was there crossed on the bright sky so startlingly blue and the white clouds puffed like giants breathing on a cold day, it was so soft on the–a small tortured Jesus twisted on wood dear god they should take him off there after all these years as long as he could remember nailed on so crooked, and a nail, it drove into him, a nail spiked into his head just above the eyes and he gasped with pain sitting up, he was on his knees,

"Keep shooting, I'm okay, I can feel everything, don't let them get away! Cut them off!"

Riel was holding his shoulders, his huge grey-streaked beard against his shoulder and his cousin Auguste Laframboise tipped over him too, the few blond hairs on his cheek streaked black with powder.

"Little cousin, use Le Petit." Gabriel found it still in his right hand, thrust it forward. "Its good to 800 yards, just lead them a little, as they move. Twelve shoots...ten now...then you have to reload..."

He could hear the sharp crack of his rifle again, good; he opened his eyes to Riel's face so close and hunched, almost into tears,

"I'm okay, just let me lie, you go with your cross, show yourself."

"Gabriel." Riel's eyes were flaming black, bending.

"Go! You have to, tell Edouard to lead them, go!"

He lay perfectly still on his back a moment surrounded by the fighting; heard shots, screams, the terrified horses of the police still struggling to get by on the ruined trail. And he felt a kind of peace; he knew he would not die, not yet. It was a cut, nothing broken, a cut much deeper than he got Crozier but the snow would hold the bleeding and the sky was so blue there was even a bird, yes it was a bird flying so high he could barely see it, could not distinguish any colour at all but its lazy, drifting, motion.

"Uncle...Uncle..."

A small voice, a child? But it was Auguste, Le Petit no more than inert iron in one hand now, his left clutching himself; face contorted in agony. Gabriel lunged up, began crawling, called to him,

"Courage, my little cousin...courage, the good Lord...."

He was beside him in the snow, the boy's eyes already glazing and he wanted to lift his arm and make the cross over him but his right shoulder and arm, they weren't there, nothing and he strained his left arm up and lost his balance and fell face down beside Auguste in the stinging snow and the groan shuddered against his left hand fallen across the ripped, sodden jacket and he heaved desperately on his dead shoulder, got his head up and almost laughing a little for shame of his body's betrayal before the last terrifying distance that the boy's eyes suddenly fixed open before him. Saying lightly, so dreadfully ashamed,

"Auguste, I want to pray, but I'll...have to owe it...." but he was praying. His prayer, even while he continued in this last moment the silly joking words he had always spoken with his many cousins who stared after him and listened as if to God, the many words which he could not have changed now in the face of death, his own head throbbing prayer: Lord, strengthen my courage and my honour and my faith, the prayer he thought every morning and every evening since he had knelt with Riel;

he would pray it forever and recognized a tree like a gallows, and Father take him Auguste was certainly painless now, dead. Give him peace, so young, eternal peace.

He hoisted himself over and peeled the fingers from his Winchester; someone else would have to use it. Edouard. Edouard was there, above him, and he could sit up suddenly. Across the clearing the last police sleighs were dragging away, frantic horses whipped by frantic drivers and the Métis spread like a fan after them, shooting yes but not moving. Yelling in derision.

"They're getting away for god's sake! You let them get away!"

Edouard was screaming back, his coat ripped open to a long slash down his left side, face dripping sweat and gunpowder and melted snow,

"We could have wiped them out and got the gun, killed them all—"

"No!" Riel was whirling Edouard around, voice tight as wound steel. "In the name of God, there has been enough bloodshed!"

"But their gun, ammunition, and hostages and Lor—"

"Isn't Crozier at the back?" Gabriel groaned. "Get Crozier at least, he's worth all—"

"He stopped us," Edouard tore himself from Riel. "All these people killed and hurt and noth–Guilliame!"

He was charging across the snow but he was too late; the Métis soldier had already pulled the trigger and volunteer Captain Morton jerked out stiff in the snow. They both looked down at him for a moment; the twitching stopped.

"He was screaming and screaming," Guilliame said at last. "His back was broken. Anyway, he killed Baptiste and Joseph Montour."

"Both?"

"By the cabin. He could really shoot."

Napoléon Nault joined them as they walked back to Gabriel, a fancy fur hat stuck on the point of his gun.

"That big-mouth Lawrence Clarke," he muttered.

Edouard said, "I saw him run out from under it."

"His head should be in it, nothing else just his yapping head."

There were five sleighs and eight unwounded police horses left behind, thirteen rifles and a little ammunition, and nine dead Prince Albert volunteers, most of them near the cabin. All the dead policemen, three at least Edouard reported, maybe four, had been removed in the retreat. They tied Gabriel on a horse and carrying their own dead, four since Aseeyewin was taken by Beardy and his warriors back to their camp on the reserve, they rode back the way you do from a fight: both happy and sad, you cannot tell which. In Duck Lake prisoner Hillyard Mitchell dressed Gabriel's wound in his own house with his own medical supplies.

"Your skull is thick. Like a buffalo's," Mitchell said; "that bullet just glanced off the top."

"It feels like horns, yeah." Gabriel sat rigid, head propped on his hands, "Like it was split in half."

The blackness rolled out, returned in waves; he knew they should be doing things quickly, because if they annihilated the police quickly now the Indians would rise with them, the half-breeds at Battleford and Bresaylor and Pitt and Victoria and perhaps even St. Albert and Lac St. Anne and Lac La Biche and –God grant such a miracle– all the Brelands and Bonneaus in Cypress Hills and Willow Bunch, not standing in line for police guide money but picking up their guns for The Nation, listen: the intrepid, totally invincible North-West Mounted Police, who in ten years have never killed so much as one Métis or Indian but forced hundreds behind stone walls to come out just before they die to avoid delivering a body to a family, who never back down, almost any officer of which would dare to kick Sitting Bull out of his own lodge or demand a warrior from Big Bear and Little Pixie as if he had made the world and every pebble in it, these mighty police blundered into both Métis and Indian and were stopped dead and Superintendent Crozier, toughest of the tough, has lost a quarter of his men and had his own face nicked and run for Carlton and the dignity of Commissioner Irvine himself, small stiff man always mounted on a large stiff horse, with one hundred and eight men on forced march from Prince Albert arriving on the bluffs overlooking the so-called fort which is nothing but several wooden Company buildings surrounded by a spruce palisade, arrived just in time to see them hauling the last of their wounded behind the huge, useless gate, and all their volunteer dead, but no police dead of course, left behind for the coyotes. Patrice Tourond reported this last to Gabriel that night; he had it from Ambroise Desjarlais who was driving a sleigh for Irvine, and Gabriel had to laugh a little, drinking whisky and holding his bound head in his hands. What stories these were to laugh at around a campfire! And he tried to convince Riel; for he had seen Irvine's thick, cropped beard and stiff walk, as if he had not bent knee or elbow in forty years. He could not imagine the report in officialese:

> It appears to me a matter of regret that with the knowledge that both myself and command were within a few miles of and en route to Carlton, Superintendent Crozier should have marched out as he did in the face of what had transpired earlier, but I am led to believe that this officer's better judgement was overruled by the impetuousness of both police and volunteers and Factor Clarke to go and take the stores and, if necessary, fight for them.

But he could very well imagine Crozier's total humiliation, the demand for three different reports each longer and each stating again and again: "with prompt action I certainly expected to succeed...I admit I was deceived as to their strength...how the prestige of the rebel half-breeds would have suffered and ours gained among the Indians had I succeeded in getting the provisions...." For Crozier was, Gabriel knew, destroyed in the force; he could not remain in it, leave alone become the Commissioner, as he certainly expected. It would be several years before he saw Crozier again, close enough to see the white diamond on the right cheek which would be all that remained then of the passage of his bullet; but he would have enjoyed destroying Irvine even more, and he easily might have if he could have convinced Riel.

"Can't you understand! They have to leave Carlton, all of them; they have to protect the women and children in Prince Albert."

"We're not fighting women and children," Riel said; "what—"

"They won't think that, we're savages, all those volunteers, god my head." Gabriel dared not clutch it though he longed to tear it off his shoulders. "Stiff on the snow and the rest shivering in Carlton, they think we're just riding like hell to rape their goddam women. Carlton isn't defensible, the police...look, we send Michel and Edouard with the horsemen, they didn't get much today, on the Prince Albert trail there's a dozen places, ambush...a few men...."

The room tilted, swam like fish diving; the whisky thundered in his head, almost spilled.

"That does you no good," Riel said anxiously.

"Send them, destroy Irvine," he muttered.

"Gabriel, we don't want to destroy people. I have nothing against the police or the volunteers—"

"They were killing us...pretty good...today."

"The invincible police are destroyed, you did that today! We don't have to kill any more, Macdonald will listen, he has to. We've got the guns like you said, remember? At Red River, you've given me the guns again, and they'll listen to me now. They have to!"

"I wish we had that gun," Gabriel groaned; but he was past caring just then. And so that night everyone pulled out of Carlton, police, volunteers, Company, shortly after midnight and the fort burst into flame just as they were leaving; and Patrice Tourond with his watching scouts galloped in, saved some burning stores as the last of the sleighs disappeared above the cemetery ridge. They would have salvaged more had they waited in the darkness of the spruced ravines and picked off driver after driver as the sleighs crawled through single file; they might have even captured the three big guns and the ammunition to go with them which the police now dragged up and down the snow-iced hills to Prince Albert but Riel had forbidden them what had always been our greatest military strength, ambush, and they had to content themselves with fighting burning buildings with snow and discovering kerosene-soaked flour intact, some rat-gnawed bacon. Riel was right of course, Sir John was listening now, very carefully indeed, but he had not considered well that Sir John also had guns; a great many. That they, rather than negotiation, might be his answer was not in Riel's mind as he organized the march back to Batoche next day and the funeral there of the four men fallen so gloriously in battle for the sake of the New Nation and the high calling of the Métis.

"These are the terrible decisions, O God," he was praying alone at Mitchell's kitchen table. "Give me courage to make them, you helped me face killing yesterday, give me courage to say what has to be said. As you in your Holy Spirit guide me. For by the memory of my sainted Sara I will fulfil the mission to which you have called me!"

And he was writing; words to fill the leather suitcase, to give his unwritten people a place on paper before the frozen earth closed them away one by one and no one would hear them, the words they cried to each other lost like the cry of gulls turning trackless over the river, words to be used against him, for every written word called to judgement:

And I heard the Spirit of God saying, The battle has taken place two miles from Duck Lake, and the Crees were of great help to you. If you miss the police by that road you will have time enough to capture them, you need only to take them at the rise. And I saw the rise above Batoche, where the road passes St. Anthony's church. O my God, assist me that I may not endanger anything, support me that I may remain free. And comfort Gabriel Dumont, who is now weak and ashamed, who will not look at me. He is looking at his bare table. And the Spirit of God showed me eight young Métis running toward me, without coats, in blue and white striped cotton shirts, running very fast–one would think they are racing but they are not at play: they are occupied with making their salvation, they are winning paradise! The land that some would take from them.

We will wait for the enemy, I have seen our people lying in ambush. I prayed, grant that I may know who is the enemy, and it was answered me: Charles Nolin who deserted you and fled to Prince Albert in his sister-in-law's sleigh. And I understood; we must tie up the prisoners.

For in a misty sublime our Riel's great vision was at last shaping itself on earth: nothing less than God's perfect kingdom. It was a vision he had caught in glimmers since his vow, but feared even to dream in the most terrifying days of Longue Point, one whose vague dimension he had begun to see again when he talked to the Indians in Montana while Evelina wrote him such blood-thirsty letters beyond any possible knowledge of its taste; and at that time only with a desperate hopelessness. As this vision now crystallized out of his prayers and reading the Old Testament prophets and defiance of the priests and writing and in the long slow procession of mourners winding down the hollow toward the cemetery at Batoche overlooking the still, grey bend of the frozen South Saskatchewan River, he gradually forgot what he had known of Montreal and Ottawa and the strength of Canadians crowded large and violent in Ontario.

He even forgot Napoléon Nault's proffered apprehension about three hundred Winnipeg Rifles Napoléon had seen drill with such machine-like smoothness on the summer Sunday grass of rotting Fort Osborne on the Red River. And though Riel could not yet know that Major-General Frederick Middleton, commander for all Canadian militia, had not only arrived in Winnipeg upon Dewdney's hasty telegram "Situation looks very serious," but on the day before Duck Lake had already reached Qu'Appelle, the point nearest Batoche on the Canadian Pacific Railway with two hundred men of the Rifles, Riel's past might at least have taught him that a single rifle shot in a wilderness is more immediately and ultimately activating to a safely distant politician grown old in power than any petition with a thousand signatures–"no amount of concession will prevent people from grumbling and agitating"–and that after sixteen years of persistence from a pemmican-eating, moccasin-shod half-caste who would certainly get elected to Parliament any time a seat was created near his people–"hasn't he been elected four times already, and barely kept out of the house?"–and then could legally show up in Ottawa with parliamentary immunity and rouse all kinds of French clatter while insisting he was and had always been elected a Conservative–"a Conservative so easily elected, who cannot be bought with a title or a few dollars or at worst both?": given the incredible opportunity of numberless rifle-shots, of popular police and courageous white Ontario pioneer volunteers dead on the Saskatchewan snow–"everyone in Ontario knows a prairie winter is barely fit for buffalo"–this was no pretend execution; this was most easily *war*. And one must call it that, as Macdonald said smiling his patented double House of Commons smile which in one expression could contain regret for the sorrow of mothers and wives and children weeping their dear hearts out when men are called to arms and at the same time the blessed relief that finally something drastic has been perpetrated and even the dullest voter will comprehend that now guns can provide their simple, direct solution and with any luck most of the problem will be blown apart altogether and one thing at least is confoundedly certain: no picayunish Opposition will have the gall to yell about budget deficits! Even though Liberal Edward Blake, sitting as always in glum self-rightousness across the Commons, would refuse to accept the clean lie: "We are not aware of any causes for discontent in the North-West," even Blake would have to agree that insurrection cannot be justified, that there can be no negotiation with an imported American *rebel* who not regarding the duty of his allegiance, nor having the fear of God in his heart, but moved and seduced by the instigation of the devil to subvert and destroy the constitution and government of this realm, in contempt of our Lady the Queen, her Crown and dignity. Because that is treason.

And the political capstone: no Opposition would now dare vote against the last gigantic loan which could complete the financing of the Canadian Pacific Railway for the massive benefit of Canada from Sea to Sea and, quite incidentally, for the benefit of CPR shareholders. Riel had created the catastrophe, an outbreak worthy for Conservative purposes of elevation to rebellion, as the Prime Minister would explain carefully to the Governor General as soon as the fighting was over: "In respect to the character of the outbreak, we have certainly made it assume large proportions in the public eye. This has been done, however, for our own purposes, and I think, wisely done." So wisely indeed that 383 men from Nova Scotia, 1012 men from Quebec, 1929 men from Ontario and 2011 from Winnipeg and West were mustered and hauled on the CPR to Qu'Appelle, and Swift Current and Calgary, to say nothing of 2684 staff, transport, commissarial and medical corps and thousands of horses and beef cattle and wagons, and nine guns and two special imports from the United States: seven tons of Armour Canned Meat from Chicago; and Lieutenant A. L. Howard from Boston, who wanted to test the performance of two Gatling guns–known affectionately as 'patented killing machines'–under live conditions. Out of the total bankruptcy, again, which President George Stephen wrote Macdonald about on March 26, 1885, the Canadian Pacific Railway exploded from the so-called Second Riel Rebellion to rival the Hudson's Bay Company itself as the most powerful business empire in Canada; one of the most perfect monopolies on earth. I have often felt the CPR might at least have named a hotel after Riel; at the very least given him what they gave Father Lacombe for the relatively puny service of talking Crowfoot out of a railroad right-of-way across the Blackfoot Reserve: a lifetime train pass. But I'm being peevish, I suppose. Riel could have used a pass only once, in May, 1885, riding twenty-five miles from Moose Jaw to Regina, and the government was paying then anyway. Coffins hauled in box cars travel as freight, though Riel could not have afforded even that, had it been possible to demand payment of him the December night his was loaded.

But in March the Exovedate sat about Mitchell's kitchen table in Duck Lake and listened while Riel dictated and Jaxon wrote, swiftly,

"...God gave us victory over the Mounted Police; they attacked us, we defended ourselves and they ran. Justice commanded us to take up arms. For fifteen years Ottawa has made sport of our rights; the Police are so corrupt our wives and daughters are no longer safe. The English half-breeds of the Saskatchewan are with us, heart and soul; the Indians are joining us. Listen to no offers from Ottawa; sign no petitions: we must preserve for our children that liberty, that possession of soil, without which there is no happiness for anyone. Rise, face the enemy; if you see police passing, destroy them if necessary, but take their arms. All you do, do it for the love of God and in the protection of Jesus Christ and St. Joseph, and be certain that faith does wonders."

Ambroise Jobin said, "I move we send that letter to both

French and English half-breeds at Qu'Appelle, Bresaylor and Frog Lake."

That was passed in a unanimous rumble. Gabriel raised his hand above his heavy bandage. "There are all the bodies of these volunteers," he said. "Lying in the snow."

President Parenteau looked at Riel. "Yes," Riel said.

"Some of them maybe had nothing more against us than we had against them; they never expected us to—"

"Then why were they with the police with loaded guns?" Moïse Ouellette asked.

"Okay," Gabriel agreed, "okay, but they were brave, and we killed them, and the police left their bodies for the wolves. I think we should send a message they can get those bodies, we won't harm them."

"They've all run for Prince Albert," Albert Monkman said. "Who'd go there with a message?"

"We should have sent it with Charlie Nolin," Moïse said sardonically and everyone stared, paralysed, at Riel; only his eyebrow twitched, and Gabriel broke the tension with an easy guffaw.

"He left a little early!" He clutched his head at his own laughter, "Saint!—" and stopped. "Send a hostage, one of them...Sanderson, he can ride."

"Yes," said Riel. "Write a safe-conduct to whoever comes to claim the bodies. Anyway, the bodies should be placed inside that shack."

"Yeah." Gabriel rose, grimacing with pain. "I'll get it done."

Parenteau said quickly, looking about the table, "Are we all agreed, then?"

Gabriel hesitated at the door, heard their consent and left; Henri Jaxon was writing furiously, but Gabriel had no head to think about why he should be when they had been speaking only French. He didn't much like the small English settler, so feverish all the time, eager. Tom Sanderson in the store attic which served as prison was more than willing to carry a safe conduct to Prince Albert; he even promised to return and give himself up again as a hostage but Crozier—god Gabriel thought, when he heard, that fight really smashed him—Crozier jailed Sanderson as soon as he appeared in Prince Albert on suspicion of being a spy; as he had also already jailed Charles Nolin. It was only when Irvine overruled Crozier on the pleas of wives whose husbands were frozen stiff in that cabin on the edge of the Beardy Reserve, that the two settlers came with sleighs and the safe-conduct. One of them was Thomas Jackson come to fetch his brother back to his parents, and Methodism if possible. But the Exovedate had left Duck Lake by then and Jackson could do nothing except help load bodies while at Batoche the Exovedate was passing resolutions.

"If the hundred and fifty police could be isolated from the people at Prince Albert, we could make them surrender easily and keep them hostage until we have a fair agreement with Ottawa. All emigrants as well as natives have a clear case against the Government and the monstrous monopoly of the Hudson's Bay Company. Join us against both, without taking up arms if you find that repugnant; join us in our opposition by separating from them and sending delegates to meet ours. We will then discuss the condition of our entering confederation as a province."

Further: "That the Canadian half-breed Exovedate acknowledges Louis David Riel as a prophet in the service of Jesus Christ: a prophet at the feet of Mary Immaculate; under the visible safeguard of St. Joseph, the beloved patron of the half-breeds; as a prophet, the humble imitator of St. John the Baptist, glorious patron of the French-Canadians and the French-Canadian half-breeds."

Parenteau said, into the silence, "Anyone want to say more about this."

Albert Monkman shifted slightly in his chair. Old Parenteau sat across the table from him so when he raised his eyes for a moment he could avoid looking at Riel, little Jean motionless on his lap.

"I don't know," Monkman said at last. "We're talking about a province, getting the English and Protestants who're mad enough to join us now, sure, but if we get talking pro– prophets are...we're just ordinary people."

"Who else can know?" Riel said gently.

"Well, maybe the—" Monkman felt Moïse's elbow in his ribs, caught himself on the word, 'priest': "I don't know, but... farmers, hunters." He shrugged.

"The blessed Apostles were just fishermen, workers but they first declared the Saviour of the world," Riel said. "True prophets are known by what they do."

"He has led us to victory over the police," old Parenteau said, "when the priests would have stopped us."

"The police arrested Nolin," Jobin said, "as soon as he drove into Prince Albert."

"And Archbishop Bourget's letter," Démase Carrière said. "The little priests here, what do they know of something new for our people? They just want us to stay down," his voice was suddenly very bitter, "on our knees, legs together and hands folded, down, that's what they want. Make a fancy altar for the church, they say, just make it and God will bless your crop a hundred-fold. But He hasn't. And the Company takes even that! And Louis has told us why; he knows. You got some rain last year on the west side, Albert, and you read and write English but I'm poor, fourteen mouths opening empty every meal. I know a prophet when he tells me something will happen and it does! And I'll work myself to–yes, I'll shoot the Devil's police. I know how they ride around here cocky and fat, like they rubbed them-selves down in oil every night and stare at my daughters as if they–I'll shoot them again, God give me strength!"

At the vote every hand went up except Moïse Ouellette's; he did not move even when Parenteau called the "nays."

"I can't," he said, his glance lifting for the first time; he was pleading with Riel, the long prairie days from Montana and the summer rain and sun oh if only Gabriel were here now; a glance and he could know. But Gabriel was riding, head still bandaged but riding; and Riel's eyes above young Jean's curly hair left him helpless. "I can't vote, today. If I can, soon, I'll...."

"You can record it then," Riel said, gently as though he had been thinking of something else.

They would eat together as they now often did; the women entered one by one with food but the men did not talk among themselves, or joke. This had been the first break in their unanimity, and so drastic a...they had made a religious decision? What Métis had ever dreamt it possible to decide anything religious? Ambroise Jobin stared at Riel as though he would leap up screaming for happiness. Henri Jaxon, writing furiously as Garnot translated into English, seemed about to explode: this was beyond comprehension, revelation! And Jean sat so still in Riel's lap, the child did not quite breathe, his strangely pale fingers lay motionless on the edge of the table beside his father's papers always covered with writing, but abruptly his eyes opened to one man or the other, unblinking, sharp bits of obsidian arrowhead caught in the pallor of his round, unhealthy face; one by one the men about the table stiffened in wordless amazement at their incredible act.

The women were waiting, and suddenly Riel raised his hands:

"Spirit of God who maintains all living thing; You are the prime substance of this food and drink. Bless it mercifully. Change this lowly milk into celestial milk, that in drinking we find it richer than all earthly drinks, that in being quenched we drink the milk of Your divinity; that in absorbing it there is created in us the same pure blood which fills the heart of Jesus Christ resurrected and raised into heaven."

Steadily, the men swallowed their beef and bannock, drank their milk. Only occasionally would someone glance involuntarily at Riel dipping bannock in the boiled blood and milk which was all anyone had seen him eat since the Novena.

While Riel and the Exovedate sent their message asking the English half-breeds to help take Irvine and Crozier in Prince Albert–after all, 455 of them had signed a statement to Dewdney on March 22 which declared they would have either a negotiated treaty or a war–Gabriel organized his camp. The twenty hostages, all storekeepers or volunteers or government snoopers, were guarded in St. Anthony's Rectory and cared for by Fourmond and Vegreville, virtually prisoners themselves now that André had disappeared to Prince Albert. Early in April the tobacco Gabriel sent to the reserves brought him a message: the two hundred people of Battleford had fled to the police when Poundmaker rode up with Crees and Stonies to parley; the Indian Agent had refused to come out and talk, so the warriors sacked the town; all the whites of the district now cowered with the police behind a stockade on the flats between the rivers. It was growing, growing. The same day Thomas Jackson arrived from Prince Albert to get his younger brother; however, Riel told him not everyone who saw the night filled with angels and renounced Methodism and believed his duty other than comforting his mother was necessarily sick and so Gabriel locked Thomas up, separately, where he was in no danger of getting information out to Irvine. For Gabriel's scouts told him Middleton had started north from Qu'Appelle with a hundred and twenty wagons and over four hundred men; more were arriving every day by train, hundreds of horses and men in shining uniforms. On Easter Sunday, April 5, at the church door as Riel was leaving mass Fourmond screamed after him he was a heretic; Gabriel set a tighter guard on priests and hostages, had his men bring in to Batoche the Grey Sisters of the Cross from St. Laurent and all the priests left in their parishes; there were only three. André remained with the police behind the hastily erected spruce stockade now surrounding Prince Albert.

And then the tobacco brought news from Frog Lake: Wandering Spirit had led the Rattlers of Big Bear's band and killed the Indian Agent, two priests, and all six other white men on the Cree reserve there, taken the white women prisoner, and Four Sky Thunder had burned the church over the bodies. Old Big Bear had tried to stop the killing but he was being laughed at now; Wandering Spirit and the Rattlers were eating government ox and dancing for the right time to ride to the police barricaded in Fort Pitt forty miles away.

"Fort Pitt!" Gabriel roared. "It's no better than Carlton, they'd have to nail a steel roof over–how many police in there?"

"Maybe twice my hands, maybe three," said Johnny Saskatchewan.

"Nine unarmed whites?" asked Riel. "Including priests?"

"They'll never stop Spirit's bullets," Gabriel laughed, turning to Riel. "And four years ago he was licking Dewdney's boots in Battleford. Starving's done him good!"

The spirit of God showed me Father André; he was tiny, far away, his back was towards me. And the Spirit said, the enemy has arrived.

"They sent tobacco to Saddle Lake and Lac la Biche too," Johnny said. "There's enough in Pitt for all of them."

"André was right," Riel said.

"What?" Gabriel stopped laughing.

"Neither the English half-breeds nor the settlers who were so loud last summer will come to us now. They're terrified of Indian war."

"Did the English message come in?"

"They don't answer."

"And they won't," Gabriel was furious, "because they've all run into Prince Albert. Well, let them peek around behind the police, just like Red River we'll do the work for all the cowardly bastards!"

"Are you sending tobacco to the Indians?"

"Yes! And I'll send more now, Poundmaker can take Battleford and Wandering Spirit will burn Pitt and they can come help us bugger Middleton. Louis, listen," Gabriel rushed against Riel's strong expression, "this English general is so fat he knows everything and rides a horse sixteen hands—"

"How do you know?"

"Jerome Henry," Gabriel laughed. "He was with us at Duck Lake and after I told him to get to Qu'Appelle, his family lives there, and he got himself hired by Middleton as a carter! His personal carter, he gets two dollars a day and his team the same."

"We would all make a fine living," Riel said, "if Macdonald thought we were fighting ourselves."

"God damn me if—" Gabriel caught himself. "Sorry, I can't help it, if they'd put a handful of money into finding out how to help us but they'd rather pay a stupid Englishman to–listen, we don't need the English half-breeds. Middleton has to drag himself and all that stuff two hundred and fifty miles, it took them two days to get out of the Qu'Appelle Valley."

"It's pretty deep," said Johnny Saskatchewan; and they laughed, though Riel very quietly.

"His troops are green," Gabriel said, "and I'll take some men down and we'll harrass them every night, we'll shoot tea pots off campfires, pick off sentries, stampede horses, in daylight nothing but at night," Gabriel snapped his fingers like sparks, "they'll never see us, never, and after three nights they'll be so jumpy they'll be shooting each other and Middleton, he doesn't know anything but an English square and steady advance, march march, he'll be yanking his white moustache out of his fat face. And that's when–listen," Gabriel said over objection darkening Riel's face, "it'll be so easy for us, they won't even nick one of us, and when they're at each other's throats and half their horses gone, Jerome will steal Middleton!"

"Dead dog!" said Johnny Saskatchewan in awe.

"Forget about Crozier, Irvine–once we've got Middleton

hostage, Macdonald will stop everything and talk. He can't let that English bladder get bust."

If you do not take them by that road past St. Anthony's, you will still have time to take them at the ridge above Batoche.

Johnny Saskatchewan was scratching himself for happiness but Riel said heavily,

"No."

After a momentary silence, Gabriel turned to the scout. "Johnny, you didn't hear nothing here. Go get some sleep; you have to ride before sun-up."

The scout nodded, dragged his hand through the horse-trough and wiped icy water across his face. "Yeah Gabriel," he said, going. "I gotta get back to Pitt, tell Dickens what he wants to know. If he's still there, and has his ears."

Riel watched the scout go. "He carries messages for the police?"

"He has to make a living," Gabriel said. "And he'll tell Wandering Spirit what we're doing, everybody hears what they need to."

"And we too?"

"No," Gabriel said slowly fingering the white cloth about his head. "No, we hear exactly what's happening, because he and I hunted buffalo and Blackfeet together and he's my brother. Louis, that Middleton, that's the way to stop him. I know the land; our men can ride circles around them, and there's not a bush on that prairie for them, we'd blow up the railroad, and not another—"

"It's too Indian; it'll just make Canada madder."

"You want me to face them with an English square?" Gabriel burst out. "You'll cover that whole damn hill with our graves!"

"I don't want any more killing!" Riel cried.

"There'll have to be more," Gabriel said simply. "And better them than us. Besides the scouts I have twenty-six companies of ten men, and only two hundred rifles; I couldn't make a square even if I knew how. They have cannon, all the ammunition. We have to slow them down until our friends get here, the Sioux, Poundmaker, Wandering Spirit has at least four hundred men but he has to have the supplies at Pitt and come over two hundred miles with all his people—"

"And talk and dance," Riel grinned humourlessly.

"Yeah, you know what Indians have to do; it could take him all summer – or Poundmaker too if all of a sudden in June they need a Thirst Dance. Duck Lake was good, but they need a little more encouragement. If we tangled up Middleton their young men wouldn't wait; they'd gallop in here and—"

"That's what's wrong," Riel broke in, his face twisted, "you say we should fight them like Indians and that will only make the whites madder and I can't—"

"I don't care if they're mad, I want them so scared they'll leave us alone!"

"You listen!" Riel cried. "I know that! And I know we haven't the guns, but I can't *see* it, my prayers, I cannot see ambush and night raids and the Indians mutilating Christian bodies. Gabriel, I wake screaming some nights, Marguerite has to hold me or I'd run outside screaming."

Gabriel stared at him. Finally he asked, "What do you see?"

"Only the ridge, here." Riel pointed to the spire of St. Anthony's flashing silver a mile away. "Above Batoche."

"Where we live, all the women and...?"

"Gabriel, I don't know, I don't see it yet. I am praying and praying but–anyway," Riel broke out of his indecision, "you still need that bandage on your head, I have seen you reel, and still you ride half the day, you—"

"That was a scratch," Gabriel muttered. "I can fix Middleton without my head, all I need—"

"No," said Riel softly, "not before you heal. You are too reckless, and without you we are surely lost. You know that."

"But we could reach out, pick them like berries!"

"Even if you went, your head is so hard, what about Irvine with his three hundred men in Prince Albert. With you all gone south what would happen here?"

"Goddamn those English half-breeds," Gabriel muttered.

"We don't need them," Riel said; "we will get our work done in unity and faith by those who believe. Believe me, Gabriel, God has promised me."

"There'd be less killing my way."

"God will show us the way," Riel's face was serene again, almost content in the pale spring sunlight. "Each day no one gets killed is another day of salvation for us all. Have confidence and pray."

Gabriel turned, not at all happy. "My hands and feet do my praying."

Riel chuckled, walking rapidly beside him down the street through Batoche, the ground under their feet still frozen hard as stone. "You know something odd? Macdonald's minister of militia, the man who's organizing the army against us is a Quebec lawyer exactly my age named Adolphe Caron."

"You go to school with that bastard too?"

Riel's laughter rang from house to house and bounced against the cliffs across the river. "No! He's Quebec Conservative, not Montreal, but I did meet him once, a slim quiet man ten years ago; we became quite good friends."

"God save us from your friends."

"If you knew them," Riel's voice had the distance of memory in it, "you would not judge them so harshly."

But in this Gabriel understood humanity far better than Riel who, though he might in the heat of battle cry "Return their fire," was still puzzled that a man could find it within himself to kill another. I know the vicious man is rarely the best killer, nor the most frequent; Gabriel knew this too because he himself had killed more than any vicious man he had ever met. So, though he was convinced that, as he declared years later "from a humane standpoint mine was the better plan," he did not harrass Bladder Middleton and his mostly pea-green troops, partly for military reasons–Irvine was behind them, poised impatiently–but largely because he believed in Riel's faith. You find that strange? No believer would, since faith is the essence of things hoped for, the evidence of things *not* seen.

O Mary! I am not worthy that God guide and assist me, but for the love and mercy of Jesus Christ, pray him that he continue his perfect guidance to me. I pray through Jesus and Joseph and your servant John the Baptist, grant me and all the Exovedates and all the volunteers for your cause the holiness of obedience, to act for your great glory imme-diately, quickly for the salvation of souls and our society. And the Spirit showed me a small boat on the South Saskatchewan river, in it two or three men, one with a red toque. They were coming downstream, keeping close to the left bank, and I saw the cable broken and I heard: Be careful at the ferry; keep close watch on it night and day. O God, I have been called David! Renew me, find me worthy for great faith, for the covenant so that I may bless your people.

Gabriel knew he must have more men if he was to stop Middle-ton's cannon with rifles. He again sent tobacco south to White Cap, east to One Arrow, and west to Beardy and also Poundmaker still leading a huge band of Plains Crees and Stonies and now living wherever they pleased in Eagle Hills since all their gov-ernment people had fled when the Stonies killed their brutal farm instructor. But they were mostly eating settlers' cattle and talking; they did not move to clean the few police out of Fort

Battleford even when Gabriel sent them a message to do it fast because Irvine was going to send some police from Prince Albert to help there. For the first time in six years their bellies were round full, it was almost as if they agreed with Riel: each day no one gets killed is another day of salvation. And far in the northwest Wandering Spirit did not stir either until all the Frog Lake cattle were eaten: he and his Plains Cree sacked Pitt after they forced Inspector Dickens to retreat on a scow down the ice-clogged North Saskatchewan River but by the time Gabriel heard of this, and that Dickens had arrived at Fort Battleford with one man dead and another wounded and was trying to get his official reasons together why twenty-six policemen could be safe while the forty-eight civilians that had been with them in Fort Pitt were all now captives of Big Bear's band, it was already April 18 and Middleton and his growing army had reached the South Saskatchewan River at Clarke's Crossing. Only forty miles south of Batoche.

And Riel was in that strange outward stasis which cycled in him throughout his life; it was not the boyish year-long sorrow at his father's death, nor the total inertia as Wolseley advanced: here there could be no hope of sudden amnesty, or peaceful intentions; rather, though he walked about every day and made innumerable small daily decisions, gradually the people who watched him, everyone in Batoche, understood that he was living somewhere where they would never follow him. He pored over the Bible, his prayerbook, he prayed hour for hour on the splintered floor of St. Anthony's and no one but the child Jean accompanied him up the long chilly hill which had not yet started to green. The day the first ducks flew north in an almost warm breeze he was laughing soundlessly as he passed. But that was only for that day; often the women mending clothes or cooking in the smoky chimneys of their cabins would hear the door scrape behind them and would turn to find him standing in the doorway, contemplating them in heavy silence. Then the children began to follow him and Jean, as they walked along the line of river hills in the April sunshine or to St. Anthony's for prayer; they would play silently, as Métis children sometimes play, with bits of sticks for riders and small stones for carts or sleighs in the sand against the lee of the church and when Riel emerged from prayer, his face gaunt and empty almost like a sleep-walker who will not wake, though shaken, because he already knows he is sleep-walking and refuses anything else, Jean holding his hand as if to guide him through the door, the children would follow the tall man and the child like a small grey shroud moving relentlessly down the lighter grey of the slope towards the white Council House where the Exovedate still met daily for prayers and resolutions, where Riel sat at the long table and read and wrote and prayed into the night, where twice a day he ate the blood and milk Marguerite boiled for him.

The spirit of God showed me the Métis Nation in the likeness of Geneviève Arcand coming to me on the street of Batoche. Her body revealed her pleasure in the flesh, her face the certain marks of carnality. O my Métis Nation, how your lust disfigures you! You are not worthy, not worthy. And yet you long for the right. You thirst for God's truth as the dying thirst for water, you suffer, fast, pray, and I see your face turn to me and you are so tall and strong, you are so beautiful I long to embrace you. O what fasting and prayer can work in a nation whose God is the Lord! From dwarfs they are transformed into giants, your body moves with the graceful purity of the Virgin worthy to conceive the Saviour of the World. O Lord my God, who is worthy, who is worthy?

"There is evil in this room," Riel pronounced. "Deceit, mockery! Like a stink soaking up the air, it is here, who is it, who? Confess!"

Under his glittering eyes the Exovedate sat as if nailed at the table, consternation on their faces.

"Confess!" The room echoed, "Confess, or God will strike you!"

"I–I—" Patrice Fleury began, and everyone at the table stared in horror at the youngest man there. "I must confess—"

"No," said Riel, "it is not you; this evil is older. And deadly."

The Exovedate had been considering a new eruption among the hostages; they had spoken only French since Jaxon had begun to weep uncontrollably over his brother Thomas's refusal to be baptized and Riel had ordered him put away where his cries would not disturb anyone, but now Riel was speaking a phrase in English, a phrase in French as if he read his terrifying words burned into the log wall.

"I resisted it, Brother Riel," young Fleury said in French, "yes, but the day after Beardy's Indians came to our command across the river it was suggested to me that I desert. And to Abraham Belanger too."

"Is the man who made that suggestion at this table?"

"Yes."

"Confess!" thundered Riel. Albert Monkman, Gabriel's captain across the river, English and Protestant, sat with eyes down on the table.

Gabriel said sadly, "You confess, Albert?"

"Yes." Monkman suddenly looked up; his weathered face was serene, almost happy. "It is true; but I did not intend to desert. I had said in my heart, I will prove if Louis Riel is a prophet."

The men stared from Monkman to Gabriel to Riel; the older, simpler men did not know what to say; there were temptations every day to desert: the priests caring for the hostages, nuns talking to women, always, but here again was their prophet who led them; who knew and suddenly old Parenteau murmured,

"You have proven it; now do you believe?"

"Yes," Monkman said, then carefully in English, "I believe Louis Riel to be a prophet by the grace of God for our movement."

"You would have been jailed like Charles Nolin if you had reached Prince Albert," said Jobin.

"And you tempted two young men," Parenteau added, "to desert their brothers."

Gabriel stood up heavily. "You will be bound, Albert," he said. "You must have had it in your heart to do what you said."

That afternoon White Cap arrived with his Sioux warriors from the Round Hills. Thirty of them in ragged leather and feathers, but they fired their rifles and shotguns into the air from their whirling, dancing horses and the people ran into the street, followed them shouting to the Council House. "We are come," White Cap shouted to Gabriel on the porch, "Bladder Middleton has ferried half his men across the river at Clarke's Crossing."

"It took him four days," Gabriel laughed. "Clarke's old scow between the ice! Did he get the guns over?"

"Two, only one sank for half a day. But they have a big boat coming down the river, loaded with everything. They told us, the whites in Saskatoon."

"How long till it gets here?"

"So much running ice and sand banks," White Cap chuckled, "they say it's coming mostly on its levers, by land!"

"How long?" Gabriel asked impatiently.

White Cap shrugged. "Who can say." Among his silent men he sat contemplating the distant spire of St. Anthony's. "They want to come against you on both sides of the river, so they have divided their soldiers. Bladder Middleton has never heard of Longhair Custer."

I have seen the giant coming: he is coming, he is hideous. It is Goliath, but he will not reach the place he intends. He loses his body, I see him left with nothing but his head. He will not humble himself, he is beheaded. O God, you have shown me the beautiful prairie and the people who will live here! O my God, fight for us, give us grace to conquer them one after the other; send us Irvine twenty-four hours before Middleton and Middleton twenty-four hours after Irvine. Send us the steam boat when we can best take her at leisure. O my God! Make haste, hurry the Cree as fast as possible, send us Crowfoot and the Blackfeet, all the Indians we need to help us triumph in the mission you have assigned us in this holy place. I pray in the name of Jesus and Mary and Joseph.

Reasons had nothing to do with it; Riel could not doubt that he had seen only the ridge above Batoche; inevitable advance, divided men and guns, the loss of every advantage, the sinking morale of the men: he had not yet been given to see! But Gabriel was suddenly adamant: if he did not go now, the Nation was finished; some Indians had come and Middleton was within forty miles of Batoche. Then suddenly, as if light had struck him, Riel said, "All right, do as you wish." And he added, "I will pray God, that he fight for you."

"That's who I need to face those big guns," Gabriel said, and left Riel laughing in the darkening room. At noon the next day, April 23, Gabriel rode at the head of his men ranked in their companies with the scouts ahead and the Cree from One Arrow and Beardy and White Cap's Sioux flanked on either side; he rode up the street of Batoche to the Council House. The people flocked after him, only the children shouting as they ran; Riel came out, peered into the bright sunlight at the waves of mounted men spreading down the fall of the street, the river flecked with running ice and the spruce-black banks beyond the women and children and old men craning behind them. And Father Fourmond was there: Gabriel had brought him to bless the troops and the tall priest, now emaciated and pale from over a month's close watch with the hostages, did indeed step forward, his crucifix clutched against his cassock. But as the Métis bowed their heads to the lifting cross, suddenly Fourmond shouted, this was wrong, they were being led astray! All the priests held so long against their sacred office without charge in the rectory would refuse the last rites to every person killed or wounded in this unholy and—Gabriel was roaring, and Riel on the platform exploded: "Listen to this priest who dares tell you it is a crime to fulfil your sacred mission!"—and Fourmond was swept away, Riel had the brown crucifix that had led them to victory at Duck Lake lifted high over them with his prayer book gripped against the suffering Jesus and the Métis soldiers and the women and children were kneeling in the street of Batoche, praying as his blessing rolled over them, the silent Indians on their horses as motionless as wood above them.

"God is our refuge and strength, a present help in trouble, therefore we will not fear though the mountains slide into the depths of the sea. The Lord breaks the bow, he cuts the spear, he burns the chariot with fire; the Lord God goes before us!"

Then they rode up the hill past St. Anthony's Church, and turned south on the ridge road above the bend of the river. O to have seen our people riding against our enemies then, the flag of the Virgin flying over them and Riel and Gabriel at their head. It was the greatest army we ever had, and it was the last. As I grew older the glory of fighting and war which I loved and sang in my youth slowly soured for me, as you may have gathered, but to see our people ride like that: excitement, pride, brotherhood, and ceremony all together are not easily found on earth, especially by the poor; they must be enjoyed for that fleeting moment in which they touch us, for pain and perhaps agony are then never far away. At every halt the soldiers dismounted and knelt with Riel for a decade of the rosary, and they had almost reached Gabriel's house—he and Madeleine and Annie had been living in Batoche since Duck Lake—when Edouard Dumont, who had remained with thirty men to guard Batoche, sent a messenger saying Irvine and Crozier were marching south out of Prince Albert: he must have thirty more men, and Brother Riel, immediately. So Riel reluctantly returned to Batoche to help Edouard face Irvine while Gabriel rode south against Middleton with one hundred and fifty men. Dusk was falling then; it was too late to find the Canadians and attack them at night, but they could set an ambush for the morning. Napoléon Nault rode beside Gabriel; on their right below them the river gleamed between its black banks like a flat pink and golden snake.

But Irvine and Crozier did not come; six miles out of Prince Albert they suddenly turned back. And about ten o'clock next morning strange thuds began in the south; the people of Batoche gathered about Riel on the ridge beyond the church and listened. An April day sharp with spring as I had seen it so often over the Assiniboine, the clouds white puffs, and clearly through the absolute silence of hundreds of people they heard: it must be the Canadian cannon. Riel knelt, all the people with him, and they began to pray. Riel turned his face upwards and raised his arms like a cross towards the south. When he could no longer hold them up, two men, then women, then the children kneeling about him supported them, so that hour after hour they implored heaven. O God you are our God, hear us, fight for us. The guns continued, wavering faint and clear as distant thunder. At noon Edouard Dumont came to Riel and said he was riding to help Gabriel with his eighty men; deserters were coming in one by one, and the fighting at Fish Creek was terrible.

"Fish Creek?"

"They're fighting where the road goes down there and up to Touronds. If Irvine and Crozier come, let the deserters face them, I'm going to Gabriel."

"Find him, and tell him I am praying."

"Yes," said Edouard, going, "prayer will have to do more than small bullets."

O St. John the Baptist, glorious patron of all French Canadians, be praised for having been immolated, for the sacrifice of your living flesh. Intercede for me. O my God, forgive

me the offences I committed among the Cree and Sioux and
Blackfeet, the Bloods, the Saulteux, the Sarcees, the Stonies,
the Gros Ventres, the Piegans and Nez Percés, the Pendants
d'Oreilles and the Flatheads. In your endless mercy.

By the middle of the afternoon a low bank of rain, perhaps
sleet, had moved over the river south; they could no longer hear
the guns but Riel remained praying on the ridge. There were
only children left around him when Madeleine Dumont brought
his food up the ridge, now windy with cold. He dropped his
arms then from the shoulders of the two children supporting
them; the hours of prayer for miracle in the spring sun had
burned him dry, fleshless she thought, like a single tree on the
prairie slit by lightning. His hands, when he reached for her
bowl seemed like carved wood, transparent as ice–almost she
expected, prayed to see marks on the palms, the terrifying
marks; but there was nothing.

"You are beautiful," he said, his voice hoarse and flat among
the circled children. Her profile was all he could see, facing
steadily south. "I have not seen many souls going up to paradise there, the Lord has chosen very few Métis today on the field
of battle."

"How many?" she asked harshly.

"Only enough to give us victory today."

"Today isn't over," she said; when his mouth closed over the
first spoonful of blood-milk broth Marguerite had given her for
him, Marguerite who had too little breath in her chest from her
morning sickness to carry a tin pail a mile through the wind,
Madeleine abruptly felt anger at him. She could not have
explained why; men did what they did, women had their place.
But still she was angry, his voice, his male assurance. He was
studying her when she finally glanced at him, quickly; the
empty spoon forgotten in his hand.

"The Lord shall fight for you, and you shall hold your peace."

"They don't have any—" she was gesturing south and her eyes tightened in amazement; she had countered him twice; no one spoke like that to him, she had never spoken to him at all.

"I have seen that today, on this hill," Riel said. "We will see the glory of God beat down our enemies here, and those that hate us shall plague us no more." She seemed to be shaking her head, looking at the children clustered about him and hearing his words reluctantly, almost impatient; he said, "You can say anything here; they believe in me."

"Then why...why are they shooting at Fish Creek, and all the men running back here so ashamed?"

"Gabriel isn't running, Edouard rode with eighty men."

"Dumonts never run." There was almost disdain in her voice; the daughter of Jean-Baptiste Wilkie, captain of the Red River buffalo hunt, and wife of Gabriel Dumont for twenty-seven years would never see a miracle in blind bravery.

"Yes," he said eagerly, "yes, God needs only a handful, let the rest run away and we will see a great miracle at Fish Creek; the unbelief of all our people will be turned into faith. That is the miracle! Those deserters today will repent of their doubt and believe and then the power of God will give us the greatest victory of all over our enemies, here on this ridge."

"Here," Madeleine asked, "at Batoche?"

"I saw that long ago, Gabriel and I talked of it."

"This isn't a good place for men to fight," Madeleine said slowly. "They'll lose their nerve, the children crying, and women."

"No Madeleine, no." Riel thrust the spoon into her hand, leaning forward; "it is the best, the only place, because God has shown it to me, because he will fight for us all here and break our enemies and it will not be men alone fighting far away. We are a community together," his fierce black eyes held her rigidly, "and these children and you women will give the men strength; you will fight too because faith alone will give us the victory.

You think we can destroy Middleton's hundreds with our few bullets?"

"Are there so many?" Fear flickered in her face.

"Yes! And Gabriel will stop them at Fish Creek."

"So we can all believe?"

"Yes," he said softly, his hand on a small girl's head, fondling her as she sorted grey grass from green in her hand. "I had not seen that before. I finally understood from Gabriel, we are all brothers, we are all led, that he must fight and I thought I had to go along, like Duck Lake; but the message came from Edouard and I had to return, and I was asking, 'Why, Lord, why?' and he showed me, why."

"God made the police go back, into Prince Albert?"

"Yes, they had done their job, kept me here and made us send fewer men against Middleton."

"How can Irvine and Crozier do God's—"

"Everyone does God's job, but some don't know it yet."

Madeleine sat with him, circled by the silent children, the bowl of his food cold in her hand from the wind bringing the black weather north towards them. Gabriel had said, again and again, "You've heard him talk to all the people; well you should hear him alone, there's no way to shake him. He knows what he's been since he was born, it's grown in him forever like roots." The power of words–he was praying suddenly, his arms crossed above his head against the thunderheads boiling over the wind-blurred river, sun strokes and gusts pushing down even flatter the gnarled trees simmering faintly green below them and in the river ravines.

"Then why is it so hard for us?" she said, defying his prayer, "and so easy for Canadians?" But he continued to pray in that torturous posture; she felt overwhelmingly that the whispering priests–he prays to impress you, a trickster keeping you in his power to lead you to destruction–were wrong; such prayer had nothing to do with listeners.

After eating at Roger Goulet's, we sent the Sioux out as scouts. We then went to Tourond's Coulee, and I, myself, rode on further. I went out of the moonlight into a tuft of trees and then came back again because I could hear nothing but Calixte's flute from our camp. When I got back to our people they were on their knees praying; I also knelt down. The scouts had not come in when we finished, so I said we should leave that place and go out to the enemy's camp. We set out and went through the ravine as far as McIntosh's but it was turning day and I saw it would be impossible to get at them during the dark. I told my people to return to Tourond's Coulee while I went forward with Napoléon Nault to try and make them follow us. We rode within half a mile of their camp, and it seemed to be very disturbed. So we rode back to our people. They had killed an ox for break-fast, and I told them, "We shall wait for them here. Do not fire until they are all in the coulee." I then took twenty horsemen to cover on the left of the trail; I wanted to treat the enemy as we would the buffalo. O Holy Virgin Mary, Queen of the Eucharist, you have prayed for us, pray for us now.

"All creation groans for redemption," said Riel. "We cannot imagine, the world has never seen, what would happen if a whole people would sacrifice to truly love God and do his will. Israel was called, the Holy Church was called, but they would not. They could never face the terrible demand of faith. Always only a saint, one solitary saint here or there far from each other, but a whole nation believing, holy enough to carry God's will into the world, that would turn winter into spring. We would not recognize the goodness and love that would run everywhere like water raining from heaven, every man love every woman, every woman every man, in purity like a mother her child, like a brother his sister. Now I can hold a child in my arms and love it without sin because of the child's purity, not my own; but then I would have that purity, and you, if we had faith, if we would repent of all our sins, we...."

Riel stopped as suddenly as he had begun; perhaps he had been answering her question, Madeleine was not certain. He was looking into her eyes with a strange, terrifying intensity which squeezed her head, her body, into a numb awareness of flesh and longing. As if her limbs sang.

"Then I could love you," Riel said, "the wife of my dearest friend, with the complete holy love Jesus gave to the women who fed him every day he was on earth."

Tension broke in Madeleine and she laughed, her full woman's body shaking as she sat with her hard hands clasped in her lap; and the children one by one lifted their faces to her and contemplated her with wide, expressionless eyes. After a moment she stopped, a catch in her voice almost like a sob,

"Gabriel has nearly killed men for—" she stopped herself. "He is a good husband," she said, "he could not...."

"Gabriel is perhaps better than you think," Riel murmured softly. "It is on his faith, on his faith and goodness..."

O gracious God strengthen me, they were riding down alongside the wood and we started firing before they were all down, it was that Boulton we almost shot in Fort Garry leading scouts and I encouraged our people, "God is strong; fire!" Then I went to the Sioux, the place where a Teton was lying on his back. I asked him, "Are you dead?" and he answered me, "Not yet," but he was singing his death song, and so I left him to his last happiness and went down the coulee past our horses and passing near our people and encouraging them and there I was told Jerome Henry had been hit. When I came near Maxime Lépine he said he was troubled about what he ought to do. I thought it was because of the crucifix he held in his hands, so I said, "Pray for the cause of our faith and for its glory." Just then someone shouted they were going to charge. We drew back into more shelter, and cannon balls were crashing through the woods like hail, but we were firing and they fell and their horses broke and I heard the cry, "They are going to run!" and we shouted for joy. Then we went back up the coulee after them, and I was knocking them around, one by one, one of my men loading Le Petit while I used another rifle and I showed my young men how to shoot and not waste bullets. I said, "Don't be afraid of their bullets, they won't hurt you." There was a heavy man with moustaches shouting orders from a grey horse, so I took his fur hat off–I was aiming a little lower, but he dropped his head–and my young men started to shout for joy. Then Napoléon Nault said, "Uncle, I think the Indians are going to run, you had better stop them." So I said, "Yes, I'll follow them," and when I got near where we tied the horses I found a lot of Cree and Sioux and Métis and I said, "Come with me and we'll knock down some pretty police," and some of us went down the coulee and around to head them off. An Indian said to me, "Don't leave us or we'll run away," so I held on for a while, and then I said, "Try to fight by yourselves, I'll go and see how God is helping our other people and I promise I'll come back." Then I went down the coulee, but the soldiers had already moved far into it. They were firing cannon and rifles and had killed almost all the horses and I stopped where there were large trees beside the creek, the risk was too great O blessed Joseph and St. John the Baptist pray for us and I wondered what I could do, there were so many of them. And then I heard our young men singing the song of the Bois-brûlés, Grandfather Falcon's song laughing between cannon. That gave me courage and I kept shouting to them, "Take courage, take courage, pray to God!" So we held them there, their cannon could not break through, and

*in the afternoon it began to rain, harder after a time, and
finally sleet. Jesu, Maria, shield us.*

"...world will be at peace like Eden, and we will love each
other holy and pure as Adam and Eve before the snake, like the
angels in heaven, without sin shining in God's holy light."

"Angels and heaven. I don't know," Madeleine said slowly,
"anything about them. I dream about them, and the angels protect us every day but I just wish I had given Gabriel a child."

"You have found love together," Riel began but she interrupted; she could not wait for his slow affirmation.

"Oh, love, I'm an old woman but when his seed leaps in me I
have such happiness, such—"

She broke off, staggered by her confession, so clearly impossible for a Métis woman, a strange man surrounded by a few
silent children. She could only laugh a little as he waited, saying
nothing, not looking at her now she knew at the corner of her eye.

"God never gave us that happiness together," she said.

"He gave you other gifts," Riel said slowly.

"The priests say children—"

"The priests are forbidden much," Riel's voice was hard and
clipped, "and so they're ignorant of much. Children are God's
great gift, but there are others, perhaps rarer and more holy."

"You don't think I'm...cursed?"

"Those priests!" And for an instant it seemed he could tear
his hair, but that passed. "Our women have so many children,
God must have given you a very great faith to have none at all."

He was praying in the thin cold rain that spilled over them
off the river. Only three children were left, one of them tiny Jean
squatting, perhaps asleep, under his father's jacket; after some
time Madeleine supported Riel's arms. One was on her shoulder,
the other on her two hands propped on her knees and so she
had to sit tight against his back, felt him shudder against her,
whether from cold or the overpowering necessity of prayer she

could not tell; after some time all her pain was gone, her long bitterness and her fear for Gabriel and all the fathers and sons and husbands gone and she felt only that she was part of him, this hard, solid rock.

By the mercy of Jesus I went back to the little group I had left, and only a few of them were there. The Sioux and some of the half-breeds were leaving, they would not listen to me any longer. But my brave men said to me, "Let's see if we cannot get to our people," and we went down, but as soon as the soldiers saw us they opened fire with cannon and rifles. "We have to stay till night, then we can rescue them," I said, so we went up to Widow Tourond's place and took some chickens from Isaac's hen-house and roasted them. Shortly after we began to eat, Moïse Ouellette and Philippe Gariepy joined us, and soon others came from the woods where they had been hiding. Two rode on a wounded mare, they had tried to go to the fight, but one of them, a Cree, said it was impossible to go there now. I said, "We must wait, our people will come from Batoche, and when it is dark we can get our boys and the wounded," so some of us waited, but others went away. It was raining heavily, but then Edouard came with the men from Batoche, and we greeted them. Then we dried their guns at Tourond's and set out all together though some of our men wanted to hang back. Near the coulee I went in front, and some of our people were on the left side, some on the right, and I found two horses alive and led them up the coulee through the creek and said to Yellow Blanket whom I found there, "Saddle them both, come nephew," but he said, "You saddle them, I'll watch for you here," and while I was saddling them Philippe Gariepy came up and I gave him the halter strap saying, "You take this one," and I tied the other with the reins to the saddle and started them all off towards our people, behind

us. Someone there was shouting, "They're going to charge,
watch out, the coulee!" but Edouard and our people charged
them, firing across the creek and they dived into bushes and
when they heard our shouting they ran leaving a lot of bag-
gage. Their medical officer left his box of medicines and two
bottles of brandy, with which we happily drank his health. I
told my people though we had lost so many good horses it
was the power of God that had saved our lives. Of the
whole day's fighting we had only four dead, and Maxime
Lépine said, "Yes, prayer did more than the bullets." Then I
shook hands with them and said, "Now we can go after
them and take everything else they drop," and some of our
people were ready, but others shouted, "That's enough,
don't go," so I said, 'It's enough, yes, but we must find all
the bodies and rifles.' The soldiers had fled but they had
removed everything, all we found were the tracks of the
carts they had used for their bodies. Then we all went back
to Tourond's together and warmed ourselves and got two
wagons to carry our dead and wounded. I said, "The people
on foot will walk ahead of the wagons, and those who have
horses will follow them," and they started that way, and
Edouard and Joseph Boucher and I remained in the rear
until we were well started. Then I said, "My friends, I am
cold, I think my head will suffer. Will you let me ride on in
front?" They said a great many would follow me. I said,
"No, I will prevent them," and urged them not to separate,
and rode ahead. When I got to the people in front five or six
wanted to follow me, but I stopped my horse and said,
"Since you will not listen, I'll stay here." Then André
Letendre said, "Go yourself, we'll stay." So I rode in, and
when I got here I found some of our men who had left us
long before, though I was not aware of it then. I at once
went to the Council House and after shaking hands with the
Exovedate there I asked for some hot tea. There was none to

be had. So I made my report, and if there is anything incorrect in it I ask pardon of God for it will not be by my fault.
—*A true copy, Philip Garnot, Secretary*

"By the power of God," Riel said, "you stopped Middleton with about a hundred men and held him with fifty-four."

"Those that run," Gabriel said, "they'd never been shot at before. You can't blame them much now, they feel—"

"This fight proved God's power," Riel said. "I don't blame them; no one should."

"Well," Gabriel drawled, holding a warm cloth to his aching head; the morning sunlight was creeping under the veranda roof across the table, "a few of us had to stay there to draw Canadian bullets. And we needed Edouard and the others to get those they had pinned down." He laughed outright, "White Cap was right! If Bladder Middleton hadn't sent four hundred men to the other side of the river, they'd have broken through. They were trying all day to come back; one of our Cree scouts said they all damn near drowned trying so hard on that one leaky scow, with horses and guns!"

"The clear hand of God." Riel stood with his hand like a blessing over Gabriel's shaven, gashed head. "Go to your house and your warm bed, we will care for the men. Tomorrow we'll bury our dead and dedicate ourselves to our next commitment of faith. Go my great strong brother, and rest."

"I'll rest," said Gabriel, "but you have to send messages now to Poundmaker and Big Bear, they have to come here."

"Yes," said Riel, "yes, now go."

No Englishman can possibly rest when stopped by natives. Middleton had suffered fifty casualties, including ten dead, of whom five were officers; the "affair with rebels twenty-five miles north of Clarke's Crossing on east bank of River," as he telegraphed the Honorable Caron in Ottawa, jarred him; its personal effect grew, the longer he thought about it. At first he telegraphed confidently: "Lord Melgund joined me as soon as he could from the other side of the river [it actually took two days to get all the troops and supplies back again], and we shall march tomorrow united on Batoche." But that confidence was soon staggered by the seriously wounded, the hospital ship *Northcote* still hung up on river sandbars, the growing knowledge that the Métis had almost routed him. Further west matters were not going well: Middleton finally agreed to let Colonel Otter march north with 540 troops from Swift Current to relieve Fort Battleford, still afraid of Poundmaker though no Indians had been seen there for two weeks; in Calgary Thomas B. Strange, a retired British general attempting to raise cows near the Blackfoot reserve, was ordered to organize troops and march north through Edmonton to Fort Pitt and teach Big Bear whatever lesson he could. "I think we have taught the Rebels a lesson," Middleton telegraphed Caron four days after the fight, and still camped at Fish Creek, "and am pretty sure I could march on Batoche, but it would not be politic for me to lose too many men. We actually had in action about 280 men and the Rebels must have outnumbered or at least equalled us. Need more men, mine are nearly without training and require management."

The general refused to believe Boulton's scouts that as few as a hundred and fifty of our men, perhaps fewer, had stopped him; he walked along the coulees again and stared at what he would call "excellently prepared rifle pits," which Gabriel years later would disdainfully identify as "nothing more than footpaths hollowed out by animals in the woods." Middleton's personal bravery in New Zealand and the Sepoy mutiny in India, where he was twice nominated for the Victoria Cross, was such that the bullet Gabriel had given him meant nothing, but he was sixty years old and ambitious for a padded civilian ending to his career; his young and beautiful French-Canadian wife should make almost anything possible if he impressed the Ottawa politicians with the size of his achievement.

"No, no," he declared to Boulton, mounting his horse; "there were at least three hundred there, and their casualties were equal to ours."

"One thing is certain," Boulton offered with careful diplomacy, "they lost sixty-four horses, some very fine ones. It's been a hard winter, I wonder how—"

"Shows they know nothing of cannon, tied down in groups like that in the coulee." Middleton snorted, kicked his mount into a canter. "You badly overestimate their prowess."

But he sent Lord Melgund, the only member of his staff he really trusted (after all, Melgund was experienced, British, and "of good birth") back to Qu'Appelle with secret orders to begin plans for an army of British regulars in case the Rebels shattered him and his Canadian volunteers at their next encounter; another fifty casualties out of a possible 280 (by lowering the number of his troops he had worsened his casualty rate) was too heavy to gain him anything, in Ottawa or anywhere else. And he ordered up the Gatling guns from the steamer *Northcote* and also the Midland Battalion from Swift Current. It was commanded by Lieutenant-Colonel Williams, a Canadian unfortunately, but every available man was now needed for the march on Batoche. Nine hundred seventeen men in all, not nearly enough Middleton knew; but he had to move. He could not stay at Fish Creek forever with his impatient, green, troops.

I have always agreed with my father who told me when my mother died, if your faith does not help you in time of death, then to hell with it. The expectant faces of our people were lifted to Riel, tear-stained, three coffins in a row of white pine just below the pulpit in St. Anthony's.

"But God, who has always led you and assisted you to the present time, will not abandon you in the darkest hours of your life. For he has called you to a mission which you must fulfil in every respect. May the grace of God keep you."

He closed the prayer book over the letter, the memory of

Sara on his fingers, in the eyes of his mind– O Louis let us be saints together–and our people, waiting to hear comfort, to be assured again that they were human beings, known to God who cared for them like a father, who would hold them in his arms and bless them and wipe their tears from their eyes.

"The words of Bishop Bourget to me are the words he has for everyone today. Many times I spoke to him, and he wrote to me when I fled for my life. Bishop Bourget knows us; he was obedient to the successor of St. Peter in Rome when he sent me these blessed words. If Rome is the truth, then it is Rome which promises us through the faithful bishop it has blessed that we have been called. And if we have been called, we will fulfil God's mission for us. We are not then deceived by anyone; we will not stray from the path God has traced for us, through which we will bless not only ourselves but also this country and all peoples. Though we will suffer for it, and though some of us will have to die.

"To die in the act of living our faith is no death at all. We sorrow for St. Pierre Dumont and José Vermette and Michel Desjarlais, and the two Indian brothers who died with them and were taken to their people, we sorrow for their suffering and for the love which they could have given now gone from our life, but we do not sorrow that they are dead. To die living your faith is no death, and the mouth of Bishop Bourget has told me that it is the religious faith of the Métis people which will lift them out of oppression and poverty to be an honour and blessing among the nations. By the grace of God, we must ardently serve God and advance his glory if need be to the very point of giving our lives. As these have done.

"Do not weep for these three; they went into battle with prayer, and no Canadian bullet can hurt them further. Weep for ourselves, and our lack of faith! That God gave us victory with fifty men set against hundreds supported by cannon, is a certain sign of his mercy towards us; that if we turn from sin and believe him, he will stop those that are coming against us and make them believe: the Métis people are called of God; who dares to touch God's people? Weep for ourselves, and our lack of faith! O my Métis Nation, you have long offended the kindness of God with your horse races, your gambling, your quarrels and feuds over the swiftness of your runners. The Eternal says, 'I know your sinful attachment to your horses and that is why yesterday, while sparing so many of you, I let your horses die.' He has touched us in our sin, but punished us lightly, and for this he asks our full faith, our full obedience."

The Widow Tourond, Madeleine, Marguerite with the two children, Patrice and Francois Tourond, Annie Dumont, old Pierre Parenteau and the older José Ouellette, Donald Ross, Moïse Ouellette, Philippe Gariepy, Patrice Fleury, Philip Garnot, Démase Carrière, Michel Dumas and Baptiste Boucher and Ambroise Jobin and Joseph Delorme, doubting Joseph Arcand, the strong brothers of the Dumonts, Gabriel and Eli and Edouard and Jean only left now, with old Father Isidore, brought from his sickbed to his grandson's funeral; and Maxime Lépine...Oh, Ambroise and beautiful Red River...and the scores of children and women and girls and Geneviève Arcand and Isaac Tourond, he could have named everyone listening to his words, those few hundred of our people whom he longed so tremendously to inspire by his faith to a faith that could, would have to, move mountains. But most of all he saw Gabriel there, seated at the head of his captains; O that God would stand like lightning and thunder in the clouds to brand them forever with the greatness that would be theirs if they steadfastly believed, guns were nothing, if they only–Gabriel's oaken, weathered face set on his immense shoulders, the cropped grey curls of his sheared head growing in over his wound like a buffalo bull's forehead, power and rage that could move the world–O my brother Gabriel, without you we are lost, with you we may be destroyed–he needed Will Jaxon, broken and crying in a small room; he needed Louis Schmidt, held perhaps not completely against his will behind the barricade of Prince Albert; he needed Father Ritchot; he needed the songs of–dearest God how?–but the words came to him then; he could continue, for the light of his vision shone like a single fire blazing in a night storm:

"The Lord shall fight for you, and you shall hold your peace! That is his promise to those who believe in him and in our mission. And hear these words, once spoken to David, words of new promise to us in this new land for our New Nation and our renewed Church: 'I took you from the sheepcote and from following the herds to be ruler over my people, Israel. And I was with you wherever you went and I will cut off all your enemies and will make of you a great name among the people of this land, and you will be remembered, the day of your birth and the day when you lie down with your fathers will be known from now and forever. For I will appoint a place for my people, and will plant them that they may live in a place of their own and move no more, nor run from oppressors, neither shall their children and their children's children be afflicted by the wicked. And if they commit iniquities I will chasten them with the rod of men and the stripes of the children of men, but my mercy shall not depart from them, neither now and forevermore says the Lord of Hosts, your Redeemer. Try me and see; wait on the Lord, and you will see his overwhelming glory revealed against all your enemies. For I would have you a blessing to all the nations, a light to the heathen who oppress you.'

"Many of you fear, some of you have doubts; God in his mercy understands our weakness, but do not tempt him. Commit your doubt to faith. Duck Lake and Fish Creek have shown us God's mighty hand. He will fight for us! Woe! Three times woe to the soldiers who fight on the side of wrong! The Lord will crush them like sticks broken for a fire! But joy to them who wage war for the love of truth and justice and right! Blessed to the Lord is the death of his faithful, for in the midst of life we are always in death. I am the resurrection and the life, saith the Lord. He that believeth in me, though he were dead, yet...."

And while Riel was trying, with his own vaulting and yet sometimes so prostratingly doubt-ridden faith, to lift our people from their guilt and apprehension to their final leap into the abyss–before them he knew there could not be destruction; there could only be the outstretched arms of God ready to raise them into a new paradise of belief untouchable by earth's mud and horrors–Caron's Canadian militia came slowly, inexorably forward. Colonel Otter at the head of 574 troops reached Fort Battleford to the cheers of the settlers packed in there with the police for over a month; on May 1, General Strange led the first division of his troops into Edmonton; the *Northcote*, filled with medical supplies and hay, was walking its way over the gravel bars of the slowly rising South Saskatchewan towards Clarke's Crossing; the Midland Battalion under Lieutenant-Colonel A. Williams, MP, reached Middleton's camp at Fish Creek; on May 2, without contacting Middleton and for unknown reasons, Otter marched out of Fort Battleford and attacked Poundmaker's camp on his reserve at Cutknife Hill and after four hours of fighting escaped annihilation only because the chief would not allow his warriors to complete their ambush of the retreating soldiers. "We have killed enough," Poundmaker said; "we may need more of them tomorrow." The poor fool; like all Indian chiefs except the Blackfoot Crowfoot, who listened to Father Lacombe long enough not to fight, and the Cree Big Bear who had lived and looked and pondered long and wisely, Poundmaker had no true concept of the dead weight of white bodies and of white stuff that could fall on him; that 314 poorly commanded soldiers equipped with repeating rifles and two seven-pounder guns which broke apart under steady fire would create a mere skirmish for whites but a life-and-death glorious battle for an Indian band protecting its women and children. For his misplaced magnanimity, within four months the handsome Poundmaker would be bolted inside Stony Mountain Penitentiary, and dead at the age of forty of a sickness that worked its way out of the wet lime-stone walls into his very bones.

But now in bright May the warriors had tasted glory and they decided in council to smoke Riel's tobacco and then go find out how long Bladder Middleton's hair was under his fur hat. Two thousand people to move over a hundred miles as the trails ran, but much farther in actuality for every night there was a new glaze of ice on the sloughs–why did Riel start it so early, before there was new grass for the horses?–and the few carts breaking down, and the children crying for hunger as they walked or waited while the hunters scoured the empty land. By mid-May they were southeast in the Eagle Hills again and a wagon-train intended for Otter at Battleford blundered into them; suddenly they had thirty carts of food and ammunition and twenty-two prisoners, and they were still eating and talking about what should be done with them when they heard from Batoche again.

Two hundred miles north-west, Wandering Spirit and his four hundred warriors and fifteen hundred women and children and old men had finished eating Hudson's Bay cattle between Frog Lake and Fort Pitt. There was no new grass for their horses either, but Little Bad Man, Big Bear's son who had replaced him as chief, was leading them slowly to Frenchman's Butte where he hoped a Thirst Dance, it was really too early, but still possible, would unite both Plains and Woods Cree, so they could begin the long march to Batoche.

Our old people left in St. Boniface and St. Vital and St. Norbert and White Horse Plains read what Louis Schmidt wrote in our French paper and did not know what to think about Riel and Gabriel on the Saskatchewan. A few young people, like wild dreamer Napoléon Nault had gone there, but mostly they had made whatever hard peace they could with white Manitoba; John Norquay had been premier for seven years, after all, one of our own and only three years older than Riel. I would have liked

to tell them again about our particular dreams when we were
young with Cuthbert Grant, of a peculiar people and the pride
of yourself as a self, not turning the small circle of making whatever living it barely can and sitting every night in the bar for that
one comforting beer before a soft bed. But I could never make
songs about an idea: a happening or a person was all I was ever
given to sing in the long years of my life (though it is enough,
the song at Fish Creek is enough), and you had to think like Riel
and see the exact problem standing where you could reach out
your hand and touch it as Gabriel must in order to understand
Duck Lake and Fish Creek and Batoche and the necessity of
rejecting Father André with all his church clutter. Louis Schmidt
helped nothing; he had stopped writing for the Métis. The only
news of Saskatchewan heard at White Horse Plains was the
English Winnipeg news of the Conservative and Liberal papers,
that and the Brelands coming from Wood Mountain and the
Cypress Hills for their spring trade and telling us Riel was mad
and their young men were already rich scouting for the Government and hauling poor slough hay to feed the Government
horses they had sold them too. There are always such, just give
them some excuse; in 1870 the Saulteux who were our blood relatives would gladly have shot us for, as Doctor Schultz assured
them, the honour of the Queen, a woman they would never see
and who never knew they existed.

The Spirit of God had me in a carriage with Michel Dumas.
He was leaving for the United States, I accompanied him a
certain distance. As I looked after him going on his way I
saw a large flowered snake following him, it had no retinue
but it was big–O, in America there are so many snakes. O
my God, keep us from the misfortune of having to join the
United States! I have lived miserably there, the United
States is hell for an honest man. He is made the object of
ridicule and scoffing. May the United States help us indi-

rectly, according to the disposition of your Providence, but never through union, never through our agreement.

To an extent Gabriel would always think like a hunter: at any moment Poundmaker's horsemen might appear on the west bank of the river and double his troops; or Wandering Spirit more than triple them. But he did not wait for that; he knew the Canadian guns now, and his resolute men had all been tried by fire: he told Riel they must strike. Fast, while Middleton sat immobile. If they stampeded all those horses chewing expensive hay, as they easily might, and killed a dozen soldiers while raiding their supplies for more rifles and the ammunition they had to have for a stand-up fight, Middleton would have to retreat and wait even longer for supplies and more troops. Day after day that big camp simply sat there on the river-bank, prac- tising a few horse manoeuvres, shooting at targets, and chewing up supplies. They had not so much as dared cross Fish Creek Coulee to look into Isaac Tourond's hen-house!

But Riel would not hear of that; Batoche was the place, the road beyond St. Anthony's Church where God would help them bring the Canadian troops to a standstill and Sir John would have to negotiate with them as a free and independent people who had their rights and would have, God grant it, their own western nation without benefit of Ottawa or Protestant Ontario or even French Quebec. There were Frenchmen with the Canadians; the men had heard them swearing in French at Fish Creek: well, let the wrath of God fall on them too; it was at Batoche where God would reveal the true strength of his arm against all who would oppress his people. This is the place! And though, in a long dragging moment of doubt that almost broke him on the hill above Batoche, he wrote a letter–"to all those in the United States who love freedom," there was now no means by which he could send it anywhere–he would not send Michel Dumas away now–and no one but he knew of it until it appeared in the paper that had always been O'Donoghue's favourite, *The Irish World* of New York; on November 21, 1885.

For Michel Dumas was with Gabriel, laying out the pattern of rifle pits with which to defend the peninsula of Batoche. God will have to fight for us, Gabriel told Riel, but we'll have to do some shooting too and I'd rather do that from behind something. When Riel told him how God had once so terrified a huge Persian army with thunder and lightning that it fled in the middle of the night without attacking Israel, Gabriel stared across the river a moment, grasping at last what Riel was waiting for and then turned to go up the hill to where his men were digging.

"I don't think God could scare Canadians with thunder," he said. "They've got too many guns."

The front line of the pits was almost two miles long and followed the broken line of prairie taking its first dip into the valley. Both the cemetery above the river bending west through shallow rapids and St. Anthony's with the rectory beside it, where the priests and nuns were still guarded, stood on the flat prairie and therefore both were outside the pits, unprotected and not even within shotgun range of the second line of pits scattered below the first. From their second line, the top of the spire was barely visible against the sky. That was the only way it could be, Gabriel explained; they had to be below the dips and hollows of the ridge where the Canadians' cannon was of no use and so the soldiers would have to attack them against open sky as they had at Fish Creek. In the ravines and brush knolls, the pits had to be dug at angles to each other so when the soldiers came in close the single- and double-barrelled shotguns and the muzzle-loaders could be used in cross-fire. They had to draw the soldiers in close; there were too few Winchesters and even fewer Sniders, and the cartridges for both were low after Fish Creek, they should have captured more ammunition there. But they had plenty of powder, and as long as that lasted the muzzle-loaders could use iron scraps or even bent nails when the shot was gone; they just had to get the Canadians in close enough, thirty to fifty yards like at Fish Creek.

And the volunteer Canadian soldiers camped before Fish Creek and seeing the horrible, jagged holes of wounds their comrades had suffered, had plenty of time to wonder what sort of "bloodthirsty savages" (as they had been told) these might truly be they had left their comfortable homes in all patriotism to subdue. Surely bloodthirsty men planning "all-out war" (as they had been told) would better prepare themselves than with such a relic of a smooth-bore fowling piece they had found in the coulee; it must be at least a hundred years old. As the Liberal *Globe* declared in Toronto on May 6: "The very strength of our citizen soldiery lies in this: That it thinks, and while it obeys, it has not ceased to have the right of asking the reason why, aye, and of pondering the weight of that reason when it is given." And when the *Northcote* finally staggered around the last bend and orders to march came at last, after two long weeks, their first encounter with Métis homes did little to assure them of their righteous cause against "savages."

It was the Tourond place on the bank above Fish Creek; the seven sons and two daughters, with their widowed mother had built, as Father André would soon passionately declare, his hand on the Bible, "the nicest kept farm in the settlement, plenty of cattle and horses." The latter were gone from the barns, either scattered or dead, and when Colonel Williams arrived at the house there was nothing left there either, its whitewashed log walls bare, pine table and chairs and beds thrown about, cupboards hanging empty and only in one corner of the kitchen, near the fireplace, a picture of the Virgin intact and beside it a Sacred Heart of Jesus from which the white muslin curtains had been torn aside, dangling on the string that had held them.

"Private!" Williams barked.

"Yes, sir!" The soldier wheeled, a small book in his hand, fumbling to drop it behind the broken table.

"General Middleton gave orders, no looting."

"Yes sir! I haven't got anything, sir; it was all gone by the time—"

"What's that book?"

"It's French, sir, I can't read a word, I swear I wasn't trying to—"

Williams interrupted across the open fear on the soldier's face; a very young man, nineteen perhaps.

"I'm sure a French prayer book would do you no good. Just leave it, get back to your regiment."

The private dropped it, coming for the door where several other soldiers looked in and hastily withdrew upon seeing the officer.

"What's that, sir?" the private gestured to the corner.

"That's a shrine, a Roman Catholic shrine."

The private stared incredulously at the impossible perfection of the woman's face, then the other; outside there was bellowing. "Prepare to mount!" but in the low, destroyed room the rounded valentine, as it appeared to them, seemed to glisten redly, almost as if it were wet.

"What do they...?"

"It helps them to pray," Williams said gruffly. "They are Christians, you know."

By afternoon next day when the Canadians reached Gabriel's landing, they were artists at clandestine looting; the officers, including Williams finally, though as Conservative Member of Parliament for East Durham he had a particular need to be careful, made sure they noticed nothing. Gabriel's barns they tore apart, his house crumbled to their whoops and they dragged the logs of both down to the ferry to barricade the *Northcote*; Middleton had decided that if he did not have enough men to advance on both sides of the river, the barely mobile steamer must become a gunboat and run down the river past Batoche, men aboard with rifles blazing, and so divert the

Métis with their simultaneous frontal attack. Every log made the stern-wheeler sink a little deeper in the shallow river, but Gabriel's billiard table was exactly what the captain needed for protection at the wheel; Madeleine's washing machine was less useful perhaps, and Annie's violin even more problematic–savages play violin?–but they also escaped the fire that somehow exploded almost immediately, among the ruins. The Canadian soldiers cheered as the smoke billowed behind them marching the last few miles north before setting camp on May 8; they could not quite believe how Gabriel Dumont, who had commanded the Rebels with "wonderful skill" at Fish Creek, could have left them so completely unharassed during their long march and even now as they "cut through the heart of the Rebel country" appeared only as distant horsemen vanishing on horizon hills.

Over the Council House at the edge of the river trees in Batoche floated the white Métis flag of the Virgin: on one side a sewn picture of Our Lady of Lourdes, on the other a poem written carefully in ink that smudged gradually in the quick spring showers:

> *Pray our divine Master*
> *Jesus Christ to prove now that He alone*
> *Is Lord,*
> *Emperor, King, Monarch, President, Czar,*
> *Prime Minister.*
> *Pray our divine Master*
> *That He mark us with the seal*
> *Of His Elect,*
> *At the foot of His Altar.*

Around the long table inside the Exovedate had considered a motion by Ambroise Jobin,

That Hell will not last forever, that the doctrine of ever-lasting punishment is contrary to the divine mercy and to the charity of Jesus Christ our Saviour,

and passed it unanimously; however a further motion by Baptiste Boucher:

That the heathen names of the days of the week be changed as follows:

To be named:

Monday	*Christ Aurore*
Tuesday	*Vierge Aurore*
Wednesday	*Joseph Aube*
Thursday	*Dieu Aurore*
Friday	*Deuil Aurore*
Saturday	*Calme Aurore*
Sunday	*Vive Aurore*

old Donald Ross could not agree, despite a long, careful explanation by Riel. Finally, though the other eleven voted "Aye," Ross was recorded as "Nay." And when President of the Exovedate Pierre Parenteau moved the next motion:

That the Lord's Day be put back to the seventh day of the week as the Holy Spirit appointed it through his servant Moses, to restore, in God's name, the Holy Day of the Lord's Rest

Ross was again opposed; and Maxime Lépine, still shivering at night from the memory of Fish Creek; and Moïse Ouellette. Gabriel was glaring at him, but Moïse would not lift his head. Not even when Riel suggested they might add, "though some delay their adhesion, it shall be accepted when it comes as freely as if it were given today," would Moïse raise his hand in agreement. So Gabriel turned to White Cap who had replaced Monkman; he began to translate into Sioux, struggling with concepts he could barely understand in French and about which no Sioux had ever dreamt, leave alone invented words for. But White Cap had already voted his agreement and was now watching Riel's long-bearded head bend over Garnot's papers with an expression like fear on his crumpled brown face. Finally Gabriel stopped, looked at the old chief in silence.

"Bladder Middleton marches, tomorrow we will be fighting but today he still..." White Cap shook his head in profound awe. "He is the holiest man I have ever known."

Gabriel stood abruptly, nodded as Riel looked up, signalled to Patrice Tourond and Démase Carrière and went out. From the porch, between the mounds of the inner rifle pits he could see a purple haze of crocuses scattered up the slope; children were playing there; ducks whistled up suddenly from the near marches along the river. A horseman came galloping down the bend of the street: Michel Dumas.

"They've burned all the farms south of Gabriel's Crossing," Michel reported. "And Vandal's and Poitras' north. That boat, he's covered it with logs from your house. It's tied up for night five miles south of here, and the army's digging in north-east from the river now, on Jean Caron's big field near the lake."

"Careful old bugger," said Gabriel. "You think they can run the boat down the rapids below the cemetery?"

"If we had some Winchesters below there," Patrice said, "we could wreck it anyway; the guy steering has to see out, just pick him off."

"We need that ammunition they'll have on there," Démase said. "We need it."

"And if they get through anyway, we snag them with the ferry cable, right here," Gabriel gestured down the street to the river. "All the ammunition just where we want it."

"It's too high," Michel said, "the cable's too high."

"Then we lower it, quick! Démase, you command the front pits tonight. I'll be up on the cemetery to signal you and the Winchesters down below."

"They probably want to attack at the same time," Démase said. "The boat and Bladder Middleton coming down the east trail."

"Sure," Gabriel said, already going. "So Michel and his scouts have to be out on the prairie, east, and I'll see his signals and also how the boat comes. We need that boat. Give all your men a good feed, kill cows, and I'll come around tonight."

"Better bring Riel," Démase said.

"We'll both come, sure." Gabriel stopped abruptly by Michel, sitting so still on his exhausted horse. "Get some rest tonight, we'll rub them out tomorrow. White Cap says."

"I just hope it doesn't rain." Michel looked into the cloudless sky. The late afternoon sun was still high above the north-west cliffs of the river; it was almost the season of mosquitoes. "When Wolseley come down the Red River, it was raining like all hell."

Gabriel put his broad, heavy hand on Michel's knee. "Middleton's no Wolseley," he said very softly. "We are the Nation now, and Riel is our prophet."

"Gabriel, you really believe him?"

"Like my salvation," Gabriel said, looking up steady as rock into Michel's troubled eyes. "God speaks with him."

I see the white one coming with his war helmet. The white one wavers, his feet slip slowly to the wrong side, he cannot stand, he slides little by little, down, down, down; he vanishes. Because his heart is great only for evil. Holy Virgin Mary, pray for us! I see the red soldiers, I pass ten feet from their guns and they do me no harm; they are stunned. Our men are only little boys, our women little girls fit only to play together, but they have been in front of these soldiers. God alone has saved us. O my God, what must I do to

appease your justice? O blessed Saviour, drive from us our
sin and save us from death, wounds. O Mary Immaculate
help us to show pity on the wounded, charity on the dead.

Riel and Gabriel with two or three hundred fathers and sons
and five or six hundred women and children – less than a thousand people, O what a Mighty Nation we were on May 8,
1885!–were dug into the slopes above Batoche waiting for the
Canadian army that night. Only fifty or sixty Cree and Sioux
were with them; the Blackfoot and the Bloods far away in the
south on their huge empty reserves, so long broken by smallpox
and moldy flour and stinking salt pork, if any, by disease and
inactivity and by missionaries' comforting words; the Cree scattered in small bands over bush and prairie so long broken by the
same that only Poundmaker and Big Bear's warriors started
anything, and even they could not finish it because of their own
lack of purpose unless faced directly by a hated white, their own
weakness and poverty and ignorance; because neither Big Bear
nor Poundmaker personally thought they could gain anything
by fighting except a little momentary glory for a few warriors.
And the people of Batoche whom Riel had abruptly forced not
only to think about when to hunt and plow and what to do with
their children–they had also always known that–but also to
decide about police and Company and bad government and,
most terrifying of all, whether Hell should be burning eternally
for them; whether they personally had the confidence in themselves to decide they would believe something they had not been
taught always to believe, that a personal decision about faith not
dictated by a priest but directly and personally communicated by
God was even possible, and that a priest could then only corrob-
orate or, if he refused to do that, he was damnably *wrong* – our
people themselves decide that in a matter of faith a priest could
be *wrong!*–how can I sing this sad, last act of our people when I
found my greatest strength at the altar of our merciful Lord in

St. François Xavier and when I died was buried with the full blessing of Holy Mother Church and every priest within two days' travel? The word and understanding is very near you: you need no revelation from beyond the grave; as our Jesus said when he was on earth, if you will not believe what is already discernible on earth, then neither will you believe that which comes extraordinarily from beyond.

The word and understanding are ancient: if with all your hearts you truly seek God, you will surely find him. Our people at Batoche had despaired in the advice of the priests; justice, right, worship after the pattern of the priests had become impossible (it never became impossible for me, though I sometimes wondered a good deal). And Riel had shown them they could change their thinking, they had to change their thinking not only about politics but also about their religious faith if they were truly to gain justice. In 1869 at Red River the priests stood with us, though even there Riel already questioned Taché's–not Ritchot's–true understanding of the people's needs and the hard world in which they lived; in 1885 the priests could no longer–or perhaps they did not want to–fathom our people; the crisis became more religious than political, and the long testimonies of the priests when a few months later our people stood on trial proved that. Riel could never have cajoled our people away from the Church, as the priests swore again and again he did, if he had not understood better than the priests their problems of faith. For our people, like true believers everywhere, Indian or white, when they are faced with seemingly insurmountable problems of faith, do not curse God and die; they begin to search within themselves whether their understanding of God is too small. Riel offered them a new and larger vision of God and his destiny for them; they in all sincerity believed–though at times doubting: the thoughtless are always certain–that God in his mercy would help them find.

The women and girls bedding down the excited children in the crowded settlement–there were not nearly enough houses;

tents and such shelters stood everywhere under the trees–felt the fears and doubts most deeply. Since March 23 many had slipped away once or twice to the priests and nuns in St. Anthony's Rectory; perhaps there was a word, something, but there was nothing to be heard up there except "Persuade your man, leave," and now even if they had wanted to go up the hill, it was impossible because the men were already in the rifle pits, waiting. Whatever the problems, and however their situation might have been changed if this or that had not happened, the men now faced a particular job; it was a job they could do, and at last they were doing it. Some muttered they wished they had a better rifle; some grumbled that, just like at Red River, a few had to pick up the guns and if they succeeded, all the cowards of the West hiding under their beds would benefit, they had already with that fat army spreading more money and work around than there had ever been in the West, why hadn't that drunk Macdonald given it to them instead of fat English generals, no one would have had to be killed? They were not too concerned about dying, though the rifle pits dug into the hill looked strangely like graves when they settled into them; death was always there, children falling in fires or gone with a stomach pain, women in childbirth, men hunting or lost in the snow, or everyone with disease. If you lived, you died; and some like Donald Ross or Pierre Parenteau lived to be old, or Old Ouellette ancient, he had ridden with Cuthbert Grant in 1816 and fought the Sioux on the Missouri Couteau in 1852, and here he was in a trench at Batoche, ninety-three years and still laughing and telling stories, his muzzle-loader that had shot white man and buffalo and Sioux worn smooth as calf's leather in his gnarled, still-steady hand.

"There were all the women and little children with us then too," his Cree words running soft and thoughtful in the long twilight. "And only enough rifles for seventy-seven men and boys over twelve. Women won't disturb us fighting; they'll pray and encourage us, that's what we're fighting about. This is the

346

biggest army our people has ever had, only thirty of us rode with Grant. But we were masters of the plains, the fiercest Indians left us alone."

"Lépine had more," Napoléon Nault said. "At Red River."

"Sure." Old Ouellette's hands began searching his pockets, "Seven hundred armed men plus the Company cannon, but we never fought anyone, never fired a shot even at the Portage party." He found the tobacco, began shaving it into his pipe. "Not a shot."

"We didn't have to," Moïse Ouellette suddenly answered his father from the darkness of the next pit. "We were too strong, they didn't dare."

"Maybe, maybe," the old man's pipe glowed with a coal from their tiny smokeless fire. "We rode all over with Lépine, armed like robbers and never fired a shot, but we were ready to do it."

"Well, I'm ready too," declared Patrice Tourond beside Napoléon.

"And if you get shot tomorrow?" Napoléon asked.

"Or you?" Patrice laughed a little. "One or the other, Annie won't have to make up her mind."

All the listening men laughed quietly with two young men. Down in the valley, from Isidore Dumont's field which Gabriel had assigned them for a camp, the Indians were beginning to drum; only a single beat now but it would be chant soon.

"That's a Sioux drum," Old Ouellette said. "Now they're with us."

"Would it be better, Grandfather," Napoléon said, "if it were only Crees?"

"I'm so old everything seems to have changed at least four times since I lived." The old man chuckled softly in the corner of the rifle pit. "But I've never questioned anybody who wants to fight beside me. Friends are better than relatives."

"But what if what you're fighting for is different," Napoléon insisted, "like the Sioux wanted to kill all the hostages and Gabriel wouldn't—"

"So did the Crees," the old man interrupted.

"Okay, okay, I'm not Sioux or Cree; I'm more like the French-Canadians in Middleton's army, why are Sioux and Cree with me, shooting them?"

"You're not French-Canadian either, Napoléon," Patrice said, "You're Métis, like Louis Riel. And you always will be."

"You never see what I really mean," Napoléon muttered.

"Then why don't you say it better?" Patrice asked.

The Indian drums were very loud in the May twilight now, and the air felt cool, almost cold through their thin clothes. The old man shifted a little against the warm earth.

"We are who we are," Moïse said from the other pit.

"And God is on the side of justice," Old Ouellette said. "That's always true, ninety-three years that's true."

"What if," Napoléon said slowly, "if your cause isn't just?"

Old Ouellette, strangely, laughed at the question they all had asked, and their wives had asked, and they had seen it in each other's eyes as they lay flat among the ravine bushes that long day at Fish Creek. He laughed his soft, worn old laugh as if it grumbled deep inside himself somewhere for very happiness.

"Then you say to God, I didn't know better, haven't you got a little mercy left for me? I don't need much, I was never big enough to do anything big and terrible, just a little will be enough."

Albert Monkman spoke for the first time all evening. "Yes. If God ever gives us what we deserve, we'll all hang."

"I think I'd rather be shot," Patrice said.

O holy Father, I love you! My great Redeemer, glory be to you, and a hundred thousand million thanksgivings, O my God, for all eternity, for your mercy toward my wife, toward my two blessed children, toward my mother and my family, toward all my enemies. Help us find a way to be good to our enemies, O God, while giving us from this moment and forevermore your success, your victories and your tri-

umphs. Dearest Saviour, it is my sins that will wound us,
it is our grievous fault that will annihilate our nation,
though we will not cease to pray, no, never cease to pray.

"You two should go on your own business for a little," Old Ouellette said. "Go. You want to do something."

Napoléon and Patrice looked at each other across the fire, then to the old man squatted almost invisible in the shadows. Finally Napoléon said,

"We are supposed to watch...."

"I'm too old to sleep before dawn. Go."

When they were gone, noiselessly into the night which was deepening from red to purple over the cliffs across the river, Moïse said.

"Gabriel won't like that. Or Démase when he comes."

The old man bent forward; his gnarled hands sank toward the tiny firelight, cupped it between them. Under the wild drumming and chant a new sound arose, as it seemed from the dark mass of trees outlined against the north-western sky.

"I wish I could make confession," Moïse said.

"There will be no priests," the old man said. "We must do as Riel told us, the old way of the plains, and the way of the Indians too, before battle."

"Yes," said Moïse. "Will you hear my confession?"

"Yes.

The Canadian soldiers on picket four miles east also heard the sound; a stray wisp of it carried clear and strong, and for a moment they thought they heard the distant organ chimes of home, or bells at least ringing them to worship. But it was like the enormous sky over them, strange and faintly terrifying in its restlessness, its gigantic moving lights that flickered sometimes like fire; and the Indian drums. Those they heard plainly, could recognize of course, as they could not have the women singing, even had they been close enough as the Métis men were in the pits stretched for two miles just below the edge of the prairie. The women of Batoche singing the song our people had always loved. It is in the first conscious memory I have of the prairie; I was a baby lying on the fur of green hides in the cart and I remember the peeled vertical poles of the cart's side and the spokes turning beyond them against a grey-green line smudged by heat between land and sky, the cart bumping and squealing under me on the green, rubbing hides and my mother above me driving the horse, singing,

We praise thee, O God,
We acknowledge thee to be the Lord.
All the earth doth worship thee, the Father everlasting.
To thee all Angels cry aloud.

"You're supposed to be on the ridge," Annie hissed. "All the men are!"

Before Patrice or Napoléon could answer she had pushed them out of the firelight into the darkness, behind bushes; the women sang on, oblivious, their heads bowed before a small picture of the Virgin nailed to a tree, the wispy cloth that framed it swaying a little in the night air.

"Grandfather Ouellette said we wanted to do something," Napoléon whispered.

"He said go, he'd watch till dawn," Patrice added.

"He's with you, in your pit?"

"Yes."

"Well." They could almost see her face, her leanness outlined by firelight between spidery trees. After a long moment, she said, "What do you want to do then?"

Patrice said slowly, "We both want to see you...."

"And Gabriel would never let either one of us see you alone in the dark," Napoléon said.

"He won't come to the house tonight," Annie began, but Napoléon interrupted.

"He'd kill us if he found out, and he'll find out."

"Oh, he'll find out," Annie said. "You can't come to the house anyway, they've put the hostages in the cellar again and there's stones piled on the cellar door and Old Man Rochleau sits there with a double-bitted axe."

"There's two of us anyway," Patrice said disconsolately.

"I could start with one," Annie teased, "then the other."

"And how'd you choose who visited first, eh?" Napoléon demanded. "Maybe they'll attack at night and we'd have to run before the second one got any time—"

"I'd let Rebecca decide," Annie said solemnly, but her voice betrayed her.

"Sure," said Patrice, "that's real—"

"That's not fair—" Napoléon burst out, and Annie clapped her hand over his mouth; she had once let the mare decide but since Patrice had often fed the horses, he then had the advantage.

"Anyway," she said, "we can't go there, because Mama's with Mrs. Riel."

"He kissed you, didn't he?" Patrice said.

"What?"

"Your hand, when you shut him up."

"Oh!" She slapped Patrice, lightly. "There's a kiss, you're supposed to be soldiers facing ugly Canadians and you're like... like...."

"You?" Napoléon offered. "We're as grown up as you?"

Lord have mercy upon us;
Lord let thy mercy lighten upon us,
As our trust is in thee.
Lord, in thee have I trusted; let me never
Be confounded.

"Come," she said suddenly, her voice shaking as if she might cry. She led them quickly down a path, away from the singing and nearer the ceaseless drumming of the Indians that wavered, rose and fell in the spring night like warmth and coolness. Then just below Isidore's house she turned left, into the willows towards the river; she moved so swiftly in the darkness the two men could barely follow her; the willows stung their faces, and several times one or the other stopped uncertain in the brush-filled darkness, and only the sound of her plunging ahead guided them on. Then they stumbled against her; they seemed to be in a hollow under willows. They could see nothing, only hear her quick, deep breath taken between her teeth.

"Sit down," she said, and they hardly knew her voice, it was so abrasive. "This is where Mama and I will stay if they shell Batoche. Hush!" she cut across them both, starting to protest, "if Daddy's wrong, he's wrong, but I doubt it. Just sit down, both of you."

They sat down, as literally at her command now as they had been emotionally for seven months and had hardly noticed the laughter of the other Métis young men who would never, but never be caught like that by one little female, goddamn never; the sand and smell of the river; they must be near it, as their breathing quietened they could hear the secret, endless, slipping of river over stones. The drumming was not so loud here, and the Te Deum was lost altogether, swallowed by dark.

"I don't want you to say anything," she began slowly, then plunged on very quickly, "we've talked so much all winter and I don't know which of you I love more because I love you both and you've been so good, both of you, always considerate and gentle and not fighting and I love you for that too because I've felt so different from other girls the men are chasing and they want only one thing, but you have been so–good—" her voice was almost a sob momentarily but she controlled herself, "–no, don't say anything, either of you, we've said enough, I have too, and I want...I want you—" she stopped; Patrice and Napoléon were not so much as breathing for they knew Annie was holding them both, one arm around each of their shoulders and they knew she could do that only because of the darkness, the words she was going to say said to each of them and together as if they were only two people alone in the world.

"Mama once told me a story," she said very quietly, almost happily, "about a man and a woman who could not...could not make love together, it was forbidden, and so they slept together one night with his long sword lying between them, and they—"

"I don't want *him*," Patrice began, "I want that sw—"

"You never understand anything!" Napoléon said in disgust.

"Shut up, both of you! They lay like that all night and loved each other so much and the rule that forbade them was so holy to them, they did not touch each other all—"

"You can't love us bo—"

"Don't you start," Patrice said.

"Don't argue!" Annie joggled them by the scruff of their long hair. "Just shut up and listen! It's a lie, a woman can only love one man, why can't she love two? I do! Sometimes I like to be with you," her hand caressed Patrice, "riding and laughing about horses or farm cows and sometimes I like to talk about stupid governments and word games," she brushed Napoléon's bristly beard. "And sometimes I can't stand either of you, always watching me. I want to be alone, myself, be myself and a woman who doesn't need anybody and sure not a man acting so big and strong like he owned the world and every woman in it with one look from him would curl up and warm his dirty feet! And I get so fed up with the girls who go twitching their rear at the—"

"That Geneviève Arcand walks like she has eggs up her—"

"You're far more beautiful then Gen—"

"Hissst!" Annie's hands closed over their mouths. "I've said enough, that's all. I just want to be with you, with you both till you have to go again. I didn't think I'd see you," she laughed softly, her full laugh that tumbled the men's feelings over and over, they would have taken her in their arms but they could not, did not dare. "Grandfather Ouellette is so good, so really good. O, I wish I could love you both, love you, O...we'll lie down, right here...no, just lie beside me. Don't say anything! Just together."

Through the bare willows crossed above them they could see the pale red glow of the spring sky, the stars like devil's eyes peering at them. The girl breathed between them; her arms held them close but her long slender body lay between them like an untouchable naked sword.

The Spirit of God has instructed me: the Lord lets himself be moved by fasting and prayer. You will not be wounded. O my God! Give me your Holy Spirit of courage, your Holy Spirit of strength and of good intentions, from now until my last breath so that our people all may have the joy of doing your holy will and that we accomplish the good work you have given us, in every respect.

The Canadian soldiers waiting for dawn in the ring of their zereba of oats and hay and earth under the enormous prairie sky could still hear, very faintly, the Indian drums beating.

3

THE Battle of Batoche began on Saturday, May 9, 1885 at ten minutes after eight in the morning.

Gabriel was on the height above the cemetery and saw the *Northcote*, blocked round with logs from his own barns and house, and his billiard table against the wheelhouse, inch its way around a bend and halt at anchor in the middle of the river about seven o'clock. The two loaded barges it was towing gradually drifted forward past it on either side in the current, and he studied them for a few moments; supplies, tons of them. Through his glass he could just see a metal contraption on a three-legged stand which must be the small Gatling gun mounted on the blunt prow; men in uniform moving around it, behind sacks and logs piled there. There were hoof-beats behind him; Michel galloped up: Middleton was moving in straight from the east, Boulton's scouts first, then Howard with the Gatling, and then the infantry on foot, at least nine hundred men. How far? Three miles. Gabriel looked at the steamer: it was starting to move again. He signalled to Edouard below and Patrice Fleury across the river. Immediately a Winchester cracked, then several, and white steam blasted from the *Northcote's* stack, its dull whistle blaring into the cloudless morning sky.

"By God!" Michel said, "Good thing it's spring or they'd stampede the rutting moose on us."

"Tell Démase to get the pits ready." Gabriel was flat on his belly with his Winchester. "We'll finish Bladder's navy before he gets here."

To the east a cannon boomed, and the *Northcote* whistled again. But the Gatling on its prow was clattering too, an enormous alarm clock sound rocketing between the cliffs as the boat came on and Gabriel fired Le Petit, carefully, at that machine so stupidly exposed. Let those down on shore pick off the pilot in the wheelhouse; he wanted that American with his murdering machine. But it was too fast, and bad light coming directly towards him to where the river bent at right angles into rapids, paddles churning and the Winchesters below and across the river wasting bullets furiously, the Canadian soldiers on board firing back and they were dragging the Gatling behind flour sacks piled on the deck: Gabriel got one good shot down into the boat's open wheelhouse where the pilot was lying flat on his back, his head hidden by sacks and trying to steer with his feet as the clumsy boat swung crazily around, helpless, and slid fast into the current ripping against the far shore. He thought for a moment it might ram the bank, but the river was too swift and high, the boat hooked the bank an instant but the current swung it completely around, backwards, and carried it high over the rocks of the rapids, its bottom thudding down, the steamer shuddered, bounced, paddle-wheels still churning with the barge lines snarled in the paddles; and Gabriel was laughing aloud, cheering on the cliff, then leaped up, sprinted for his horse. The cable! At a dead gallop he was down the river trail, firing two fast shots, then two again into the air; but the current was too fast with the crippled boat: it swirled around the bend and into the long north stretch of river almost at the speed of his good grey, and the men could not lower the ferry cable fast enough.

"Lower! Lower!" Gabriel was screaming as he galloped but the cable barely hooked, tore off the smoke stacks, dragged them in flames the length of the boat; if they had caught the wheel-house, the whole boat would have floundered, shoved under by the current and thrown up on shore, somewhere. As it was, fire burst in hay and splintered wood and while the boat swept on down the river and around the northern bend some of the men aboard were fighting that furiously while others kept shooting at the shore.

"They can't signal any more with that whistle," Eli said. "Too bad, we could have swamped them."

"All those supplies!" Gabriel could barely control his rage. "At least get five men down the river, shoot at them so they don't come back."

"We couldn't hear your shots, Gabriel," Eli began, but Gabriel wheeled, ran to his horse.

"Forget it! I was too long watching that goddam thing fall ass-end over the rapids!" He sent his sweaty grey up the road and through Batoche, yelling at the staring women and children, "Get down, Middleton's coming!" And their white faces were whipped away from him as he lunged on up the slope toward the silver spire of St. Anthony's and the rifle pits.

He was just in time: Démase Carrière was in the dip between church and cemetery, the men snug in their pits, rifles ready, heads high and staring. They could hear the distant rumble of horses and wagons; dust drifted up where poplars and the hill bent the road under the morning sun already high towards the south-east. Suddenly there was a rattle of gun-fire; all the men listened, breathless, and then the boom of a cannon. Gabriel yelled to the nearest, "That first's the Gatling, you've got to watch that," and the word spread along the pits. Abruptly smoke bil-lowed up, then more; dreadfully black in the blue sunlight.

"There goes Baptiste's house," Gabriel said. "And his barn too."

"Weren't Michel's men there?" Démase asked.

"I hope they knew enough to get—" but horsemen were galloping over the crest of the hill down the road: the last of Michel's scouts.

"They're spreading out," the foremost rider yelled, "their guns in front!"

"Ride down the line," Gabriel gestured, "and get four companies from the north pits down here, double up behind the church. Just single men in the north pits, we need everyone here."

"The church," said Démase, "the priests and nuns are still in the rectory."

Gabriel stared at him. "What?"

"Louis said, 'Leave them there, let the Canadians have them,' so I just took the hostages down to the cellar yesterday."

"Okay," Gabriel was watching the road. "Okay then. I hope they get shot for all they helped us, those black bastards."

Démase nudged him; Riel was coming along the line of pits, the long Duck Lake cross high in his hands. The men knelt as he came, and Gabriel slid to one knee and heel, his eyes intent still on the bent road over the hill, but his lips moving in prayer, with Riel's deep chant,

Our father who art in heaven,
Hallowed be thy name.
Thy kingdom come, thy will be done
On earth....

Riel was past then, the shadow of his cross passing over the men dug into the earth, his voice moving on so that the whole hillside murmured after him. For a moment Gabriel could not remember his special prayer; he knew he should be praying it and vowing to do so as soon as–why couldn't he find the words so automatically on his tongue–and then the first of the soldiers topped the hill: red uniforms like the police, and in the very centre drawn by two big horses, was the four-wheeled wagon with ammunition box between the front, a barrelled contraption between the back pair: the big Gatling gun. And a fat rider on a tall bay horse: Middleton sure. They were wheeling the team around on the hill, not coming nearer. At twelve hundred yards away, much too far.

"Démase, nobody shoots till I signal. Not one shot, no matter what they do," Gabriel said, and climbed up to a knoll, well forward on the prairie. The gun was being turned into place, the broad spread of the army invisible behind the hill: only the few men there, and the gun searching, being twisted about into line with something.

"Get down!" Gabriel yelled. "Keep your heads down!"

Démase was signalling down the line, and suddenly smoke began churning about the gun, then the high scream of bullets and the chatter of explosions. Gabriel couldn't believe it: they were shooting at the church, the rectory! The bullets drummed into the wood with a sharp clear *thud! thud!* and then the revolving gun muzzles moved ponderously sideways and the bullets screamed overhead, far away into the blue sky over the rifle pits. But the muzzle was swinging back again, *thud! thud! thud!* like a quick hammer pounding on the grey rectory, the boards of the church so high they must be hitting above the window, by god, those priests were–a white handkerchief shook frantically at the gable window of the rectory and immediately the mounted officer signalled and the Gatling stopped. Gabriel looked back down the line of pits. All the men stood there erect, staring in amazement at that unbelievable machine cranking around to wipe them out. Gabriel laughed, waving to them.

And they all watched as the officer group rode forward towards the church and the white flag; the group stayed well back from the rifle pits, at least a thousand yards and when they arrived at the rectory, nuns and priests billowed out in a black cloud: Gabriel could see Father Moulin clutching his shoulder: the first casualty from the Gatling; he must have been upstairs praying. After a moment the priests and nuns were going off with the Canadians, they would of course, and Middleton was signalling behind him and then, for the first time, the Métis in the pits saw the army advancing towards them; the scouts had seen this, and talked time and again; and Fish Creek had been a wash of red through smoke and rain, but this–they had never seen so many men, and horses, and carts, and none of them ever, so many beautiful rifles.

The Canadians advanced in a block, the scarlet Royal Grenadiers in the centre, the green 90th Battalion on the left, and the Midlanders, scarlet and white, on the right. But they halted out of rifle range. Orders barked, and then the Grenadiers advanced alone, swinging out in a long thin skirmish line around the church and down the ravine in front of the cemetery. On one knee, Le Petit butted in the spring-soft ground, Gabriel watched them come; scarlet coats and round flat caps, their gold braid glinting in sunlight against the shimmery green poplars and the sharp steel of their bayonets; his heart was hammering in his chest so he could hardly breathe. He glanced at Démase; the big man stared at him desperately for the signal and for a moment Gabriel did not give it, waited those few more yards and not breathing felt in his bones the tramp of the hard boots smashing grass into mud to the skirl, skirl of their rattling drum, their colours proud as conquering flags above them and then he jerked Le Petit above his head, screamed,

"Now, now! In the name of God!"

And he leaped down to the rifle pits, his mind gasping, "O God strengthen our courage, our courage..." but the Winchester was already blazing, there was nothing to aim at, just the red wall, even as the men in the ravine stood up at Démase's signal and fired their first withering volley over the edge of their pits into the human wall advancing upon them.

Every Canadian who died at Batoche or Fish Creek was described as a kind, considerate son or father, gentle with all who met him; only twenty-five Métis stood trial at Regina, known to our people as The Place Where the Bones Lie; only eighteen of them were convicted of taking up arms and fighting Her Majesty's troops, and every one of them had testimonies, sometimes very moving, of their decency, their individual kindness to particular prisoners and hostages. Where was all this kindness, this goodness on the ridge above Batoche? I should have to tell you! The Grenadiers hurled themselves to the ground and but for Howard, furiously working his Gatling over them, still far too high to saw down any more than the tops of the trees in the ravine—it seemed lie wanted to bury our men in mangled sticks—but too low also to advance into, the Grenadiers would have lost a dozen men and more rifles and ammunition. As it was, our men dared not advance but they cheered wildly as they continued to fire from the pits and the bright uniforms crawled back through the grass they had trampled so boldly, here and there a scarlet splotch left behind.

"Napoléon!" Gabriel was down in their pit, "Give me some cartridges, Winchester cartridges!"

But the young man was staring out of his hole, Winchester motionless in his hand. Beside him, Old Ouellette fired, whooped, and methodically withdrew his long muzzle-loader from between logs, poured in more powder.

"What's the matter?" Gabriel asked. "Napoléon."

"I...I think I shot, that man...."

Gabriel peered over the notched logs; a redcoat lay there, fifty yards, head and chest jerking but his legs lying strangely motionless; out of his mouth, they could hear it over the gunfire, came a thin, high sound; nothing human, more like steel drawn across a saw.

"That's what you're supposed to do here," Gabriel growled, digging cartridges out of Napoléon's pockets. "Now you know."

He scrambled out, found his place well forward on the prairie; there, seated on one heel with his knee to the ground, he fired carefully, directed the defence. The Midlanders advanced on the Grenadiers right, so Démase set fire to the bushes there and drove that battalion back; the Ninetieth advanced in skirmish line left of the church but by then the companies from the north pits were in place and they held them off easily, not a single man touched by Canadian bullets because the Canadians had to come in against the blue sky unable to see anything in the ground below their feet. They were brave enough, and moved forward steadily in company groups to carry off their wounded, but given the positions, as one of their correspondents noted, "one rebel was as good as ten volunteers, just as it was at Fish Creek." The Gatling could not seem to crank itself low enough to place any bullets near the pits so finally it raised its attention to the houses almost a mile down the valley. About that time Michel Dumas led a company up a ravine around the cemetery against the guns of A Battery set on a knoll behind the infantry lines now dug in on the prairie paralleling the Métis line; the two big guns had done no damage, the men in the pits could see and hear the commands as easily as the gunners and on the word "Fire!" they simply crouched low in their pits and though the balls landed along the line, the earth swallowed them harmlessly. Michel's attack killed a gunner and wounded three; Patrice Tourond and two others came within sixty yards and they would have carried the gun if Boulton's scouts had not galloped up and driven them all back. So Middleton, still on his horse out of range behind the church, ordered the guns pulled to a hill half a mile behind the lines; from there they also began to fire into Batoche.

The Gatling had accomplished nothing in the village either, its bullets very nearly spent when they thumped against walls and trees; however, the nine-pounder balls screaming through tree-tops and exploding into the river cliffs beyond terrified the children and the women with them. They fled from the houses of Batoche into the woods. Middleton halted the firing for five minutes when he noticed; he would not deliberately gun down non-combatants, but with that warning pause he ordered, "Carry on firing."

One of the guns concentrated on the white Baker store on the west cliffs above the river where Riel now had posted the Virgin flag. One ball did hit the house, another tore through it end to end and fire burst from the wooden walls. The people watching groaned, the white flag waving so stiffly out of the climbing black smoke; but suddenly as though wiped away by a hand, the smoke and fire were gone. Riel, at the Batoche shore loading the ferry with women and children to take them to the shelter of more trees on the west side, looked up as a mother screamed,

"Look! Look! The fire, it's a miracle!"

"No cannon ball," Riel laughed, handing her baby up to her, "can destroy the goodness of the Holy Virgin. Go there."

The flag of Our Lord, which the people called the "Fish Flag" because of the picture sewn on one side, flew over the Council House. No ball touched it during the first three days of fighting. Night and day Gabriel sat forward in the pits with the men, Riel either walked unarmed along the line with his cross carried high in prayer or with the boys and girls brought up water and the food the women cooked over fires in the densest trees. Neither on that first Saturday, May 9, nor on Sunday nor Monday following was any Métis killed, only two were wounded slightly as every day Middleton's troops advanced to exactly the same gouges on the prairie they had held before, fired steadily at nothing they could see below the break of the land in front of them, paused for lunch, returned to the same business, and every evening, as Gabriel said, "they crept back into their holes," in the zereba they had formed a mile from the church. Middleton had found the enemy in a valley, not on a hill; he seemed to have no idea what to do, and by the morning of the third day he was convinced he had too few troops, or supplies, even to starve the rebels out. The weather was beautiful, clear with occasional showers; one night the pickets and the exhausted men in the pits saw the rare beauty of a lunar rainbow. Middleton spoke loudly to his wounded (they now used St. Anthony's as a hospital) and telegraphed to Caron "I fancy the rebels must have lost a fair average, judging from our own killed and wounded and the amount of fire kept up by us," but it truly was his fancy. The Canadian rifles were hitting grass dummies hoisted out of the Métis pits for their convenience; the cannon blasted trees and log walls; in three days the Gatling hit nothing except a baby, struck by a spent bullet as it lay beside the women's cooking fire. When the mother turned from stirring a cauldron of beef, she saw the red splash on its body. She screamed; the other women came running, but in its last spasm the infant was already dead.

By Monday evening the Canadian soldiers were talking so loudly and furiously about this "doddering old man's war" that was steadily wounding and killing them without ever once having *seen* the enemy, that Middleton could hardly pretend not to hear them. He had wired long ago for more men; in Winnipeg by now Lord Melgund must be working like the devil to get British regulars; but all that could be certainly weeks, perhaps a month away. After three days here there were two encouraging factors however: one, the released priests and nuns, doing a damn fine job with the wounded, damn fine, insisted that many Métis were deeply discouraged; two: they must be running out of ammunition for most of the wounds, as the doctors explained in detail, were now made with slugs, even bits of blacksmith iron. After five dead and over thirty wounded in three days, and still in exactly the same position as when they first arrived, that was encouraging.

The nights were very cold for May, and our men suffered in the rifle pits, but not more than their women and children hiding in the woods with a few blankets and robes, in the small caves

they had dug in the ground or into the sides of ravines and covered with brush. The gun bombardment, though it hurt no one,
had destroyed their homes. Riel went everywhere, praying and
leading in prayers. In the thickest stand of the poplars and spruce
near the river, where the women had sung that night before the
battle–it seemed so endlessly long ago now–he had added a
Sacred Heart of Jesus to the Virgin picture. Day and night groups
knelt there in prayer. But the endless balls and bullets of the
Canadians drove them towards despair; during the night the
dirty, bearded men came down from the rifle pits, one by one,
asked about their families, ate what little broth there was, and
dug the Gatling gun bullets out of the destroyed house walls, the
splintered trees. They had some powder, but nothing left to shoot;
there were no Poundmaker or Big Bear Indians suddenly on the
west cliffs, and there would not be. Both Riel and Gabriel knew
that as Monday faded into Tuesday morning.

His officers reminded Middleton that he had men and
resources within sixty miles: North-West Mounted Police Commissioner Irvine with three hundred police and volunteers in
Prince Albert. If the *Northcote* were sent down to Prince Albert
and Irvine marched up from the rebel rear–No! The vaunted
police were nothing but gophers; they had done nothing in this
rebellion except get blasted and then dig in like gophers, waiting
to be relieved. And he would relieve them, let them stay where
they were! With that, General Middleton finished a last bit of the
fresh bread his personal cook had produced for him and retired
to the comforts of tent and feather bed; May dawn comes early
in these wild northern latitudes; even English generals know
that.

Gabriel had pulled in every man from the west side of the
river, from shooting at the *Northcote* (which after two days at
anchor protecting its supplies just around the north bend had
suddenly steamed downstream and promptly run onto a gravel
bar); a few older Indians were making arrows to receive the

Canadian soldiers–if they only had ammunition! One more day, maybe enough for that.

"All the people are tired," Riel said. "This is too long. The cannon balls, the endless shooting. Always the women stare at me; I will tell them their man is killed."

"God's been good, I couldn't believe it if someone told me." Gabriel wolfed bannock. His massive hunched shape loomed in the firelight of the rifle pits, his proud, dark face gouged with fatigue but his eyes glaring sharp, unnaturally vivid as coals. "Three days and nobody dead."

"The Canadians shoot no better than the Sioux on the Coteau," Old Ouellette said. "But those sure rode better."

"We need a miracle," Patrice Tourond said quietly.

"They have shot three days with all their guns and not hit us, or the flags," Démase said.

But Patrice was studying Riel.

Riel was contemplating the fire. All the fires he had looked into; he was remembering the fire in rain he had seen at Seven Oaks; and the one in celebration that December in Fort Garry, our people dancing and laughing then while he saw wood burning like crossed sticks, perhaps a white cross of ash in the flames. They had always needed a miracle, and sometimes God in his mercy had given that, though not always. Vision God gave, and sometimes miracle; last night he had seen a rider on a horse, the horse so pure white it flashed in the sunlight as the rider turned it off the road, a high road over a hill and out onto the level plains; he had heard himself say words, "My nation holds my life, my wife holds my life, my family, my nation has no other life than mine. A hundred years is but a spoke in the wheel of eternity, a hundred years, a hundred..." but he did not know what that meant; he had not been given to understand the white horse yet, and he would not recognize the rider now fading smaller and smaller on the enormous, open plain. The fire twitched, leaped and died, and flickered up again as the life in the wood and air drove it.

Riel looked up into Patrice's earnest, longing face. They had done what men could; they would now suffer what they must.

"Tomorrow is the day," he said. "If God gives us sunshine, he will also give us victory."

"We'll wipe out Bladder Middleton?" Patrice said in amazement.

"God will give us victory," Riel said.

And that was the word that went down the muddy line of rifle pits that night, stinking from all the battering of three days and four sodden nights. The moon rose out of the poplar and spruce, red like a brutal face. Still anticipating a possible night attack, the men kept watch or wrapped their soggy blankets around head and feet, longing to remember and dream of warm arms holding them, soft breasts, and waking at a terror of bullets flying, but there was only the silent night, the far groan of another sleeper.

Big Bear once said, "When the sun rises on this land, the shadow I cast is longer than any river." When the rim of the sun bulged red over the horizon on May 12 a small man's shadow might have touched the shining mountains: the air shone so clear, still. And if I had been there, our men that dawn would have been singing a song of Bladder Middleton, so beloved by the Macdonald government and so detested by the Canadian volunteers he commanded that the former would award him $20,000 after the campaign and the latter eventually force a special commission of Parliament to investigate him for the theft of furs valued at $4634.66 and belonging to a half-breed he had arrested for complicity in the rebellion but whose innocence was so obvious the matter was dismissed without trial; an investigation that would leave his plans for his final years as chairman of a large Canadian insurance company in ruins. He had not yet, of course, stolen anything so blatantly that volunteers could testify against him but he had begun the morning in his usual fashion: after breakfast he ordered the soldiers forward to their well-known positions under the first barrage of the guns, none of them any more accurate than before; and he himself with scouts and all mounted brigades rode around north as if they intended an attack there. Gabriel of course moved most of his men parallel behind his lines to repulse them, where necessary, and when Middleton met with the usual steady resistance: less firing now, but still accurate shooting, he retired again the two miles back to his zereba. He had, however, left orders that as soon as he "created a diversion" in the north, the troops around the church were to charge the Métis line. Unfortunately, rifle fire over a mile away could not be heard at the church, the big guns booming twice could hardly be a "diversion" and when he returned to find the Midlanders and the Royal Grenadiers still obediently shooting into the sky off the rim of the prairie, he exploded in one unrehearsed oath and retired to his tent for lunch.

The officers of the two battalions were, if possible, more furious with Middleton than he with them. A messenger might have galloped the mile in five minutes, but throughout the campaign a total lack of signals had destroyed any troop co-ordination. So Lieutenant-Colonel Williams of the Midlanders and Grassett of the Royal Grenadiers reached an agreement: when the expected standard order came from Middleton after lunch for "Forward reconnaissance in force," they would advance, and they did so to their original positions out on the prairie. But they did not stop there, hunker down, and start shooting futilely. With a wild cheer of "Charge!" Williams led his fifty Midlanders in a dash through the trenches they had occupied for three days and down the ravine against our line on the right; Grassett with a yell and waving the colours led two hundred and fifty Royal Grenadiers charging forward into the centre of our rifle pits. Middleton heard shouts, firing, and burst from his tent, his jam bread in his hand, bellowing to the astonished officers surrounding him, "Why in the name of God don't they stop firing? They're just wasting—" and then he realized what had happened. "Stop!" he was rushing forward, "Stop!" His bugler was blasting "Retire!

Retire!" but not a Canadian on the front line obeyed, or heard for that matter. The Royal Grenadiers were already above the first line of our rifle pits in the centre below St. Anthony's, firing into them; the Midlanders below the ravine at the cemetery had already driven us back into the trees on our right, O Jesus, Mary and Joseph.

Middleton knew several things Williams and Grassett, lying with their men in shallow trenches and being shot at and dragging away groaning wounded every day without ever seeing an enemy, did not; that morning Riel had written a note:

"If you massacre our families, we will kill the hostages we hold," and sent one of the hostages, Astley, scrambling up the hill with a white flag to deliver it. The general did not bother to read into the note either a hint at a cease fire nor negotiation for terms should the Canadians overrun Batoche; he merely wrote in his most polite, British fair-play fashion:

Mr. Riel–Put your women and children in one place, let me know where it is, and no shot shall be fired on them. I trust to your honour not to put men with them.

It seemed this Riel knew how war between men must be proceeded with; Astley was sent back fast and had just reached Middleton's luncheon table with a reply when the charge exploded on the line.

Riel was still sitting at the deserted Exovedate table staring down at the replies he had torn up, not really thinking of the one he had finally sent to the general on the hill, "General your prompt answer to my note shows I was right in mentioning to you the cause of humanity. We will gather our families in one place..." nor what he had suddenly, furiously, scrawled on the envelope as Astley stood there, pale and gaunt from two months' sunless imprisonment, already exhausted but waiting to carry again:

"I do not like war, and if you do not retreat, and refuse an interview, the question remains the same concerning the prisoners. Louis David Riel."

The notes suggesting negotiation, terms of surrender, pleas for surrender, lay about his feet; the flag of our Lord, the Fish Flag, still hung from the standard above the house but there was no breeze to lift it now, and though it was barely noon, the room had gradually grown darker. The prayer book and the worn letter were in his hands, folded on the table. It was only after a long time that he realized it was so dark in the room he could not have read anything, even if he had needed to. He was comprehending that, the low ceiling of the familiar room shaping itself into dim log rafters, gradually, and his heart slowly beginning to quicken in a dreadful comprehension and then the corner of the room exploded: the house shuddered as if it were a ship smashing against rocks. He staggered to his feet, was charging through dust, smoke. Outside smoke burst here and there along the ridge, thunder of the guns; as it had been for three days but more now, dreadfully more: there were tiny figures of Métis, running, running in terror, and pursued by splots of red, as if patterns of blood were dribbling over the slope below St. Anthony's, towards him.

Riel leaped from the porch into the street, staring up into the heavens. Women were screaming somewhere as water struck his face. One cloud, single as any prairie rain, one small cloud but black enough, quite enough.

The charge drove our men from the trenches, as it would have had it been made that first Saturday, but now they had less ammunition with which to defend themselves. Between the first and second line of rifle pits were killed Michel Trottier, André Batoche, Calixte Tourond and his brother Elzéar, two Sioux warriors, all by bayonet, José Vandal who had both arms broken first and then was finished off by bayonet; Donald Ross and Isidore Boyer, both over seventy-five and killed by bayonet; John Swan, and also Démase Carrière, shooting until his rifle was empty and then clubbing the red soldiers bellowing over him as his leg was shattered by a ball, and finally a cavalryman threw a rope around his neck and dragged him at a gallop through ravines and brush and stones up the slope again and into the zereba before he tried to control his foaming horse. By that time most of the men had been driven back to the trees before Batoche and four houses, including the Council House, were on fire.

Gabriel was on high ground in the second line; with Patrice and Napoléon and Old Ouellette he stopped the centre of the Royal Grenadiers for a time. There was, as Gabriel laughed, no shortage of targets; it was just a problem of selection. The inevitable red crept gradually closer as behind them the flanking troops already thundered, cheered in the woods and finally he sent Patrice back, then Napoléon to rally our men across the river, reluctantly but he went when Gabriel swung Le Petit around at him in threat, and then there was only Old Ouellette to convince; three times, but he refused.

"Father," Gabriel shouted in his ear again, "we have to retreat! Come now! "

The old man was pouring powder into his muzzle-loader with the same steady deliberation he had for four days; a bullet splintered the top of the log, the earth sprayed at them; the bullets singing lower and lower did not so much as quiver his bony hand.

"Wait a minute," he said. "I won't get another chance." He was already taking aim over the logs. "I want to kill one more Englishman."

He was ninety-three, ten years older than Gabriel's father; he could not be carried back, even if that had been possible in the barrage.

"All right," Gabriel levered Le Petit again. "We can die here."

There was a movement in the near brush, right, and he waited, behind him Ouellette's rifle fired, waited while a Snider protruded there and gradually a shape and then until he was certain, and he fired; that Snider jerked into the brush, crashed, gotcha bastard; and he was laughing, turning. But there was the old man hurled against the wall of the pit and he remembered the *thud!* familiar enough; he had recognized it, somewhere, just as he pulled the trigger. He crept forward, cursing himself for that split second of certainty, the trap so baited; and the old man grinned at him.

"I got that Englishman," he grimaced momentarily. "I think, anyway. But there's too many more...now you go."

"I can carry you to—"

"No. In two minutes I'll be dead, so, they need...."

There was red burping at the corner of his lip, something sloshing red as it seemed through his slow words.

"I've lived long enough.. longer than our nation."

Gabriel was firing with one hand, low, ahead into the unstoppable Canadians, his left hand on Ouellette's hair, it was so fine it felt like a child's, praying that prayer he had spoken so often and so thankful for this old man's courage, faith and honour; he longed suddenly to kiss him. And he did that, with fierce commitment, that shrunken dirty face already glazed in death. Then he was running, crouched down and running as he had never run, through rain that slashed against him with the blessing of the Indian Thunderbird to hide him from his enemies and he ran erect, heaving Le Petit up into the driving rain and bellowing in fury as something tore in him he had not known was there, was ripped apart as he ran roaring through the thunder and rain towards his men firing gravel at the Canadians already bayonetting their way into the trees.

He screamed the men under the trees into turning around; when Moïse Ouellette suggested they retreat Gabriel smashed him to the ground with his fist. "We stop them here! Anybody runs I'll kill him myself!" So they held the Canadians at the edge of the trees for half an hour. Charles Tourond ran barefoot through a fusilade to the Council House and returned with an unopened barrel of powder. They fired bent nails, gravel, even chewed metal buttons at the Canadians with it. Gabriel still had a dozen Winchester bullets and when a Canadian captain peered around the Council House corner, Gabriel shot him; a soldier dashed toward the body and he killed him too. But then the ammunition was finished and they retreated to the ferry where Gabriel had hidden two boxes of bullets; Riel was there shouting orders as the women and children jostled, crammed onto the ferry. It was strangely quiet there as the drenched, dirty men dashed out of the trees; the women screamed in terror momentarily but fell silent as the men surrounded them, tried to heave the ferry, almost awash, out into the river still flowing imperturbably on.

"What are we going to do?" Riel shouted at Gabriel. "They have broken through, we are beaten!" He was lifting his arms to heaven and Gabriel knocked him aside, heaved up a stone beside the cable support.

"We die, that's what we do!" He was clawing at the mud, finding one then another box of bullets. "I told you once you start shooting you have to take whatever they shoot back. Well, let them kill us!"

Patrice Tourond staggered out of the muddy river, keeping his balance on the cable, his open face running blood. "We need a miracle, now, Brother Louis!"

"Gabriel—Gabriel!" Riel was clawing at his shoulder, his face contorted but not with fear, even in his fury Gabriel recognized that, only pain. He pushed Patrice away, grabbed Riel's hand, crushed it,

"Shut up, and get all the women across. I've got forty bullets left, I'll do the killing."

"Gabriel, don't expose yourself so much, don't—"

"You'll need blankets. I'll send some back from the houses, just get them all away, over!"

"If you get killed, what—"

"No Canadian'll kill me, and never no Englishman!"

His pockets were stuffed tight with bullets, Le Petit slammed full, and he ran up the trail, smashed two soldiers down as they came out of a rifled tent, and threw out the blankets there. He was breathing thunderously; he charged out, ripped the bullet-belts off the still-twitching soldiers–goddamn it, Winchesters!– and sprinted up through the trees where red troops were running from house to house trailing blankets, dropping dishes, furs, and sacred pictures—

"Gabriel!"

It was Madeleine, God in heaven! He seized her; she was sobbing against his chest, and he thrust her away, not seeing her, his eyes leaping here and there as he spoke, almost shouting,

"There's blankets by that tent, there, take them to the ferry. Louis's getting the women over, they'll need blankets, you get over it's too hot here—"

"Gabriel!" she cried into his face, "Gabriel!"

But he had already knocked her hands aside, was running towards the edge of the woods where rifles still sputtered, the heavy thump of bullets so good in his pockets, by jesus he'd kill them, they'd all be crawling for holes, god help him!

And for two days he flickered through the valley of Batoche a killer haunt in tattered shirt and pants; he shot at and perhaps killed more men than he knew: a sentry he whistled into terror first; a teamster feeding horses; a looter looking carefully out of a house, his arms full; an officer on a stroll kicking idly through the ash of a burned house. He saw the soldiers carry armfuls of paper out of the Council House, still only partially burned but the Flag of Our Lord gone from the mast, and he picked off two, Louis's papers exploding over dust and mud holes like goose feathers before they drove him off, deeper into the woods. The second night he found a camp of women and children still on the east side of the river, Madeleine among them, and Eli too. His brother had killed a cow to feed them around their tiny fire hidden in a hole and the children were lying under damp hay Eli had cut, burrowed down like animals, their naked feet blue in the night air. As he wolfed some beef he cut the rawhide into pieces, tied it to the children's feet with strips of leather.

"Please stop, Gabriel," Madeleine begged him. "It's over, over."

"Where's Riel?"

"It's over. Ride to the States, they'll—"

"Where's Riel?" he glared at her. "With him I can still kill them all! All summer some here, some there, and we'll go to the Indians. I'll kill every white myself."

"Gabriel!" Madeleine wailed.

"Shut up then." He was already going, "tell me nothing. At least if you see him, I'll be at my father's place tomorrow night. Just shut up." She could not recognize him now, he who so gently, momentarily, had cut bootlets for children and had always loved her, she knew it, but he was in some savagery beyond her worst experience of any man. "If the soldiers find you, you haven't seen me. Understand?" He wheeled on her as if he would tear her apart. "No shit police can handle me, and neither can you. Just shut up!"

He found a herd of horses and jumped a wild pinto and stampeded the herd through the Canadian zereba, riding the pinto like a devil in the intermittent moonlight and laughing; the very wolves stopped howling under the cold stars.

All the next day while he looked for Riel he watched the horsemen ride in troops, looking for them both; the white flags of our people appearing everywhere, surrendering. The Sioux-Cree camp was empty; their horses gone; fled. From the river willows he saw Napoléon Nault with seven others, Patrice Fleury too, come down the opposite bank to the ferry now controlled by the Canadians; hand over their rifles. He fired a shot across at them, saw the Redcoats jump for cover but Napoléon stood motionless, staring across the river, wiping his sleeve across his eyes as though he could not see something at his feet. There was commotion below, at the ferry anchor, horsemen mounting, wheeling towards him and when he saw Napoléon dive into the muddy river he turned, ran through the willows and across the bottom of Isidore's pasture and through the thickets: three men were circling five horses on foot. Jim Short and two Trottier brothers. He hallooed them and they each caught a horse. They would not come with him, but riding alone he could circle more easily. From cover he saw three Canadian officers stand discreetly beside the church steps while Fourmond and Vegreville and even stupid old wounded Moulin stood in a line on it and accepted guns and handshakes from our people, their heads hanging, their torn clothes filthy. Le Petit found the cross on the silver steeple, splattering them with it as they all scattered like feathers, and then he outran three scouts into the ravines northeast of the zereba. They wouldn't come close enough there, and by the time one of them returned with an entire troop, he had circled them south and was among the river trees below the cemetery. There he found his grey grazing among crocuses below the cemetery and he changed his winded horse for it. He was suddenly exhausted then; when he felt the good grey between his legs a log seemed to hit him over the head, split it again, hammered, hammered and he rode along the edge of the trees, north, almost collapsed for sleep and not caring who saw him until the horse carried him to the thickets below Emmanuel Champagne's house and he slid off, slept. He awoke at the grey nuzzling him, the reins still wrapped around his wrist. The sun was a livid strip along the top of the cliffs across the river. Someone was singing.

Emmanuel Champagne's glass windows – the wonder of the settlement – had been smashed, a trail of broken dishes led through the door torn from its leather hinges; Michel Dumas and Patrice Tourond lay against the logs of the house in the last bit of evening warmth. They passed a crock carefully between them while Michel tried to teach young Patrice a song. Michel was patience itself; he would sing one line very clearly, almost tunelessly so there would be less to remember:

"Pierriche Falcon est un brave homme."

And Patrice would sing it alone, confident, certain of it; then Michel would mumble the next, last, line:

"Pascal Breland est un cochon."

And Patrice would sing that too, words and tuneless tune perfectly accurate; and they both laughed, quietly, happily, at their emphasis on the last word. Then Michel said, again,

"Awright Patrissh, sing it all, all alone now."

But Patrice could not remember; the first name was there, even "homme," but the second was too hard. Who could remember all those old bastards, huh?

"You shits," Gabriel said and took the crock away from Patrice. They lifted their eyes to him without surprise.

"The Canadians did it all," Michel gestured toward the ruined house. "But they'd never find the place Emmanuel kept that, nope, nope."

"Did he surrender?"

"Yeah, he'll drink Canadian piss now, till they hang him."

"Pascal," Patrice said. "Just like my name, it starts just...." His voice faded.

There was barely a trickle down the logs as Gabriel smashed the crock against the corner.

"We were saving it for you, Gabriel," Michel said self-righteously. "Honest."

"I'm gonna marry Annie," Patrice muttered against the wall, "I'm gonna, you'll see."

Gabriel hunkered down beside Michel, "Do you know if Riel...did he go to Middleton?"

"Pascal Breland est un—"

"Louis, did you see Louis today? Michel!" Gabriel thumped the big man's head against the wall.

"Hey!" Michel shook himself free. "I can hear you, you know. We shoulda shot the hostages, one at a time, starting with Jackson and then Hillyard Mitchell and then—"

"Jackson was no hostage, you idiot, what—"

"One at a time, every two hours out in the open, lotsa people, till they stopped shooting, they'da stopped shooting, one at a..."

"I'll tell that Napoléon!" Patrice jerked upright, glaring about the darkness. "I'll kill him and I'll marry Annie and kiss her all I want, and I'll–I'll–I will so help me God!"

"That's all we're good for," Gabriel heaved himself up. "Drunk swearing, Jesus Christ if I don't kill all the Canadians that's all we'll–" he stopped abruptly, drenched suddenly in despair. All these strong men of our New Nation.

Michel was calling, "Didn't Isidore's widow have some hid in their root cellar, Gabriel, hey!" But he was going, blundering through the willows, the slash of their green branches good, pain across his face.

"I'm proud you haven't given up," his blind father's fingertips searched his head, face, tender and knowing here and there. The Stander sat shrunken in his hide and spruce chair, open eyes glazed to a white, impenetrable inwardness. "But it is all over. If you keep on killing people, you will only be considered a savage and a fool. It is all over now."

"Where's Riel?"

"I brought him a letter today," Moïse Ouellette said, "from Middleton and he—"

Gabriel cursed. "Where is he!"

"He was north, in the copse below Fisher's, and—"

"Is he still there?"

"No, he was going to—"

Gabriel's black face foamed curses, and Madeleine could not hold him down; he was on his feet glaring into Moïse's face.

"What did the letter say, you read it, Moïse!"

"Yes," Moïse stood his ground, quietly. "Middleton said he'd protect him and you and the council until everything was decided by Government; if you'd give yourselves up, he'd do everything—"

"You carry letters for Middleton?"

Moïse looked at him steadily; his weathered face was grey, his bearded—my God, he's over fifty year old, Gabriel thought.

"I love my wife and children, I have to think of them now."

"Go to the devil! Macdonald's skinned you like a sheep, and taken your gun, and you'll just do as you're told. What do you think we were fighting for? Fun? Holy Jesus and Mary we were going to teach them a lesson: you can't smash little people forever and kick them any time you feel like it or forget them, and now you—children, sweet Jesus, what am I killing for?"

"Gabriel," Madeleine said.

"You...*messenger*, you tell Bladder Middleton I'm in the woods with twice as many bullets as I had two days ago, eightynine for his men and one for him. That's all I'll need, just one!"

"Gabriel," Moïse said slowly, "Riel took the letter and went to Middleton. This afternoon."

Gabriel stared at him.

"It's all over," The Stander murmured. "Finished."

The yellow coal-oil light gouged their faces into solid black shadows. After a while Gabriel said,

"Where's Napoléon."

"Gone, in the river some say."

"Annie?"

"With Marguerite and the children," Madeleine said softly beside him. "They're hiding across the river."

It was nearly dawn when Gabriel awoke. The darkness of the room wavered in sounds of breathing; his arm was numb, when he moved it Madeleine came against him, groaning a little, trying to hold him even more tightly. Her warmth, softness, her known body was a blessing, soothing him out of the dream; the grey spring dawn at his father's small window still seemed to shiver of it. He had been in a blank white space with black stars shooting over him and he had to shoot them down, explode each as it streaked past him through whiteness and he could not so much as lift his Winchester but he had to shoot, shoot–by the merciful grace of God it was just a dream.

Moïse was sitting by the door, but asleep.

He lay for a moment, awake in Madeleine's strong arms; there was something–the dream had told him–and then he heard a sound outside, a dog scratching perhaps but he knew it was something else and he unfolded Madeleine's arms so gently she barely moaned, turning, her face empty in sleep as he would remember it and he was past Moïse snoring at the door: there were soldiers out there. Not yet in the cabin's clearing, the shadows shifted near trees and he was outside, around the house, crouched and running in his stocking feet and only Le Petit warm in his hands in the cold dawn. In the greyness against the cow shed he stopped; twenty, thirty scouts, who could tell in the darkness, they must have been detailed to watch The Stander's cabin; they were coming around – maybe someone had informed – it was Boulton on the lead horse! Gabriel wheeled, sprinted through light, around left and under the nearest poplars found a log, enough light, he could pick off that son of a bitch like a squirrel chattering and waving his arms as the scouts circled the cabin, rifles ready. He would simply–be an idiot! Kill Boulton and everyone in the cabin. He lay there and chewed green poplar twig, shivering a little as Boulton dismounted, hammered on the door, and Moïse opened it, then Madeleine too. He could not hear what she said; after a few moments Boulton and three men went in; light moved past the window and he was chewing the stick, shredding it between his teeth, clenching his hands into fists between his legs to keep them off the Winchester, if Riel had surrendered there was no one left but him for several thousand soldiers–Boulton came out; they all mounted and rode off. Except two; by the cabin settling down, watching.

He wouldn't even need the noise of a shot; a knife for both and then–his face was wet; he was sweating in his cold shirt. He had sworn to Crozier no army would ever again make Riel run, and he was not. If he could believe Moïse suddenly old and weak–he had to believe Madeleine, his father. Riel was not running, and not because of any army either. God? To Middleton? He tried to think of going to Bladder Middleton with Le Petit in hand, holding it out butt first and as the soldiers reached for it spinning it around and wiping him out before–the man meant nothing now, was nothing. A bullet into a pillow. It was Macdonald, sitting somewhere in glory, all the white-bearded gentlemen of–shit, he could not imagine them, they were–seagulls swarming after a plow, squawking and clawing each other for the rain worms, gulping, if Louis couldn't handle them, how could he? There was a new world camped on the ridge above St. Anthony's, no New Nation, and ninety bullets for his one Winchester: the horses. He had to get away; across the railroad tracks.

He found he was watching gulls wheel and flash in the first light of dawn; their cries circling above him and he was saying words he had lost for three days, "O my Lord, strengthen my faith, my faith," and when he finally comprehended himself, frenzy draining from him like blood from an unknown wound, "my honour...my courage." Poplar buds moved against the sunlight. Perhaps Riel would want him to surrender; if that was God's will then what else could he do? Riel and God together were too much for him; surrender to that–thank God, he had to get across the railroad and the line, back to Montana. From where they had gotten Riel; not even a year ago. Dear God.

The sun was barely over the trees and he was riding east along a ravine to get around their zereba and the sprawling Canadian camp already breaking up, moving north to Prince Albert; his nephew Alexis had gone for him to The Stander's cabin to tell them and returned past the unsuspecting guards with his leather jacket and moccasins and eight dry galettes; it was all Madeleine and his father had to eat, between them. He told Alexis to take them back four and had barely said goodbye to the boy, who stood there crying, ridden to the edge of the clearing when a shout rang behind him: Michel Dumas, riding hard.

"You going to Montana?" Michel asked.

"Sure. Regular spring trip." Gabriel thrust his Winchester back in his stirrup.

"I'm coming too."

Gabriel looked at him a moment. "Where's your rifle?" he said finally.

Michel rubbed his bare head, the long night snoring on cold ground still caught in the sag of his shoulders. "I guess I lost it somewheres, last coupla days. But I got," he patted the pocket of his cotton shirt, "two galettes."

Gabriel swung his horse about. "I've got four, and ninety bullets," he said. "That's enough for savages, it's just six hundred miles."

He said nothing more but continued east, south, then west again and down into the valley, until just before noon they swung through the trees and came upon the slashed cable of his ferry drifting in the swollen river at Gabriel's Crossing. They rode up the trail to the blackened ruins of the house and barns. The oat field was sprouting weeds and the manure pile bright nettle. The soldiers had dragged Madeleine's washer out before they burned the house, but then they'd smashed it under the clothesline. Gabriel said nothing at all; and Michel, who had kept watch from the rise in the trail, pulled his horse around and followed him silently as he rode away, south.

That was Saturday, May 16, 1885; about noon. On Friday, May 15, 1885, about noon near a rail fence on an unused trail four miles north of Batoche Louis Riel had identified himself to Tom Houri, William Diehl and Robert Armstrong, all Canadian scouts searching for him though Houri was, of course, half Cree.

There were three armed Métis with Riel at the time, but he sent them away when the scouts assured him they would honour Middleton's letter, which he showed them, of safe-conduct. So the general's early afternoon rest was interrupted by this "mild-spoken and mild-looking man with a long brown beard and a haggard look about his eyes which gradually disappeared as I talked to him. He was dressed in poorer fashion than most captured half-breeds, in fact he was shivering without a coat as it was still chilly out of the sun and I commenced proceedings by giving him a military great coat of my own. I concluded he was sane enough in general everyday subjects, but he was imbued with a strong, morbid religious feeling, and that mingled with intense personal vanity."

"I come to fulfil God's will," Riel pronounced in careful English. "Through the grace of God I believe I am a prophet of the new world."

Middleton leaned back, stretched his legs out straight under the camp table; they were still a bit stiff from riding every blasted day in this cold–heavens, it *was* May! –staring over his vast stomach at the shaggy man almost hidden in his brilliant blue, epauletted coat.

"All my papers are gone," Riel was leaning forward, earnestly. "I told Pierre Parenteau to put all my books underground but he did not do it; they are all gone, even my prayer book, my letter, my letter is gone!"

"Letter?"

"From the blessed Bishop Bourget in Montreal which affirmed me in my mission, 'You have a mission to complete which you must fulfil in every respect.'" Riel was bent to the general, his face quivering perhaps from cold, perhaps intensity. "My mission is to bring about practical results."

Strange, truly powerful eyes. Almost hypnotic, really. But mad of course, quite mad.

"I had it the day of the charge, in my...." Riel stopped, so close to Middleton now several officers at the door of the tent moved imperceptibly nearer. "Did your men find my letter?"

Middleton slowly folded his legs under him, suddenly stood up.

"Anything we have is evidence for your trial," he said. "For or against you."

"But this letter, no one has a right to see it, if you are gentlemen and see this letter, they will surely not read or touch—"

"Captain Young," Middleton said, "he is in your particular custody. Take him away."

Young separated himself from the cluster of officers, coming forward with his arm out almost as his father might have when he accompanied Thomas Scott, years ago, assisting him to the wall. But Riel was studying Middleton unswervingly.

"General," he said steadily, "I have been thinking. Whether, if the Lord had granted me as decided a victory as he has you, whether I should have been able to put it to good use."

"Take him away," Middleton said.

4

"HE shall hang though all the dogs of Quebec howl in his favour."

Who could have been in doubt about what Prime Minister Sir John A. Macdonald had decided must happen or, since Riel had never personally killed anyone, what the charge would have to be? If they had caught Gabriel the whole matter would have been more complicated but thank God the United States had given him political asylum–the several thousand soldiers and police between Batoche and the border had known the circuitous trail Gabriel and Michel Dumas rode two or three days after they rode it but had never quite managed to catch up with them, their one Winchester and ninety bullets–so the blame for the rebellion could be placed on Riel, those two exiles, and the men already killed in the battles–Démase Carrière and Old Ross and Old Ouellette were obviously vicious, incorrigible rebels. If the Exovedate and a few others prominent in the shooting could be persuaded to plead guilty to lesser charges of treason-felony–intending to levy war against the Queen but not *actually* doing so, that is, for purposes of their trial the battles could be considered as intentions only and not actualities which had claimed at least fifty-three Canadian dead and over a hundred wounded–they could be given relatively short jail sentences and the only life-and-death trial then would be Riel's. He must be totally to blame, for everything; for purposes of his trial the shooting was blatant, open rebellion. I know of no historian who has commented on this to say the least strange legal distinction that the men who shot and killed Canadian soldiers only *intended* to wage war while Riel, whom no witness had ever seen with anything more than a cross or a pen in his hand, that he and he alone had actually waged war. I presume everyone in Canada accepts, as even the dullest Quebec backbencher did in 1885, that blessings shouted to men being shot at or hand-written letters which can be laid as facts before a judge are far more lethal to the Queen, her crown and dignity, than outright lies or even Winchesters. Le Petit not excluded.

The Conservative Cabinet therefore decided the charge would have to be treason; the strategy, not to allow Riel to conduct his own defence. Charles Nolin, Riel's cousin, remembered everything Riel had done from July 1, 1884, to March 23, 1885 and despite the small slip of holding him in a police jail from the time he fled the fighting at Duck Lake to Middleton's arrival in Prince Albert on May 20, he was still more than willing to be the Crown's star witness; Riel must not be allowed to cross-examine him. Fortunately again, Riel had many Liberal Quebec friends: Masson was now Lieutenant-Governor and so out of the way but Fiset and Desjarlais and David and LaFlamme and others quickly formed a Riel Defence Committee and financed three lawyers. They were all under thirty-five, brilliant, and would go very far as soon as the Liberals came to power; one of them was Adolphe Caron's brother-in-law and worked for the Defence Minister's law firm. However, a hundred years later they would be known only for the fact that they travelled from Quebec City and Montreal to St. Boniface and saw the Mrs. Riels, mother and daughter-in-law, and received from them some water from the shrine at Lourdes to take to the famous prisoner held in the new guardhouse built especially for him in the North-West Mounted Police Barracks on the flat plains west of Regina. The Métis who drove them the two-and-a-half totally empty miles in the scorching sun might have told them that Lieutenant-Governor Dewdney was the reason for their discomfort–he had owned the property on Wascana Creek where the barracks were built and Van Horne of the CPR had declared he'd be damned if he'd let that Conservative pet speculate in any more corner lots–but they did not ask him; Lemieux, Fitzpatrick and Greenshields had not the faintest notion that the stoic driver understood their every French grumble. No Métis talked to them in St. Boniface either.

"I am most grateful that my friends remember me," Riel said to them. The crossed shadows of the window lay across the table in Commissioner Irvine's vacant office at which he was allowed to sit every day, the table cluttered with notes, bits of poetry, prayers, rewritten letters to Sir John A. and Dewdney and U.S. Consul Taylor in Winnipeg, crumpled paper covered with words, words, if he could only find enough words. "I have no resources to mount a defence, I have never had anything and now even the little I had has been taken. I am very grateful to you, who are I am told the ablest counsels in the land, that you should consent to come so far, for me. I am certain therefore, that you recognize the importance of this trial, that it must take place before the Supreme Court of Canada where everything I have done, in making Manitoba and in services to the Conservative Party and the deprivation of my human rights and the suffering of those dear to me, and my mission, that the clarity of my mission is revealed to every person in Canada. There cannot be a single person who will not hear and understand the message God has given me and that Macdonald must be called as—"

"It is not possible," said Lemieux, Fitzpatrick and Greenshields, "that this case be heard in the Supreme Court."

Riel laughed, suddenly; out of the fever that had welled up

in him there was this swift calm, almost happiness. But his words were as incisive, "And I appreciate your brilliant legal minds, but surely that you are all Liberals is a problem for me. I have always been a Conservative. As such I was elected four times Member of Parliament for Provencher. With God's help my victory over the party of Mr. Blake, you will excuse me but he has in times past laid particularly shameful indignities upon me and my companions, our victory will be complete, and to avoid all this partyism I insist my counsel should consist of one French-Canadian and one Irish-Canadian Liberal, one French-Canadian and Irish-Canadian Conservative, and one English-Canadian Protestant who enjoys the confidence, particularly, of Sir John who has been my opposition all my life and is yet chief of my—"

"Your friends are now all Liberals."

"But I gave up my seat for Cartier, I persuaded the Métis to repel the Fenians in 1871, I administered Red River for months for the good of—"

"You also sh–had Thomas Scott shot," said Lemieux, Fitzpatrick and Greenshields. "But 1869–70 matters nothing here, this is—"

"Oh?" said Riel. "Nothing? My creation of Manitoba and my exile for it, the destruction of my life in Canada is nothing to Ontario, but Thomas Scott still is? How very selective."

"You are now charged with treason, levying war against your rightful Sovereign."

"Even though I am an American citizen, and I have the papers, they are with papers they took at—"

"That cannot matter. If you are a citizen of a country at peace with Her Majesty and are living within the Dominion, it behooves you to keep Her Majesty's laws, as every citizen must."

"Very well." And for a moment the three lawyers saw as we had in Fort Garry and on the snowy hills west of Duck Lake the sharp, hard brilliance of concentrated fire in those unforgettable eyes. "Then I must have the material for my defence, the letters and petitions and papers which Middleton's soldiers stole from me before I could hide them during the charge; and I need Gabriel Dumont and Michel Dumas, and Napoléon Nault is now in Montana also; they must testify what the conditions were that necessitated our actions. When Lawrence Clarke bragged to our people that five hundred police were coming to arrest me, they reached for their guns; is Clarke on trial? When Crozier and his men fired on us first at Duck Lake, we fired back in the name of the great God who made us; are Crozier and McKay on trial? I was never captured, I gave myself up; my trial must stand on the merit of my actions, and I will prove—"

"No matter what the circumstances, high treason can *never* be justified. If that charge is proven against you, there is only one possible defence."

"What?"

"That you did not know right from wrong at the time of your treasonous behaviour."

"In other words, that I am insane."

"Yes," said Lemieux, Fitzpatrick and Greenshields.

There was a prairie summer brightness in the room, cut by the whine of a solitary mosquito. Judge Hugh Richardson had disposed of the case against Henri Jaxon, or William H. Jackson as the Crown insisted, in thirty minutes; and Jaxon, still thundering his sanity, had been muffled off to the asylum in Selkirk, Manitoba. Within two weeks he would escape from there and from Chicago telegraph Sir John that he would return, gladly, if they agreed to hang him and let Riel go free; to a laughing Ottawa that would only prove the correctness of swift judgement. Riel would never hear of that telegram, though it would not have surprised him; his lawyers did. And angered him also, that they who had heard nothing of his case except through newspapers should so swiftly assume his guilt.

"Do you believe in God, who made the earth and all that is in it?"

The three lawyers shifted slightly in their chairs. Such a personal question could only, in polite company, be regarded as rhetorical. Embarrassing nevertheless.

"I have always believed," Riel went on carefully, his anger quite controlled now; in fact he was gazing out the window, almost musing, "that to hear, and obey, the voice of God who made us all is the highest possible form of human wisdom. And when that voice speaks again and again, calling you to help the weak find justice, the hungry food, that oppressed, guilty consciences must find liberty, how could any human being refuse to obey it? To try, anyway?"

The lawyers could only clear their throats, thoughtfully. Then patiently begin again:

"Will the prosecution, however, be able to present evidence that you did encourage the Métis to fire on the police? That with your prayers and blessing they shot and killed soldiers you all knew were proper Government Militia, commanded by officers lawfully appointed by Her Majesty's properly elected government? Will they be able to table notes and letters in your handwriting urging Indian bands to foment war on the police?"

"The Indians are our brothers! Have you seen the hunger and scrofula on the reserves, have you seen?"

Lemieux, Fitzpatrick and Greenshields sighed. "An Indian war is a terrible thing, terrible. Mutilation, rampage, destruction of property, priests and innocent settlers ravaged and mutilated, how—"

"Not one settler, not a single woman or child was so much as touched! What kind of war is that? Not even Mrs. Gowenlock and Delaney, who were held prisoner for two months by the fighting Cree. Haven't you read the papers? The Indians killed police, government agents, soldiers that attacked them and crooked traders—they never touched one honest man."

"Nevertheless, they were Indians, killing whites."

"And Canada finds that particularly wrong? The Indian

Department can slowly starve them to death, but when they strike back that is, quite suddenly, murder?"

The lawyers found it unnecessary to so much as clear their throats; they sat motionless, monolithic.

"Well then." For a moment Riel held his head in his hands; his voice was muffled, almost as if his body had retreated far away from the grey prison shape seated in the afternoon sunlight. "I am now to be placed on public trial, the whole world will hear of the mission which God gave me, which I *must* complete in every respect – the world must hear it in order for me to complete it, and I thank God he has given me this opportunity; it was for this reason I gave myself up to Middleton. I could have run, but Canada must hear this message, now–but if I am to live I–that I was, am–that my mission was that of a madman?"

"The Crown has very strong evidence for high treason."

Riel's brilliant eyes studied their tanned, healthy faces, one by one. "This case is extraordinary. The prosecution with its great talents would show I am guilty and you, counsellors sent here by my friends whom I respect, would show I am insane." They remained silent; Riel gazed out the window, at the heat smudging the prairie horizon.

"This has happened before," he murmured. "My enemies respect and fear me, my brothers honour me, but my learned friends insist I am mad."

"If we are to work on this case," said Lemieux, Fitzpatrick and Greenshields steadily, "you must place it entirely in our hands; you will instruct us, but everything must be done through us. It is your only possible hope."

"Hope?" said Riel. "Hope, that is hope? To abandon human dignity? I defend myself against high treason or I have to consent to the–I have been there before, gentlemen, I know the brute life of an asylum and I—"

"We know," said Lemieux, Fitzpatrick and Greenshields. "We know."

"I have lived in situations you would be horrified to dream of, but I cannot again live an animal life if I am not allowed to carry with it the moral existence of an intellectual being."

It has always seemed to me that Riel made a mistake here: he protested and argued with them in the very courtroom itself, but he could not bring himself to dismiss those three white brains. Had he conducted his defence himself, with a single lawyer to tutor him in the niceties of the law, cross-examined every witness himself and forced McKay and Crozier to declare under oath who had fired first at Duck Lake; forced Father André to state how many Macdonald bribes he had turned down before talking of the possibility of $35,000 as payment for his lost land claims and services rendered at Red River; exposed star witness Charles Nolin in his lies as only he could who had lived with him for months, who could nail our shifty Charles to the wall with the very power of his eyes; above all, challenged the jury of four farmers and two merchants and every one of them totally English and Protestant: he might have forced a mistrial or a hung jury. Or he might have shown such extenuating circumstances that the jury could not find him guilty by reason of excessive provocation and so forced the Government to recognize the inadequacy of a legal definition formulated over four hundred years ago to help English kings eliminate enemies who quite possibly had a better claim to the throne than they; or, if desperation had reached the most desperate, Riel, given scope to express himself in the trial, might have convinced the jury to bring in a true verdict of "not guilty by reason of insanity." Who can know, now?

But Riel did not dare. At the critical moment of his life he did not trust his best sense; the mysteries of a treason trial were suddenly all overwhelming white mysteries to him: too deep to be waded into without white guidance. It was his life-long sense of inadequacy in the face of white custom, lurking in him like a snake since his arrival in Montreal, since facing Marie-Julie

Guernon, and that betrayed him here–oh, I know how he felt, I have known that fear of living in my own country and suddenly, dreadfully, not *knowing*; that inner betrayal–why do you think the Métis loved my silly, ironic, ribald songs so much? Why do you think I loved to compose them? We all need to experience our own, complete superiority, even momentarily; even half-breeds. Riel could write powerful letters to Macdonald and Taché and Taylor as slowly and forcefully as if he carved a totem out of the hard wood of his prayers; but to face English whites every day with their all-knowing judgement already stamped on their steady stares: night after night he cried to God in his cell, but he could not win through to that resolution. So, confidently assisted by Lemieux, Fitzpatrick and Greenshields, old Macdonald got his jury verdict: "Guilty of high treason."

At that moment of verdict, standing in the box with the stifling courtroom crushed full to the very corners with judges, jurymen, police officers, newspaper reporters and sweating, titillated spectators, Riel heard only words like hammer blows, one after the other. Feeling nothing more than movement in air, the distance of sound. But he became aware then, slowly, of the jury foreman, a dark bearded Irishman who still stood, refusing to sit while the court murmured, sang with relief at the verdict and finally Richardson looked up to see the foreman standing still, sobbing audibly into the suddenly soundless room. Finally the foreman could control his voice.

"Your Honours, I have been asked by my brother jurors to recommend the prisoner to the mercy of the Crown."

In 1925 one of the jurymen would relive on his deathbed those moments in the courtroom that had haunted him for forty years. Edwin Brooks would tell his daughter: "We were western farmers, and we knew there never would have been a rebellion, and consequently no prisoner to try, if the Government had done its duty. But we could not justify rebellion, and we could not pass judgement on the Prime Minister because he was, unfortunately, not in the dock. We had to give our finding on Riel according to the evidence. We refused to find him insane, dear God how often had we ourselves prayed for someone to do something desperate to get at last that old Ottawa bastard's attention! Riel was not insane; we believed him when he told us that by its absolute lack of responsibility the government had proven its own insanity, complicated by paralysis. But what could we do? We added the clause recommending mercy. For us that was no empty, formal expression. It expressed the serious desire of every one of the six of us."

But Riel, now standing in the dock where he had knelt in steady, audible prayer during the hour the jury reached its verdict in the most memorable state trial Canada would ever have, heard this verdict with tears of happiness streaming down his face.

"It is a great advantage for me, that now I will cease to be called a fool," he said when Judge Richardson, with personal impatience but bound by legal necessity, allowed him to speak before sentence. "Do I appear excited? Am I very irritable? Can I control myself at this moment of great contradiction?" He looked about at the expectant courtroom, at the beautifully dressed ladies dabbing their eyes as his powerful voice rolled over them, and he smiled; an ironic lift of his lip at Nolin and André, who of all the people there, knew him, knew, as he knew, that their testimony had condemned him; and still he was in complete control though his reasonable words now would help him less than the faintest vision, the most violent anger. "I thank the gentlemen of the jury. Should I be executed –at least I will not be executed as an insane man. That will be a great comfort for my mother, my wife, for my children, for my brothers and relatives, and for all my countrymen. The verdict against me is proof that I am more than ordinary myself; that I have a right to believe that by the will of God, by the circumstances which surrounded me for fifteen years, I have been called to do something in the North-West that nobody has yet done in this world. My learned counsel, sent by my friends, tried to prove me mad: 'If he had simply exercised the ordinary dictates of prudence, caution and common sense and maintained his influence over the Métis, of absolute necessity he would have reached the highest pinnacle of his ambition, whatever it might have been!' If I had ambition, I did go most stupidly about achieving it. But this verdict today is proof that, perhaps, Riel is a prophet. Certainly he has suffered enough for it. I have been hunted like an elk for fifteen years. David was hunted seventeen, so I think I may also have two more years. For the troubles of the Saskatchewan are not to be taken as an isolated fact. They are the result of fifteen years' war between us, the Métis, and you, the invaders from the east who think you own this country simply because you have managed to get here. In 1869 we did to easterners what we used to do to Sioux when they invaded us from the south: we took up arms, we made hundreds of prisoners, and we negotiated. And as a body tribal we were recognized by Macdonald and Cartier, and we gained what we wanted; we gained The Manitoba Act. In it we were given one-seventh of all the lands in Manitoba, and that is what I want in all the North-West. I want a seventh of the land for the French and English Half-breeds.

"Who starts nations? The master of the universe, God, and as a good father he gives a portion of his lands to each nation. This is a principle: God cannot create a tribe without locating it. Even birds have a place; we have to walk upon the ground, and when that ground is too large for us alone we are willing to share it with those whose country is too crowded. When those come to us, they ought to say, My little sisters, you Cree people, you Scorched-wood people, you each keep a seventh of your land, but let us cultivate what you do not use. I think that is fair sharing, when two of us have seven pairs of socks, to keep only two."

Through the oppressive heat of August 1, 1885, his voice sounded in the sweating room; the spectators listened patiently enough, but the verdict had ended the drama and the Indian trials were coming, soon they promised, including hoary old Big Bear and the dreadful Sioux White Cap, and tall, elegant Poundmaker with thick braids like snakes almost to his knees; he looked just like every Indian should, you could see that, oh, it would be so savage! Riel's careful explanation of how five-sevenths of the North-West should go to the landless believers of the world to create a new Bavaria and a new Italy and a new Poland and a new Ireland and a new French Canada; how British Columbia, which was of course also part of the North-West, should likewise become a new Norway and Sweden and Denmark of beautiful mountains and sea; and how the Belgians would also find a new land there, and especially the Jews, searching for a country for eighteen hundred years and rich, landless lords of finance would find a new Judaea of consolation for their centuries of wandering in the sweet chanting music of the Pacific lapping against the mountains; to build a paradise for the world's deprived on the thousands of square miles of the North-West: this was barely interesting, especially since the Hudson's Bay Company and the Canadian Pacific Railroad and numberless Canadian land companies and private speculators already knew exactly what they were going to do with all the land, endlessly large though it seemed; it would never be too large for their developed white ambitions.

"Is that all?" Judge Richardson asked wearily, fingering the sweat from his tiny round glasses.

"No, excuse me," said Riel. "I feel weak, and if I stop at times, I wish you would be kind enough to..."

And he spoke on, and on, but it was no use; the vision was ungraspable by any but himself. At last he declared categorically they had fought the battle of Batoche, so correct in the line of military art as Middleton had declared, on the place where the Spirit had instructed him. "It did not come from me or Dumont," he stated. And there were two reasons why the sentence of the court should not be passed on him: he was led by the Spirit. But

Richardson had been prepared with his sentence all afternoon; simply waiting. Riel seated himself for a moment, exhaustion written in age over his face and the steel clasp of his chained ball like a band of fire around his ankle, but he had to stand immediately, the sentence so implacably necessary; and unjudicially cruel:

"I cannot hold out any hope to you," declared Richardson, "that her Majesty will, after what you have been the cause of doing, the most pernicious crime a man can commit, that she will open her hand of clemency to you. All I can suggest or advise you is that you prepare to meet your end. It is now my painful duty to pass the sentence of the court upon you, and that is that you be taken to the police guardroom at Regina, which is the gaol and the place from whence you came, and that you be kept there till the 18th of September next, that on the 18th of September next you be taken to the place appointed for your execution, and there be hanged by the neck till you are dead.

"And may God have mercy on your soul."

The mercy of God. All his life he had prayed for that, and been blessed with it again and again when forced to despair. The mercy of queens, of prime ministers slowly dying in power, of millions of Protestants still remembering that blasphemer Thomas Scott though they had never actually known him; as soon expect mercy from the steel ball chained to his ankle, the iron bars in the door whose pattern the sun laid across the floor and over his feet like delicate strips of tar. The cubicle blackness of the hospital; he could almost hear the distant subterranean thunder of fists beating, beating against stone walls; only the walls here were wood, the sounds shouts of officers drilling recruits, the steady whine of mosquitoes nosing through the heat.

"And what was my insanity?" Riel said to Father Fourmond, seated there in the shadows of the sunlight before him. "I declared Rome had fallen. Why? Not to set myself up; because the Pope, though he calls himself the Vicar of Christ, has never paid any attention to us; and Bishop Bourget, he did pay attention. The Spirit revealed this to me. In spirit and truth, he was our pope, not Leo XIII."

"But Bourget has died now, he is buried and—"

"And as Archbishop Taché preached the funeral sermon the blessing of Bourget passed upon him. Today Rome is like the ravished spouse of Jesus Christ, is it so mad to believe his vicar must come to St. Boniface? What is Rome but the eternal cause of strife, of war between Protestant and Catholic? Do you think Jesus Christ would wish the Indians of one reserve to be taught by Catholic priests, the Indians of the reserve next to it, many of them related to each other, taught by Methodists, and both taught to believe the other is going to hell eternally? The devils of Europe are being forced upon us. Is it so insane for me to want my children to shake the hands of the Protestants? My mission is to bring about practical results, and even if it takes two hundred years to achieve it, what does that matter? God's time is not ours."

"But you have been sentenced," Fourmond said slowly, his gaunt face sincere, so completely dedicated. "We pray for you every night, Father André and I and thousands of believers, everywhere. Make your peace with God and the Church. Will you sign the formula of faith we have prepared? Don't let Satan have you, Louis! The Church longs to give you her comfort."

While this lean priest spouted words like fire he had lifted him from the pulpit through the power of that vision in St. Anthony's Church. Riel stared at him, at the paper he held in his hand. Rome might fall, but it always triumphed; it held the weight of centuries thoughtlessly, effortlessly, in its soft, manicured hands.

"A formula for faith." After a long moment he added, "It was Father André, with our Charles, who destroyed my defence."

"Not so much as you did yourself," Fourmond countered.

"You were so clear, so reasonable no one in the court could believe...the defence, then."

"But you know better, don't you?"

"Louis," Fourmond leaned forward offering the white paper, "this is no place to argue, now. We love you, we want you to have peace again, to feel the strength of the sacraments."

"Yes," said Riel eagerly, "yes, I need the sacraments. But your abjuration opposes what the Spirit has revealed to me."

"You have always been such a fervent child of the Church," Fourmond said softly. "Just these last few months...obedience is the greatest gift we can offer God. You know this, you have heard this from your youth. Accept obedience again, obedience."

In the bright, squared sunlight, Riel was reading; words. He had himself written so many words, years of them, and they had all been taken from him at Batoche and now he was writing frantically every day, letters, poems, prayers, visions, cries for help out of the new grey clapboard jail on the police square set in the flat seemingly endless prairie. But these words "...solemnly abjure all the errors I have taught...errors...against the Holy Roman Church...errors...the infallibility of the Holy Church...its visible head the Holy Father...errors...his infallibility...I believe that the holy day Sunday...I believe...." His gaze kept slipping off the page; he could not concentrate on the awesome denials, the weight of renunciation here expected of him, and finally he stared at his hands. Surrounded, hemmed in, sentenced. At last he said,

"Obedience is the bread which I must now eat. Will it be nourishing, Father, do you think?"

Fourmond's face flickered with the possibility of an impossible hope. They had all prayed again and again, endless nights of prayer, even Father Dugast who had returned to St. Boniface and Bishop Taché with his message that Riel was "mad as a hatter." To win this wandering, misleading sheep back into the—

"Obedience is the only true, complete nourishment of the soul!"

And Riel was reaching for the pen on his small table. Dipping it, writing swiftly, "Louis" and then he looked up into the lean priest's sombre face hesitating on the edge of an overwhelming happiness.

"You will leave me this, won't you?" Riel said, and then quickly finished his signature, "David Riel."

"Of course," Fourmond was almost ecstatic, though he tried to control himself. "Of course!"

Much has been made of this abjuration: was made by the priests who used it to convince the last implacable Métis left in Canada that Riel had confessed his grievous sins and returned to the eternally forgiving bosom of the Church and so they too must repent, return, obey. The lost rebellion of course quite destroyed our people. Not only had their farms been burned, their crops not been planted, their animals slaughtered, and sons and fathers either wounded or fled to the United States or in prison or killed, but the religious commitment they had given Riel had been, apparently, destroyed. What could they do but return to the priests? Riel had no way left to speak to them, even if they could have listened. This is a sad song I cannot sing, no more than the machinations of eastern politicians who were now making certain Riel would hang and our people be crushed so they would never dare declare themselves again. Eighty years later they would be known simply as "road allowance people", having no place whatever except in their clanking wagons, their rusted cars on the placeless public roads. In his stifling summer cell Riel saw this coming horror; cried and prayed long against it, though he knew even as he signed that abjuration composed by the priests to destroy forever the concept of his mission and the mission of our people, that "the logic of obedience is infinite," as he wrote, "infinite like the will of God." And that those who had truly believed in him would believe in him still, no matter what the priests said he had signed.

For his visions did not stop. In fact, it seemed after he signed his Sara-given prophetic name to the all-inclusive words of the priests that the spirit which had guided him came to him more awesomely than ever. He had entered the holy obedience of the Church and every morning he assisted at the Mass in complete calmness and devotion so that André, who had been very disgruntled at Fourmond for allowing the "David" signature, wrote to Taché, "He is a phenomenon, strange, I don't really know how to take him. To see him one would take him to be a saint." And a saint the grizzlied old Breton would never know what to do with.

The visions came to Riel sleeping, sitting on his bed or at his table, when he walked in the yard – R. Burton Deane, the police officer in command, had removed the ball and chain after public outcry in the press about it and Riel could walk easily now without carrying the steel ball–where the guards stood squared around the square, treeless enclosure, their rifles butted on the ground; even at Mass he heard voices, the same voices he had always heard. And gradually out of the long desperate prayers for deliverance, his meditations on death which soon sang lyric the way his poems never had, the necessities of his poor Marguerite and his people and the summer days that were flying away more quickly than snow before a burning spring chinook, beyond the hope that burst in him again and again that his vision for the North-West which had been printed so clearly in the newspapers of the world would suddenly blossom into the massive uprising of the oppressed of the world, an incredible movement of peoples which the miserable, corrupt governments of nations would find unstoppable, especially out of his profound fear that in signing the abjuration and in finding the Mass as deeply comforting now as in his most desperate hours of exile, through all this the voices again came to him; and gradually he understood that he had not been deserted. The strength of the hills and of the Lord of Hosts was still with him; even without the Bourget letter and his sainted Sara's prayer book.

Anyway, he knew them by heart; when he concentrated, the exact words in their exact place on the paper came to him as if he held letter or book in hand, was turning the holy pages with his fingers, one by one, the exact prayers rising like incense in his soul. The priests' comprehension of God was bound by the Church, by the necessity of formula, but the revelation of those who dared believe took the believer far beyond that.

He was sitting with his head in his hands, staring at the floor, when he began to understand. The infinity of God in relation to the set formulas of the priests was like sunlight on the open prairie in relation to the patterns of barred light on the floor at his feet. To burst out, into the infinity of God! He cried aloud for sheer joy, the incredible knowledge broke from him like a spring flood. To die and explore the infinity, the freedom of that measureless wisdom! The silly contradictions of his life—he seized his pen, wrote frantically,

> *My God, I offer you through Jesus Christ my condemnation to death, my imprisonment, the weight of my chains, my privations, my pain and suffering and the suffering of my loved ones and all my people. I unite them to the passion of my beloved Saviour, that it may please you, because of his infinite merit and your infinite, endless and unmeasurable wisdom existing since before the foundations of the earth were laid, and so far beyond our feeble comprehension, to pour your divine spirit on all. By the grace and foolishness and scandal of the cross of our Lord, accept my foolish suffering. Renew the face of the earth!*

The way of the cross was humiliation; the prophet must die to reveal his ultimate vision, and this conviction transfigured Riel's understanding of himself even as he heard workmen at the end of the guardhouse begin to hammer together what he knew must be his scaffold.

Poor fool; it was immoral to hang him; clearly he was mad. The necessity of hanging him was simply, clearly Sir John A.'s Conservative politics. You believe that? Many Canadians, even many Métis believe and will believe it; but I cannot. I agree with white-haired Dr. Augustus Jukes, senior surgeon of the North-West Mounted Police, that we are too likely to call men whose understanding of life goes counter to our usual opinion, insane. Sanity becomes then a mere matter of majority opinion, not a test of the wisdom of what is spoken. When Jukes was asked during the trial, "If it could be proved that a man is labouring under an insane delusion that he is in direct communication with the Holy Ghost (I would ask, why should that be an *insane* delusion? Cannot the Holy Ghost communicate, directly, to whomsoever he–it–wishes?), would he be responsible for that act?", he replied,

"Men have held very strange, remarkable views on religion and have been declared insane until they gathered great numbers of followers and became leaders of a new sect and then, suddenly, they were great prophets and great men. Take Muhammed, for instance. Few believed him, most thought him mad, but he carried out his belief at the point of the sword and so convinced half the world of that which, if he had failed, would have been considered simply a delusion of his mind. Is this direct fraud, honest delusion, organizational power, or truly guidance from the divine? I would not be qualified to say."

And if the prosecution had asked, as they did not, whether earthly success was then ultimate proof of divine inspiration, Jukes would have answered that if immediate success were proof, then surely Alexander, Attila, Ghenghis Khan, and Napoleon were the most divinely inspired of men while Jesus and St. Francis must be very questionable indeed since they were long dead before their teachings were widely established with the masses. Am I mad to think Riel the most sane man in that court-room in Regina, the most saintly man in the North-West when he found peace with himself and with whatever purposes God had for his mission, and so could receive his family in that jail for the last time with calm, with happiness? If so, I prefer madness to the sanity of Sir John, of Sir Wilfrid Laurier who used Riel when he was safely dead as the cornerstone on which to build a Liberal wall around Quebec which would last a century.

What more is there to say? The whole Canadian world–never before and never again had Canada been so united in thought about one subject–was screaming to Macdonald about Riel: absolutely, he must hang; absolutely, he must be pardoned. The appeal to the Manitoba Court of Queen's Bench in Winnipeg proved fruitless: the court in Regina was competent; its decisions stood. When Riel's mother and Marguerite and three-year-old Jean came to Regina with Joseph Riel, they were coming to say goodbye. Execution, Riel told them, was not so terrible a thing because unlike most men he would not be surprised by death.

"We should bless the judge, together," Riel said, "who appointed my last day."

They were in the orderly room of the guardhouse, Riel seated on one side of the table and the four visitors on the other. Two guards with Winchesters at ease stood before the doors and the officer in command at the window, watching them. They had been ordered to keep their hands on the table, not touching, but it was too wide for Riel to reach across to tiny Jean in any case. The boy was very pale, coughed steadily, and now he was crying without a sound, his hands clasped in front of him and tears running down his cheeks.

"Jean," Marguerite said in Cree, "that white police is watching you."

The boy stopped sobbing, though the cough was beyond his control. They could speak in French or Cree, neither of which the guards understood, but what could they say? After they had explained all the small news of St. Vital, the sickness, the poverty, how the family was struggling and the neighbours were good, the words caught in their teeth. Everything that truly mattered could not be said across that long spruce table. The love and misery that hardened their faces was less than what they might dream of each other, each alone and five hundred prairie miles apart as they had been. Marguerite's black dress hid her pregnancy. Mrs. Riel's dark Cree-like face, though she was completely French-Canadian, was gaunt, hollow as a skull. Joseph said nothing at all, and to the end of his life forty-seven years later he would say nothing to anyone about that older brother he had seen, hair cropped and pale from a summer in the tiny cell beside the guardroom; he would live all forty-seven years in the house in St. Vital, silent, with the bare spruce coffin in which Riel's body was brought from Regina to St. Vital standing in the corner of his living room.

Father André burst into their heavy vigil: God is good, there has been a reprieve! Ecstasy leaped into faces, bodies: a whole month! Glory be to God! But Riel was struck as if dumb; the women stared at him, but dared not fall about his neck, crying for happiness.

"It is the 17th today?" was what he asked André.

"Yes," André was almost laughing. "Yes!"

"Today is Angélique's birthday," Riel said, and he remembered the golden fall day two years before when a girl had come running towards him at St. Peter's, her skirts spreading behind her like crimson Birdtail Rock jagged on the distant skyline, crying, "Mr. Riel, Mr. Riel, it's a girl! She's beautiful like an angel, girl!" The long warm summer of Manitoba had not loosened the cold of Batoche from her tiny lungs; perhaps no summer every would. But he said, trying to smile, "On her birthday God looks upon me with favour; may his blessing fall on her too."

Mrs. Riel was studying his face with tears of happiness in her eyes, but his quiet, gentle words could not hide from her that he was near breaking under a new despair.

"Louis, Louis," she was leaning forward. "Thirty days, surely it means they will not, at all..." she stopped, unable to say that terrible word.

"It is thirty more days of purgatory," Riel murmured. "God give me grace."

But it was Joseph who spoke when they had to leave. The guards, at a gesture from the officer, all turned their backs. Momentarily Marguerite could cling to Riel and he could hold her thin, swollen body; he thought he felt the child move within her and his heart leaped; he whispered, "Be strong, it will be a boy to care for you, a boy," but she was sobbing, for an instant she could not control herself and Joseph bent to him, words were in his ear he could not gather them, they overwhelmed him while he held Marguerite so dreadfully thin in his arms,

"... Montana, they'll get you out, Gabriel and Michel and Napoléon, I had a message and sent a little money—"

The guards had wheeled about to face them again, almost sheepishly hesitant, their decent young faces so unaccustomed to the barbarity of this required intrusion. But they were North-West Mounted Police, they must, it was the duty laid on them by the mechanical brilliance of their uniforms in the long, gloomy barracks. And then the four with Father André were ushered out, the memory of their presence in the room vanishing like dust in streaks of sunlight, nothing there but the tyrannical sameness of the orderly room, the boards and small windows of the long corridor, his cell door, the grey blanket that could smother his hysterical sobs; breaking from him because of this final parting, the new purgatory of reprieve, the possible agony of Gabriel's rescue an unbelievable–terrifying? he would have to believe himself back into living, and mission, again–hope: for what reason he could not grasp then, the coarse blanket stuffed in his mouth, the wooden shelf of the bed shuddering under him. O merciful Father, O merciful.

Sir John would have been relieved of his worst political crisis–compared to this possible collapse the money of the Pacific

Scandal was no more than a single brick falling out of his arch of confederation from sea to sea–if Riel had broken out of prison. Then the old man could have stood up in the House, raised his eyes to heaven and sighed, "Ah, Louis Riel: I wish to God I knew where he was!" and let the United States Government wrestle with political asylum, his own eventual successor with a possible amnesty; he would then have avoided everything, as he had in 1870. But he was getting very tired of this implacable little half-caste, persistent as a droning mosquito about his people, his religion, his adherence to the Conservative party. Surely a Scot who had come to North America at age five, had helped create an entire country and had pulled it together despite a grasping United States on one side and silly continentalism on the other, who would remain prime minister until the day he died, surely he deserved some relief from this endless small-minded western insistence. Besides, the police were absolutely immovable. Irvine and Crozier had men standing shoulder to shoulder around that guardroom, had horsemen circling the entire North-West Mounted Police barracks night and day and on several occasions almost shot their own men who, well into their cups, returned late from Regina, the password forgotten; immediately when the thirty-day reprieve was announced the police clamped a fifty-pound ball about Riel's leg again: before all Canada Middleton had called them "gophers" and if Riel escaped them now what was left of the ten-year honour and glory of the Mounted Police would be hooted away forever. There was no approaching Irvine, Dewdney made that clear; and Macdonald's most politically useful characteristic was his ability to recognize incorruptible honesty and to leave it strictly alone.

Finally on October 22 the Judicial Committee of the Privy Council in London ruled on the defence appeal: the court had been competent, Riel was clearly guilty, it remained for the Canadian Executive to decide as a matter of policy whether the capital sentence must be enforced. By this time a second long reprieve had been granted into November, but Macdonald was growing hard, and he was hardening his Quebec ministers with him, Militia Minister Caron, Public Works Minister Langevin, Secretary of State Chapleau whose younger brother was Sheriff of Regina and who now informed Riel and Father André that Tuesday, November 10 was the day set.

Riel was writing. He was no longer allowed the commissioner's office and table; the only time he left his cell carrying the heavy ball was for mass or an hour's daily diagonal of the yard when the mud churned up by the fall rain was passable; police stood at ease, rifles butted, every four yards. At the tiny table of his cell where the light fell through the grating in the door he worked on letters, statements, visions which came to him at night or as he stared against the black wall, on his history of the North-West. Who would write it if he didn't? There were so few days left, and he wrote and wrote. Dr. Jukes allowed him all the paper he wished and sometimes when he leaned back exhausted on his stool, the faces of the Mounted Police guards were hooked in the gratings of the door, staring at the paper snowed about him on the floor, the fury of his hand moving in French or English, his body bent to the tiny table like a child crouched over hard lessons.

"...'Métis' is derived from the Latin participle *mixtus*, which means 'mixed', in French 'mêlé'; it expresses well the idea that is sought to convey. However appropriate the English expression 'Half-breed' might have been for the first generation, now that the European and Indian blood are mixed in every degree, it is no longer general enough. The French word 'Métis' expresses this idea of mixture well, and thus becomes a proper race name.... Why should we care to what degree exactly of mixture we possess European and Indian blood? If we feel ever so little gratitude and filial love towards one or the other, do they not constrain us to say, 'WE ARE MÉTIS!'?

"The Indian blood in our veins established our possession of the North-West conjointly with the Indians...our wars with the Indians were not aggression but self-protection of our rights....As a primitive, simple and plain-dealing people, placed by providence in a happy abundance of riches, and not endowed with any aggressive ambition, the Métis needed almost no government. Nevertheless, when they went buffalo-hunting...as much to maintain order as to guard...they organized and composed a camp. A chief would be chosen, twelve counselors...soldiers formed groups of ten, and every group chose a captain....I have seen and taken part in these buffalo runs; they are terrible, the skill...."

So much had to be written; there was so little time. The new yet in their own way civilized Métis people had been formed on true concepts of public liberty and equity, they had peacefully traded with the Hudson's Bay Company, prevented the horrible Indian wars and savagery that had been perpetrated again and again in the United States; and they had rightly resisted Canada laying hands on their country. At gun-point they demanded justice when they were about to be robbed of the future they had created for themselves but oddly, despite forcing The Manitoba Act into existence, that same act seemed to have given every advantage only to the immigrant. Métis land titles seemed never to arrive; their leaders were arrested, some brutally killed by rioting soldiers, some exiled and even thrown out of the Parliament to which they were legally elected, again and again! Was it just that a greater people destroy a smaller people's leaders, tear from them their country? Humanity answers no. God who is our Father, in his mercy has granted that every people shall live in their own place so that they may bless their Creator, forever. Those who wrest from its people a country commit sacrilege!

"The Government of Ottawa is guilty of conscienceless sacrilege towards the Métis!

"And then the Dominion at last put aside whatever small moderation it had exercised. On the Saskatchewan it gave an entire parish, St. Louis de Langevin, church land, school lands, and all the property of thirty-five families to a land speculation company. Is it astonishing that the Métis rose in revolt? That they sent for me? I crossed the line without arms or ammunition, taking my wife and children with me. I did not think of war; I came to draw up petitions. I had been the free choice of the Métis people in Manitoba, and on the Saskatchewan they chose me again. In 1874 the Dominion's own Governor Archibald of Manitoba wrote to Ottawa in disgust: 'You give representative institutions to people, and then you expel the representatives they elect; for their chiefs you raise scaffolds. You will never gather grapes on the thorns of your conduct!' But if Ottawa changes, it is to become more tyrannical; instead of so much as writing a letter in response to our petition, Ottawa sent several hundred Mounted Police to arrest me! What is this but—"

He had written all this so often! He had declared it in public court and the eager Liberal newspapers had scattered it across lands and oceans, they were reading this in London and Paris and Boston and Washington and—and he was here in a black cell still writing, writing! He was pounding on the walls until the wood rang, where was justice, were the educated whites of the world such conscienceless bigots that one blaspheming Protestant could eliminate the longings of thousands whose rights–he was hammering so hard, screaming too, the board door clattered on its iron hinges and the grate over the hole–the guard was roaring at him, long rifle braced across the grate to hold the door shut and for a moment he could have ripped that white face away like a sheet of paper under his fist, but then Father André was there, his beard flying over his greasy cassock and the door open, light, people. He was lying rigid on his bed, the cool hand of the priest soothing him, the good, quiet voice murmuring a psalm in his ear fresh as a spring bird song in the blue, delicate air above Saskatchewan willows. Be still, be still, say nothing of your agony.

"...my strength and my salvation. Of whom shall I be afraid." After a moment André said, "Perhaps writing is not good for you. You should rather think of God, make your preparations and not—"

Riel jerked erect; he knew every crack in the cell longer than an inch, and out of his rage he now felt only an awesome–he knew it would pass soon, but he thanked God not to disturb it–lassitude.

"Preparation." He looked past André's face, the whiskery outline smudged and gone against the closing door. "I've had three months longer than Thomas Scott, my whole life was mostly a—" he stopped. This priest was a great comfort; the church was so solidly planted on his round shoulders, in the bend of his body and in every confident whisper of his voice. But to understand vision or dying was so far beyond his grasping, pudgy fingers, so–Gabriel understood better, a bloody hunter, killer. Gabriel, my brother, where are you? Will you come a third time, will I dare go with you, again, God in Heaven, will I?

"The word has just arrived," André said. "It is postponed again."

Riel said nothing and the priest continued, quickly in the silence,

"The sheriff has to have a letter, signed by the Governor General, and the messenger hasn't left Ottawa, the letter can't reach here by..." André's voice faded at Riel's still motionless silence, then began again, so heartily, "The fourth time, I have the assurance they won't...do it, now, at all...."

"When is the date?"

"November sixteen, but I—"

"Monday. Macdonald has to hang me," Riel said. "The Spirit has told me. Then the people can make me a saint."

André sat so still, his face solidified into stone.

"And I have made a prayer, you can give it to our good Bishop Taché," Riel's voice was precise and cool as the click of poplar leaves in a quiet summer. "When the Church recognizes what the people already know, you can teach them my prayer."

André could not move; he was silently crying to God at the horrible travesty of hanging this poor mad fool.

"Third Monday of the month," said Riel dreamily, drawing words as it seemed out of the gloomy cell air, "to be prayed three times.

"O Saint Louis David the Métis, who through the goodness of God and to give us an example of obedience, wished to climb the scaffold on this day to bring to God the merit of your sufferings in life–now that you are near God, be our advocate and carry to the Father of Heaven and Earth the little sufferings which we endure in our desire to follow the path you have traced before us. We beg you, through Jesus Christ our Lord, give us strength to achieve the great work you began for the Métis people, and for the whole world.

"Saint Louis David the Métis, pray for us."

After a moment, Riel said, "I'll write it down for you, so you can give it to Father Taché." But the priest could not say anything.

Three hundred and fifty miles away as a bird would fly, at Fort Benton, Montana, Gabriel had both his hands clamped on Michel Dumas' dirty buffalo jacket and was hoisting him erect, slamming him down on the table again. Michel shoved one hand away, slowly raised his head to peer at Gabriel.

"I can hear you," he said, rubbing his big hand thoughtfully over the unshaven blackness of his heavy jaw, a trace of blood on his cheekbone. "I hear you."

"Then c'mon," Gabriel muttered, turning, "we gotta ride."

Michel very deliberately moved his hand six inches, fit his fingers around the bottle glinting in the smoky light. "No," he said.

Gabriel's arms swung down, the bottle leaped away, crashed somewhere, but the men from the surrounding tables were on him. For a few moments there was nothing but men cursing, grunting, the crash of tables and shriek of bodies tearing, convulsing as the saloon lights swung uneasily, slamming shadows ugh! on shadows; then Gabriel heaved himself up against the bar, hurled one last man against the twenty surrounding, moving in on him, and his long skinning knife glinted at his fist.

"C'mon, c'mon!" he hissed. But no one moved, suddenly.

"You can put your shotgun away, Frank," he said over his shoulder to the bartender raising his head carefully over the bar. "These shits won't touch me again."

Major John Burke detached himself from the pillar he had hastily stepped behind, his blue uniform as immaculate as his drawling voice,

"Now, now Gabriel." Burke was moving carefully, hand out as to a spooked horse. "I don't know what you want of Michel," he winked elaborately at the men circled there, panting, wiping their hands over cuts, testing the movement of their fingers, "...my friend Michel to do, but you can't take a man's drink and—"

"Shut up!" Gabriel seemed to be hunching his huge body together for a leap and Burke stood motionless; said carefully over heads,

"We bring the Best of the Great West to all Amer—"

"Shut your mouth! He was all right till you son-of-a-bitch coward started soaking him in whisky and talking money!"

"Gabriel, Gabriel," Napoléon Nault whispered from the side of the bar, "don't."

Burke was laughing easily, friendly as ever. "It's just Michel knows a fun job when it's offered. The Buffalo Bill Wild West Show is the finest, most beautiful—"

"Michel!" Gabriel roared. "C'mon, we have to ride now!"

From behind the ring of men came a sound. "No." And all the hard faces before him who had sworn the secrecy, the commitment, said nothing more. For a moment blackness swung over him; he had his free hand on the bar and he barely swayed but when he could see them again, he knew they knew his weakness. And that his plan was hopeless. He looked at them, his fury coiled in the centre of a terrifying calm.

"I'll ride alone then," he said softly. "And I'll pray God every day he freeze you all in the deepest pit of hell."

The sky was black with stars outside; he could not see anything, strangely, his eyes seemed clouded even beyond the hard darkness and the furtive, slipping sound of the Missouri River cut below him and the tied horses. He found their hitch but tangled the knots, stupidly, and then he wheeled, arm up and clamped and his knife dead certain—

"Gabriel—" Napoléon gasped.

"You stupid kid." He dropped his arm, bent to the tangle reins, hooked his knife point there and jerked. "At least you're coming."

"Gabriel," Napoléon had his hand on his shoulder, trying to find him somehow in the darkness between the breathing horses.

"We've got all the relays set, horses ready, everything."

"But it's hopeless!" Napoléon jerked him around. "You got Pascal Bonneau's message, I know it, three troops of police day and night mounted guard, three hundred men with cannon, Gabriel, we'd need an army to break into there on the flat prairie!"

"So we'll get an army, Jesus Christ we'll hire all the killers in Montana and bust...."

"Hire with what? Our people are so poor...."

Gabriel stood, still between his two horses, the saddled grey with the Winchester butt sticking up above it, the other roped down with a pack. Below them the river ran on relentlessly; a shadow on a mule ambled by, mourning,

"...O bury me not, oh no, on the lone prairie-e-e-e...." the lights of saloons wavered the length of the street, in distant shouting, laughter.

"You think...." Gabriel's voice was so small it seemed to Napoléon he heard a child, far away. "You...they'll really hang him?"

"Yes. They have to."

And after a time in the darkness Napoléon understood that Gabriel had his hands up, clenched on the rifle butt, that his gigantic shoulders were bulging rigid as stone because he would twist that wood and steel, crush it between his hands into tiny splinters; that he was leaning his head against his patient grey; crying.

Father André had written three times to Bishop Taché asking that he be relieved of the Regina cell duty; to testify against Riel, to wait and wait and know him so intimately, his confessor now: it was too much for him. Taché sent Father Charles McWilliams, whom Riel had known as a boy at the Collège de Montréal, to assist André, but would not agree that the latter leave; Riel too wanted André to stay. "How can I convert you to believe in me if you go back to Prince Albert?" he asked, laughing a little at his own irony; and André had to turn his head, leave. Despite his violent opposition only a few months before, he found himself writing letters to Taché attacking Macdonald and praising Riel in a way that embarrassed him when he read them later. André was a strong person but he found, like so many of us, Riel irresistible on long acquaintance. Even in a death cell, even as a visionary. Which made the messages he must carry all the more difficult.

"The baby, it was a boy. It lived only four hours."

After a moment Riel whispered, "Was it baptized?"

"Yes, and Marguerite is fine, fine."

Riel lay back on the shelf of his bed. "It's as well then they postponed this to Monday. The son I have never seen will welcome me to heaven." His voice moving upward into the air absolutely rigid, thin as if he were threading it through a relentless needle. "Tell me, Marguerite?"

"She–she survived the birth," André said slowly, "but she still coughs. But the birth, the birth, was fine, fine."

"They shelled the houses, they had to sleep for two weeks in the woods, in holes in the cold ground. She will not," Riel stopped;

he saw in the gloomy air that she would not survive him by six months. "She gave me herself, so completely; it was all she had, and I have nothing to leave her but—" he sat up suddenly, leaped to the little desk, his hands frantic over papers. "Father! You must send her these, every word I have written, the words and words; they must have them, publish them, sell them so they can live, you must promise me, promise!"

He had the priest's shoulders in his grip, was shaking him so that the old man's tears splashed, sparkling in the tiny light of the grated door.

"Yes, Louis, y—"

"On God's Holy Book, you swear!"

"Yes, yes, I swear!"

Riel sat down abruptly; only his breathing, and the priest's long drawn sniffing.

"And jean? Angélique?"

"They are better, almost healthy now; the fall was—"

"Tell me!"

"On God's Holy Book Louis, it is true! Joseph's and your mother's letters, I saw the policeman reading them, they are, they are getting stronger."

And the letters when he got them that Sunday afternoon did say as much. So he could prepare himself; he had heard them again hammering outside the south entrance of the guardhouse; whatever he had left undone was too late now, he had to prepare himself. Colonel Irvine and Sheriff Chapleau and Dr. Jukes were standing in the doorway; it seemed the sentence must be carried out at eight o'clock tomorrow morning. Riel said quietly,

"I thought I had twenty-four hours."

But Father André was furious. After all these months of hesitation, now suddenly, a rush, a–but the messenger from Ottawa had just arrived with the letter; how could they–Riel laughed. He sat bent on his bed, the cell crammed tight with all this officialdom arguing about him. He was gripping his left leg with his two hands, just above the knees, and he felt himself so usual, so simply himself as he had been all his life. And yet there were the mighty of the world sending messages, puzzling their great heads over–he laughed a little, the feeling of himself so absolute between the fingers of his own hand.

"I was glad when they said unto me, 'We will go into the house of the Lord.'"

The doctor, the soldier, the sheriff, the priest all stared at him in amazement; like all people still totally committed–perhaps "bound", "tied down" would be better words–to earth, they could not quite comprehend this tremendous calm, this–almost happiness. This man was the divisive talk of the civilized world. Petitions for clemency, demands for the "full rigour of the law," tens of thousands of signatures, were piling up in Ottawa. The London *Times* had declared: "Riel not only raised the standard of revolt against the Queen, and when defeated and pardoned raised it again; he is a murderer and the instigator of murder, foul, wholesale, and pitiless;" the Paris *Telegraph*: "Riel is not as pure a martyr as John Brown, but he is a mystic in daily converse with angels whose strategic advice is unequal to that of Joan of Arc's voices, possibly because he has no Dunois to interpret them;" the New York *Herald*: "By converting Riel from a lunatic into a martyr they have retarded, perhaps forever, the reconciliation of races and the fusion of the Canadians into one harmonious people;" *La Presse* of Montreal: "If Riel must expiate the crime of having demanded the rights of his compatriots, if he must expiate above all the crime of belonging to our race...then he destroys all the party lines formed in the past; there are now no longer Conservatives or Liberals, only Patriots and Traitors;" and The Toronto *Mail*: "If the collapse of the cabinet should result from the withdrawal of its French Riel partisans, then let it be known that we, British subjects, are convinced that it will be necessary to undertake the Conquest again, and Quebec may be assured there will be no 1763 treaty; this time the conqueror will *not* capitulate."

But Riel sat silently, content, near submission on his face; if government would fall and people riot, let them; it was God's will. The Spirit had told him that there would be a terrible shaking throughout the land, that many would die, and he prayed now that those he loved, those who had believed in his mission, though sometimes doubting, would be spared. When he knelt before André and McWilliams in the Mass he placed his mother's last letter on his head so that the priests' hands united in blessing with hers. He prayed for all who were dear to him, his nieces, nephews, sisters, brothers, for Jean and Angélique...I leave neither gold nor silver, but pray God in his infinite mercy to pour on you my paternal blessing, that you devote yourselves to the will of God...and his mother...may you be blessed from generation to generation for having been such a good mother, when your last days come may God be pleased to carry your pious spirit from earth on the loving wings of angels...and Marguerite. He was crying, remembering the rare small tension of her mouth when she was angry, though she would not say a word; the quick smile of happiness whenever she saw him, always in the four short years they had been married—dear God, when have you allowed me the sweetness of family life, only those few months on the mission in Montana—

> Ah, Marguerite be fair and good
>> Consider now the sacred wood
> On which the perfect Jesus
>> Died willingly to save us.

...and her fingers moving easily over his body, her own body tightening like a bow bending as he held her, drove into her, loved her to the roots of his soul, her body shuddering suddenly so completely and terribly, the first time he thought he tortured her and he lurched out of his own ecstasy into terror, "Marguerite! Marguerite! What—?" but she opened her eyes to him, smiling, her face like a Madonna to be worshipped forever. "Oh Louis, I love you." They were lying under his cart in the whorled tangles of the Missouri brakes, the horses snuffling over their hay as the spring moon rose higher. Montana...Montana...there were three persons standing on Birdtail Rock, outlined against the sky like crosses, perhaps, and they were talking together: a priest, his brother– Joseph, it was Joseph clearly and Father André, and one more, a third. They are talking of his death, the third person says to Joseph, pointing down to him, "God will be with him. Though they cause him to die, God will raise him up again on the third day." It is Gabriel! Brother Gabriel, namesake of the blessed angel who brought blessed tidings to Mary. O my brother, where are your strong shoulders and arms, your gashed head and relentlessly honest eyes, your wild raucous laughter, your gentleness, your gnarled ugly face welcoming me into your open arms. You brought me blessed tidings; you are blessed beyond all men for you saw with me the gallows on the hill and you have now declared I shall be–he laughed aloud for joy for he saw Gabriel's giant fist like the hammer of God smashing through earth and rock, rolling away stones, smashing open barred cells that had sealed him in all his life, the miserable sweating stone and green wood and haystacks and muddy willows and filthy shacks that had held him shivering in the dogged terror of his flesh and bone body, O praise God, blessed brother Gabriel, your dreadful arm has broken through my fear; because of your courage at last I am free! O my saviour Lord Jesus, I obey, I give you my endless thanks.

"Mr. Riel."

The English voice at the open door; a faint lightness outlined the corridor beyond the yellow lamp.

"Mr. Chapleau?" he asked.

"He would n—," Deputy-Sheriff Gibson stopped abruptly. "I am to officiate."

"Yes," Riel said in English, and turned to André and McWilliams rising from their knees. "If you would give us a few minutes, Mr. Gibson."

He was dressing himself, carefully. And he remembered that dressing in Fort Garry, the exact ruffles on the shirt, the frock coat so elegantly black against the wall, his face stone white then in the stained silver of the Hudson's Bay mirror betraying nothing of his ancestry; and Gabriel's voice in the next room. The men laughing with his gigantic laughter as they walked out between the Métis soldiers, rifles and vivid blue sashes and dark bearded faces, a long human wall embracing them, he and Ritchot side by side into the growing roar of The New Nation declaring itself in their welcome–into the house of the Lord for there is the seat of Judgement, even the seat of the house of David who shall judge–but he had no mirror now, nor did he need one for the grey homespun trousers, the grey jacket, with the rigid police at the door, his own feet slurring a steady prayer down the corridor and André in a white surplice beside him, staggering from a psalm into sobs, almost breaking.

"Courage, Father," he said. And André, clamped to his arms a moment, answered,

"Go then, to heaven."

No faces, only the open door at the end of the corridor, the wooden steps leading up there, the platform and the man waiting beside the knotted rope. He was suddenly aware of the ivory crucifix in his hands and he raised it, the contorted body twisted like–he crushed it against his chest, he could not bear to see it but then he raised it again, he wanted the next moments to go, quickly. He had waited so long and in an instant he would be beyond this body at last, he would see, he would see Jesus and his father and his tiny son and—

"Do you," said McWilliams, "offer your life a sacrifice to God?"

"With all my heart."

"For the love of God do you forgive all those who desired and worked for your death?"

"I forgive them as I pray God to forgive me."

"Is your conscience at peace?"

"Yes. Thank God yes."

His body was singing. He felt it so tremendously from his toes stretching in his moccasins to his thighs and chest distended, his fingers clenched about the tiny ivory cross, his shoulders, head powerful, gigantic, he was this instant so completely himself God had given him the earth and all that was in it, a honeyed sweetness singing his body for this instant before it was broken, left, thank God forever and he would look into the face of God Himself and ask him why, why, and he would touch Sara. Ineffably beautiful, pure into all timeless eternity, dearest God. He was kneeling, prayer rising in him, "Holy Lord Jesus, strengthen my faith, help me to love my people according to your mercy which is beautiful beyond measure," and the priests' hands on his head seemed to be Gabriel kneeling beside him in that little church in Fort Benton, the wagon with Marguerite and Jean and Angélique and the three riders waiting to carry him north to his mission in Canada. And he stood again, ready, his body lifting itself in perfect, powerful grace, and McWilliams had the cross, his arms were seized, gripped together behind him like steel.

"Louis Riel, do you know me?"

The man at his shoulder: sixteen years. For an instant he wondered how this man could be there on this small, unsteady platform with two priests and the deputy-sheriff, this rabid cell companion of John Farmer and Dr. John Christian Schultz, and Thomas Scott; but then his hands were immovable, the white hood was lifting up past the savage eyes, the bearded face contorted now as it had always been with clenched, implacable Orange hatred, and he said,

"God have mercy on you, Jack Henderson."

And in the peace of that moment as the white hood hesitated, then lifted higher, he looked out over the pale witnesses pressed together below, the barrier of the red police squared shoulder to shoulder and faced away, the distant pickets mounted and fencing off a cluster of people and wagons, the far, tiny clumps of Regina; and he saw again the immense circle of prairie, the bulging sun's glare over the horizon. The sky was blue as crystal, the earth a line drawn and in the silence the level light of the sun burned the hoarfrost into gold, even the meanest grassblade in every split and bend stood gilded, flashed, glistened in a straight, golden path waiting for him, the whole great world itself rolled up into this final glorious beauty. And he tasted that as the hood fell vicious as snow, the rope twisted, coiled tight about his neck. The knot nudged snug against his spinal cord.

"Say 'Our Father,'" said McWilliams' voice. Someone was sobbing, he could hear, and he began into whiteness,

"Our Father who art in heaven, hallowed be..." and he was kneeling beside his mother and saying those words carefully, with complete concentration one by one, his soul bent before our Father God in adoration and at the tiniest corner of his eye as he concentrated straight ahead he could discern the edge of the Golden Moccasins and if he dared lift his head he would...and he would in an instant, he would dare now, yes! and the king-doms of the world were a map spread at his feet as the glory of vision blazed up before him again, burst around him, consumed him in searing, eternal fire

"....as we forgive those—"
and the earth fell away, he was free, O God free.

Even the police faced rigidly away heard when the rope struck. A nine-foot drop. Those mounted on the prairie saw the white-hooded figure vanish; perhaps their straining ears heard a sound. Someone said,

"The son of a bitch is gone at last."

Below the scaffold the body shuddered, swayed gently to and fro, turning slowly until it stopped facing north. The two doctors reported that its toes came within six inches of the ground, that is, they brushed the dead prairie grass.

Riel and Gabriel

"*Death lies beside me in my bed;*
when sleep begins to close my eyes, her
whisper sinks to the bottom of my heart.
She says, 'This is how I will greet you on
the day you must meet me. I will close your
eyes like sleep. And I will wake you also,
but not to this world. For when we meet,
I will introduce you to eternity.'"

— Louis Riel, 1885

THAT is all the story I can tell you. Our New Nation blossomed and faded for a few short months in Manitoba in 1869-70, it blazed up in 1885 and in less than two months died on the Saskatchewan. Our prairie vision was too strong, too destructive of all that was; it had to be borne away by the violent. And though he was dead, the very body of our chief was worried by the dogs of hatred, prejudice, ambition. Honoré Mercier, the Liberal leader of Quebec, screamed to fifty thousand people in Montreal, "Riel, our brother, is dead! Victim of the fanaticism of Sir John A. Macdonald!" Wilfrid Laurier delivered the greatest speech on judicial murder ever heard in the House of Commons, Riel being safely dead, and eventually rode that oratory into the prime minister's office where he stayed for fifteen years. Orange lodges sent letters of satisfaction at last to Sir John; when Taché wrote the Prime Minister that Riel had prayed for him the night of the execution, Old Tomorrow said nothing at all; he knew he was safe, that Ontario Liberals would vote for him now even if Quebec Conservatives did not. André sent all of Riel's prison papers to Taché, and it was 1932 before Joseph Riel could get them out of the Archdiocese of St. Boniface. Riel's crucifix was stolen, perhaps by a policeman; by the time Sheriff Chapleau got the body, bits of its clothing, beard, hair, even eyebrows had been cut off; the very shavings of the coffin in which it was placed had disappeared. It was three weeks before the Sheriff and Colonel Irvine and Lieutenant–Governor Dewdney and Secretary of State Chapleau and Prime Minister Macdonald could agree that Riel's last request be honoured: that he be buried beside his father in the cemetery of St. Boniface Cathedral. At eleven o'clock on the evening of December 8, 1885, four perfect fours of years to the day after the declaration of the Fort Garry Provisional Government, ten years to the day after Riel's vision came to him during the Grand Mass of the Immaculate Conception, Pascal Bonneau placed his coffin in an empty boxcar, climbed in with a loaded Winchester. Next evening that car was nudged onto a siding behind St. Boniface Cathedral. Joseph and his brothers were there with a sleigh, waiting in the winter darkness.

For three nights the Riel family slept in their house while the body lay in its polished oak coffin in the living room; for two days our people came, the tall candles on the altar bending their flames to them as they filed past endlessly, silently. On Saturday, December 12 the men came with a white sash each across the breast of their buffalo coats; they closed the coffin and lifted it to their shoulders. Charles Nault, Eli Nault, Pierre Harrison, William Lagimodière, Norbert Landry, Roman Nault, Alfred Nault, Martin Nault, André Nault, Louisson Lagimodière, St. Pierre Parisien, François Marion, Louis Blondeau, Romain Lagimodière, Frances Poitras, and Joseph Lagimodière carried it on their shoulders, four and four and again four and four by turn the six miles through the snow north to St. Boniface. At first Mother Riel walked, but the drifted snow soon exhausted her and they placed her in the sleigh with the children; Marguerite walked all the way between Joseph and Alexandre Riel, leading the hundreds of our people, the last great procession of our people behind the last of our chiefs.

To the Cathedral, where the whites of Manitoba waited below Alexandre Taché on his high Archbishop's throne; before aged Noël Ritchot with his domed head bowed at the altar, his immense white beard bent down to the cross at his waist. The sixteen men with the coffin led the people in, up the aisle, and placed their burden down before the altar. Then they formed a tight circle around the coffin, at attention and shoulder to shoulder; Ambroise Lépine came forward and stood with them at the head. Slowly, through muffled sobbing, Ritchot's deep voice began to intone:

"Grant him eternal rest, O Lord, and may perpetual light shine...."

It would be three years before Gabriel saw the brown granite shaft they placed over the grave, words laconic as for an emperor:

RIEL NOVEMBRE 16, 1885

And he would remember Lief Crozier's slightly scarred face over the beer glasses in a Staten Island, New York, bar, July 28, 1886. Buffalo Bill's Wild West Show was then touring eastern America.

"I didn't expect you to be shooting blue balls out of the air," Crozier said, "not with Le Petit."

"Cody had to work out an act for me." Gabriel hoisted a long swallow of beer. "They don't know nothing about Saskatchewan here. Political exile don't mean much, to Americans."

Crozier said nothing; his green eyes glinted above his blue civilian suit, the white shirt. Gabriel chuckled suddenly,

"At least it pays pretty good! You out of a job too?"

"Yes," said Crozier. "I might go to Oklahoma, I don't know."

"Shoot more Indians?"

"Maybe," Crozier said expressionlessly. "If I have to. Madeleine with you here?"

"She died in April, in Montana."

"I'm sorry. But Annie is—"

"Oh, she's alive," Gabriel said curtly. After a moment Crozier shifted a little in the dim light.

"Marguerite Riel died too, in April."

"Those weeks in the bush, that was too much." Gabriel raised his head, studied Crozier a long moment; when Crozier's eyes came up at last, Gabriel said without any emotion whatever, 'You finished us, real good."

Crozier just stared into grey eyes; all the letters he had written, curses he had bellered, rage and war he had outfaced again and again; ten good years on the Saskatchewan, a way of life and a country destroyed for them both. He raised a glass, and drained it slowly.

"You can go back now," he said. "Macdonald declared a general amnesty to all Métis."

"What! You mean Parenteau and Monkman and–all of them in the pen will get out?"

"Sure, they'll all get sent back in empty boxcars, like the Indians. All is forgiven."

"Dear God." Gabriel sat with his huge head in his hands. Crozier could see the long line through the grizzled hair across the top of his skull. "I tried for two days to find Riel, to get him not to surrender. The good Lord..." his voice fell; perhaps he was musing, perhaps again the recurring momentary blackness of his wound had washed over him. "...I couldn't find him, he would have won me over to his way of thinking. They were right, they had to hang him, yes. They were right."

"What?" Crozier tilted across the table, half-standing. "They were right?"

"Sure. All his life he tried to show how the government was destroying us in the West. He got away from them once, to the States, so he could fight them again, but he wouldn't run this time. You know why, you know?" Gabriel's big hand was clenched in Crozier's collar; their faces bent slowly together until the darkness of the bar found no passage between them. "So his body on the end of that rope would prove forever how Canada destroyed us!"

"But you really are finished now, what good—?"

Gabriel opened his fist, sat back heavily. "You think like a white," he said after a moment. "You can't help it, that's okay, but you think Riel is finished? He said a hundred years is just a spoke in the wheel of eternity. We'll remember. A hundred years and whites still won't know what to do with him. The smart whites will say, like Laurier now the cheap bastard that never said a word for us when it mattered, they'll say it's judicial murder; Riel was mad. But it wasn't, and he wasn't mad. There's no white country can hold a man with a vision like Riel, with people like us who would understand it and believe it, and follow. Canada couldn't handle that, not Ontario, and not Quebec, they're just using him against the English. They all think he was cracked, mad."

"He wasn't...mad?"

Gabriel sat motionless; staring at the drained glasses before him.

"You knew him better than anyone," Crozier said quietly. "You know men...."

"By the grace of God," Gabriel said, "he received the vision."

"You had us! That disaster retreat from Carlton, Middleton plugging along, Gabriel you could have killed us and had a hundred hostages in Prince Albert and forced Macdonald into anything, but you listened to Riel, listen...."

And suddenly Gabriel Dumont began to laugh. He leaned back, his Wild West rawhide jacket open on his red shirt, his grizzled chest; the jacket's preposterous dangling fringes shook all over him like poplar leaves in a wind. He saw that poor white who had never, would never find such a man to know stare at him in consternation, and he roared with laughter as only our Gabriel could when he was completely, overwhelmingly happy. The huge bar rang.

O God I pray again, let our people not be confounded. Give them that faith again.